SEEING RED

ALSO BY DAMIEN BOYD

DI NICK DIXON

As the Crow Flies

Head in the Sand

Kickback

Swansong

Dead Level

Death Sentence

Heads or Tails

Dead Lock

Beyond the Point

Down Among the Dead

Dying Inside

Carnival Blues

Death Message

From the Ashes

Blue Blood

DI BOB WILLIS

Deceived by the Light

Blast from the Past

A DI Nick Dixon Novel

SEEING RED

DAMIEN BOYD

THOMAS & MERCER

This is a work of fiction. Names, characters, organizations, places, events, and incidents are either products of the author's imagination or used fictitiously. Any resemblance to actual persons, living or dead, or actual events is purely coincidental.

Published by Thomas & Mercer, Seattle

www.apub.com

EU Product Safety Contact:
Amazon Media EU S.à r.l.
38, avenue John F. Kennedy, L-1855 Luxembourg
amazonpublishing-gpsr@amazon.com

ISBN-13: 9781662524677
eISBN: 9781662524684

Cover design by @blacksheep-uk.com
Cover image: © Evgeniya Litovchenko © DFog © Ruud Morijn Photographer
© New Africa / Shutterstock; James Macey

Printed in the United States of America

For Andy

Prologue

'It's pitch bloody dark, for heaven's sake.'

'He's got to go out,' she snapped. 'You've been working from home, Paul, and I bet you haven't taken him out.'

'He's been asleep under my feet most of the day.' The voice was coming from the open dining room door, a laptop visible on the table. 'I let him out in the garden a couple of times.'

'Whatever.' She leaned over, clipped the lead on to the dog's harness; switched on the flashing red light. She'd got it online, so people could see him in the dark.

A black Labrador, at night. Cars travelling too fast in the lane. Some bugger had hit him once before, but then that idiot boyfriend of hers had let him off the lead.

Paul was a prat sometimes.

She took her phone out of her pocket, opened the tracker app and clicked 'Walk'. Boomer had to get his steps in for the day.

'You're not going round by the church, are you?'

'Just the usual loop.'

'There was that body found in the churchyard at Kingston. He'd killed her with a ham—'

'Don't be ridiculous.' She was putting on her coat, checking the pockets for dog bags. 'He picked her up in town, late at night.'

'Yes, but churchyards. Just be careful, that's all I'm saying.'

'You could come with us.'

'Got to finish this, sorry.'

She thrust her hand into her coat pocket, pulled out her attack alarm, felt for the defensive spray in her other pocket. It was there, in among the dog bags.

'We'll be fine.'

She let the front door slam behind her, Boomer already halfway down the garden path on his extending lead.

Forgotten her hat. Sod it. Still, it was dark and no one would see her bald patches.

Bloody chemo.

'We're not going far, Boomer. And for God's sake don't pull me over.'

Along the lane, past the allotments. She could see through the hedge on her left, people moving about in kitchens and conservatories at the backs of the bungalows. One had been burgled a couple of months earlier, a handbag taken through an open window. It had been on Facebook, caused quite a stir.

Boomer was pulling her now, barking at something in the hedge; a cat, probably.

That bloody idiot, Paul, had taught him to chase cats, not that Boomer would know what to do with one, if he caught up with it.

St George's was just around the corner now, the spire silhouetted against a starry sky, the flashing lights of a jet heading west, high overhead. America, most likely.

She knew she'd never fly again; might just live to see Boomer out. The dog was ten and a bit and she'd been given six months to a year. Must hang on for Boomer's sake.

Hadn't told anyone, not even Paul.

Especially not Paul, actually.

Her eyes welled up at the thought – of leaving her dog behind.

With him.

Somebody was moving about in the churchyard. Boomer had heard it.

Another dog walker. Some went that way; never picked up. It had been in the parish newsletter. Kicked off a mighty row online too.

Parking and dog poo. She'd got fed up with it in the end, left the Spotted Modbury Facebook group.

The lane widened by the entrance to the churchyard, parking either side, although there was only the one car. Nothing going on in the church, so that was to be expected, perhaps.

Footsteps behind her, soft, moving fast.

Pain exploded across the back of her head.

She dropped Boomer's lead. 'Not my dog. Please don't hurt my dog.'

Leaning over now, trying to shield the back of her head with her hands. Another blow; the top of her head this time.

She fell forward into a puddle, the water splashing her face, slowing the blackness that was overtaking her.

Just enough to see Boomer's red light fade into the distance.

Chapter One

'Gravedigging?'

'What did you think "Cemetery Operative" meant? You didn't read the job description, did you?'

'I thought it would be cutting the grass, gardening and stuff.' He was sitting in the passenger seat of his mother's car, staring through the lychgate at the tarmac path leading up to the churchyard, gravestones emerging from the morning mist. 'Dad said it would get me outdoors, and it was either that or the solicitor's office. Photocopying and making the tea, he said.'

'You shouldn't have left it so late.' His mother was drumming her fingers on the steering wheel. 'Now hop out, or I'll be late for work.'

'Gravedigging, though.'

'It's only a week's work experience.' Then she gave that irritating laugh he knew only too well. 'And you never know, you might see a ghost.'

'Yeah, right.'

'You look like you've seen one already.' She cackled again. 'Serves you right for watching that *Stranger Things* rubbish on Netflix.'

He slid out of the passenger seat into the drizzle.

'And don't forget your coat. It's on the back seat.'

He resisted the temptation to slam the car door, watched as his mother sped off, her tail lights disappearing into the damp grey morning.

Water clung to empty cobwebs hanging under the slate roof of the lychgate as he slid on his coat, enjoying a moment's respite from the rain.

His mother was right. Maybe he shouldn't have binged *Stranger Things* the day before work experience in a cemetery?

West Bagborough church. His dad had looked it up on Wikipedia; something to do with the Black Death, he'd said. Probably just been taking the piss though.

Then a van pulled up by the war memorial behind him.

'Are you Luke?' asked the passenger.

'Yes.'

'Good. We've got an internment at eleven, so you'll be helping us get ready for that. Then we've got a dig over at Galmpton.' The man grimaced. 'Just a small one, that.'

'Oh, right.'

'Then we come back here and fill this one in.' He tried a reassuring smile. 'Don't look so scared. You get used to it.'

The driver had got out and opened the back of the van. A tall man, greying beard, steel toe-capped boots caked in mud. 'I'm Tony and this is Ray,' he said, putting a hard hat on Luke's head, giving it two solid taps on the top. 'Always wear a hard hat on site, young fella. We're both fully trained under the Cemetery Operatives Training Scheme, so you're in safe hands.'

The hat slid down on to the bridge of the boy's nose.

'There's an adjuster thing on the back,' said Tony. 'You can tighten it. Then you can help me get the ladder off the roof.'

'You always have to have a ladder in a grave whenever an operative is working. As an emergency exit in case of collapse. That's the Confined Spaces Regulations 1997.'

'He really doesn't need to know all that stuff, Ray.'

The ladder was short, aluminium, the rungs muddy despite being on the roof of the van in the rain.

'Didn't you bring any gloves?' asked Tony.

'No one said,' replied Luke, nervously.

'There might be some in the back.'

Turned out there were. Thick rubber, cold and damp inside. It didn't bear thinking about. He really shouldn't have left it to the last minute to choose his work experience placement; hadn't wanted to appear too keen.

At least he didn't drop the ladder.

'Right, follow me,' said Tony, taking it off him. 'You carry this.' He handed him a large bag of sawdust. 'It's a bit of a flog up this path, then we're round the back of the church.'

They followed the path around the church tower and began weaving between the gravestones, Luke following Tony, trainers getting soaked in the long wet grass.

'You got any boots?'

'Wellies.'

'Wear those tomorrow.'

Ray was walking behind. 'There has to be two of us if we're digging deeper than three feet,' he said. 'That's the Confined Spaces regs and the Manual Handling—'

'You're boring the pants off the poor lad,' interrupted Tony.

'He needs to know these things.'

'It's fine,' mumbled Luke.

'Then you've got to do your risk assessment before you start digging. Ground conditions, hazards. We dug this one on Friday and I had to move a couple of memorials, so we'll put those back this afternoon, when everybody's gone.'

Tony stopped, resting the end of the ladder on the ground. 'Right, here's one I made earlier.' He laughed at his own joke.

'Nobody watches *Blue Peter* anymore,' said Ray.

'Don't they?'

Luke shrugged. 'Not really.'

'Your Thermos is still here, Ray,' said Tony.

'Thought I'd left it. The coffee will be stone cold by now.'

'What's the sawdust for?' asked Luke.

'We put it in the bottom of the grave, last thing, to soak up any water. Just makes it a bit nicer for the family,' replied Ray.

'It's their loved one's last resting place,' said Tony. 'So, anything we can do to make it a bit nicer, we do.'

Large pieces of chipboard had been placed on the ground to one side of the grave, the huge pile of earth on them boxed in by planks and covered in green matting that had been pegged down. More green matting had been placed on all four sides of the grave, underneath thick planks that covered the hole in the ground.

Ray was busy rolling up bright orange tape that had been looped around a traffic cone at each corner. 'Don't want anyone falling in, do we?' he said, with a toothy grin. Then he began stacking the cones.

'Right then.' Tony was standing at the far end of the grave. 'You help me lift off these planks, Luke. We've got some blue satin to cover the sides – never like leaving bare earth for the family to see – and the sawdust goes in the bottom. Then we put two bits of wood across the top for the funeral directors to put the coffin on when they get here. Ray's got the flowers and off we go. All right?'

'Whose grave is it?' asked Luke.

Tony slid a piece of paper out of his pocket, unfolded it. 'Dorothy Henley. She was . . .' He paused, doing the maths in his head. 'Eighty-two.'

'Can't grumble then.'

'You won't be saying that when you're eighty-one,' said Ray.

'I suppose not.' Luke could feel his face reddening.

‘Let’s get these planks off,’ said Tony, squatting down. ‘Middle one first.’

Luke leaned over, slid his fingers under the leading edge of the plank, lifting it a few inches. Then he dropped it, straightened up sharply.

‘Sorry, I should’ve warned you,’ said Tony. ‘They’re a bit heavy.’

‘It’s not that.’ Luke was breathing hard. ‘There’s someone in there.’

◆ ◆ ◆

Nine weeks old and he still hadn’t been outside the hospital.

Acting Detective Superintendent Nick Dixon was looking through the small window in the door of the private room at the Ashcombe Birth Centre, watching his wife, Jane, sitting on the edge of the bed, cradling their newborn son Peter in her arms.

It had been an odd couple of months. Jane on maternity leave, him suspended on full pay; all day every day spent at the neonatal unit with Peter. Jane had stayed the nights there too, leaving him to sort out their cottage. A deep clean, new carpets, redecoration.

It had been an interesting conversation with the insurance company, but they’d got there in the end, authorised the work without too much fuss.

‘How did it happen?’

‘I shot an intruder in the neck with a 3D printed gun.’

‘How d’you spell that?’

His call had been transferred to a supervisor after that. ‘Well, that’s a first for me,’ she’d said.

‘For me too,’ Dixon had replied.

Jane still hadn’t been back to the cottage since that night. Hadn’t mentioned going back to work, either, although a detective sergeant's salary might come in useful if he was shown the door by Avon and Somerset Police.

That was just the gross misconduct investigation. There were criminal charges pending too.

The best he could say, looking through that small pane of glass at his wife and son, was that it had been worth it. The man had been holding the barrel of a gun to the back of his wife's head. She'd been heavily pregnant at the time, and bleeding profusely.

What else was he supposed to do?

He'd been asked that question often enough in the weeks since.

'What else were you supposed to do?'

His problem was that he'd taken the gun with him, and if they could prove that, and prove he had taken it intending to kill, then he was in difficulty. That was the word his solicitor had used – *difficulty*. He hadn't felt the need to explain further. Dixon knew the score.

It had been a heat of the moment thing. The man had been on his way to Dixon's cottage, armed. So, Dixon had picked up a gun, gone after him. No one knew that, of course, except Jane.

And the Armed Response officer Dixon had followed into the house in Burtle. He'd said there were two guns on the table by the computer, when the Scientific Services inventory had recorded only one.

It had been Jane's idea. 'He turned up here with two guns, one in each hand. We fought and he dropped one on the rug. You saw it, picked it up and shot him.'

Yes, it had been a very strange couple of months. A husband and father, but with all of that hanging over him. Hanging over *them*, actually. If the Professional Standards Department could prove Jane had lied . . .

That was an outcome they'd never discussed.

Dixon had got into a routine of sorts. A walk on the beach with Monty in the morning, then off to the hospital; all going to come to an end tomorrow, he thought, one way or the other.

The consultant had said they might be allowed to take Peter home at long last.

Then there was the meeting at the PSD in the afternoon.

Gits.

Dixon pushed open the door, smiled at Jane when she looked up.

'How is he this morning?' he asked.

'Feeding tube's gone and I fed him myself.'

'Bottle?'

'No.' She grinned. 'He's up to seven pounds, eight ounces. That's what they said he needed to be to go home. Feeding normally and gaining weight.'

'When's the consultant coming round?'

'She's been round, said we'd look at it tomorrow.' Jane glanced over her shoulder at a bulging holdall on an armchair in the corner. 'I'd even packed up, ready to go.'

'One more night then.' Dixon was watching Peter sucking the tip of Jane's little finger. The boy was wearing yet another new romper, blue with his name embroidered on the chest. 'Is that new?'

'Mum came in earlier. Said she couldn't help herself, got three more for him to grow into.'

'Nice.'

'Any news about tomorrow?'

Dixon shook his head.

'If we're allowed home, it'll be about five o'clock, I reckon,' continued Jane. 'So, you can pick us up afterwards.'

'Better have your dad standing by just in case.'

'Really?'

'If they're going to arrest me, it'll be then.' He sat down next to Jane on the edge of the bed, put his arm around her.

'They can't, not the day we're bringing Peter home.'

'I'll leave Monty at the cottage. No point in him sitting in the back of my car. If you're staying here, someone will need to go to the cottage and feed him, let him have a run in the field.'

'I'll get my dad to—' The words caught in the back of Jane's throat. 'But they've got no evidence, for fuck's sake!'

'The statement from the Armed Response officer conflicts with what we say, doesn't it?'

'Then it's his word against ours, surely?'

'Pretty much.' Dixon reached out to take Peter from Jane's arms. 'Here, let me have him,' he said.

'He needs changing.'

'I pick up after the dog,' he said, recoiling.

'You still haven't changed a nappy, have you?'

'I don't know how.'

'Well, now's a good time to learn.'

Chapter Two

Detective Constable Mark Pearce was in Bristol when he got the message. Didn't mention his new living arrangements – that he was at least an hour away, depending on the traffic on the M5. It was his day off anyway, and he was left wondering what could possibly be *that* urgent.

He left Helen in bed. Meeting DC Helen McMahon had been the one good thing to come out of the 3D printed gun investigation. Sitting opposite her in the incident room, by chance to begin with. Then he'd always made sure he got that workstation.

Now he was doing the daily commute, staying at her flat in Clifton. Not that he'd actually moved in. He just slept there every night.

The message was short and not terribly enlightening: *Meet Detective Sergeant Louise Willmott. West Bagborough church. TA4 3EF. ASAP.*

He'd put the postcode into his satnav and clicked 'Go Now' before he realised. Detective *Sergeant* Louise Willmott.

She'd kept that quiet. He hadn't even known she was sitting her exams. Conveniently failed to mention that. Not that he'd seen her for a couple of months. Not since Nick Dixon had been suspended from duty. Mark had stayed in Bristol for a few weeks to close down the 3D printed gun thing, get the files ready for the coroner, and

Louise had gone back to Bridgwater. She'd been moved to Taunton by the time he got back. No one had thought to mention why.

Not that he was bothered, and certainly not jealous. He had other things on his mind at the moment – his interrupted lie-in, for starters.

He parked in the lane behind Louise's car, walked down the outside of the line of vans and patrol cars parked in the lay-by in front of the war memorial. There was an ambulance too, the paramedics chatting, one smoking, the other with his hands in his pockets.

A dead body then.

A bright light was visible on the side of the hill above, partially hidden behind trees.

'The body's up there,' said the uniformed officer at the lychgate. 'Follow this path up to the church, then round to the left. Young woman. In a grave.'

Mark resisted the temptation, followed the path, his breathing becoming laboured.

A Scientific Services tent was visible in the churchyard; it seemed to hover – almost – the bright light creating miniature rainbows in the drizzle as he approached on the path that led across the wet grass from the corner of the church tower.

'No stepping plates?' he asked, raising his voice to announce his arrival.

'There are some in here, but the ground's too steep outside,' replied Louise, poking her head through the tent flap. 'According to the crime scene manager.'

'Oh God, he's here, is he.'

'I heard that.'

Mark recognised the voice. Louise was wearing full overalls, so he should've known the crime scene manager had got there first.

Pursuit trained possibly, either that or he was a former rally driver; Harinder 'call me Hari' Patel always seemed to get there first.

'You made it then,' she said.

'Just about,' Mark replied, stepping on to the first plate inside the tent. Then added 'Sarge', his voice dripping with sarcasm.

Louise knew him well enough. 'Don't take the piss.'

'You. Out!' Hari was waving his clipboard at him. 'This is a controlled area.' Hari squeezed past Mark without either of them falling off the stepping plate – a well-rehearsed manoeuvre. 'You'll need overalls, boots and gloves. Then I can sign you in.'

Louise was standing in the entrance to the tent, watching Mark wriggling into a set of overalls.

'Those have got a hood, please use it,' said Hari, an impatient edge to his voice. He waited for Mark to do as he was told, then ticked a box on his clipboard with a flourish. 'Right, now you can go in.'

'She's not a pretty sight,' said Louise, softly.

'I take it the grave wasn't meant for her.'

'No.'

Mark took a deep breath, stepped inside the tent.

'There was a funeral booked for eleven, but it's been cancelled,' continued Louise. 'It was dug on Friday, apparently. I let the gravediggers go. They've gone over to Galmpton to dig one over there, said they'd come back later.'

Mark walked on the stepping plates around to the far side of the grave, careful not to get in the background of the photographs being taken by the Scientific Services officer.

'The gravediggers found her?' he asked.

'They came to get it ready for the funeral. Lifted the planks they'd left covering the hole, and there she was. They've got some lad doing work experience and he saw her. Then they dialled 999 and waited.'

'Is the pathologist on his way?'

'Roger Poland is coming. Said he'd be here in about half an hour,' replied Hari, peeling back the elasticated cuff of his overalls to look at his watch. 'Detective Chief Superintendent Potter is on her way, and she's got the ACC in tow as well.'

Mark looked at Louise, raised his eyebrows. 'Why us?' he mouthed.

'There's no one else.'

'There's a DCI coming from Devon too,' continued Hari. 'You'll find out,' he added, before either of them had a chance to ask.

The planks that had been covering the grave had been moved to one side and were resting on the pile of earth, next to a stack of four traffic cones. An arc lamp had been positioned shining directly down at the body. The photographer straightened up, gestured to Mark. 'You'd better see what you're dealing with,' he said, his face much the same colour as his overalls.

Mark leaned over. 'Did the boy doing work experience see her?'

'Just the feet, he said,' replied Louise.

'What else did he say?'

'He wants to be cremated when his time comes.'

'Me too.'

'The gravediggers said they'd take him home; the mother's leaving work early, will meet them there. Uniform have got his details, but he just lifted the plank, saw her feet and dropped it again. Can't really add much.'

'Where are her clothes?'

'We've checked the graveyard,' replied Hari. 'No sign. No murder weapon either, but that's just a first sweep.'

Mark stared down into the grave. Regulation six feet deep, a small amount of muddy water had seeped into the bottom and was covering the fingernails of the left hand. The body was lying face down, her short blonde hair matted with blood, her right hand hidden underneath her.

'Looks like blunt force trauma to the back of the head,' said Louise.

There was loose mud on the backs of her legs, corresponding scuff marks visible on the side walls of the grave. 'Someone climbed out,' offered the Scientific Services officer when he saw Mark looking at them. 'Probably pulled himself up on a plank, scrabbling with his feet.'

'No wedding ring,' Mark said.

'I can't see an impression on the skin where one's been either, but I haven't been down there for a close look. Not yet.'

'Any footprints?'

'It's too wet in the bottom of the grave; there's nothing in scuff marks, and everywhere else it's long grass and footpath, so that's a no.'

A loud cough from outside, then a uniformed officer appeared. 'D'you want us to start house to house in the village?'

'We'll wait until we've got a time of death from the pathologist,' replied Louise.

'Of course. Sorry.' He backed out of the tent, walked off along the path.

'What's that tattoo on her left shoulder blade?' asked Louise.

'I took a photo, zoomed in,' replied the Scientific Services officer. 'It looks like a red rose. Should make her easier to identify. Can't really do much more until the pathologist gets here.'

'Was there a church service yesterday morning?' asked Mark.

'The usual Sunday morning Communion,' replied Louise. 'We need to speak to the vicar.'

'She could've been in here the whole time.'

Heavy breathing outside. 'Right, what've we got?'

'One in, one out,' said Hari.

'I've finished. For now,' replied the Scientific Services officer, ducking out of the tent.

'You can come in, Dr Poland,' said Hari.

'I gather congratulations are in order, Sergeant,' said Poland. He was already suited and booted, but then he'd brought his own.

'Thank you.'

Poland had left his case on a stepping plate just inside the tent and was staring into the grave, pulling a facemask over his mouth. 'Better get a ladder. I can't do much from up here.'

'The gravediggers took theirs with them,' said Louise.

'Scientific will have one. Give me a minute.' Hari ducked out of the tent.

'No clothes?' asked Poland.

'Unless they're underneath her,' replied Louise. 'Scientific have searched the churchyard.'

Poland turned when the end of an aluminium ladder appeared through the doorway of the tent. 'Perfect,' he said, taking hold of it. Then he lowered one end into the grave. 'Feet end first. There's more room.'

Mark and Louise stepped forward to watch Poland climb down, place his feet carefully, start examining the body.

'She's about five foot seven. Slim build.' He leaned over, talking into a Dictaphone. 'No apparent piercings. Rose tattoo on left scapula. Injury to the back of the head. No obviously broken bones, apart from the skull.' He lifted her left arm in a gloved hand. 'Rigor mortis all but gone.' He straightened. 'Where are we now? Monday morning, so sometime Saturday evening into night. I can give you a better idea when I get her back to the lab, but say between eight and midnight on Saturday, possibly early hours of Sunday.'

'That gives us something to work with,' said Louise. 'We can start house to house in the village, at least.'

'What about an ID?' asked Mark.

'She's not wearing a name badge, if that's what you're asking, but we can run fingerprints, DNA and dental records. We'll know more when we get her out of here, but let's have the photographer down here first.'

It took about three hours in the end. Every stage meticulously photographed, swabs taken, before the body was lifted out and into a large crate that had been placed beside the grave.

'There was nothing underneath her,' said Poland, when Mark and Louise were allowed back into the tent. 'Mid to late thirties. No sign of sexual activity. No other obvious injuries.'

Lying on her back now, her hands sealed in plastic bags, they got their first look at her face, through the mud. Her skin was grey, lips blackened; eyes wide open, muddy water trickling into the crate from her nostrils. Her mouth was contorted into a scream. Of sorts.

'So, she was hit over the back of the head and pushed into the grave?' asked Mark.

'It's not quite as simple as that,' replied Poland. 'Hit over the back of the head, yes; pushed into the grave, yes. But there's petechial haemorrhaging in her eyes. Tiny little blood vessels that have burst under pressure. My thinking is she was still alive, so her killer jumped in and suffocated her in the mud. That explains the muddy water in the nose and the mouth, if she was still breathing. I'm guessing I'll find more water in her airways when I open her up.'

Louise took a sharp breath.

'A real piece of work, this one,' continued Poland. 'And I think her clothes were removed after death.'

'How can you tell?'

'The mud spatter on the body isn't consistent with a fall from six feet. There's very little of it on the backs of her legs, for a start. My view is she was lying here, dead, and the clothes were carefully removed.'

'That would've taken time,' said Louise.

'It's a remote churchyard. One thing he had was time.'

◆ ◆ ◆

'Brace yourself,' whispered Mark.

Two of the voices outside the tent were unmistakable. Detective Chief Superintendent Deborah Potter and Assistant Chief Constable David Charlesworth. The third sounded older; must be the DCI from Devon, thought Mark, which meant there had been other victims.

Come to stick his oar in, no doubt. Charlesworth and Potter there to make sure their arses were covered, although Potter was technically the senior investigating officer unless and until she found someone else.

'We'd better go and face the music,' said Louise, her voice hushed.

Mark followed her out into the drizzle that had started falling again, the tiny droplets blowing on the wind in the light from the arc lamps.

Potter was standing under an umbrella, teetering on tiptoe to stop her high heels sinking into the soft ground of the graveyard. Charlesworth was standing behind her, his a large golf umbrella.

'This is DCI Hatch. From Plymouth.' Charlesworth finished making the introductions while Hatch was wriggling into a hazmat suit, not that the bloke was listening.

'They're getting ready to move the body, Ma'am,' said Louise. 'Scientific will be here for the rest of the day. Longer, probably. Dr Poland will be doing the post mortem this evening.'

Mark listened while Louise filled them in on what they knew so far, which was actually bugger all. It didn't take long.

‘House to house?’ asked Potter. She’d shifted on to a gravestone that was lying flat, most of it hidden in the long grass.

‘Yes, Ma’am. Started as soon as we had a timeframe from Dr Poland.’

‘Traffic cameras?’

‘Not yet.’

‘Why not?’ demanded Charlesworth.

‘There isn’t anyone to do it,’ replied Louise. ‘There’s only us, and we’re both here.’

Put that in your pipe and smoke it, you tosser, thought Mark.

Raindrops were starting to settle on Deborah Potter’s pinstriped trouser suit, glistening in the bright light. Obviously hadn’t had time to put on a coat. Charlesworth was in uniform; hadn’t seen fit to offer her his coat either.

Potter turned her back on Louise, spoke to Charlesworth. ‘Staffing this is going to be a real problem,’ she said. ‘And that’s before we have to think about liaising with Devon and Cornwall.’

‘We can deal with it, if that would assist,’ said Hatch. His face was framed by the elasticated hood of the suit, his smirk betrayed by his moustache. ‘If all you’ve got available is a DS and DC. We’ve got a major investigation team in place and would be happy to take it on.’ He gave a dismissive wave in Mark and Louise’s direction. ‘We can take these two for liaison.’

Fuck off.

For a second Mark thought he’d said that out loud, was relieved to see he hadn’t, although the sentiment was clearly shared by Charlesworth if the look on his face was anything to go by.

‘A kind offer, Geoff, thank you,’ said Potter, before Charlesworth had a chance to say something he might regret. ‘Let’s see if it’s connected to your investigation first, take it from there, perhaps. You said your victims had been posed in the bottom of the graves?’

‘Yes, they had.’

'This body wasn't posed.' Poland's voice carrying from inside the tent. 'She lay as she fell into the grave.'

Potter looked at Hatch. 'The pathologist,' she said. 'Dr Poland.'

'Cause of death?' demanded Hatch.

'He drowned her in the mud.'

'I'd better have a look,' said Hatch, disappearing inside the tent. He ignored the stepping plates, but then he was wearing sterilised boots.

Potter waited until Hatch was intercepted by Hari Patel and his clipboard. 'This is his fourth attack,' she said, over the raised voices. 'The first outside Devon, and it would be on our patch, wouldn't it.'

It was a rhetorical question.

'And it would be now,' she continued, under her breath.

'Sorry,' said Louise. 'He's done this three times before?'

'One survived, but she was found unconscious in almost identical circumstances, in the bottom of a fresh grave dug in a rural churchyard. Naked, blunt force trauma to the back of the head, no sign of sexual assault.'

'When?'

'Two early last year, January and March, then another in November.' Potter turned. 'Devon and Cornwall have got a team on it out of Crownhill. That's Plymouth to you and me.'

'Do you want me to deal with them?' asked Louise.

'Leave that to me for the time being,' replied Potter. 'You just concentrate on getting an ID for her. Somebody, somewhere, is going to be wondering where she is and we need to find them. You've checked missing persons?'

'We've put a call into the MPU, Ma'am.'

Potter turned back to Charlesworth. 'It couldn't have come at a worse time,' she said.

Mark knew how it worked. Unconfirmed reports of a body found at West Bagborough church, so someone from CID needed to attend. Louise twiddling her thumbs at Taunton, waiting for a sergeant's job to come up. He could imagine the conversation now.

'Send DS Willmott. She's got nothing else to do at the moment.'

'She can't go on her own. Isn't there anyone else?'

'Mark Pearce. No one will miss him.'

He knew his own reputation well enough. Fine when someone was directing him. No real initiative shown. That seemed to be a regular comment on his performance reviews. Bit too keen on his beer. It had never bothered him. Teams needed foot soldiers, someone to do the legwork. He was good at doing what he was told; all it took was the right SIO telling him what to do.

Then two mortuary assistants appeared, ducking under the tent flap, each carrying one end of a stretcher, a trolley waiting on the tarmac path below to take the body to the van parked in the lane.

Roger Poland was walking at the side, the procession following the narrow track in the long grass between the gravestones.

Charlesworth held up his hand. 'Can I see her, Roger?' he asked.

Poland unzipped the body bag a short way, then stepped to one side, allowing Charlesworth to lean over. 'We haven't cleaned her up yet, I'm afraid,' he said. 'She's still covered in mud.'

Mark was known for being free with his opinions too. Never one to hold back, even if they were usually expressed anonymously from behind workstation partitioning, a computer to duck behind. Now there was nowhere to hide, but he'd known the time was coming, that he'd take his chance when it did. Have his say.

'We'll have to take people off other teams,' said Potter, her voice hushed. Hatch was still in the tent, and the less he knew, the better.

Charlesworth watched Poland zip up the body bag.

'Why don't you just put a stop to all this 3D printed gun bollocks?' said Mark, his voice little more than a whisper. 'Then we can all get back to normal. And Nick Dixon can get on with finding the bastard who killed her.'

'You've said enough, Constable, I think,' hissed Potter.

Poland fixed Charlesworth with a cold stare. 'He has a point, David.'

'There's a process that has to be followed, Roger. I can't just—'

Mark had retreated to the safety of the tent. 'Yeah, right,' he muttered, just loud enough, as it turned out.

Chapter Three

Charlesworth adjusted his horn-rimmed glasses, glanced down at the speech the press officer had thrust into his hand only moments before. It was the usual stuff, and he'd heard it many times before. Far too many to mention, actually.

He'd been standing in the porch at West Bagborough church, sheltering from the rain, when he got the call.

'The Chief Constable is ill, so you'll have to stand in at the awards ceremony.'

Mercifully, Charlesworth's driver was pursuit trained and blue-lighted it up the M5, swept into the car park in front of the sports hall at Portishead HQ with a few minutes to spare.

No Police and Crime Commissioner sitting next to him on the dais this time, but then there were a few days to go till polling day, so there'd soon be a new one to break in. Always a pain in the backside, that. They arrived, newly elected, full of their own ideas and self-importance. Usually made for an irritating few months until it was knocked out of them. Still, this would be the last one, apparently, the government having announced the role was to be abolished. Charlesworth would believe it when it happened, though. And there'd be some other bureaucrat to contend with, no doubt.

It was a good photo opportunity all the same. A chance to fly the flag.

The sports hall was pretty much full. The award recipients, their family and friends, mainly. The official police photographer. Journalists tended not to bother coming these days, unless there was something really high profile. They just relied on the press release and the official photographs. Lazy buggers.

Hard-working police officers deserved better, really.

Deborah Potter had been right. The body in the grave couldn't have come at a worse time. Every team working on every case was just about as small as they could get away with. Any smaller and there'd be complaints. Now there was a murder to deal with. One that required liaison and cooperation with another force.

He'd spent much of the drive north stewing on it. Now, here he was, sitting in a sports hall, his best player on the bench. That had been Deborah Potter's analogy, although he was about to present awards to police colleagues, rather than play a game of five-a-side.

The press officer looked at her watch, turned to Charlesworth and nodded.

He stood in front of the lectern, glanced down the list of award recipients.

Nigel Cole. Again.

Police Sergeant Rhys Webber; a Chief Constable Commendation.

Maybe this wasn't going to be a complete waste of time after all?

'Ladies and gentlemen, it is always humbling to recognise those of our colleagues who have demonstrated exceptional commitment to public service, be it acts of bravery, lifesaving interventions, or initiative and teamwork. These are colleagues who have gone above and beyond, and it is only right that their efforts and dedication are acknowledged. At the very core of our profession is a determination to make a difference, and those being recognised this evening have indeed made a very real difference.' Charlesworth glanced at the press officer, who was shaking her head. He must've gone off script, he thought. 'We also recognise this evening two members of the public with the Waley Cohen award for their bravery in assisting officers detain violent offenders. Both showed extraordinary courage, rare in this day and age when most people's initial reaction seems to be to reach for their phone and film the incident.'

Charlesworth ignored the press officer's violent coughing, which had seemed to come out of nowhere. Perhaps it wasn't such a bad thing there were no journalists present?

'So, without further ado, our first recipient of the Waley Cohen award witnessed the street robbery of an elderly woman at knifepoint, gave chase, summoning police as he went, and then assisted officers in apprehending the offender. The incident resulted in a conviction for the offence of robbery. David Taylor, if you'd like to come up and receive your award, please.'

Charlesworth turned Taylor around to face the audience and the police photographer. Big smiles all round, much applause.

'An extraordinary effort. On behalf of Avon and Somerset Police, thank you.'

Taylor seemed lost for words, so Charlesworth pointed him in the direction of his seat in the front row.

'Our next recipient of the Waley Cohen award accompanied a lone officer into a house where a suspected burglar was hiding, and assisted in making the arrest . . .'

Charlesworth was going through the motions now, and he knew it. The knack was not to let anyone else know, and certainly not the recipients.

Pats on the back, vigorous handshakes. It was a well-rehearsed routine. It wasn't the first time he'd stood in for the Chief Constable and it wouldn't be the last. The previous Chief Con had been suspended for eighteen months – something to do with an inappropriate relationship – and Charlesworth had done the award ceremonies then. Twice yearly; he'd lost count of them.

'Our first Chief Constable Commendation goes to Police Constable Nigel Cole. Actually, I should add that this is Nigel's second commendation. His first was awarded last year for extraordinary bravery in helping to disarm an offender wielding a loaded crossbow. On this occasion, Nigel yet again showed exemplary courage. His hands tied behind his back, he deliberately threw himself on to glass bottles, suffering grievous injury to free himself and save the life of a young colleague, a probationary constable who is here tonight and also receiving a Chief Constable Commendation. Nigel, where are you?'

Cole stood up, to cheers and applause from the audience.

'All right to shake hands?' asked Charlesworth, when Cole reached the dais.

'Fine, thank you, Sir,' replied Cole. 'Healing well.'

'Good.'

More smiles, more photographs, then Charlesworth leaned into the microphone on the lectern. 'I probably shouldn't say anything, ladies and gentlemen, but I thought you might be interested to know that the Chief Constable has also nominated Nigel for the George Cross, which is awarded to recognise an act of the most conspicuous courage in circumstances of extreme danger.' He stepped back, leading the applause.

Cole was applauded all the way back to his seat.

'Now, for outstanding initiative and determination in the apprehension of a serial murderer, a commendation goes to Police Constable Sarah Loveday, who was herself grievously injured in the process.' Charlesworth watched her approach the dais nervously. 'Making a good recovery, as I understand it, Sarah,' he said.

'Yes, Sir.'

He hadn't seen her since Dixon's wedding more than two months earlier. 'No wheelchair?'

'That's long gone, Sir.'

Several Royal Humane Society awards followed. Then Charlesworth looked around the sports hall.

'Lastly, we have a Chief Constable Commendation awarded last year, but the recipient was unable to attend the relevant ceremony. So, for outstanding coolness and dedication to duty in bringing to an end an armed siege at the top of a crane at the Hinkley Point C construction site, Police Sergeant Rhys Webber of the Armed Response Unit.'

That was as much detail as Charlesworth could share about the incident; as much as he *would* share. After all, a man had died. He presented the award to Webber, then leaned in, whispering under cover of the applause, 'Are you coming to the drinks reception afterwards, Rhys?'

'Yes, Sir.'

'Good. I'd like to have a word with you in private, if I may.'

◆ ◆ ◆

Mark looked at his reflection in the pane of glass in the door of the pathology lab at Musgrove Park Hospital. Pale, much like the morning after the night before and a few too many beers.

'I can't remember the last time I came to a PM,' he mumbled. 'I'm usually watching ANPR footage. Safely out of the way. You can't go wrong with cars.'

'You look like death warmed up,' said Louise. 'Are you going to be sick?'

'I hope not.'

She opened the top drawer of the filing cabinet in the anteroom, took out a jar of Vick's VapoRub. 'Put a blob of that under your nose and wear a mask,' she said, gesturing to a box on the top. Then she turned and looked through the large window into the lab. 'There's a window on the far side, so just go and stand near that.'

'Do I have to go in?'

'You'll never live it down if you don't.'

'You wouldn't tell anyone?' Mark was smearing a blob of VapoRub on his top lip.

'I wouldn't,' replied Louise. 'But *he* would.'

The door opened and Roger Poland appeared, blood smeared on his green smock. 'You're just in time,' he said. 'I've opened up the skull and the blow to the back of the head wasn't fatal. It would've been, eventually, but something else killed her. I'm just about to open up the chest cavity, check her lungs.'

'He's a bit . . .' Louise let her voice tail off.

'You've surely been to a post mortem before, Mark?' asked Poland.

'I do CCTV and stuff.'

'Have you eaten?'

'No.'

'You'll be fine.' There was mischief in Poland's voice. 'Stand by the window, and for God's sake lean out of it if you're going to be sick.'

'I'll keep an eye on him,' said Louise.

'He doesn't look any worse than he did the morning after Nick's stag do.'

'That was grim enough,' said Mark.

They followed Poland into the lab, Mark keeping well back from the slab where the body was lying. Various samples had been taken and were arranged neatly on a worktop on the far side. Jars and stainless steel bowls.

'You got anywhere with an ID?' asked Poland.

'Not yet,' replied Louise.

'A DNA sample's gone off, and we've done the fingerprinting. There was quite a lot of debris under her fingernails, so that's going off for examination too.'

Mark was standing in front of the window, ready to turn his back to the slab quickly if things took a turn for the worse. Her head was at the far end, and he wanted to keep it that way, averting his gaze as he'd walked past. He'd thought the top of her skull was missing, although her forehead was covered with a sheet.

Oddly square. Best not to look too closely.

Mid-thirties. Remarkably like Helen – a vision that would take some shifting.

'Definitely the presence of petechial haemorrhaging,' said Poland. 'She broke her tibia at some point. An x-ray shows plates and screws, so I'll see if there's a serial number on the plate. Otherwise, fit and healthy on the face of it. I've done a tox screen and bloods, so we'll see what that turns up.'

'Any other injuries?' asked Mark, mainly because he thought he ought to make it look as though he was paying attention, rather than just fighting the urge to puke.

'There's some bruising on the upper back, in between her shoulder blades, consistent with a large shoe or a boot. My working hypothesis is he pushed her down into the mud in the bottom of the grave with his foot. There was no evidence of the back of her head being held. Hatch's theory was that he'd left the last victim alive and wasn't making the same mistake again.'

'Might explain why he took the clothes,' said Louise. 'If there was a boot print on her coat.'

'He took the clothes off the other victims,' replied Poland. 'They were posed, according to Hatch. Two killed outright by the blow to the head; the survivor's been left with a permanent brain injury.'

'Would she have been unconscious?' asked Mark.

'Oh yes.'

'Then a foot in the middle of her back could've done it. She wouldn't have been able to turn her head.'

‘You might want to turn yours, old chap.’ Poland was standing over the body, a scalpel in his right hand. ‘I’m going to make the incision—’

Mark waved his hand, silencing Poland mid-sentence, then he turned to look out of the window.

The incision was fine. What came next was something else. A dentist’s drill on steroids. Actually, it was an electric saw, and Poland was using it to open up the chest cavity, cutting down through the breastbone. Mark knew that much; could’ve done without the commentary.

‘Scalpel,’ said Poland. ‘Yes, there’s muddy water in her lungs. She drowned.’

Mark headed for the door. ‘I’m sorry, I’ve got to . . .’

‘Well done today, Mark.’ Poland pulled his mask below his chin. ‘You said what we’ve all been thinking.’

‘Thank you.’

‘Let’s hope David Charlesworth was listening.’

Chapter Four

Canapés and a glass of something fizzy.

Charlesworth was doing his duty, making all the right noises.

Circulating, congratulating each award recipient in turn, telling their families how proud they should be of their son/daughter/husband/father.

Nigel Cole's wife was there.

Sarah Loveday's parents.

'Have you thought about joining the police?' It was his standard, half-joking question to civilians receiving the Waley Cohen award. It always got a laugh, was a good icebreaker.

Then he got to Rhys Webber and his family. Wife, two teenage children. Better spare them the details of what their father had done. The wife looked like she knew anyway.

It had been quite something. A dark and stormy night, Webber had climbed a crane at Hinkley Point to bring an armed siege to an end at the top of an adjacent crane. Nick Dixon had been up there, trying to get the crane operator away from a serial killer armed with a shotgun. Both cranes had been swaying violently, turning on the wind.

A fine shot on a night like that. On any night for that matter.

'You should be very proud of your father,' said Charlesworth, towering over Webber's children.

'We are,' said the older child, hesitantly.

'I wonder if we might have a word, Rhys?' Charlesworth gestured to the door.

'Of course, Sir.' Webber went to hand his glass of sparkling wine to his wife.

'Bring that.'

Webber returned his wife's puzzled look.

The clocks had gone forward a few weeks earlier and it was a balmy spring evening, shouts carrying from the all-weather football pitch behind the sports hall.

Charlesworth closed the door. 'That was a hell of a shot from that crane. How are you coping?'

'I had a few months off while the IOPC did their bit. I knew who it was when I went up there, which made it easier.'

'It's never easy.'

'No, Sir.'

'Well done.'

'Thank you, Sir.'

Charlesworth took a swig of sparkling wine. 'I wanted to talk to you about that business with Acting Superintendent Dixon and the 3D printed guns.'

'Yes, Sir.'

'Is there any chance you could have been mistaken about there being two guns?'

'Well, I—'

'You'd just gone into a house where you thought the occupant was armed, you were doing the first sweep, expecting contact to be made. You were hardly noticing every item that might have been lying around, were you?' Charlesworth was shifting from one foot to the other, trying to appear casual. 'Where was your partner at this point?'

'Downstairs, Sir. Mr Dixon was right behind me when we went up.'

'You went in the front room first?'

'Yes, Sir.'

'So, when that was clear, if the offender was going to be there, it would have to have been the back room?'

'I suppose so.'

'You were tense then?'

'Definitely.'

'Gun raised?'

'Yes.'

'So, I ask you again. Is there a chance you could have been mistaken about there being two guns on the table in the back room?'

Webber hesitated. Charlesworth felt sure a light bulb was flickering somewhere.

'That's what you're going to be asked if and when this comes to court, Rhys,' he continued. 'And it would be in all our interests if it didn't.'

'I suppose I could have been mistaken in that case, Sir.' Webber spoke hesitantly, watching for a reaction.

Charlesworth breathed a sigh of relief, loud and deliberately so. Webber had got there in the end. 'Would you like to contact the Professional Standards Department and tell them that then?'

'I can do that, Sir.'

'First thing in the morning, perhaps?'

'Yes, Sir.'

'Good man.' Charlesworth smiled, clinked his glass against Webber's, took another swig. 'Have you thought about applying for promotion, Rhys?'

'Not really. My wife wants me to.'

'I'd be happy to throw my weight behind your application, if that would assist.'

'Thank you very much, Sir.'

Chapter Five

'You'd better go. The consultant won't be round till five, and you don't want to be late for your interview.'

Dixon was sitting in the armchair in the corner of the room, holding his son over his shoulder, gently patting him on the back, a towel strategically placed to protect his best suit. Just in case.

'I don't want to go smelling of baby sick,' he'd said.

'Why not? It might remind them you've just become a father.'

Hardly a relevant consideration, but Dixon had thought it best not to argue the point. Jane knew. Deep down, Jane knew.

'I've got plenty of time,' he replied.

He'd walked nearly the whole way along the beach from Berrow to Brean Down and back that morning; left Monty at home, fast asleep in front of the TV. He'd parked at Berrow Church, the dregs of the confetti thrown at their wedding only a couple of months earlier sodden and littering the graves either side of the path, some of it blown as far as the hedge. Come to think of it, Dixon could understand the churchwarden's fury. 'We thought you were joking,' Poland had replied, with a mischievous grin. It was supposed to have been biodegradable too.

'The only thing they've got is what that Armed Response officer said. So, it's our word against his.' Jane was trying to sound encouraging. 'And you're a highly respected – and decorated – senior police officer, for fuck's sake.'

That just made his fall from grace all the more spectacular; that old joke about traffic officers and Ferraris being worth double the points.

Detective Superintendent Carlisle and DI Larkin. In fairness, they'd just been responding to the evidence. Forensics had found one 3D printed gun and the Armed Response officer had said there were two. So, where had the other one gone?

It was an inconsistency that needed to be investigated. He knew that, even if Jane didn't.

The fact that Dixon had taken it with him when he went after the gunsmith was the problem, not that he'd killed the gunsmith.

He could live with it, all the same.

It may not have been legal.

But it was right.

Sitting there with his son asleep on his shoulder, he knew it was right.

'I'd better go,' he said, standing up. He handed Peter to Jane.

'Just stick to what we agreed, and you'll be fine.' She pulled Dixon towards her with her free arm. 'You'll be back before the consultant comes round at five. I'll see you then.'

'You will,' he replied, trying to sound confident.

Trying not to notice that her kiss lingered a little longer than usual.

◆ ◆ ◆

Dixon's solicitor was waiting for him in the reception area at Express Park when he arrived half an hour later. He'd parked in the visitors' car park, acknowledged the nod from Charlesworth's chauffeur, a newspaper stretched out across the steering wheel.

'Good luck, Sir,' said the receptionist when Dixon walked in.

'Thanks, Reg.'

'Superintendent Carlisle asks that you wait down here. He said he'll come and get you when he's ready.'

'We're not members of the public. Tell him we'll be in the seating area at the top of the atrium.'

Then Dixon punched in the code on the security door at the bottom of the stairs, held it open for his solicitor.

'And if he's not ready at two o'clock sharp, we're leaving.'

Reg smirked, 'He's going to love that' just carrying over their footsteps on the stairs as the door slammed behind them.

Ten minutes early, as it happened. Dixon had glanced across at the open plan CID area as he walked up the stairs, most of the workstations empty, no familiar faces. The canteen had been all but deserted too.

Now on the floor above, the space used as an incident room at the far end of the atrium was lit only by sunlight streaming in through the windows. Empty workstations, clean whiteboards in the darkness at the other end, near the door to the staff car park.

The Professional Standards Department had proper offices, with walls and doors, just like the Safeguarding Unit on the landing to his right, where Jane had worked before she went on maternity leave. The soundproofing needed a bit of work, raised voices carrying on to the landing outside, even with the doors closed.

The plush chairs in the seating area were new; so was the water tower. There was even a copy of *Somerset Life* on a coffee table.

Dixon stood up and walked over to the glass balustrade, looked down into the atrium below, figures visible walking on the landing on the first floor, uniformed officers milling about on the ground floor.

His solicitor was helping himself to water from the tower when the door opened sharply and Charlesworth strode along the landing towards the stairs at the far end. He must've seen Dixon, but there was no acknowledgement, the raised voices dulling to a murmur as the door closed behind him.

'I wonder what that was all about,' said the solicitor.

Dixon knew it was about him. Charlesworth had been at his wedding, for heaven's sake. He'd have said something, surely?

Unless he didn't want to be seen to be saying something.

That could be it.

That must be it.

The solicitor dropped his plastic cup in a recycling bin. 'It's two o'clock.'

'We'll wait.'

'I think we should.'

Dixon walked over to the floor to ceiling window, watched Charlesworth walking across to his car. He paused at the rear passenger door, glanced up at the window. Then was gone.

Ten past two.

Dixon took out his phone, texted Jane.

Still not gone in. Something's going on. Nx

He was watching the speech bubble, waiting for whatever it was Jane was typing to arrive, when the door of the Professional Standards Department opened behind him.

She's an admin assistant, thought Dixon. He'd seen her a couple of times in the canteen. Civilian staff.

She handed an envelope to his solicitor, then walked back to the PSD, closing the door behind her.

The solicitor tore open the envelope, read the letter, then handed it to Dixon.

Standing there at the top of the atrium, his hand shaking, speed reading, but certain phrases leapt off the page.

. . . we have concluded that Acting Detective Superintendent Dixon honestly believed that the deceased posed an imminent threat and responded accordingly . . .

. . . picked up the weapon and fired . . .

. . . no further investigation . . . will now be treated as a witness . . .

. . . the file will be referred to the coroner . . .

. . . the IOPC report will contain no recommendations for misconduct proceedings against your client or remedial action on his part . . .

. . . Acting Detective Superintendent Dixon is free to return to work.

◆ ◆ ◆

Jane was sitting on the edge of the hospital bed, saw him through the pane of glass in the door, closed her eyes, her chest heaving. She'd recovered her composure by the time he opened the door, threw her arms round him and lost it again, sobbing uncontrollably into his shoulder.

Dixon was rubbing her back, hoping she wouldn't be sick all down his suit. He glanced across at Peter, fast asleep in his cot.

'You're back early,' Jane gasped. 'What happened?'

'I'm not entirely sure, to be honest.' He had his arms around her waist, holding her tight. 'We were sitting there waiting to go in when one of the admin team came out and handed a letter to my solicitor. No further action, it said. The file's going to the coroner for the inquest, and I'll be hearing from the IOPC with their report in due course. In the meantime, I'm free to return to work.'

'Exonerated?'

'So it seems.'

'That means I'm off the hook too.'

'We both are.'

She leaned back, looked him in the eye. 'D'you want to go back to work? Back to the police, I mean?'

'I'm not sure I'm going to have a lot of choice.' Dixon was looking over Jane's shoulder, through the open door at the unmistakable figure of Charlesworth, in full dress uniform, standing out by the nurses' station, his cap tucked under his arm. He watched the nurse point in their direction, Charlesworth turn, stride towards them.

'Let's have a look at him then.'

'I've just got him off to—' Jane thought better of it, lifted Peter out of the cot. 'Would you like to hold him, Sir?' she asked.

'Lord, no. I'm not very good with babies, I'm afraid. He'll start squawking straightaway if I hold him.'

'We're hoping to be able to take him home today, Sir,' said Dixon. 'We're just waiting for the consultant to do her rounds.'

'It must have been a long nine weeks.' Charlesworth nodded, then added, 'In more ways than one.'

Dixon hadn't told Jane he'd seen Charlesworth in the Professional Standards Department earlier, hadn't got round to it before he appeared in the neonatal unit. Charlesworth must have been behind the letter though. The only question now was how he'd done it.

'What time does the consultant come round?'

'About five, usually, Sir,' replied Jane.

Charlesworth looked at his watch. 'Might we have a word in private, Nick?' he asked. 'You've got plenty of time.'

Dixon followed Charlesworth down the stairs, out of the double doors and around the corner, away from prying eyes in the car park; Charlesworth's driver, for one.

'What did the letter say?' asked Charlesworth, his eyes darting from side to side.

'I can return to work.' Best poker face on. 'I'm not surprised they dropped it, Sir. They had no evidence of any wrongdoing on my part. They'd certainly never have got a conviction, probably not even a finding of misconduct.'

'It would have been pursued to the full extent of the law, Nick. You should be in no doubt about that. There was a clear statement from Rhys Webber: two guns on the table.'

'What changed their minds?'

'I did.'

Dixon had thought as much; wondered about the price to be paid.

'Five magic words,' continued Charlesworth, with a wry smile. '*I may have been mistaken.*'

'Webber?'

'He changed his statement this morning. At my behest, I might add. I'm going to have to promote the oaf, but I wasn't going to risk having our best officer thrown out on his say-so. It left them nowhere to go. They checked with the CPS – *no prospect of a conviction* – and that was that.'

'I'm grateful for your intervention, Sir,' said Dixon.

'I should think you bloody well are.' Charlesworth put on his hat. 'When are you planning to return to work?'

'I thought I might take a couple of weeks' maternity support leave, Sir. As I said, we're hoping to take Peter home today and . . .' Dixon let his voice tail off when Charlesworth appeared unmoved.

'A touching family scene, I'm sure. But we've got a woman, mid-thirties, naked in a freshly dug grave at West Bagborough, the back of her skull bashed in. He used his foot to push her face into the mud, make sure she was dead. Not only that, but we've got some sanctimonious twerp of a DCI from Plymouth trying to tell us they'll be happy to take it on if we can't find the staff.'

'Tell them I'm on my way.'

'Thank you, Nick. I knew you'd understand the gravity of the situation. I'm afraid *them* is only DS Willmott and that Pearce fellow. There's no one else, for the time being anyway. And try not to fall out with Devon and Cornwall; there have been some similar attacks down there, two fatal and one near as damn it.' Charlesworth turned for his car, hesitated, looked over his shoulder. 'You can keep your acting superintendent rank. If we take that away from you it'll look like we think you did something wrong.'

'Thank you, Sir.'

'You owe me one, remember.'

'I think you'll find that makes us even, Sir,' said Dixon, matter of fact.

Charlesworth's face reddened. Then he disappeared around the corner of the hospital.

Chapter Six

Not telling anyone about Charlesworth tampering with that file had seemed the right thing to do at the time. Dixon couldn't say he'd done it deliberately to give himself leverage with the ACC, although it had turned out to have been a smart move all the same. He'd have to be careful he didn't say anything to Jane. He'd never told her, although that had been for her sake rather than Charlesworth's.

'Has he gone?' she asked, when Dixon reappeared at her bedside.

'There's been a murder and there's no one else, apparently.'

'You'd best get on with it then, hadn't you,' said Jane, smiling. 'It'll be nice to get back to normal.'

'A new normal.' Dixon took Peter from Jane's arms, held him aloft, the boy staring at him. 'We've still got to introduce him to Monty, don't forget.'

'Somebody asked me if we were going to rehome him when we took Peter home,' said Jane. 'I told them you'd be more likely to put Peter up for adoption.'

'Monty will be fine.'

'Right then.' They turned to find the consultant standing in the doorway, flicking through the pages on a clipboard. 'Weight's there or thereabouts. I reckon he'll have caught up in about three months. He's done well.'

Jane reached across the bed, took Dixon's hand.

'Feeding normally, I'm told.'

'Yes, fine,' said Jane.

'Everything else working as it should.' The consultant looked up. 'He got off to a bumpy start, didn't he, but the less said about that the better. I think he'd be better off at home now.' She slid the clipboard under her arm, beaming at Jane. 'We don't always get to give good news, but when we do it makes it all worthwhile. You go, but you know where we are if you have any problems.'

'Thank you.' Jane was crying again, but then it was an emotional business, motherhood; Dixon had made the mistake of mentioning it once before.

He'd left his Land Rover near the entrance, just in case, and Jane sat in the back with Peter in his car seat for the short drive home.

'You told them, didn't you,' he said, leaning forward to look at the front of the cottage. His father-in-law's car parked outside had been the first sign, then he'd spotted the 'Welcome Home' banner and the balloons.

'I texted Lucy to let her know we were on the way,' said Jane, stifling a sigh.

Dixon parked behind the cottage, the back door flying open, Jane's half-sister running out into the yard.

'They're here!' Lucy shouted.

Monty was jumping up at the driver's door. Jane's father, Rod, standing in the kitchen doorway, examining the fingers of his right hand. 'I had him by the collar,' he said, when Dixon got out of the car. 'The little bugger nearly broke my fingers.'

Jane's mother, Sue, had opened the rear passenger door, was leaning in. 'Here, let me take Peter,' she said, undoing the car seat.

'Just give us a minute, will you, Sue,' said Dixon. 'I want him to meet Monty before we do anything else.'

'Oh, right.'

Dixon knew what people would think. A large white Staffordshire Terrier and a newborn baby. In the same house.

He took Peter out of the car seat, carried him into the cottage and sat down on the sofa, Monty following, sniffing the new arrival. Then the dog hopped up on to the seat next to Dixon, took a closer look at the boy before curling up next to them.

Jane was standing behind the sofa, watching what was going on, Rod, Sue and Lucy watching from the kitchen.

Dixon stood up slowly, placed Peter in his new cot, blinking away the moisture in the corners of his eyes as his dog jumped off the sofa and curled up on the floor next to his son.

'Friends for life,' said Rod.

'Looks like it.' Only then did Jane take a moment to glance at the bottom of the stairs. Just to check the blood had gone. She turned to the champagne and cake on the dining table. 'You shouldn't have, Mum.'

'Of course we should. If this isn't something to celebrate, I don't know what is.'

Dixon made his excuses after that. Left them to it. After all, cake and type 1 diabetes didn't go together anyway. That and the fact there were a few hours of daylight left.

Enough for a trip to West Bagborough.

◆ ◆ ◆

'Well, Cato, I'm back on the force.'

'Shut up, Mark.'

'Yes, Sir.' Mark looked at Louise, grinned. His Clouseau impersonation hadn't been much good anyway.

Dixon was standing in the churchyard at West Bagborough when they arrived, sheltering under an oak tree a few paces from the grave. The traffic cones had been replaced in each corner, the tape blue this time.

POLICE LINE DO NOT CROSS.

Mark looked relieved, Louise nervous. Dixon hadn't seen her since her promotion had been confirmed.

'How's Jane?' she asked. 'And Peter?'

'Home today,' replied Dixon.

'Good.' Louise gave an anxious smile. She'd spent much of their last case questioning his every move; was probably wondering how he'd react to her promotion.

'Talk to me about the Devon cases,' he said. He stepped out from under the tree, collar up, hands thrust deep into coat pockets.

'There are three of them,' replied Louise. 'All found naked in freshly dug graves. Blows to the back of the head, one survived. There are DNA samples believed to be their attacker's; same individual, no match on the database.'

'They were all taken off the street late at night or in the early hours,' said Mark. 'One in Plymouth, one in Tavistock, and one walking her dog in Modbury.'

'Where were the graves?'

'Small villages in that sort of area, edge of Dartmoor, the churches are carbon copies of this one, really.' Louise shrugged. 'One was at a place called Peter Tavy. Deborah Potter was liaising with Devon and Cornwall. We'll need to go down there and see what they've got. It was a DCI Hatch, something like that. Bit of a knob, if you ask me.'

'Not until we've got an ID for our victim.'

'Nothing yet, Sir,' said Mark.

'No missing persons matching the description?'

'Nothing from the house to house either.'

'Empty properties?'

Louise took out her notebook, began flicking through the pages. 'There were three. The Old Rectory over there was one,' she said, gesturing over her shoulder at the large house on the far side of the churchyard. 'We got uniform to try them all again today, but there was still no answer. Neighbours said the occupants of two of them are away on holiday, no one knew anything about the third, just that it hadn't long been sold.'

'Let's go and have a look then, shall we?'

Dixon followed Mark and Louise, pulling up behind them outside an overgrown property on the edge of the village. A manmade earth bank with a fence of sorts along the top adjacent to the roadside, bodged from offcuts of wood and old pallets. Dixon thought it was probably a passing-place in the narrow lane in front of the house, but he parked there anyway.

Large trees overhanging the property plunged it into darkness, although the light was going now anyway; a bungalow, wood construction with a large conservatory on the side, the glass tinged green, the roof covered in pine needles.

Louise was standing in the lane, typing something into her phone.

On Rightmove, probably.

'I'm doing a search,' she said. 'If I include properties sold subject to contract, it should come up, unless the agent's taken down the listing.' She spoke without looking up from her phone. 'No, the agent's taken it down. Let me try something else.'

Mark was squinting into the darkness, his hand on the rusting garden gate. 'I think it's what they call a "fixer-upper". Looks like there's a large garden behind it.' He pushed the gate, which opened under protest, had to be lifted and dragged across the path behind it. 'No wonder there's a post box.'

An old tin box, nailed to a bit of wood. Not even straight. Dixon had checked it. Empty.

'Ah, here we go,' said Louise. 'I'm on the planning portal. There's full planning permission for demolition and construction of a three-bedroom house. Nice. Some of these trees look like they're for the chop, but there are preservation orders on the oaks at the back.'

'Any contact details?'

'There's a planning agent listed, but they'll be closed now. It was granted last year, so probably to the vendor anyway. They'll have sold it with the permission.'

Dixon was walking on the flower beds around the front garden, keeping clear of the long wet grass of the lawn, such as it was; clumps of grass, dock leaves, stinging nettles and thistles. Then he leaned over and looked under the hedge, reaching in behind the thick tangle of brambles and dragging out an estate agent's 'For Sale' board.

'Wragges,' said Louise. 'They'll monitor their emails out of hours. I'll ask someone to call me straightaway.'

Dixon left Louise in the front garden, followed the path down the side of the conservatory, several buckets on the floor inside overflowing.

'It's nice to have you back, Sir,' said Mark.

'Thank you.'

'I'm glad they saw sense in the end. Wankers.'

It was an old conservatory, several panes of glass cracked, the window frames rotten. Dixon tried the door. Locked, but he could see the key in the lock on the inside.

'Here,' said Mark, a large stone in his outstretched hand. 'Look at the state of it. No one's going to know, are they?' He gestured to the large window, adjacent to the door. 'That crack could go at any time.'

Tempting, but then Louise appeared around the corner, talking on her phone. 'Thank you for coming back to me so quickly,' she said. 'We're outside a property in West Bagborough and need to know who bought it, please . . . That's it, The Oaks . . . Routine enquiries. There's been an incident in the area and we're doing house to house . . . Thank you . . . No, I'll hold. How much did it go for, by the way?'

Dixon sighed. Their resident property expert clearly couldn't help herself.

'Really. That's a bargain.' She held the phone to her shoulder. 'He's going back through his emails, Sir, seeing if he's got anything.'

Dixon was still holding the stone Mark had given him.

'Victoria Smith. Something to do with the Navy . . . Thank you. When did it complete?' Louise nodded. 'Was she moving in on completion? . . . Yes, thank you. I'll be in touch.' Louise rang off, noticed the stone in Dixon's hand. 'It completed a couple of weeks ago. He thinks she's a naval officer, Sir. Shall I do a search?'

Dixon had beaten her to it. He held his phone out to Mark and Louise. 'Is that her?' he asked.

'It is.' In unison.

'Lieutenant Commander Victoria Smith RN. That's her profile picture on LinkedIn.'

'She was going to live here until the work started,' said Louise. 'He said she wanted to get some changes to the planning permission first.'

'We'd better get Scientific out here,' said Dixon, dropping the stone into the undergrowth.

Chapter Seven

Poland was sitting at his desk, nursing a plastic cup, a whisky bottle on top of the filing cabinet behind him, when Dixon walked into the pathology lab at Musgrove Park.

'Deborah Potter rang me, told me you've got the dead woman,' said Poland. 'They saw sense at last then?'

'Something like that,' replied Dixon.

'How's Peter?'

'Took him home today.'

'Good. We must fix a date for the christening.' Poland stood up. 'Fancy a nip?'

'Can I see her first?'

Poland led the way. 'We haven't got an ID for her yet, I'm afraid.'

'Lieutenant Commander Victoria Smith, Royal Navy.' Dixon held up his phone, her profile picture filling the screen.

'Yes, that's her.' Poland was standing with his back to the door of the morgue. 'Any family?'

'Louise and Mark are getting on to the Joint Casualty and Compassionate Centre now.' Dixon had left them at West Bagborough, waiting for Scientific Services to go into the house, making calls. 'We'll get her service record – that'll name a next of kin – do the usual trawl of social media.'

'I'll get on to the dental team at Plymouth. See what records they've got.'

Dixon followed Poland into the morgue. White tiled floor, smaller white tiles on the walls, bright white lights reflecting off eight stainless steel doors in four rows of two.

'Didn't take you long to find her,' said Poland.

'There was a "For Sale" board under the hedge at an empty property in West Bagborough. Louise spoke to the estate agent.'

'Simple, really. She's in this one.' Poland opened the door, slid out a stainless steel tray. 'What d'you want to see?'

'Just her face.'

Poland unzipped the black body bag. 'We've cleaned her up a bit. There was mud in her nose and mouth, bruising between her shoulder blades consistent with a boot print.'

'Any ideas on the blow to the back of the head?'

'No wood splinters. Didn't find any paint traces either.' Poland was patting the back of his head with his hand. 'It was about here. Do you want me to lift—'

'No.'

'The blow would've been fatal within a few minutes, I expect. The parietal bone is crushed, pushed into the brain.'

'How many blows?'

'Just the one. The back of a ball peen hammer, possibly. The wound is round, there are no sharp edges; about an inch across. They concluded it was a ball peen hammer in the Devon attacks and it fits.'

'What's a ball peen hammer when it's at home?' asked Dixon.

'They're used in metalworking. It's got a round, flat face, and the back of it is ball shaped. A woodworking hammer has those two prongs for pulling out nails.'

'So, he—'

'Yes, *he*,' interrupted Poland. 'A woman could've done it, but it was a mighty blow, took a good deal of strength.'

'He hit her over the head, pushed her into the grave, then climbed in and held her face into the mud with his foot.'

'Stamped on her, more like,' said Poland. 'Judging by the bruising.'

'Then he took her clothes off?'

'Yes. There's not enough mud spatter for her to have been naked when she went into the grave. There was quite a bit of water in the bottom, and she'd have been covered in it. The gravediggers had even brought a bag of sawdust to mop it up.'

'Why take the clothes, I wonder?' asked Dixon, idly.

'Maybe he thought his DNA was on them?'

'Have you got any samples?'

'Several samples have gone off to the lab. Fingernail scrapings, hair.'

'No sexual assault?'

'No.'

Dixon raised his hand, stopping Poland when he reached for the zip on the body bag. Her head had been shaved for the post mortem examination, large stitches across the top of her forehead where Poland had examined the skull. He'd never have made a plastic surgeon, but then his patients were past caring.

Her eyes were closed, mouth pinched. It looked unnatural, but then it was.

'A lieutenant commander in the Royal Navy,' said Poland. 'That fits. She's strong, athletic.'

'Would've fought back.'

'If she had the chance.'

'Took her by surprise then.' Dixon stepped back, watched Poland zip up the black bag, slide the tray back into the fridge. 'Was she struck at the graveside?' he asked.

'Scientific found no evidence of it.'

'Struck elsewhere, incapacitated and then carried there.'

'Might explain why the clothes were taken, if he thought fibres would have been left behind.'

'Everybody's a bloody expert these days,' muttered Dixon.

'You can thank Netflix for that.'

'Scientific will be going into her house, shortly, if they haven't already. She'd just bought a place in West Bagborough.'

'He must've known about the grave too, don't forget that. And this is his fourth attack.'

'Funeral notices are easily checked.'

Poland slammed the fridge door. 'How about that drink?'

Dixon perched on the windowsill, watched Poland pour two small whiskies into plastic cups. He'd got a stack of them on top of the filing cabinet. A jug of water too; just to keep up appearances, probably.

'Cheers,' Poland said, slumping into his chair and taking a swig. 'D'you get to keep your rank?'

'Can't take it off me, really. No grounds.'

'What happened at your interview today?'

'Nothing. It didn't happen. We were handed a letter saying the investigation was over and the file was being passed to the coroner.'

Poland frowned. 'I wonder what changed?'

'The Armed Response officer said he might have been mistaken about there being two guns.'

'Of course he was. There couldn't have been two guns, could there?'

Dixon took a sip of whisky, letting the silence hang.

'Well, how does it feel to be back in the saddle?' Poland asked, changing the subject.

'Surprisingly good.'

'Then you can put that other business behind you. You did what you had to do and there's nothing more to be said.'

'You won't tell anyone, will you, Roger?'

'Tell anyone what?'

◆ ◆ ◆

Dixon arrived back at West Bagborough to find Louise and Mark sitting in her car.

'They still won't let us in,' said Mark, opening the passenger door.

'Was she attacked in there?' asked Dixon.

'Looks like it.' Louise had climbed out of the driver's seat, was standing by the open car door. 'There's blood spatter on the wall and skirting board in the hall. Not much, but enough.'

Arc lamps had been set up in the conservatory, light streaming into the overgrown back garden where several uniformed officers were conducting a fingertip search.

'We've had a bit of luck with the Navy,' continued Louise. 'I had a call back and she lists her next of kin as her father, Michael Kenneth Smith. It's a Minehead address and the Navy are sending a casualty notification officer to tell him.'

Dixon recognised the senior Scientific Services officer, Donald Watson, in the front porch, walked up the garden path and tapped on the glass.

'Is it the crime scene?'

'I thought we'd seen the last of you.' Watson was dusting the inside of the front door for fingerprints, a plastic pot of grey powder in one hand and a brush in the other.

'No such luck.'

'Pleased to hear it. Yes, is the short answer. I've had a look at several areas with luminol, and there's traces of blood spatter here. More on the living room door frame.' Watson opened the door from the inside, gesturing to the wall. 'My guess is she turned her back on him to walk in there, and wallop. There's very little blood on the carpet, which you'd expect, possibly. You can come in now, just stick to the stepping plates in the hall. She was still living out of suitcases, by the looks of things. Boxes everywhere, as you can see. There's a pile of post on the kitchen table, and a folder with all the correspondence about her purchase of this place.'

'Does it give her previous address?' asked Dixon.

'From what I can see, she was living down at HMS *Drake*, and her stuff was in store. There's a letter from her solicitor about the stamp duty, telling her she was eligible for the reduced rate as a first-time buyer.'

'Any sign of her phone?'

Watson shook his head. 'We'll get what we can from the phone company, there's a bill with her number on it. She hasn't had the internet connected yet. There's a letter with a date for installation next week. The rest is letters from utility companies wanting her details. Council tax. Crap like that.'

'Bank statements?'

'Can't see any. She'd probably gone paperless and had an app on her phone.'

'The solicitor will have the details.'

Dixon was standing in the living room door. A two-seater sofa against the back wall, a rug with missing tassels, a corner TV unit but nothing on it.

'The chest of drawers is empty,' said Watson. 'Looks like mice have been at that rug. That sewing box is nice, although the inlay is lifting a bit in places. Must've been a bit damp in storage. Wouldn't take much to fix it, then you might get five hundred or so at auction. My bet is it was her grandmother's. That's usually the way of it.'

'Anything else?'

'Nothing of note. We'll have those ashes out of the fireplace just in case. Kitchen's through there. Conservatory roof needs a bit of work, but I think the plan was to knock the place down anyway.'

'Bedroom?'

'Just a mattress on the floor.' Watson was following Dixon into the kitchen. 'And a few suitcases full of clothes.'

'No jewellery?'

'Nothing to speak of, but then I'm not sure they allow that in the Navy, do they?'

An electric oven, the rings on the hob rusting. Torn lino on the floor, a chipped Belfast sink. The units had delaminated in places, the pine-effect coating stuck down with tape, handles hanging off.

Then a Scientific Services officer walked in through the open back door, holding a small, camouflaged box. 'The garden's huge, Don,' he said. 'I found this trail camera strapped to a tree at the bottom end, near a gap in the hedge. She probably set it to see what sort of wildlife she's got visiting her.' He released the clips, opened it, then flicked a switch. 'Batteries are still good. There we go. Three hundred and twelve clips.' He was scrolling through the videos, each click greeted with a bleep. 'That's a fox. Badger. That's a Muntjac deer.'

'We haven't got time for that now,' said Watson. 'Bag it up. If there's anything on it, High Tech will let you know, Nick.'

'Thanks.' Dixon started flicking through the post on the kitchen table, although it looked more like a camping table, and the letters were mostly junk, or addressed to the previous occupant. He looked up. 'Is there a handbag? Purse, wallet, anything like that?'

'No,' replied Watson.

'What about car keys?'

'There's no car. Those two in the lane are accounted for. They belong to the people in the cottage on the corner. No off-street parking, apparently.'

Dixon dropped the pile of post, picked up the file marked 'Purchase'. He knew his way around a solicitor's file, knew which letters and documents were important. He'd spent two years as a trainee solicitor, then left the legal profession the day he qualified. He liked to think he'd never looked back, but actually he had. Even gone for job interviews.

'Who's Evelyn Clark?' asked Watson. He was sorting through the pile of post.

'The previous occupant,' replied Dixon.

'Wonder where she is?'

'Dead.' Dixon held up a piece of paper. 'This is her grant of probate. Our victim bought it off the executors.'

'Explains a lot.'

A voice outside. 'He's through there.'

'Thanks.'

Dixon turned to find Louise in the corridor.

'I've spoken to the desk sergeant at Minehead, Sir,' she said. 'There's a mother and a father, mid to late sixties. Not taken the news very well, by all accounts. Our victim's got a sister and she's driving down from Bristol to be with them. The casualty notification officer has gone and left our family liaison officer to it. The father is asking to see whoever is in charge of the investigation.'

'Of course, I'll go and see them, probably in the morning now.'

'That's what I said, and they were fine with that.'

Then Mark appeared in the corridor behind Louise. 'There's been a missing persons report, Sir,' he said. 'A woman just rang; says she can't get hold of her friend and she's worried. Not seen her since Saturday night. They were on a girls' night out in Taunton. Her friend got in a taxi just after midnight. Now she's not answering her phone. Nothing.'

'Name?'

'It's our victim, Victoria Smith.'

Dixon knew precious little about the three attacks in Devon, but he knew that much: two of the women had been on their way home alone after a night out. 'You'd better stay here, Lou,' he said. 'Get a lift back with Scientific. I'll need you for cameras, Mark.'

Chapter Eight

'This is it,' said Mark. 'You might as well leave it here.'

A wide grass verge, drive leading to black gates in a high red-brick wall; no latch, so they must be electric, a camera mounted on top of the pillar.

It seemed a nice village, Corfe; plenty of money. Dixon had driven past Taunton Racecourse, so he knew roughly where he was – the posh side of town.

He turned on to the drive, stopped at the gates and held his warrant card up to the camera. He still had it, had remembered to drop it into his pocket before he'd left home.

The gates opened slowly, revealing a long winding drive up to the house, the gravel crunching under the wheels of his Land Rover, no doubt filling up the tread on his tyres.

'Wow,' said Mark. 'Where's Louise when you need her?'

'One-point-two.' Dixon parked behind the Range Rover Sport. 'One-point-five million if there's land with it.' He sighed. 'She's turning me into a property expert as well.'

The front door of the house opened before Dixon switched off the engine. 'What's her name?' he asked.

'Katherine Huxtable,' replied Mark. 'She rang just after five, was put through to missing persons at Express Park. They passed it on to us.'

'And she doesn't know what's happened?'

'No, Sir.'

Dixon glanced across at a life-sized statue of a galloping horse on the lawn; made from driftwood, it was lit by lamps in the glass plinth beneath it.

'Huxtable,' said Mark. 'Isn't he the bloke who runs Taunton Racecourse?'

Dixon couldn't remember the name, even though eighteen months earlier he'd brought a race meeting to a standstill. A tweed jacket and tie had been less than impressed, but Dixon had left it to someone else to placate him. The blood on the concourse might have had something to do with it.

He glanced at the couple standing in the porch. First day back on the job, delivering a death message. Nice.

'Mrs Huxtable?' he asked, warrant card at the ready.

'Yes.'

'Detective Superintendent Dixon. And this is—'

'A detective superintendent for a missing person case?' demanded the man standing next to her. 'I know you, don't I?'

It was him.

Bollocks.

Dixon turned to Mrs Huxtable. 'You reported your friend, Victoria Smith, missing?'

'What's happened to her?'

'Shall we go inside?'

'What's happened to her?' Louder this time, almost shrill.

Doorstep it is then. 'I'm sorry to have to tell you that a body was found yesterday morning in West Bagborough. There's been no formal identification yet, but we believe it to be the body of Victoria Smith.'

Her knees buckled; her husband's arm clamped around her waist, holding her up. She started to sob.

'That explains the superintendent.' The husband turned, helping his wife inside. 'You'd better come in. Shut the door behind you, will you?'

Dixon and Mark followed them into the large kitchen, an open bottle of red wine and two glasses on the worktop. Something was in the oven; a foil tray, the smell of garlic.

The husband sat his wife down at the table, placed her glass of wine in front of her.

'Switch the oven off, Pat,' she said, her face buried in her hands. She was regaining her composure, slowly, although she'd probably lose it again when Dixon answered her first question. She hadn't asked it yet, but it was inevitable.

'What happened to her?'

And there it was.

'I'm sorry to have to tell you, Victoria was murdered.'

'Murdered?' The husband this time. 'How?'

'We're waiting for the post mortem report at the moment.' Technically true. Dixon hadn't had Poland's formal written report yet.

'When was this?'

'Sometime between ten o'clock on Saturday night and the early hours of Sunday, two o'clock, something like that.'

Mrs Huxtable took a deep breath, followed by a large swig of wine. Then she straightened. 'She'd want me to be strong; to help you find who did it.' She slid her empty glass across the table to her husband. 'Whatever you need to know.'

'Thank you, Mrs Hux—'

'Call me Kathy, please.'

'You said in your missing persons report you hadn't seen her since Saturday night.'

'We were out celebrating her house purchase. We had a meal in Taunton, then a few drinks, finished up at Labyrinth. Left about one or so. Pat picked me up.' She glanced up at her husband, who was refilling her wine glass. 'Vic got in a taxi to go back to Baggy, as she called it. It was her dream home. She had such plans.'

Mark had sat down at the kitchen table and was scribbling in his notebook.

'We'll come back to Saturday night,' said Dixon. 'How long had you known Victoria?'

'We were at school together in Minehead, been friends ever since. We both went to Bristol Uni, then she went in the Navy, and I came home. She was my bridesmaid.' Kathy dabbed her eyes with a tissue. 'Is . . . was . . . godmother to both our girls.'

'You saw her regularly?'

'As regularly as her job allowed. She did two years with NATO in Italy, but we went out a couple of times for holidays, and she came home, obviously. I saw a lot of her when she was based in Bristol, but recently she's been gone for months at a time. Then she'd get shore leave. Nature of the beast, I suppose.'

'And you got on well?'

Kathy looked at her husband.

'How is this relevant?' he asked.

'Just background,' replied Dixon, casually. 'The more I know the better.'

'Yes, we always got on, apart from once, but after that we never discussed it, never mentioned it.'

Dixon waited.

'She'd had an affair with a married man.'

'Who?'

'I don't know his name, she never said. It was someone in the Navy, though. It was a while ago, and didn't last long anyway, but I told her what I thought of the way she was behaving.'

'It was a falling out?'

'Not really. It was soon forgotten.'

'Did she have any other friends?'

'Oh God, Jenny. I'll have to tell her.'

'We can do that, if you'd prefer.'

'No, I'll do it.' Kathy puffed out her cheeks. 'Jenny lives at Bishops Lydeard. We were at school together, but she's . . . I don't know what she is, really. She's like an elderly spinster, but she's our age. Never goes out unless it's to church or the WI or hunting with the Taunton Vale. It's all drag hunting these days, but the occasional fox *gets in the way*, as she calls it. Vic let her know in no uncertain terms what she thought of that. You can imagine it, can't you?'

'She held strong views?'

'We both do, on that subject anyway, but we didn't let it get in the way of the friendship. Tried not to, anyway.'

'We'll need to speak to Jenny.'

'I'll let her know.'

'Was Victoria in a relationship?' asked Dixon.

'Didn't have time for that. All she was interested in was her career. There have been men, of course there have. Women too, although she never admitted to that.'

'Anyone at the moment?'

'Nobody would put up with her, not now.'

'Why not?'

'She's away all the time.'

'What about her parents?'

'Lovely people. I've known them for years, since the days of kiddies' sleepovers, listening to Westlife, dancing around her bedroom. They're like family; nicer than my own parents, actually, but that's another story.'

'What I'd like to do is get a timeline of your night out in Taunton, see if we can pick you up on cameras around the town.'

'Oh, right. Well, we met at eight at the Castle. Jenny came, and we had a meal there, left about ten. Jenny went home and

Vic and I walked across to the Winchester for a couple of drinks. Left there about ten-forty-five, I suppose, then walked across to Labyrinth. We went along the path by the river, round the back of the Brewhouse. Then we stayed there until one, when Pat came for me. I sent you a text.'

'The dutiful husband,' he said. He'd taken out his phone, was scrolling through his messages. 'There it is. Twelve-thirty-seven, so I jumped in the car.' He placed his phone on the table in front of Dixon.

'Was there a taxi waiting outside for Victoria?' asked Dixon, glancing at the message.

'There were a couple. It's that time of night, isn't it?'

'Can you remember the name of the taxi firm?'

'They were all Apple, I think.'

'They won't be hard to find, don't worry.' Dixon slid the phone across the table to Mark. 'Was she worried about anything? Seem bothered by anything?'

'No. She was full of this house she'd bought. Plans, what it was going to be like. I'd been with her on the second viewing, seemed like a right tip to me, but then she was going to knock it down, so I suppose that didn't matter. The plot is lovely, great views towards the Quantocks from the back, but the garden will need to be cleared. She wanted a balcony, so she could sit there with a G and T.'

'Were there any local objections to her plans?'

'No. Everyone seemed quite supportive, keen to get the place tidied up and lived in. It's been empty a while; the old bird had gone into a care home, I think.'

'Did you meet anyone on your night out? Notice anything strange, anyone following you?'

'There were a couple of young lads in the nightclub who tried it on. Got a bit arsey when she told them to fuck off.' Kathy smiled at the memory, her eyes glazing over. 'She didn't hold back, did Vic,' she said, pulling a tissue from her sleeve, dabbing her eyes.

'Did you see them again after that?'

'They were still in there when we left. I'm sure they were.'

'What was Victoria wearing?'

'Black trousers, a white blouse and a red jacket. We took a selfie outside the Winchester. My phone's here somewhere.' She was turning on her chair, then reached across to the island, picked up her phone. 'I can AirDrop it to you.'

'Thank you,' replied Dixon, sliding his phone out of his pocket.

'We were a bit tiddly by then,' said Kathy, her face reddening.

Arms round each other, pulling faces at the camera.

'No jewellery?'

'She didn't do jewellery. Hadn't even had her ears pierced.'

'We haven't found a car.'

'She hasn't got one,' replied Kathy. 'She used to have an old MGB GT, but it failed its MOT, so she sold it to someone who was going to restore it. She's never here anyway, so it didn't really matter.'

'Never here?'

She frowned. 'You don't know what she does in the Navy, do you?'

'We only identified her this afternoon,' replied Dixon. 'Her service record is on the way to us now. There's nothing on her LinkedIn profile after 2021.'

'There won't be.' Kathy raised her glass, took a sip of wine. 'That was the year she got what she always wanted. Her dolphins.'

'She was a submariner?'

'Communications officer on board HMS *Agincourt.* It's a nuclear sub.'

Chapter Nine

Mark had rung around and there'd been a couple of community support officers waiting for him at Express Park when Dixon had dropped him off. A couple of extra pairs of eyes to watch the ANPR camera footage.

'Start with a taxi leaving Taunton for West Bagborough. Work back from there,' Dixon had said.

'There's several ways he could have gone.'

'Then check them all.'

Louise had got a lift back with Donald Watson and had been ringing around the taxi firms.

Deborah Potter had been in and gone again. Left a message that she'd be back in the morning.

Eight a.m. sharp.

It was gone midnight by the time Dixon parked outside the large, detached house in Minehead. He'd telephoned the family liaison officer with the victim's parents.

'Yes, they're still up. Sitting right here. They'll wait up if you're coming tonight.'

It was a grim job, family liaison officer. Even the dress code didn't make up for that. Jeans and woolly pullover. Dixon had met Karen Marsden several times before, still didn't understand how she stayed sane; up to her neck in other people's grief, day in and day out.

Two small terriers were yapping at the window when Karen opened the front door. Lights were on next door anyway, so the barking didn't really matter. The neighbours were probably used to it. Dixon's were, although they'd had to get used to a lot more besides: gunfire, blue lights, sirens, helicopters overhead. And now a baby crying on top of everything else. They still said 'hello', though.

'How are they?' Dixon asked, when Karen pulled the inner door shut.

'He's all right. Stiff upper lip and all that. The mother's in a bit of state. Their other daughter rang, was about an hour away, but that was ten minutes ago.'

Michael Smith was standing in the hall, his outline visible behind the frosted glass of the door. Dixon nodded, Karen stepped back inside.

'Michael, this is Detective Superintendent Dixon.'

'Thank you for coming so late.'

'I knew you'd be up.'

'You're sure it's her?' Michael's eyes were wide, pleading.

'We haven't had a formal identification yet,' replied Dixon. 'We'll be asking you to do that in the morning, if you feel up to it.'

'Yes,' replied Michael, swallowing hard.

'At the moment, it's a visual, from her profile picture on LinkedIn. The pathologist is waiting for dental records from the Navy.'

Michael was holding a framed photograph in his outstretched hand. Victoria in her naval uniform, standing to attention, but beaming at the camera, all the same. 'That was the day she got her dolphins,' he said. 'You can see them there, on her uniform.'

Dixon took the picture from him, looked at it. 'Did she have a tattoo?' he asked.

'No.'

'Yes, she did.' Veronica Smith was standing in the living room door, leaning on the frame. 'She never told you because she knew you'd go ballistic.' She gave a sad smile. 'It was a red rose on her left shoulder blade. I thought it was quite nice, actually.'

'Well, I never knew that. When did she get that done?'

'At university.'

Dixon took a deep breath. 'The best I can say at this stage is that we've found a body we believe to be that of your daughter. There is a rose tattoo on her left shoulder blade.'

'Are we allowed to ask how she died?'

'Whether she suffered?' Michael had recovered his composure, was hanging on to it by a thread.

'She was struck on the back of the head, a blow which rendered her unconscious immediately.'

Veronica looked relieved. 'She'd have felt nothing after that then.'

Karen took hold of her by the arm. 'You go and sit down, Ronnie,' she said. 'I'll make us another cup of tea.'

'Something stronger for me,' said Michael, making a beeline for the drinks cabinet against the wall behind the sofa. He looked at Dixon, raised an empty glass.

'On duty, I'm afraid.'

'Of course.'

Michael picked up a decanter, the cut glass giving that familiar 'clink' when he removed the stopper. 'Ronnie?' he asked.

'Better not. I've taken a tablet.'

There was a gap on the mantelpiece next to a carriage clock and Dixon replaced the photograph, a faint line in the dust where it had stood.

'Where is she?' asked Michael.

'Musgrove Park Hospital.'

'She said she might come for lunch on Sunday, but we weren't surprised when she didn't,' said Veronica. 'She'd just bought that house and we thought she was busy with that. She was so excited.'

'When was she . . .' Michael let his voice tail off.

'The early hours of Sunday morning fits with what we know. She'd been out in Taunton, took a taxi home at about one.'

'She was out with Kathy,' said Michael.

'Kathy reported her missing at about five o'clock this evening,' said Dixon.

Veronica had sat down, her elbow on the arm of the sofa, hand across her forehead. 'She rang here a couple of times, asking if we'd seen her. Probably didn't want to worry us.'

'She was a submariner, I gather.'

'Women were allowed on Astute class subs in 2016,' replied Michael. 'That was what she always wanted. To be on the nuclear subs. They spend the whole time submerged; would you believe it? I can't imagine anything worse, but it was what she wanted. Her next deployment was on a Vanguard class; seven months under water.'

'And she was the communications officer?'

'One of them.'

'Did she ever talk about her work?'

'She wasn't allowed to.'

'We never asked either,' said Veronica. 'Didn't want to put her in an awkward position.'

'The sub is in for an extended refit.' Michael sat down on the arm of the sofa, next to his wife. 'I do know that much. About four years it's scheduled to take, something like that. She's on the skeleton crew for twelve months, then back to sea in October; doing the weekly commute thing, staying down at *Drake* in the week, then Baggy at the weekends.' He took a swig of whisky. 'I was supposed to be helping her clear the garden.'

'No car?'

'She used to have an old two-seater, but it fell to bits. She was going to get another, I think. Just a cheap runaround.' Michael shrugged. 'Hadn't got round to it.'

'Taking taxis everywhere was getting expensive, apparently,' said Veronica.

'The buses are bloody useless; goes all round the houses and takes forever,' said Michael. 'I told her to get something sensible, not sure she'd have listened.'

'Tell me about the house in West Bagborough.' Dixon was standing on the rug, with his back to the fire, his sentence punctuated by the snap and crackle of the wood.

'She bought it at auction,' replied Michael. 'I went with her for a bit of moral support.'

'Any other bidders?'

'One, but they didn't have deep enough pockets.'

'Did you help her with the deposit?'

'Didn't need to. Saving was never a problem for her. Submariners get an enhanced rate of pay and you don't spend much when you're at sea.'

Karen reappeared with a tray of tea, set it down on the coffee table.

'She only borrowed half the purchase price,' continued Michael. 'And she kept back some of her cash for the build.'

'Karen said there have been other attacks, a victim who survived.' Veronica had picked a mug and was holding it with both hands. 'Down in Devon.'

'I'll be going down there tomorrow, and we'll be liaising closely with Devon and Cornwall Police. We're much better at that than we used to be.'

'But it's true?'

'Yes, it's true. Three women found in similar circumstances.'

'What circumstances?' demanded Michael.

'Are you sure you're ready to hear the details?'

Veronica straightened, inhaled sharply through her nose. 'We are,' she said, firmly. 'We'll only be imagining all sorts otherwise.'

'Victoria was found in a grave dug for a funeral that was due to take place yesterday morning. All three of the Devon victims were also found in freshly dug graves. Each had been hit on the back of the head with a similar weapon.'

'What weapon?'

'We think it was a hammer.'

Some people wanted to know everything; others wanted to know nothing. Somehow, that seemed like enough information for Michael and Veronica Smith. They held hands tightly, their knuckles whitening; asked no more questions.

'Was she in a relationship?'

'If she was, she didn't tell us,' replied Veronica. Her eyes were fixed on the rug at her feet, and she spoke without looking up. 'She might have said something to Kathy or Jenny, but then she's always been focused on her career, never had a serious relationship. She kept a diary of sorts. Not religiously, just a line here or there about what she was doing. There might be something in that.'

Dixon was looking along the DVD collection, on a shelf next to the TV. *The Hunt for Red October*; *Above Us the Waves*; *Run Silent, Run Deep*; *Das Boot*, in among the others.

'They're Victoria's,' said Michael. '*Das Boot* was her favourite. That's when she was a teenager, mind you. Anything with submarines in it.'

'What about her sister?'

'Rebecca is a doctor in Bristol,' replied Veronica. 'She'll be here in a minute.'

'I'm going to go when she gets here, Guv,' said Karen. 'Come back in the morning.'

Dixon turned to Michael. 'Perhaps Rebecca can go with you for the identification?'

'I'd like to see Victoria,' said Veronica.

'Really, Ronnie, there's no need—'

'I want to see her, Michael.'

'Rebecca will want to see her sister as well, I'm sure,' said Michael. 'Can we all go?'

'Of course,' replied Dixon. 'I have to ask, but can you think of anyone who might've—'

'We were waiting for that question,' interrupted Michael. 'There really is no one.'

'Had she been worried about anything, said anything to make you think there was anything going on? However insignificant it might seem.'

'No.'

'I got the impression something was wrong,' said Veronica. 'She seemed distracted, but I put it down to the house purchase. Told myself that's what it was. There was something else, though. I asked her, but she shrugged it off, said there was nothing. That was Victoria.'

'And you've no idea what it was?'

'I'm assuming it was something to do with the Navy, otherwise she'd have told me.'

Chapter Ten

'The brave face was for your benefit,' Karen said, standing out by Dixon's Land Rover. 'They were in bits before you arrived, probably will be again by the time I get back in there.' Then she added, 'Nice to have you back; it means I can tell them we will get whoever killed their daughter.'

Dixon managed a mumbled 'Thanks'. His 'I wouldn't be too—' waved away with the back of a hand.

No barking when he arrived back at the cottage just before one.

Odd that.

Monty would usually be sitting on the windowsill, waiting.

Still nothing when Dixon inserted his key in the back door. Lights were on, and the television. He recognised the voices. *Goodbye, Mr. Chips*; Robert Donat's voice aged, so near the end of the film.

Jane must've fallen asleep in front of the TV again. She'd been doing that a lot lately; putting it on in the hospital for the background noise.

Monty was on the rug, next to Peter's cot, wagging his tail softly.

Dixon picked up the remote control, paused the film, Jane stirring on the sofa behind him.

'He needs to go out,' she said, sitting up. 'Hasn't moved all day. Lucy put his collar on, tried to take him round the field before Mum and Dad dropped her at the railway station on their way home, but he wouldn't budge. Dad couldn't get him to budge either.'

'Standing guard.' Dixon leaned over, scratched his dog behind the ears. 'I'll take him with me tomorrow.'

Jane rubbed her eyes, yawned. 'How did you get on?'

'It's early days.'

'Nice to be back in the saddle?'

'I suppose it is.'

Jane's grin was lost in another yawn.

'How's he been?'

'Fine.' She'd stood up, her arm around Dixon as they both leaned over the side of the cot. 'He's due another feed.' She sniffed the air. 'And a nappy change.'

'You're quite right, I'd better take the dog out.'

Dixon turned for the door, clicked his fingers.

'He won't move,' said Jane, shaking her head. 'He thinks it's his job.'

A finger hooked in the dog's collar this time. Dixon even tried the magic word – *walkies* – before admitting defeat. He leaned over, picked Monty up. Jane clipped the lead on to the dog's collar, draped it over his shoulder, then opened the front door, Dixon stepping out into the darkness just as Peter woke up and started to cry.

'That's because you switched the film off,' said Jane. 'Thank you.'

A short walk around the lane by the church. Dixon didn't feel inclined to let Monty off the lead in the churchyard this time, not that there'd been any recent burials, just the internment of ashes. He glanced over the wall at the gravestones, shone the light on his phone at the bunches of flowers and pots, most of them blown over at some point.

It felt too early to find answers – even to try.

He didn't know the questions yet. Not all of them anyway.

And he was going to have to get imaginative when it came to people too. Three wouldn't be enough. Not even close.

Deborah Potter had said she'd meet him at Express Park at eight, but she didn't have a magic wand; something she'd been at pains to emphasise.

No, it was something he'd have to sort out for himself.

Imaginative.

At this time of night.

The microwave was on when Dixon and Monty arrived home, Dixon dropping a dog bag into the small bin outside the back door, but not before he'd held it up for Jane's benefit.

'I really don't need to see it,' she said, with a heavy sigh. 'I put you a fish pie in.'

'Thanks.'

'So, are you going to tell me about it, or what?'

'A thirty-four-year-old woman on a night out in Taunton. Gets in a taxi outside Labyrinth in the early hours of Sunday; found in a freshly dug grave on Monday morning.'

'I've been to Labyrinth,' replied Jane. 'It was a while ago and I'd had a few, but I seem to remember it was all right.'

'Mark's getting the CCTV, and he's found a couple of PCSOs to help with watching it.'

'Who else have you got?'

'Lou.'

'That's it?'

Dixon unclipped Monty's lead, watched him trot into the living room and settle down on the rug next to Peter's cot. 'It gets worse. There have been three other attacks in Devon, the victims found in empty graves. All of them had a blow to the back of the head, only he stamped on mine, suffocated her in the mud in the bottom of the grave.'

'I'm sure I saw something about that on the local news. Didn't one survive?'

'The most recent one did.'

'That explains why he stamped on this one and not the others.'

It was one of the questions that needed an answer. 'Could be,' Dixon said, knowing it might not be. It was a reasonable assumption, but that was all it was.

Jane opened the fridge door, handed him a can of beer. 'So, on top of everything else, you've got to liaise with Devon and Cornwall, and you've got three people?'

'Charlesworth wasn't overly complimentary about the Devon DCI as well. A "sanctimonious twerp", apparently.'

'Brilliant.'

'Potter's meeting me at Express Park in the morning.'

'To do what?'

'Explain why there's no one else, I expect.' He took a swig of beer. 'The victim is a communications officer on a nuclear submarine.'

'Bloody hell.' Jane had dragged the fish pie out of the microwave on to a plate.

'Just leave it in the plastic thing,' said Dixon.

'What about the other victims?' she asked, handing him the tray.

Another question that needed an answer. 'I'm going down there tomorrow,' he said. 'Word has it they've got a DNA sample from the attacker, but we'll see.'

'If the nuclear sub is relevant that's a whole other can of . . .' Jane let her voice tail off.

'I know.'

'You're going to need a lot more people.'

'Have you seen Sarah Loveday recently?' Dixon was blowing on his fish pie, one eye on Monty. The dog was sitting up, shuffling closer to the edge of the tray.

'She came to the hospital last week to see Peter.'

'How was she?'

'Seemed fine.' A smile crept across Jane's face. 'Said she was ready to go back to work, but it'd have to be light duties.'

'D'you think she could run an incident room?'

'Standing on her head.' Jane was scrolling through the contacts on her phone. 'Let me give you her number.'

◆ ◆ ◆

Once in the night, just after four.

Dixon had taken Peter into Lucy's bedroom, done the honours, while Jane slept through it. It was only the second time he'd changed a nappy, and it had gone surprisingly well; taken longer than it should, possibly, but they'd both got through it unscathed.

And *once* in the night. He couldn't grumble with that. Poland had said his daughter had got them up on the hour, every hour, until she was nearly a year old.

It used to be called the spare bedroom too, and Dixon wasn't entirely sure when it had become Lucy's, but it had. She'd gone back to Manchester, dropped at Weston station by Rod and Sue – something about exams coming up – but she'd promised to be back for the weekend. It was about stability. Unlike Jane who'd been adopted at birth, Lucy had never had any. Poor sod. In and out of foster care.

Dixon had left the cottage just after seven, Jane's words ringing in his ears.

'Have you congratulated Lou on her promotion yet?'

'No.'

'Well, get on with it.'

He was walking along the corridor on the ground floor at Express Park, uniformed officers staring out of the glass partition as he went past their open plan area. Most looked bemused; wondering how he'd beaten Professional Standards again, probably.

Not that it was a game to be won or lost.

And there was the man he was looking for, sitting at a workstation on the far side, back to the window, a vacant stare at the computer screen in front of him. Top button undone. The Rural Crimes Unit reduced to this, *light duties*. Dixon had asked where he might find PC Nigel Cole. 'He's on community liaison; you'll find him in area three.'

It turned out 'community liaison' was talks to schools and local WI groups. A man who had risked his life to save the young probationary PC in his charge. A man who had stood shoulder to shoulder with Dixon, facing down a man armed with a crossbow.

He was standing in front of Cole's desk for a minute or so before he looked up, the open plan area hushed, necks craned. Nosey buggers, uniformed officers.

'How long have you been back, Nige?'

'A couple of weeks, Sir,' replied Cole. 'I could ask you the same thing.'

'Since yesterday.'

'So, it's true then. And how are Jane and Peter?'

'Home now, thanks.'

'What can I do for you, Sir? D'you know a local group that needs a talk on policing in the twenty-first century by any chance? I'm available.'

'Actually, you're not.' Dixon couldn't recall sarcasm from Cole before, but he could forgive him it. 'I have a major investigation team that needs staffing, Nige. You're with me.'

Cole didn't need asking twice. 'I'll need to clear it with Mr Bateman.' He was already shutting down his computer. 'I'm due over at Cannington Middle School for a talk later, then I've got Cheddar Secondary this afternoon.'

'I've already dealt with that.' That was a lie, but Dixon would send Bateman an email later. If he remembered. 'Get changed out of that uniform and I'll see you upstairs.'

'Is it the West Bagborough thing?' asked Cole, lifting his jacket off the back of his chair.

'It is.'

There were voices at the top of the stairs as Dixon took them two at a time up to the incident room on the second floor; vacant workstations visible through the glass balustrade. Deborah Potter was perched on the edge of one of them, talking to Louise and Mark, a very nervous looking Sarah Loveday standing off to one side.

'Have we found the taxi firm?' asked Dixon.

'Yes, Sir,' replied Mark. 'We've got a name for the driver. I spoke to the bloke at Labyrinth as well and he's sorting out the CCTV footage for us, putting us in touch with the bar staff on duty on Saturday.'

'Good,' replied Dixon. 'You'll be working with Detective Sergeant Willmott, Mark.' He smiled at Louise. 'Follow her lead, trust her instincts. She's usually right.'

'Yes, Sir.'

Dixon noticed Potter's sideways glance at Louise, and the wink. Ignored both. 'Have we got anywhere with traffic cameras?' he asked.

'We've got the taxi leaving Taunton,' replied Mark. 'But haven't picked it up coming back yet. At least, we hadn't when I left them to it half an hour ago.'

'All right. You'll have to supervise them, Mark, but we need you out and about with Lou. We also need to rerun the house to house at West Bagborough. Liaise with uniform, get them to sort it out. We're looking for anything or anyone unusual after the date the funeral notices went online and in the paper. Doorbell and dashcam footage. If he's watching the funeral notices looking for graves dug in remote churchyards, he's going to pay the church a visit, isn't he?'

'Probably in daylight,' said Louise. 'So he can check the lie of the land. Maybe somebody saw him?'

Potter stood up. 'What is PC Loveday doing here, Nick?'

'How many more staff have you got for us, Ma'am?' he asked in reply.

'None; not this week, anyway.'

'Sarah will be running the incident room in that case.'

'A probationary PC?'

'I think you'll agree Sarah is more than capable.' He turned to her. 'And you've got Jane's phone number if you've got any questions.'

'I have.' Sarah beamed.

'She's signed off for another two weeks,' protested Potter. 'Do you feel up to returning on light duties, Sarah?'

'Yes, Ma'am.'

'Well, make sure it is *light* duties.'

'Staffing is one of your jobs, Sarah,' said Dixon. 'So, start by sending an email to Inspector Bateman telling him Nigel Cole has been seconded to the MIT with immediate effect. He'll need to make other arrangements for Nige's appointments today and for the next couple of weeks.'

'Cole is on light duties as well, for heaven's sake,' grumbled Potter. 'He really shouldn't be on a major investigation team.' Her sentence was punctuated by heavy footsteps on the stairs, Cole appearing on the landing.

'I had to borrow a tie,' he said, fiddling with the knot.

'Do you want to tell him, or shall I, Ma'am?' asked Dixon.

Chapter Eleven

'Detective Chief Inspector Hatch sends his apologies, Sir. He's got a golf day over at St Mellion.' The detective sergeant had been sitting in his car outside the church on the edge of Peter Tavy, watching something on his phone, when Dixon and Cole arrived.

Aptly called St Peter's, it was an unusually large church for such a small village – granite, but then everything was on Dartmoor – the heather-clad slopes rising into low cloud away to the east.

Dixon had spent much of the drive looking at a map, folding it and unfolding it, tracing routes in and out of the village. He'd told Cole as much as he knew about the Devon attacks before they'd left Somerset. It hadn't taken long.

Cole had parked the Land Rover by the Peter Tavy war memorial, Dixon glancing up at the church tower, tall with an ornate pinnacle in each corner. Dark stone, blotched white with lichen. A gloomy place, but then it was that sort of day.

Few of the gravestones were upright, most at jaunty angles, apart from the newer ones, perhaps.

Sarah Loveday's text message hadn't done much to lift his mood either:

> *DCI Hatch on a course. DS Reddaway will meet you there. Sorry!*

Dixon hadn't been sure why she'd apologised. It was hardly her fault.

'I've got the key, Sir,' said Reddaway. 'If you'd like a look inside the church.'

Dixon had done his best to hide his irritation when Cole made the introductions. 'I'd like to see the grave,' he said, curtly.

'It's got someone in it now,' replied Reddaway. 'Last I heard, the stone had gone off to the monumental mason to have the wife's name added.'

Dixon stopped at a fork in the path. 'Which way?'

'Left, Sir. It's around the back of the church. Well hidden. They don't get many burials these days. It's usually just internment of ashes.'

'Tell me about the victim.'

'Amy Fox. She's nineteen. Was on a night out with friends in Tavistock last November. Not that there's much nightlife left in Tavistock these days, just a few pubs, good for a crawl, but that's about it. She was a student at Marjon, used to bus it down there every day. She's had to drop out now – been left with headaches, speech and movement problems, and what have you.'

'She was found quickly?'

'The next morning; last seen just before two and she was conscious when she was found at eight. The gravediggers had come back to get it ready for the burial and she was just lying there, in the bottom of the grave.' Reddaway stopped, pointed to a grave along the west wall of the graveyard, the plinth for the headstone empty, lines still visible where the turf had been replaced. 'That's it. Mrs Iris Thatcham is in there now, on top of her husband. He died in the nineties.'

'What enquiries are ongoing?'

Reddaway hesitated, his eyes fixed on the grave at his feet. 'Not a lot, to be honest, Sir. We've pretty much exhausted every line of enquiry. We've got a good DNA sample, though, and Mr Hatch says the scumbag'll turn up sooner or later. He's pretty relaxed about it.'

'Well, I am not relaxed about it.'

'No, Sir.' Reddaway looked at Cole for some reassurance. Got none.

'What about doorbell cameras?'

'There were a couple down in the village, but nothing on them.'

Dixon was standing in the long grass at the foot of the grave, listening to a car going past in the lane on the other side of the church. 'Dashcam footage?'

'None, Sir. We asked local residents, but . . .'

'When for?'

'That night. The grave was dug the day before the funeral was due to take place, so it had to have been that night.'

'When was the funeral notice placed in the local paper?'

'I don't know.'

'Check.'

'Yes, Sir.' Reddaway took out his notebook, started scribbling in it.

'And check when the notice went live on their website. It was probably a day or two earlier. Then repeat the house to house, see if there's any footage after the earlier of those two dates. Doorbell and dashcam. He'd have to have driven here.'

'You think he came on a recce?'

'Wouldn't you?'

'Fuck,' muttered Reddaway.

'Check for any footage in Mary Tavy too. If you turn off the main road there, you can come in from the north, via Horndon and Cudlipptown, avoiding Peter Tavy completely. Better check those two villages as well.'

Reddaway was still making notes.

'I'm guessing from the look on your face this wasn't done?'

'No, Sir. Once we got the DNA sample we sort of . . .' Reddaway thought better of it. 'It matches the other two attacks, so Geoff – Mr Hatch – was relying on that.'

'Was he.'

'When were the other two attacks?' asked Cole. He'd stayed on the path, Reddaway standing behind him, hiding almost.

'Before this one. They were a few weeks apart, last January and March.'

'Equally remote churches?'

'Kingston is even wilder than this one,' replied Reddaway. 'Middle of nowhere, good and proper. A lot of the local churches don't take burials anymore, some aren't even consecrated ground these days; they use graveyards, but he chose burials in churchyards for some reason. Then there's Modbury; edge of the village, lots of trees, no cameras. The lane leads out on to the main road at the edge of the village, and gone.'

'Both girls on nights out?'

'One was on a night out in Plymouth, the other was walking her dog.'

'I'll need to speak to the families,' said Dixon. 'And to Amy Fox.'

'I'd better check with Mr Hatch,' replied Reddaway.

'They are witnesses in a murder investigation.' Dixon was talking slowly, working hard on his anger management. 'I do not need DCI Hatch's permission.'

'No, Sir.'

Dixon noticed Cole stifle a grin, turn away.

'Nothing on CCTV?'

'Some from the nights in question, Sir, but it's not great.' Reddaway was shifting from one foot to the other in the wet grass, the damp creeping up the legs of his trousers. 'We'll need to go back to Kingston and Modbury, see if there's any footage after the funeral notices were placed, in case he went on a recce, as you say.'

'What's the local Plymouth rag?'

'*The Herald*. I'll check with them and the relevant funeral directors.'

'Check for any burial notices at other churches and graveyards in the area during the same period. He may have ruled them out if they're overlooked, but if they are overlooked, someone might have seen him.'

'There was one at Cornwood, from memory, the grave left all over the weekend, not touched. On-street parking only, though, houses all around.' Reddaway was writing notes again. 'I'll check for camera footage.'

'And all three were naked?'

'Yes, Sir.'

'But there was no evidence of sexual assault?'

'None. He just took the clothes. God knows why.'

'And they were posed?'

'As if they were lying in a coffin. Hands like this,' said Reddaway, crossing his hands across his chest. 'Except Amy, of course. She'd regained consciousness and was moving her arms.'

'What about their phones?'

'Gone. We think he took them with him as well, switched them off, then dumped them in water, possibly. We searched the nearest water courses, in case he threw them in. Managed to think of that.'

Dixon resisted the temptation.

'Let me ring Amy, see if she can see us now,' said Reddaway.

'Where does she live?'

'Only over in Mary Tavy.'

◆ ◆ ◆

They followed Reddaway, Cole driving, Dixon using the opportunity to send Sarah a text message:

> *We need a complete timeline of the Devon attacks, starting with when funeral notices went online and in paper.*

The bungalow backed on to open moorland, a small herd of ponies visible in among the gorse bushes on the slopes behind it.

Or was it a herd of small ponies?

Both, probably. Not that it mattered.

What mattered was that Dixon was about to meet a survivor. A young girl attacked with a ball peen hammer and left to die in a grave in a remote churchyard. And there was no doubt that Peter Tavy was remote.

Mary Tavy was at least on the main road from Okehampton to Tavistock, although the bungalow was in a side turning, one that ended at a cattle grid. Dixon had counted eight houses scattered along it, fields in between, the land falling away to Smallacombe Bottom before rising again on the far side of the valley to the glider club. Good dog walking country, the moor crisscrossed by paths. Plenty of places to park.

Plenty of places to hide.

A taxi would've dropped her outside her house, surely?

And she lived at home with her parents.

The questions were starting to come thick and fast now. Three attacks. A dog walker – opportunistic, probably. He'd been on a recce of the churchyard and suddenly there she was. That made sense. But what about the others? What about Amy Fox?

On a night out in Tavistock.

No bus at that time of night.

There'd been CCTV footage of her getting in a taxi, but Devon and Cornwall had never been able to trace the driver.

Cole parked behind Reddaway's car, watching while Dixon finished dragging the satellite images across the screen of his phone.

'If he went north, he'd have got on the A30 at Okehampton,' Cole said. 'I would.'

'Why?' asked Dixon.

'Too many cameras Lifton way.'

'What if he lives to the south?'

'I'd still go north,' replied Cole. 'Look at it. Lanes. Remote. Then you're on a dual carriageway and gone. I'd go all the way to Exeter on the A30, then south again on the A38. It might be a long way round, but you'd be lost in the crowd that way. They'll have checked the traffic cameras between here and Tavistock. There must be some in the town and the A386 goes right through the middle.'

Reddaway was standing on the drive, in front of the Land Rover, hands in his pockets, stamping his feet.

'C'mon, Nige. Let's get this over with.'

They followed Reddaway, squeezing between his car and the hedge, stopping at the back of the van parked in front of the garage. Dixon looked down at the hydraulic ramp.

'A few mobility issues?'

'That's what I was told.' Reddaway shrugged. 'I've not met the family before.'

A teenage boy was standing in the open front door of the bungalow. 'You'll be the police,' he said, nervously.

'We are,' replied Dixon. Then he made the introductions, told Reddaway to wait outside.

'DCI Hatch would want me to—'

Cole closed the front door behind them, cutting him off mid-sentence.

'Sandra's getting her ready,' said the boy.

Dixon thought it best not to ask.

'Are you her brother?' asked Cole.

'Boyfriend. My name's Anthony, but everyone calls me Ant. Sandra's her mum.'

Eighteen or nineteen, possibly. A student, judging by the Marjon hoodie; come straight from college. Dixon glanced through the open door into the dining room, a laptop and books on the table, a small rucksack on the floor by the chair. Amy had been at Marjon too. Dixon knew that much.

'How long have you and Amy been together?' he asked, more to fill the awkward silence while they waited in the hall.

'Since school.'

Childhood sweethearts then.

'Were you out with her the night of the attack?'

Ant gave a sad sigh. 'Wish I had been. This would never have happened.'

'Where were you?'

'Football. We'd had an away match, so Amy had gone for a girls' night out, met some friends down in Tavi.'

'And she'd usually take a taxi home?'

Ant folded his arms tightly across his chest. 'I'd go and pick her up, but I wasn't there, was I?'

'It's not your fault, Ant,' said Cole, his hand on the boy's shoulder.

'That's what everybody tells me.'

The door of the bedroom opened and Sandra bustled out, carrying a small plastic bag, tightly knotted at the top. 'I thought my days of changing nappies were behind me,' she whispered, a sadness to her voice. 'Let me sort myself out, I'll just be a sec.' Then she disappeared into the bathroom, locked the door behind her.

A tired face, but then she had become her only child's full-time carer. Jeans, a hand-knitted brown pullover, frayed at the cuffs and sagging at the waist. No older than forty, perhaps, so must've had Amy young.

A strong smell of lavender had wafted into the hall when she'd opened the bedroom door, more when she emerged from the bathroom, a cloud of room spray settling on the floor. 'Right then.' She finished drying her hands, draped the towel over her shoulder. 'They said on the phone you were from Somerset, so I'm guessing there's been another murder up there?'

'At the weekend,' replied Dixon.

Sandra hesitated, something left unsaid. Dixon could guess.

'Well, I'm not sure how much help Amy can be, I'm afraid, but you're welcome to see for yourself.'

'I'll wait in the dining room,' said Ant.

Sandra opened the door slowly. 'She's not been home long. They gave us this bed, and the hoist. We've got a wheelchair and the van as well, but she can't sit up in a chair. Not yet anyway.'

It was a teenager's bedroom. Once. The posters on the walls were still there; of movies Dixon hadn't seen, pop stars he didn't recognise. The wardrobe had gone, to make room for the large hydraulic bed and the hoist. The bedside table was covered in medication, a chart on the wall above it, the chest of drawers hidden under boxes of clean pads.

Cole closed the door behind them.

Amy was covered by a sheet, her head on the pillow, face turned to watch the ponies on the hillside out of the window.

'It's early days,' said Sandra. 'The doctors tell us she will get better.' There was optimism in her voice, but not her eyes. 'A physiotherapist is coming every day and we'll soon get you sitting up in a chair. Then we can go out.' Sandra was standing by the bed, holding her daughter's hand, rubbing the back of it.

Amy was still looking out of the window, her neatly combed hair covering the side of her face. Sandra leaned over and brushed it back. 'You've got a bald patch on the back, haven't you?' she said. Then she turned to Dixon, mouthed, 'Where they had to operate.'

He nodded his understanding.

'This is a police officer, Amy. He wants to know if you've remembered anything about the night you were attacked.' Sandra waited, looked down at her hand. 'One squeeze, that means no.'

Probably for the best.

Cole was breathing deeply through his nose behind Dixon, thinking about Sarah Loveday, no doubt, and the night she'd been hit on the head with a shotgun butt. A craniectomy in the back of the ambulance, a helicopter ride to Bristol. Sarah had been lucky. Not so Amy. She hadn't been found until the following morning; was lucky to be alive.

Lucky?

Dixon didn't know the answer to that one. And it was a question it felt better not to ask at all.

'Ant's a nice lad, isn't he?' he said.

'Comes every day.' Sandra gave a heavy sigh. 'We keep telling him not to, and his parents aren't too happy about it, either. Lots of lads would've run for the hills, but not Ant.'

'What about your husband?'

'HGV Class 1. He's had to go back to doing the long-distance stuff.' A flash of anger. 'We need the money. And I'd rather he did that than left us. He's not coping with it, to be honest.'

'Have you made a claim to the Criminal Injuries Compensation Authority?' asked Dixon.

'Someone did mention it, but . . .'

'Amy will be entitled to compensation, and it takes a while, so my advice would be to start the process sooner rather than later. You've got two years from the date of—'

'How do we do it?' interrupted Sandra, sparing Dixon the need to find the right words – the risk of finding the wrong words – to describe what had happened to her daughter.

'See a solicitor. A specialist. There'll be one in Plymouth.'

'I will. Thank you.'

Dixon had walked around the bed, was standing with his back to the window, blocking Amy's view of the ponies. She lifted her eyes slowly to meet his. He smiled. 'Can you remember if you rang for a taxi that night, Amy?'

'She didn't,' replied Sandra. 'They checked her calls. And there's usually no need. There's always one or two waiting in the square or opposite the Bedford.'

Tears started to trickle down Amy's cheeks on to the pillow.

'D'you remember something?' asked Dixon.

'Two squeezes,' said Sandra, her eyes wide. 'Let me get the chart they gave us.' She moved in front of Dixon, propped a large wooden board with the alphabet on it against the side rails of the bed, then began pointing to each letter in turn, all the while holding Amy's hand.

'W.' Sandra started the process again, but immediately stopped. 'A.' Again. 'L.'

'Walking?' asked Dixon.

'She says yes.'

'He stopped in Peter Tavy, told you to get out, so you started walking home?'

'Two squeezes.'

'Is that the last thing you remember?'

'Two squeezes.'

'A man then?'

'Two squeezes.'

'Is that what you *know* happened?'

'She says yes.'

'Can you picture the man?'

'No.' Sandra was holding Amy's hand tightly; hadn't noticed her eyes fixed on the alphabet chart.

'Try this again,' said Dixon gesturing to it.

'W . . . H . . . I . . .'

'He was a white man,' said Dixon.

'Yes.'

Amy blinked. Twice.

'That's our signal that she's in pain,' said Sandra, grimacing. 'I need to give her something, which means she'll sleep.'

Dixon took the hint, headed for the door. He was waiting in the hall a few moments later when Sandra emerged from the bedroom, closing the door softly behind her.

'You might as well go, Ant,' she said. 'I've had to give her something for the pain, so she'll be asleep all afternoon.'

The boy started packing up his books, closed his laptop, slid it into the top of his rucksack.

Sandra turned to Dixon. 'I know what you're going to say, and I'll keep working on it.'

'We can send over some specially trained officers if that might help.'

'It's worth another go. The Devon and Cornwall lot tried it, but she seems to be remembering more.' She watched Ant leave, then turned back to Dixon. 'He sits there all afternoon sometimes, reading to her. He's had to help me with things a boy of that age shouldn't have to deal with, but he takes it in his stride. And d'you know why?'

'Because he loves her,' replied Dixon.

'How did you know this bastard stopped in Peter Tavy, told her to get out of the car?'

'There are no streetlights there, and it's the easiest way of taking her by surprise. He tells her to get out, she does so, starts walking, and—' There was no need to spell it out. 'He probably drove her right to the church.'

'The Somerset attack, is it the same?' Sandra sounded hesitant; probably knew she shouldn't be asking.

'She was on a night out in Taunton, found in a grave at West Bagborough on Monday morning,' replied Dixon. That would do. Anything more felt like too much information.

'I've never had a lot of confidence in the Devon lot, but you . . .' Sandra shook her head. 'You're different. Find who did this to my daughter.'

'He will,' said Cole.

'It's the one thing that keeps me going, the idea that one day I'll be able to look into his eyes and watch him go down for life.' She looked down at the business card Dixon had given her. 'If she remembers anything I'll ring you first.'

Chapter Twelve

'Well?' asked Reddaway, scrambling out of his car.

'She's starting to remember things. You might want to get your family liaison officer back up here. A specialist interview team too.'

'What things?'

'The taxi driver was white,' replied Cole, sensing – quite rightly – that Dixon was going to ignore the question. 'He drove her to Peter Tavy, told her to get out of the car and walk the rest of the way. You can imagine it, can't you. Pretends he doesn't know the way to Mary Tavy, maybe he's got another pickup, tells her it's not that far. She's on foot then, and right where he wants her.'

'We thought it was probably something like that. What does she say about the driver?'

'Just that he was white.'

'Is that it?'

'Give her time,' snapped Dixon.

'Yes, Sir.' Reddaway was standing by his car, the engine running, heaters on. 'Where to now?'

'Your incident room is at Crownhill, isn't it?'

'Yes, Sir.'

'Good. We'll follow you. I'm assuming we go through the middle of Tavistock?'

'We can do.'

They drove in silence – almost – Cole following Reddaway down into Tavistock.

'What did we learn from that?' he asked Dixon.

'Nothing we didn't know already.'

'What were we doing there then?'

'Motivation.'

He pulled in behind Reddaway outside the town hall; a large ornate building, granite, much like the Dartmoor churches, with tall chimneys and what looked like a church tower. There was a wide open space in front of it, shoppers milling about.

'This is where they hold the pannier market,' said Reddaway, appearing at the passenger window. 'We're parked in the taxi rank.'

'You spoke to the taxi drivers?'

'We did. All of them. We think he was using a set of magnetic taxi signs. Stick them on the front doors and Amy would've thought for all the world she was getting in a real taxi.'

'Where's the CCTV?' asked Dixon.

'There's some on the front of the Bedford Hotel over there, but if you go up that road there you can get out of town without going past any cameras. We think that must be the way he went.'

Dixon turned in his seat to look up the narrow road behind him.

'Then it's lanes all the way across to Peter Tavy. DCI Hatch is convinced he's local and knows the roads like the back of his hand, knows where the cameras are.'

'What about the night in question?' asked Dixon. 'Did the taxi drivers report seeing anything unusual?'

'One said he saw a car parked in the taxi rank, but it pulled away each time he arrived. We think that was him. Obviously. It was a dark saloon of some sort. That was the best the bloke could say. We hunted high and low for dashcam footage but haven't come up with any.'

◆ ◆ ◆

The second floor of Crownhill police station looked much the same as any other. Open plan, meeting rooms around the outside.

The windows were smaller but that was about the only difference. That and the fact Dixon didn't know anyone. Not that there were many there. A couple of workstations were occupied, perhaps.

There were three whiteboards. One for each of the victims. A quick glance around the room to check no one was looking, then he slid his phone out of his pocket and took photos of each.

The first victim had been murdered on 31 January last year. She'd been on a night out in Plymouth, left her friends in the nightclub just before one the morning, walked out and was never seen again. Apart from on CCTV, leaving the club and then, five minutes later, walking along Union Street.

There was a photograph of her in the top middle of the first whiteboard. Her name – Kirsty Franklin – scribbled underneath in block capitals. Then came her parents, brother and sister. A picture of a hair salon in Mutley Plain.

She'd been found on the Monday morning in a grave dug at Kingston church. Dixon leaned in and looked at the red crosses that had been drawn on a map, colour printed on an A4 piece of paper and Sellotaped to the whiteboard.

Union Street, Mutley Plain, Ivybridge – which corresponded with her home address – and then Kingston on the edge of the moor.

Reddaway appeared at Dixon's elbow, mug in hand. 'Her friends said she was going to look for a cab. The statements are on the system, and we've given you read-only access, I'm told. We think it must be the same bloke pretending to be a cabbie. Takes the backstreets out into the middle of nowhere and . . .' He took a sip of coffee. 'Kirsty died pretty much at the time; a single blow to the back of the head.'

'What can you tell me about Portia Woodrow?'

'Walking her dog round Modbury, third of March last year. The poor sod had bowel cancer.' Reddaway grimaced. 'We think we know where the attack took place because that's when her dog got loose. Her partner had the Tractive app on his phone and you can see it on the map.' He gestured to the second whiteboard. 'On the lead until she gets here, by the church, and then the dog's all over the place. We're told she'd never have let him off on a road. When she didn't come home her partner went looking for her, but it never occurred to him to look in the grave. He dialled 999 a couple of hours later and two uniform teams went looking, checked the grave as soon as they found out about it, and there she was. That's it, that we know about, until the attack on Amy in November. And now we've got yours in West Bagborough.'

'What about the dog?'

'Somebody found it running loose, posted on Facebook. He got it back.'

'Our victim got in a taxi and we've found the driver,' said Dixon. 'Maybe he was lying in wait for her at home?'

'What about this CCTV footage you've got?'

Reddaway gestured to a workstation, sat down in the front of the computer. He'd got the footage ready to start by the time Dixon and Cole were standing behind him. Then he clicked Play.

Grainy, black and white; a car in the taxi rank outside the town hall in Tavistock. The timestamp read 0107, which was about right. Then a figure appeared, walking across the open space towards the car, a slight sway to her gait, tottering on high heels. She opened the rear passenger door, got in, and the car pulled away, made a U-turn in one sweep and was gone.

Reddaway paused the footage. 'That takes him straight out of town the way I said.'

'Is that it?'

'That's it. Apart from this short clip.' Reddaway selected a file from a dropdown menu, clicked Play. 'This is dashcam footage from a taxi, timed at twelve-thirty-two. Watch what happens when he comes round the corner.'

A dark saloon was parked in the taxi rank; accelerated away before the taxi had completed the turn into Bedford Square and the dashcam got a clear look at the number plate.

'We got a partial number plate, haven't matched it to any registered plates,' said Reddaway. 'DCI Hatch is fairly relaxed about it. Reckons it's almost certainly fake anyway. What you can see, if I pause it at the right spot – here – is that there's no taxi licence bolted to the rear bumper. Just the magnetic signs on the car doors, but Amy would never have noticed that, not in the state she was in.'

'Where is he?' The voice was loud, angry.

'You're back early, Guv,' said Reddaway, spinning around.

'I didn't have to stay for the prizegiving.'

'Detective Superintendent Dixon is over there, Sir,' said Cole.

'What d'you mean by interviewing my witnesses behind my back, giving my officers orders?'

Dixon stood up, turned slowly. DCI Hatch, it must be, complete with navy trousers and red pullover. Fresh off the golf course, probably. Otherwise, he had very questionable taste in casual wear, to go with the fiery temper. Red in the face too.

'And you are?'

'You know full well who I am.'

'You know full well who I am, *Sir*,' said Dixon, calmly. 'Do you have an office?'

'Yes.'

'We'll take this in there, shall we?'

It was more of a goldfish bowl than an office, the walls and door glass, hopefully soundproofed. Dixon closed the door behind him.

'Firstly, they are not *your* witnesses,' he said. 'And I do not need your permission to speak to them. Is that clear?'

Hatch coughed, didn't answer.

'Secondly,' continued Dixon. 'I am quite happy to discuss with you the orders that I gave DS Reddaway, but before we do that, we need to address why those orders were not given by you months ago.'

'We've got a DNA sample and that is our principal line of enquiry.'

'Is it.'

'It's about resources. You guys know all about that. When I went to West Bagborough you had a DS and one DC on the case.'

Dixon couldn't really argue with that, thought it best to change the subject. 'Where does this DNA sample come from?'

'We think he's forensically aware, which is why he takes the clothes. Once they've been in his car, they'll be covered in his trace DNA.'

'Did Portia Woodrow go in his car? She was attacked right by the church, surely?'

'Possibly.' Hatch sat down, gestured to the chair in front of his desk. 'Anyway, we've got samples from all three attacks. The same, to one in a hundred million, so it's him. There's nothing on the database, though. Nothing familial coming up either.'

'We've got samples off for testing. Hair and skin.'

'It's the same bloke. Open and shut.'

'There are differences,' said Dixon. He was still standing, ignoring Hatch's invitation to sit.

'What differences?'

'Victoria Smith was suffocated in the mud in the bottom of the grave.'

'Maybe he was determined not to make the same mistake he made with Amy; not to leave her alive.'

'Maybe.'

'What else?'

'We've found her taxi driver.'

'That just means her killer was waiting for her when she got home, surely?'

'Which raises more questions and answers none.'

Hatch let out a long, slow sigh. 'It's the same bloke. You'll see when you get your test results.'

'Victoria wasn't posed, either,' continued Dixon.

'She was covered in mud by then, wasn't she?' Hatch folded his arms. 'I made a couple of calls on the way over here, heard about what you did with the regional crime team at Torquay; made our lot look like a right bunch of wallies.'

Dixon turned for the door, spoke without looking back. 'They didn't need my help with that.'

Chapter Thirteen

'Did Sarah set up a meeting?' asked Dixon.

'The First Lieutenant is expecting us at five,' replied Cole. 'Which is plenty of time.' He might have been pursuit trained, but Cole was still leaning back in the passenger seat of Dixon's Land Rover. 'Shall I bring my car tomorrow?'

'Only if you don't mind Monty sitting in the back.'

The dog was curled up on his bed in the rear passenger footwell. He'd had a run on the moor before they'd left Mary Tavy; 'checking the lie of the land,' Dixon had told Reddaway, even though Amy Fox had never got home that night.

'What d'you think, Nige?'

'The DNA will prove it one way or the other.'

'Don't you start.'

'Yeah, but surely DNA proves—'

'DNA doesn't *prove* anything,' interrupted Dixon. 'It's a piece of evidence that needs to be interpreted like any other.'

'It proves a connection if the same DNA is at all three crime scenes.' Cole relaxed when traffic lights stopped Dixon on the outskirts of Plymouth. 'It'll prove a connection to our crime scene too, if the same profile turns up.'

'Yes, it will.'

'Using a stolen set of magnetic taxi plates is crafty,' continued Cole.

The lights turned green and Dixon floored the accelerator, the Land Rover lurching forward. 'What did you think of their investigation?'

'I got the impression they've pretty much exhausted every line of enquiry and they're just waiting for the DNA to turn up something now.'

'And who gave you that impression?'

'Reddaway. I reckon we'll probably end up doing the same thing.'

'Do you.'

Cole was sensible enough to know it wasn't a question, kept quiet.

'Meanwhile this person is free to kill again.'

'I rang Sarah while you were in with Hatch,' said Cole. 'She'd seen the CCTV on the system, alerted the house to house teams to look for a dark saloon. She said there's some footage on the trail camera you might be interested in as well. She's a bright kid.'

'She'd have ended up like Amy if you hadn't gone with her that night. Worth a George Cross, I reckon.'

'No, don't. It's embarrassing.' Cole reddened. 'What are you going to do about Hatch?' he asked, changing the subject.

'Work round him.'

'That must be it, down there. Sarah said to look for the clock tower.' Cole puffed out his cheeks. 'What the hell is in that shed?'

'A frigate,' replied Dixon. 'It's in for refit.'

'A whole frigate, in a shed. HMS *Agincourt* will be here somewhere as well. Victoria Smith's place of work.'

'That's the idea, Nige.'

Dixon noticed the hi-vis jackets and the machine guns first, the traffic cones and crash barrier. Only then did he take a moment to admire the entrance gates themselves. Ornate carved stone, the gatehouse and clock tower behind. He delayed his turn in a little too long, got hooted at by the car behind him, but it was difficult not to think of the men and women who had passed through these gates before him. Victoria Smith for one. Then there were the sailors who'd gone out after the *Bismarck*; on convoy duty even. Enjoyed a last G&T in the mess, never to come back.

It was a sobering thought.

Sarah must have told the First Lieutenant to look out for a green Land Rover with a white bonnet. He was a tall man, in Royal Navy uniform, and he seemed to recognise Dixon's car; waved and gestured to a parking space just behind the crash barrier as a security guard lifted it to allow Dixon to drive in.

'Superintendent Dixon?' A hand outstretched. 'Lieutenant Commander McConochie. Your assistant said mushy pea green, so I thought it must be you. We'll get you signed in first. I've arranged for Commander Vaughan to join us at five-thirty, if that's all right. He's the captain of HMS *Agincourt*, Victoria's CO, and he's come back from London specially.'

Warrant cards and driving licences did the trick, cameras watching their every move.

'We'll leave your car in the car park. I'll hop in the back, show you the way,' said McConochie. 'I thought you might like to see where she was living first. Would that suit?'

'Thank you.'

'She had a cabin in Boscawen Block. It's an en-suite room, but we call them cabins. She'd been there since *Agincourt* came in for refit. I checked and she's on leave at the moment, just bought a house, apparently, but was planning to do the weekly commute. Lots do it. Stay here during the week, go home at weekends.'

'Do you do it?'

'I do,' replied McConochie. He was sitting in the back of the Land Rover, keeping a close eye on Monty. 'I live on your patch, actually. On the edge of Wedmore. Just park in here on the right.'

'This looks like the parade ground,' said Cole.

'It is.'

'What does the First Lieutenant do?' asked Dixon.

'I'm part of the senior executive team, responsible for the day to day running of *Drake*, which is the fleet accommodation centre, basically. All these accommodation blocks you see, the mess, which is behind us, and all the facilities that go with that.' McConochie slid out of the back of the Land Rover, paused to put on his cap.

'Did you know Victoria Smith?'

'I would've met her at a mess dinner at some point. We held a dinner when they came in for decommissioning, which might have coincided with the Trafalgar Night dinner, come to think of it. I'm not sure I could put a face to the name, although I can now because I looked her up on the system, of course.'

'Was she in a relationship?'

'That's not something I'd know, to be honest, unless there was a problem of some sort that was reported to me. Boscawen Block is this way.'

Several people walked past, those in uniform saluting McConochie, their salutes returned. 'There are a lot of civilian contractors on site,' he said. 'More of them than naval personnel, actually. We've got a frigate in for refit. And *Agincourt*. That's the sub over there,' he said, pointing. 'You can just see the conning tower.'

'She's brown,' said Cole, frowning.

'That's rust,' replied McConochie. 'Which explains why she's in for refit.'

Boscawen Block turned out to be a modern building with sandstone cladding. Out of place in among the granite. Dixon stopped to read the inscription on a memorial on the grass lawn outside, a wreath of poppies resting on the marble plinth.

'Twenty-first of April 1941,' said McConochie. 'The original Boscawen Block was hit by an incendiary. We lost one hundred and thirteen that night.'

'Do you have a police presence on site?' Dixon asked.

'The armed police you saw at the gate are Ministry of Defence. They're responsible for the perimeter. Then we've got Royal Navy Police. I can take you over there later.'

'There's no need. We just need access to Victoria Smith's cabin at this stage.'

'And I have the key,' replied McConochie. 'This way.'

Through the double doors, then into the lift.

'If she'd only been staying a few nights, then she'd have been in the Wardroom, but she was living on site, so we allocated her a cabin.'

They were following McConochie along a corridor on the top floor.

'Is there any CCTV?' asked Dixon.

'Not in the accommodation blocks, and not as much elsewhere as there should be.'

He inserted the key in the lock and pushed open the door of a cabin. 'This is Victoria's. No one's been in since we were notified of her death.'

Modern. Functional.

'It looks more like a Premier Inn,' muttered Cole.

'This block's not long been refurbished.' McConochie was hovering in the doorway. 'Shall I wait out here?'

'Thank you,' replied Dixon.

'What are we looking for, Sir?' asked Cole, when McConochie had left the room.

'You'll know it when you see it.' Dixon was standing in front of the wardrobe, sliding Victoria Smith's naval uniforms along the pole, checking behind them. Her cap was sitting on a shelf, above folded white shirts. Polished shoes glinted in the bottom, next to a shoe cleaning kit.

'Ah, there they are,' said Cole. 'I thought it was odd we didn't find her uniform at West Bagborough.'

'We don't wear uniform off base,' said McConochie, raising his voice from the corridor. 'For obvious reasons.'

The chest of drawers was almost empty, but then if Victoria had gone on leave she'd have taken her more personal items of clothing with her; stuffed them in the suitcase they'd found on the floor at her house.

Dixon checked the bedside table, but there was nothing of interest. He even checked the bin.

Functional then. Anything and everything personal had gone with her to West Bagborough, and they'd found bugger all there. Her mother had said she'd kept a diary, but there'd been no sign of that. No phone, no iPad.

Cole lifted the mattress, then looked under the bed. He straightened, shrugged. 'There's nothing here.'

'Have you seen enough?' asked McConochie. 'I'm just conscious that Commander Vaughan will be waiting at my office by now.'

◆ ◆ ◆

Plush carpets, a strong smell of coffee. The office block was old on the outside, new on the inside, sailors and civilian staff sharing open plan areas. Officers with stripes on the arms of jackets hanging on coat hangers were sitting in rooms of their own, the doors ajar.

A paperless office too, judging by the desks.

Prints were hanging on the walls in between the doors along the corridor, all of them of ships at sea. Some modern, some under sail.

A woman appeared in the corridor, mouthed something to McConochie that looked like 'He's here. I put him in your office.'

Vaughan had his cap tucked under his arm, shook hands with McConochie rather than saluted. 'Hello, Alan,' he said. 'Desk jockey now, is it?'

'Winding down, Sir,' replied McConochie. 'I'll have done my thirty before your boat goes back out.'

'Quite.'

McConochie turned to Dixon, made the introductions.

'I was very sorry to hear about Lieutenant Commander Smith,' offered Vaughan. 'A first rate officer.'

Dixon hated uniforms. He could tell an awful lot about people from what they were wearing, but a uniform made that all but impossible. That was the point of it, of course. Uniformity. The military bearing had a similar effect. Vaughan was a small man, but then that just made him an ideal submariner, probably.

'Please, sit,' said McConochie.

'What can you tell me about her?' asked Dixon.

'She was a high flyer. Comms officer, might well have become the Navy's first female submarine captain. She was certainly capable of it, although my executive officer, Judith Towers, might've beaten her to it.'

'Was there any resentment towards her?'

'We've moved on a bit these days, Superintendent,' replied Vaughan. 'Diversity and all that.'

'What about on your most recent deployment – was there anything unusual? Any incident on board involving Lieutenant Commander Smith?'

'I thought she was targeted at random, on her way home from a night out?'

Dixon waited.

'No, there wasn't. I can't tell you where we went, obviously. Operational details like that are classified, but it was a routine patrol. There weren't even any disciplinary issues that I'm aware of. Everyone was very well behaved.'

McConochie leaned forward. 'The submarine service, and I'm sure Commander Vaughan would agree, does have something of a reputation for behavioural issues. USB we call it, unacceptable sexual behaviour, and there have been instances in the past—'

'There have,' interrupted Vaughan. 'But none on my boat.'

'And none involving Lieutenant Commander Smith,' added McConochie.

'How many women were on board *Agincourt*?'

'Eleven,' replied Vaughan.

'From a full complement of . . .'

'Ninety-eight.'

'And what sort of submarine is *Agincourt*?'

'We're an attack submarine. Nuclear powered, but not nuclear armed. The Vanguard class subs carry the Trident missile.'

'Lieutenant Commander Smith was due to join to HMS *Vigilant* in October,' said McConochie. 'That would've been her sixth operational deployment.'

Dixon turned to Vaughan. 'Was she in a relationship?'

'No.' He shook his head. 'Not that I'm aware of.'

Chapter Fourteen

Everyone was there when Dixon arrived back at Express Park just before eight, although *everyone* was still only Louise, Mark and Sarah.

'Did you speak to the taxi driver?' he asked, watching Cole make a beeline for the kettle.

'We did,' replied Mark. 'Went to his home. A very nice, dual-aspect dormer bungalow on a corner plot, in the region of three hundred and twenty thousand. He paid two-eighty-two for it in 2019, according to Rightmove sold prices.'

'All very good and useful background information,' said Dixon, stifling a smirk.

'Thank you,' said Louise, firmly.

'He picked Victoria up and dropped her outside the cottage in West Bagborough. Waited for a light to come on inside the property and then left.' Mark was flicking through his notebook. 'Simple as that really.'

'How did she seem?'

'A bit tipsy, was the phrase he used,' replied Louise. 'She'd been out celebrating something, but didn't say what. She spent most of the drive on her phone.'

'Which we still haven't found.'

'No, Sir. We've got her number, though, and I've put in a request to the phone company.'

'We checked his next pickup too. That was over at North Curry,' said Mark. 'An airport run and he was there on time. And he's got alibis for the Devon attacks; couldn't have been him.'

'What about the bar staff?'

'They don't remember her at all. I've got the CCTV from inside the club, and it doesn't look as if she went up to the bar. Her friend was getting the drinks in. I found the bit where those lads hassled them as well,' said Mark. 'Just looks like a couple of chancers trying their luck, to be honest, then they moved on. You can see them later, dancing with someone else anyway, so . . .'

'Something and nothing.' Cole's voice just carried over the noise of the kettle.

'One of the bouncers remembered them,' said Louise. 'Two *mature* women, he said. One got in a taxi and the other got in a car and gave the driver a kiss, so he assumed it was her husband or boyfriend picking her up.'

'Which it was.'

'When are we going to get the result of the DNA test?' asked Cole, handing Dixon a mug of coffee.

'Tomorrow morning,' replied Sarah.

'You've been busy, I see.' Dixon was standing in front of the whiteboards, both of them full. The board on the left had been divided into three sections, one for each of the Devon attacks. Dixon stared at the picture of Amy, taken from her Facebook profile, beaming at the camera on a beach somewhere exotic. A far cry from the Amy he had met earlier that day.

'How was she, Sir?' asked Sarah.

'Not good.'

'That could've been me, if you hadn't worked out where we were.'

'Best not to dwell on these things,' said Cole, a paternal arm around Sarah's shoulders.

There was even a picture of HMS *Agincourt* pinned to the whiteboard beneath Victoria Smith's photograph. Sarah had used her LinkedIn profile, in naval uniform; looking formal, stern even.

'There's this from *Devon Live* as well,' said Sarah, handing Dixon a copy of a news article. 'One day we'll get to the point when three women getting their dolphins isn't newsworthy.'

'It'll have been the Navy that put the press release out,' said Cole.

'Exactly.'

Sarah had positioned a screen to the right of the whiteboards, a large map of Devon pinned to it, more pins marking the graves at the remote churches on the edge of Dartmoor.

'Anything from the house to house, going back to when the funeral notice was placed?' asked Dixon. 'A dark saloon perhaps?'

'Nothing. There is something I think you should see, though, Sir,' Sarah replied. 'High Tech sent over the footage of the trail camera Victoria had placed at the end of her garden. There are lots of clips, each twenty seconds long, over a period of several days.'

Dixon followed her to a workstation, watched her pull up the first clip.

'They said there was nothing on it, but I think there is. This was the day before the murder,' said Sarah. 'The night, actually. The camera was set to operate between nine at night and six in the morning.' She clicked Play.

Grainy footage, black and white, hardly surprising given that it was a cheap night vision camera.

'Its motion activated, obviously.' Sarah was pointing at the screen. 'See, here. There's his snout.' Then a fox crept in through the gap in the fence, all the while keeping a careful eye on the camera.

'He knows it's there,' said Cole.

'It's something new, out of place, so he's bound to be wary of it,' said Sarah. 'But he walks past it to have a scout round the garden. We've got him coming back again seventeen minutes later. Looks at the camera, then off he goes. There's a badger too, and then three deer all file past the camera for a rummage around her garden.'

'Where is this going?' asked Cole.

Sarah ignored him, selected footage from the following night – the night of the murder. 'I reckon this is the same fox. They're supposed to be territorial, aren't they?'

The first sign of movement was the undergrowth rustling; the fox appeared, not even a sideways glance this time.

'He's expecting the camera now,' said Sarah. 'But watch what he does.'

Two steps forward, then the fox froze.

'He stands still like that for nearly a minute, then . . .' Another clip. The fox turned and slipped back out through the gap in the fence.

'He's buggered off,' said Cole.

'That was eleven-thirty-seven,' continued Sarah. 'Then, just after midnight, the deer do the same, only they don't hang around at all.'

One movement. A deer appeared, stopped, then turned and was gone back out the way it came; the sound of hooves galloping away before the short clip ended.

'There's only one thing that would make them behave like that. They're on familiar territory, don't forget,' said Sarah. 'I reckon they picked up a human scent, someone waiting in the garden.'

◆ ◆ ◆

'Has he had a run?'

'A short one on Dartmoor, and he's just had half an hour on the beach.'

'In the dark.' Jane was talking over the sound of a dog bowl being pushed around floor tiles in the kitchen.

Dixon had sat down on the sofa, watching Peter fast asleep in his cot, the little boy's chest rising and falling. 'You really need to put something else on the telly.'

'He likes *Goodbye, Mr. Chips*. It puts him to sleep.' Jane appeared in the doorway. 'I made a cottage pie earlier. Do you want some?'

'Thank you.' Dixon smiled. 'Getting thoroughly domesticated.'

'Fuck off.'

Monty trotted into the living room, stuck his nose in between the railings of Peter's cot, then curled up on the rug next to him.

'Well? How's it going?'

Dixon thought it best not to shout his reply, so he got up and tiptoed over to the kitchen door. 'I went down to Devon, met the survivor.'

Jane looked at his face, didn't need to ask.

'Do you know what's amazing? Her boyfriend hasn't run for the hills. Most lads would.'

'You wouldn't,' Jane said, without hesitation.

'I'm not most people.'

'You certainly aren't.' She handed him a can of beer from the fridge.

'He's convinced she'll get better.'

'And will she?'

'Who knows.' Dixon snapped open the ring pull as silently as he could, took a swig from the can. 'Did Sarah ring you?'

'This morning. She was working on the whiteboards and just wanted to make sure she got them right.' She handed him a tray with a plate of cottage pie on it. 'I kept it warm in the oven.'

'Where's the—?'

'If you put tomato sauce on my cottage pie I will be seriously offended.' Jane stood with her back to the fridge. 'It's mustard with cottage pie.'

'If you say so.'

'I bet you've been eating fruit pastilles all day, to keep going.'

'I got a sandwich from a garage. You can check my phone if you don't believe me.' Being diabetic was bad enough before, but now there was a sensor in his arm and an app on his phone that recorded his blood sugar levels during the day. There really was no escape.

Jane had picked up his phone, tapped in the passcode. 'What was that spike at eight o'clock?'

'Nige must've put a sugar in my coffee.' Actually, it was a Twix, but Jane didn't need to know that.

She left his phone on the arm of the sofa, leaned over the cot to check on Peter.

'How's he been?' asked Dixon.

'Fine.'

'And you?'

'What's that supposed to mean?' Jane scowled.

'I'm not daft. It can't be easy, can it? One minute you're a detective sergeant and the next you're at home on your own all day with a baby, watching *Goodbye, Mr. Chips* over and over again.'

Jane slumped on to the sofa next to him. 'It was my first day on my own. And he's been lovely, no trouble.'

'But you thought you'd go mad?'

'Something like that.' She nodded. 'Lou said she got through it by watching *Homes Under the Hammer*, *Escape to the Country*, stuff like that.'

'Explains a lot.'

'Tell me about this case then.' Jane turned in her seat, took a sip of Dixon's beer.

'You're breastfeeding.'

'It's just a sip.'

'There's not a lot to tell that Sarah hasn't already told you, I expect. One thing's bugging me, though.' Dixon took a mouthful of cottage pie, spoke with his mouth full. 'We've got a serial predator killing in a comparatively small geographic area of Devon, leaving his victims on the edge of Dartmoor, and then suddenly his next victim is in Somerset.'

'There could be any number of reasons for that,' said Jane. 'She was on a night out, wasn't she, like the others, so maybe it was just that he'd found a remote churchyard with a newly dug grave? The funeral notices will say internment at St such and such's on whatever date. Then he knows a grave will be dug in that churchyard the last working day before the funeral. He's probably checking funeral notices in Cornwall too, looking for burials. A cremation will be no good, will it?' Jane was on a roll now. 'Finds a suitable grave first, then the victim. Sarah said they were posed, the first three anyway, as if they were in a coffin, so maybe he's a funeral director, something like that?'

Dixon was feeding a large chunk of minced beef to his dog, who still hadn't budged from his place by Peter's cot.

'The DNA's due tomorrow, Sarah said,' continued Jane. 'If it's the same killer then Charlesworth will want to palm it off on to Devon and Cornwall and you don't want that. Did you meet the Devon DCI?'

'He was playing golf,' mumbled Dixon, through another mouthful of food.

'Nice work if you can get it. And the taxi driver checked out?'

'He did. It looks like the killer was hiding in her back garden when she got home. The taxi driver did the right thing; waited until he saw her go in and a light came on. Then he left.'

'Is the DNA any good?'

'It's a good profile. There was a small bloodstain on the first victim's thigh, so he must've cut himself on something. Hair and skin traces on the others. Just nothing on the database. Nothing with a sensible likelihood ratio on a familial search either.'

'Typical.'

Dixon carried his tray through to the kitchen. 'I think I'll just take Monty for a short walk, only round the block.'

'Oh, right. I was going to have a shower while you watched Peter.'

And it was a short walk. Over the road to the Red Cow and back. Jane was washing up when Dixon pushed open the back door, Monty's lead in one hand, a gin and tonic in the other. 'It's alcohol-free, so I got you a double. Rob said we can drop the glass back tomorrow.'

Chapter Fifteen

Three times in the night apparently, although Dixon slept through them all. Not that Jane minded. She understood; seemed relieved to see him 'back on the force', as Peter Sellers had put it.

Now there was a box set he hadn't replaced after his DVD collection had taken a full blast from both barrels of a twelve-bore shotgun.

He'd decided to take Cole up on his offer to drive, thought it best to leave Monty at home. 'Somebody else for me to look after,' Jane said, and Dixon let it go. He knew who was looking after who, and after last time . . .

Besides, Monty didn't seem happy unless he was standing guard by Peter's cot. He used to sleep on the end of their bed, but now it was the floor, in between the cot and the bedroom door.

'I'll go online and get him his own bed we can put there.' Jane again; common sense as always.

Dixon wasn't quite prepared for Cole's car. A BMW M3; it didn't mean much to him, not being a car person. Maybe he'd be more careful about accepting offers to drive in future?

The last one of these he'd seen had been parked in a lay-by on the Welsh side of the Severn Estuary, opposite a nice tearoom. The owner had been found by the gig rowers, floating face down in the river off Burnham-on-Sea; on Dixon's wedding day, oddly enough.

Hopefully not an omen.

Cole had reeled off the specifications, expecting Dixon to be interested. Something about six cylinders, twin turbo, three hundred and ninety-something brake horsepower. The only figure that stuck was the top speed – slightly faster than his old Land Rover.

At least Cole could drive it properly.

'I spoke to Sarah,' said Cole. 'She's chased up the DNA result, says to expect it about eleven.'

They arrived outside Jennifer Drummond's house in the middle of Bishops Lydeard just after nine, the appointment made by Sarah the day before.

'That's nice,' said Cole. 'Right opposite the pub.'

A thatched cottage, on the junction; walled garden behind. A new roof too, by the looks of things. The upstairs windows set into the thatch, dormers almost, and a little thatched porch. All newly painted white with green window frames and matching front door. For once, Dixon would've been interested in Louise's thoughts on it.

'Makes me think I should buy the wife a box of chocolates,' said Cole.

'You'd better let me out, then park tight to the wall.'

Black trousers and an orange roll neck sweater, covered in paint. 'I'm just doing the back,' she said from the porch when Dixon opened the front gate. 'I saw you coming, gives me a chance to shut the inner door before my cats get out.'

Short dark hair, black horn-rimmed glasses. She looked a lot like that character out of *Scooby-Doo*. 'Like an elderly spinster,' Katherine Huxtable had said, 'but she's our age' – which placed her mid-thirties.

She waited until they had squeezed into the porch and Cole had closed the front door behind him before opening the inner door.

Flagstone floors, a wood burner, exposed beams.

'This is lovely,' said Cole.

'I inherited it from my parents,' she said. 'They had me late. Father was over fifty and mother mid-forties. Both gone now, sadly.'

'You're painting the place yourself?'

'It's just a roller on a pole. Doesn't take long. I do it every couple of years, and it's taking my mind off what's happened.'

Dixon had counted three cats by the time they reached the kitchen at the back of the cottage.

'I don't like to let them out because of the road, but Boris comes and goes as he pleases. Little sod scratched me again yesterday. Tea?'

'Thank you,' replied Cole.

'Have you got cats?'

'A dog,' said Dixon.

'Does he chase?'

'He will if I let him. Never gets close. I'm not sure he'd know what to do with a cat if he caught up with one.'

'Let's hope he doesn't.' She flicked on the kettle, took three cups and saucers from the cupboard above it. 'You'll be wanting to talk to me about Victoria.' She sighed, took a moment. 'Kathy came round, told me. There's always been the three of us, even after Kathy married. Now there's only two.'

'Friends since school?' asked Dixon.

'Inseparable, we were. Us against the world. That is until they went to uni, then Vic joined the Navy of course.'

'You stayed at home?'

'To look after my parents.' She shrugged. 'There was no one else. I got a job that enabled me to work from home and stayed.'

Dixon sat down at the kitchen table.

'You've left the lid off your paint tin,' said Cole. He sat down opposite Dixon, took out his notebook.

'It'll be fine. How long are we going to be?'

'Not long. When was the last time you saw Victoria?' asked Dixon, watching her warming the teapot.

'Last week. I went over to Baggy to see her new place, help her move in.'

'And how was she?'

'Full of her plans for her new house. It's got planning permission on it, but she wanted to make some changes. She was off to sea again at the end of October, thought she was going to be able to get the planning sorted before then. Reckoned the builders could be in while she was away and she'd come back to a finished house.' She set down a tray on the kitchen table. 'Always the optimist was Vic. I did try to tell her.' She handed the tea strainer to Dixon. 'It's Earl Grey. I hope that's all right.'

It wasn't actually, but Dixon thought he'd keep that to himself. 'You didn't go out with them on Saturday night?'

'Clubbing isn't really my scene, I'm afraid. I joined them for dinner at the Castle, then left them to it. Sugar,' she said, placing an ornate silver sugar bowl on the table, a pair of small tongs sticking out of it. 'She'd got an architect, and he was going to manage the whole thing for her.'

'Kathy said she thought there'd been a relationship with a married man.'

'Oh, that.'

'Did you ever meet him?'

'I knew about it, but she told me it was an on-off thing, was embarrassed I think, so she was hardly going to introduce me to him, was she? I never asked, and she never suggested it.'

'Do you know where she met him?'

'The Navy. I know nothing about him at all. I asked her just the once, got fobbed off, and thought sod you then, if you don't want to tell me about him, that's fine.'

'When was this?'

'A long time ago, when she was at Dartmouth Naval College. I tried again before she went on her last deployment; something she said made me think it was still going on.'

'What did she say?'

'Just that *he* was trying to block her promotion, as if I was supposed to know who *he* was.'

'So, the relationship was still going on?'

'I assume so. I really don't know. I didn't dare ask again.' She reached for the teapot, spotting Dixon's hesitation. 'Here, let me. There's a biscuit, if you'd like one?'

On a plate with a doily, probably. 'I'd better not, thank you. I'm diabetic.' It had its uses.

She finished pouring the tea, leaned back against the worktop. 'I'm not sure there's much else I can tell you, really.'

'Did you fall out about hunting?'

'Not fall out about it, no. We disagreed. I go out with the Taunton Vale and we drag hunt, strictly by the book. Even the sabs don't bother with us anymore. There are plenty of hunts out there breaking the law every time they go out, but we don't, and they got bored, I think. To be honest, it's more of a social thing. That's what I go for, anyway. And we get to ride in places we wouldn't otherwise be allowed to go. Vic didn't like it, so we just avoided the subject. It was never an issue between us. It really wasn't.' She started cleaning a speck of paint off the lens of her glasses, scratching at it with her thumbnail. 'Friends can disagree. I'm against nuclear weapons and she was going on a Trident nuclear sub in October. We got over it.'

'When did she get back from her most recent deployment?' Dixon knew the answer to that one but asked it anyway.

'Last October. She was going to be ashore for twelve months.'

'And how many times had you seen her?'

'Quite a few. I went down to Plymouth for a decommissioning parade when they came in for refit. There was a dinner that night too, and I went as her guest. She was busy trying to buy this house of hers. She'd tried making an offer before the auction, but the seller wouldn't accept it. Executors, apparently, so it had to go to final bids. She ended up getting it for less than she'd offered.' A sad smile. 'She was cock-a-hoop. More tea?'

'No, thank you.'

'I did get the impression something was bothering her when I went down to Plymouth, but she didn't explain what it was and I didn't ask. It was just a bit of hesitation when I asked how the trip had been; she was a bit . . . *subdued*, that's the word, when she should have been excited. It was her first deployment as communications officer and it had gone well, I think. She couldn't talk about it anyway, of course, whatever it was, but I thought at the time it was probably something that had happened on the sub. Must be weird, being a woman stuck down there with all those men. Months on end too.' She shuddered. 'She was fine the next time I saw her. Back to her usual self.'

Chapter Sixteen

'They tell me the fibres and DNA are a match.'

Dixon hadn't spotted Charlesworth's car in the visitors' car park when he'd turned into Express Park. Perhaps his driver had gone off to get some petrol? Hopefully it didn't herald the start of some new tactic.

Sneaky.

Potter was there too, waiting in meeting room 2, looking sombre. Dressed in a black trouser suit, she looked like she was on her way to a funeral.

Dixon closed the door behind him, sat down.

'You caused quite a stir down in Devon,' she said.

'I made a few suggestions for further enquiries they might wish to make.'

'Are we making the same enquiries?'

'We are, Ma'am.'

'These are the supposed churchyard reconnaissance visits?' Charlesworth slid a chair out from under the table. 'Are you sure he made them?'

'Wouldn't you?' Dixon folded his arms. 'There's only so much you can get from Google Earth and Street View.'

'The DNA match puts a very different complexion on it, though, doesn't it, Nick? Devon and Cornwall have had the match for months and check the database regularly.' Potter didn't pause for breath; didn't give him a chance to answer.

'Our Devon colleagues seem to have it well in hand,' said Charlesworth.

'The only thing Hatch had in hand when I went down there was a golf club, Sir.'

Charlesworth cleared his throat. 'I've got the Devon ACC coming here at eleven for a joint press conference at twelve. Shall I tell him that?'

'I wouldn't bother if I were you, Sir,' replied Dixon. 'He was probably playing in the same golf day. St Mellion, apparently. Nice work if you can get it.'

Potter stifled a chuckle.

'He's coming to talk about the future conduct of this investigation, amongst other things, Nick.' An impatience had crept into Charlesworth's voice, at the mere mention of a meeting he was clearly dreading.

'*My* investigation.'

'It's only right that we let them take the lead on it, but I'm going to resist a regional crime team under their leadership. We'll keep our own team on it and continue to liaise as necessary.'

'Our own *small* team.'

'Quite. And you'll be pleased to learn we don't need you for the press conference. I've got all the information I need from young Sarah Loveday, who really should be on sick leave.'

'It's clearly the same killer,' said Potter. 'A serial predator, and he has to be stopped. He'll kill again; I think we'd all agree on that. And now he's on our patch . . .'

'What's causing an issue, apparently,' said Charlesworth, his eyes following someone walking along the landing outside the meeting room, 'is that you outrank their senior investigating officer.'

‘We’ve met.’ Glass partitioning. Dixon hated it. Something was coming, that much was obvious. Either he was about to lose his acting superintendent rank, or he was about to be taken off the case; just to appease some twat in a Pringle sweater.

‘I spoke to the victim’s father this morning,’ continued Charlesworth. ‘Just to reassure them we’re doing everything we can, and to make sure they have confidence in the investigation. They do.’

‘Confidence in you,’ said Potter.

‘Deborah and I have talked about this, and we make up for having a small team by having our best people on it.’ Charlesworth reached for a cup of coffee that had been going cold in the middle of the table. ‘So, if it really is a problem, I’m going to suggest they appoint someone more senior. We just thought you should be aware of the concerns raised at their end, perhaps tread a little lightly.’

Potter was smiling one of those smiles that screamed ‘fat chance’. ‘In the meantime, you’re free to conduct the investigation as you see fit, Nick,’ she said.

‘Whilst being aware of the limited resources at your disposal,’ added Charlesworth.

◆ ◆ ◆

‘What was that about?’ asked Mark, when Dixon reached the top of the stairs.

‘I’m not sure, really.’

‘They were up here before you arrived, sniffing around, having a good look at the boards. The ACC was quizzing Sarah about her health as well, I think. Kept asking her if she felt *up to it*.’

Sarah was standing at the kettle. ‘I told him I did. Do,’ she said, firmly.

‘Talk to me about the DNA,’ said Dixon.

Sarah reached for another mug. 'It's a good match. One in five-hundred million. The fibres found on Victoria Smith's body are a match for some found at the scene in Modbury; some sort of carpet, they think. I spoke to my opposite number at Crownhill. He says it's definitely the same bloke.'

Mark ducked down behind his computer; Louise picked up her phone, headed for the top of the stairs. 'I'm just nipping to the canteen,' she said.

Sarah looked worried. 'What have I said?'

'DNA is proof of nothing,' said Mark.

'It's a piece of evidence that needs to be interpreted like any other.' Louise's voice faded into the distance as she disappeared down the stairs.

Sarah's face reddened. 'It could've been planted, you mean?'

'My DNA was found on some shotgun cartridges once,' said Dixon. 'The buggers left them under my bed. Planted my fingerprints on the trigger and stock of the gun too.'

'Devon seem to think—'

'We're not interested in what Devon think.' There was mischief in Mark's voice.

'When did they run the last database search?' asked Dixon.

'They've been running a search every month. The last one for a partial match turned up the same five profiles. There are only five with a sensible likelihood ratio and all of them have been ruled out. Two are dead and the others live at the other end of the country. They've all been spoken to and eliminated from enquiries.'

'Let's run it again. Expedite it.'

'Yes, Sir.' She hesitated. 'Do I tell them?'

'No.'

Louise reappeared, a baguette in one hand, a can of pop in the other. She'd been Lewis to Dixon's Morse for long enough to know something didn't add up, at least as far as he was concerned. 'What is it, Sir?' she asked. 'Something's bugging you.'

'Look at the map and ask yourself why.'

Sarah replaced the telephone handset, turned to listen.

'Three attacks in Devon, the victims left no more than a few miles apart. Then all of a sudden he's the best part of ninety miles away, in West Bagborough.'

'I put that down to the availability of a suitable grave,' said Louise.

'Then let's check that.'

'I can do that,' said Sarah.

'How many other burials have there been in the last month at remote churchyards in Devon? Churchyards, not graveyards. Funeral notices online should tell us that. If not, we'll need to ring round funeral directors.'

'If we find one, then why didn't the killer use it, you mean?' asked Louise.

'Why did he suddenly come to Somerset?'

'We're looking for a reason why our attack might not be connected to the Devon attacks, aren't we?' asked Sarah, nervously.

'It is *connected.*' Dixon nodded. 'By the presence of the DNA and the fibres. But it's different somehow, wouldn't you say?'

A general murmur of agreement, from Louise and Mark anyway.

'Trust your gut, Sarah,' said Dixon.

'Does instinct trump DNA?' she asked.

'Every time.'

'Not for us mere mortals it doesn't,' said Mark.

◆ ◆ ◆

Dixon watched the press conference from the back of the room; ignored the frosty glances from the Devon ACC.

Vicky Thomas was there, hanging around like a bad smell. Head of corporate communications, with her starched hair. He'd had an email from her about attending a media engagement course, just before he'd been suspended; hadn't replied. No doubt she'd seen him and there'd be another email to ignore, training course to dodge. She'd definitely seen him, so it felt inevitable.

Charlesworth had done his homework. 'A thirty-four-year-old naval officer, Lieutenant Commander Victoria Smith, last seen in the early hours of Sunday morning. A connection has been made with three attacks in Devon, and we will be liaising closely with Devon and Cornwall colleagues to apprehend . . .'

'Has DNA confirmed the connection?' Shouted from the front of the press suite.

'Yes, it has.'

'Nothing on the database?'

'There is no match at the present time, but that situation is being monitored on a regular basis.'

Charlesworth made an appeal for information after that. Anyone with any dashcam or other camera footage of or on the road between Taunton and West Bagborough; anyone who had seen anything or anyone unusual in or around the churchyard either that night or in the preceding two weeks. 'In particular we are keen to interview two men seen talking to the deceased and her friend in the Labyrinth nightclub on Saturday night. I must stress this is purely to eliminate you from our enquiries.'

That was news to Dixon. Perhaps it came from the CCTV image Sarah had taped to the whiteboard; the last known picture of Victoria, talking to those two lads who'd 'tried their luck', as Mark had put it.

Charlesworth handed over to the Devon ACC to talk about progress made in their part of the investigation, just as Dixon's phone buzzed in his pocket.

A text from Sarah. *You'd better get up here, Sir. Now please.*

He slipped out of the press conference just as questions were starting, the first one asking about a serial killer on the loose – journalists did love that label – took the stairs two at a time.

'What is it?' he asked.

'I phoned through the database request to the lab,' replied Sarah. 'They said they'd done it and sent the result through to Crownhill only yesterday. Six partial matches this time. There's a new one, a *screamer* they said.'

Dixon sighed. 'Nice of our colleagues in Devon to tell us.'

'Probably want to take the credit themselves. It's a fifty per cent match with our killer, which makes this person either the brother or son.' Sarah picked up a piece of paper from the desk in front of her. 'Jordan Harris, aged nineteen, arrested over the weekend for possession of a class B drug. A small amount of cannabis, he was released pending investigation on Monday. A swab was taken and it's the best partial by far.'

'Where?'

'Exeter. He lives at 78 Ashleigh, wherever that is; with his mother, Sharon Martha Harris. I'm guessing it's his mother anyway, but it could be his wife. They're both on the electoral roll at that address.'

'And the lab phoned this through to Crownhill yesterday?'

'They did.'

'So much for close liaison with our colleagues from Devon and Cornwall,' muttered Mark.

'Right then, Nige.' Dixon turned for the door to the staff car park. 'Let's see how fast that car of yours really is, shall we?'

Chapter Seventeen

'That'll be them over there.'

The car was very fast, as it turned out. Cole had grinned, stuck the magnetic blue light on the roof and floored it.

The text from Jane had arrived when they were flashing past Taunton Deane services on the M5, cars in the outside lane pulling over to get out of the way. It was a nice picture of Peter, asleep on the sofa with Monty curled up next to him. The speech bubble was still there, and another text soon followed.

Daytime TV is doing my head in Jx

'Them over there' was two Devon and Cornwall officers watching the house. Hatch had placed it under surveillance; apologised profusely for not mentioning the partial match, according to Sarah. 'Purely an oversight,' he had assured her on the phone.

Bollocks.

And that's all familial DNA was. A partial match, but one close enough to be a relative of the target profile.

Dixon had been grateful for Sarah's call. It had given him something else to think about, apart from the Devon countryside zipping past at just over a ton.

'How long have they been watching the house?'

'Since they got the match yesterday. There are two women and a nineteen-year-old male living at the address. Mark reckons the women are a couple of—'

'I'm not interested in what Mark thinks, thank you.'

'Right. They've identified the lad as Jordan Harris anyway, so they're watching to see if his father or brother turns up. One of the women is a Sharon Harris, confirmed as Jordan's mother.'

'How long do they plan to keep watch?'

'DCI Hatch didn't say.'

The car was parked on the opposite side of the road, the officers sitting with their backs to where Cole had pulled in, the engine still running.

'I reckon number seventy-eight is that red door you can see down there,' said Cole. 'That's ninety-six there, so counting along . . .'

A 1980s development, possibly. Louise would have had the information at her fingertips – number of bedrooms, prices. Not that it mattered much. Not this time.

'Some of them are two flats,' said Cole. 'There'll be another door around the side of that entrance porch you can see.'

'Do me a favour, will you, Nige. Go and identify yourself to those two, see if they've seen anything.'

'Will do.' Cole switched off the engine, walked across to the parked car.

Dixon was looking at satellite images of the development on his phone. There was a large grass area with paths cut for dog walking; saplings had been planted, the trunks protected by tree guards. The path went round the back of the houses, right to the bottom, which gave him access to number 78 without walking past the Devon and Cornwall officers watching the house.

Cole opened the driver's door, slid into the seat. 'The lad's gone to work. He's a delivery driver. The mother's at home. Her partner is at work too. She's a carer, apparently. They haven't seen any other male visiting the property at all.'

'Do a three-point turn, Nige. Let them think we're leaving.'

'They'll be on the phone to their DCI by now,' said Cole, watching the screen in the middle of the dashboard.

Dixon was only just getting used to satnav; reversing cameras were a step too far.

'Turn right,' he said. 'Then right again up there and park where you can.'

'Where are we going?'

'To speak to Jordan Harris's mother.'

Down through the trees to the bottom of Ashleigh, then along the line of houses until they reached number 78. Cole had been right; it was the one with the red door.

'Are we just going straight in there?'

'We are, Nige.'

'What about DCI Hatch?'

'What about him?' Dixon knocked on the front door, waited.

She looked at their warrant cards before their faces, obviously used to police knocking on her door. 'What's he been up to this time?'

'It's not about Jordan, Mrs Harris,' replied Dixon.

'It's Ms.' Hands on her hips now. 'What's it about then?'

'Can we come in?'

'If you must.'

Jeans and a red fleece, the logo of a cleaning company on it. Short dark hair, tattoos on the side of her neck and the backs of her knuckles. Letters, but Dixon didn't bother to work out what they spelled.

She gestured to the leather sofa, claw marks on the arms. The sliding door to the rear garden was open a crack, a black cat stretched out on the patio. 'What's this about then? They said he was going to be let off with a caution for that bit of cannabis.'

'And he will,' replied Dixon. 'I will see to it, personally, but we're not here about that. We're investigating the murder of Victoria Smith in Somerset. She was found in a grave that had been dug at West Bagborough churchyard.'

'I saw it on the news. They said it's connected to those murders on Dartmoor.'

'That's right. There's a DNA profile of someone we wish to speak to in connection with the murders and it's turned up a partial match to Jordan. His DNA was taken when he was arrested for possession.'

'Jordan?' She reached for a packet of cigarettes on the coffee table, her hand trembling. 'Are you saying my Jordan's killed these women?'

'There's no suggestion that Jordan is involved in any way. I want to make that absolutely clear.'

'Thank fuck for that,' she mumbled.

'A search of the DNA database has turned up this partial match to him, though. Does he have any male relatives?'

'He's an only child, my father's dead and I don't have any brothers. My wife Jude has got a brother, so he's got an uncle, but they're not blood relatives, are they? That's by marriage.'

'What about his father?'

'He hasn't got a father.' She leaned over, slid open the patio door, then lit a cigarette. 'I mean, he has got a father, obviously, but not one who plays a part in his life, if that's what you mean,' she said, exhaling as she spoke.

'It's not what I mean, really,' said Dixon. 'We need to know who he is; Jordan's biological father. He's the man we need to speak to in connection with—'

She raised her hand, silencing Dixon mid-sentence. 'Just you,' she said, standing up.

Dixon followed her outside, watched her slide the patio door shut behind them. She leaned over, picked up the cat, but it jumped clear of the smoke from the cigarette in the corner of her mouth, raced up the garden path and on to the shed roof.

She coughed, spat into the flower bed. 'Jordan's father isn't named on his birth certificate for the simple reason I didn't – and don't – know his name.' She spoke quietly, her eyes darting along the backs of the neighbouring houses, looking for open windows, probably, listening for anyone in their garden. 'I met his father once.' She took a deep breath. 'Actually, he could be any one of three men I met once, and I don't know any of their names.' She flicked her ash into a flower pot full of cigarette ends. 'I wanted a child. What can I say?'

'Can you describe these men?' asked Dixon. 'Any distinguishing features?'

'No. Look, let me spell it out for you. We met in a nightclub. It was dark. We did the deed in an alley round the back. That was also dark. They might have had tattoos, but I didn't see them if they did.'

'Where was this?'

'It was twenty years ago, for fuck's sake.' She sighed. 'Plymouth. I went down there deliberately to get away from here. The last thing I wanted was to bump into him again with Jordan in a pushchair. I wouldn't have recognised him, but he might've recognised me, and I didn't want some man demanding to see my child.' She stubbed her cigarette out in the bare earth of the flower bed, dropped it in the pot. 'You got children?'

'One. He's two months old.'

'Jude wanted us to have a child, and I wanted it as well, so I did what I had to do to get pregnant. I hated it, but we got Jordan, so it was worth it in the end. Now I find the bloke who got me pregnant is a serial killer. That's what you're telling me, isn't it?'

Dixon thought it best to duck that question. 'Has Jordan ever asked you about his father? Tried to find him, perhaps?'

'He's asked, a couple of times, and I've always told him I don't know who he is, which is true.' She shrugged. 'He's talked about trying to find him, but he's got no way of doing it. One time he said he was going to go down to Plymouth and hang around outside the nightclubs, see if he recognised him, but he didn't go in the end. The idea was stupid and he knew it.'

'And you haven't got even a first name?'

'They never said and I didn't ask.' Lighting another cigarette. 'Look, all three were white, in their early twenties. That's all I remember. Just don't judge me; don't you dare judge me.'

'I can assure you I'm not judging anyone,' said Dixon. 'But you're going to need to have a serious conversation with Jordan at some point. Devon and Cornwall Police are going to want to speak to him, and I am going to find this man, which means he will find out who his father is.'

◆ ◆ ◆

Dixon tapped on the passenger window of the Devon and Cornwall car, the occupants still watching the house.

'You're wasting your time,' he said, when the female passenger got out – a DS, Dixon had met her when he'd been down to Crownhill but couldn't remember her name. 'Jordan's mother doesn't know who his father is; doesn't even have a name. You can tell DCI Hatch it's a dead end.'

'You can tell him yourself. He's in Exeter and he'll be here in a minute.'

'He's got my number.'

Dixon heard the siren approaching along the main road when he climbed into the passenger seat of Cole's car. 'Take a right at the bottom, Nige. We'll go the back roads to the M5, get on down at Kennford.'

Cole started the engine. 'So this bloke Hatch waits for a DNA match, and when it comes up it's a dead end?'

'That's why you can't rely on DNA,' replied Dixon. 'It's just one piece of evidence. Some people seem to think it's a silver bullet. It's what happens when police officers spend too much time watching true crime on Netflix. DNA and CCTV is not the answer to everything. It's just evidence, very often good evidence, but that's all it is.' Dixon was scrolling through messages on his phone. He'd only been fifteen minutes with Sharon Harris, and there were already eight in his inbox, all from Jane. 'Weeks, they've wasted.'

'That's a nice photo,' said Cole, leaning over and peering at the screen of Dixon's phone. Another one of Peter, this time asleep in his cot. 'So, she doesn't know who the father is?'

'You heard what she said?'

'Every word. I don't know why she bothered shutting the door.'

'We'll end up having to do a mass DNA test,' said Dixon, thinking out loud. 'But where? How do we narrow down an area?'

'Chuck darts at a map,' offered Cole.

Chapter Eighteen

'Who is he?'

'Wouldn't give a name,' replied Sarah. 'He's been sitting there most of the afternoon. Wants to speak to the SIO; won't speak to anyone else.'

Dixon and Cole had arrived back at Express Park just before five o'clock after a detour via West Bagborough. Scientific had finished in Victoria Smith's house and Dixon had wanted another look around. Not that he'd expected to find anything. It was more about getting a feel for the place, for her.

On the face of it, Victoria was the fourth victim of a serial predator. A random killing, selected purely because of her proximity to a vacant grave and that she'd been on a night out. A classic case of wrong place, wrong time. The killer had lain in wait for her to return. The DNA proved it.

Only it didn't feel like it.

What Dixon was missing was the reason it didn't feel like it. He'd spent much of the drive back from Exeter stewing on it and all he could say with any degree of certainty was that it wasn't just the distance, the sudden departure from the killing ground on the edge of Dartmoor.

No, there was more to it than that.

But what?'

'I offered him a cup of tea, but he said he was fine,' continued Sarah. 'I explained you were out and couldn't guarantee you'd have time to see him when you got back, but he said he'd wait anyway.'

'Did he arrive by car?'

'I checked that. There's a blue Sportage in the visitors' car park, but it's registered to a hire company in Barnstaple. I'm waiting for a call back.'

'Anything else?'

'Louise and Mark are in Taunton, going through the clubbers in Labyrinth. They haven't come up with anything exciting yet, although they have found those two lads. A couple of pillocks, according to Lou.'

A lukewarm sausage roll from the canteen; Dixon was still brushing the crumbs off his jacket when he opened the security door at the bottom of the stairs. There were several people sitting in the reception area, although Reg was pointing at a man sitting alone in the far corner.

The man was staring into the bottom of an empty plastic cup from the water tower, hadn't seen Dixon standing there.

Corduroys, deck shoes, one of those yellow waterproof sailing jackets over a navy blue pullover. A full head of thick blond hair, straggly, a pair of reading glasses acting as a hairband. Mid-forties, possibly. A wedding ring; an iPhone resting on his knee.

The man looked up. 'Are you the SIO?'

'There's an interview room through here.' Dixon galloped through the pleasantries. 'Sorry to keep you waiting. Have you been offered a tea or a coffee?' Crap like that. He'd always been quick to arrive at conclusions about people based on their appearance; a little too quick sometimes, but he was rarely wrong all the same. Somehow he could spot a time waster; knew when it was worth taking his time too. He closed the door of the interview room, introduced himself, gestured to a vacant chair at the table. Waited.

‘I heard the news on the radio. The press conference. I was out on the boat, came straight in and drove down here.’ He took a deep breath. ‘Where to start?’

‘How about with your name?’

‘Yes, of course. Sorry. Brian Finch. I run Finch Geotech with my brother.’

Dixon had noticed the logo on the sailing jacket.

‘Or at least I did,’ continued Finch. ‘Colin drowned off the coast of North Devon last September.’

‘Let me stop you there.’ Dixon picked up the phone on the table, dialled Sarah’s extension number.

‘Can you get down here, Sarah? I’m in the end room off reception. Bring your notebook.’ He replaced the handset. ‘She might be young, but she’s exceptionally bright.’

Finch was listening to the sound of footsteps running down a flight of stairs somewhere above them. Then the security door opened with that familiar creak of protest.

A knock at the door.

Finch’s face screamed ‘you weren’t joking about her age’ as Dixon made the introductions.

‘What does Finch Geotech do?’ he asked.

‘Right, yes, the beginning.’ Finch stopped fiddling with his wedding ring, sat up. ‘Basically, we do surveys for offshore wind farms. We do geophysical surveys, using sonar, to look for possible locations. Then, when we find one, we do geotechnical surveys to assess suitability. So, with the geophysical survey we’re looking for flat areas at the right depth. We need to check for cables and pipelines, any unexploded ordnance, stuff like that. It’s all done with high resolution sonar; we’ll map the seabed and provide a report.’

‘Who to?’

'Renewable energy firms are our main clients, obviously, but it's not just them. We did the seabed survey for Hinkley Point C. There was a full environmental baseline survey for that one, as well; marine habitat assessment, marine mammal monitoring, sediment analysis. Off the north coast of Devon and Cornwall it's wind farm locations, though. We provide the report and if they get the relevant licence, we move on to the next stage, which is the geotechnical survey.'

Sarah was scribbling furiously on her notepad, although Dixon didn't really need the notes. He'd wanted her to hear what Finch had to say.

'The geotechnical survey involves drilling, seabed sampling; vibrocoring, we call it, which is just taking a core sample. We're basically checking the seabed will take the weight of a wind turbine.'

'You said your brother drowned.'

'He was out with our technical operations manager, Sean Duckworth. They were off Hartland Point, maybe eight miles offshore, so out of sight of land, doing a geophysical survey on board one of our cats. It was a day trip, the sea wasn't unduly rough, the weather forecast was good, but they both drowned.' Finch raised his hands, stared at his palms. 'The catamaran was found by the Coastguard helicopter, drifting like the *Mary Celeste*. They found Sean with his life jacket on, drowned. My brother's body washed up on Saunton Sands a few days later. The inquest is fixed for the week after next.'

'What did the Marine Accident Investigation Branch report conclude?' asked Dixon.

'You've had dealings with the MAIB?'

'Don't ask.'

'They were unable to arrive at a conclusion due to insufficient evidence, but they suspected either Sean or my brother fell overboard and the other one went overboard attempting to effect a rescue. They then lost contact with the vessel, drifted away from it and drowned. All of that is utter bollocks, of course.' Finch's fist slammed down on the table. 'We've never had a man overboard in seventeen years of operations, and if we did there are strict procedures in place that Sean and my brother would've followed. Without question. The coroner's officer said the inquest verdict will either be misadventure or accidental. Misadventure I can live with because there's no negligence involved, but not accidental. That implies it was someone's fault and my brother was the company director on board.'

'Finch Geotech isn't being prosecuted by the Health and Safety Executive then, otherwise the inquest would be delayed?'

'That's right. There was an investigation, they did their bloody best to find something, but they couldn't find any evidence against us. All the risk assessments and procedures were in place, all the equipment. Everything.'

'There would have been beacons on their life jackets?'

'Yes. Sean's activated as it should have done. My brother wasn't wearing a life jacket, which is just ridiculous. He always wore his life jacket. Always.'

'Were their phones recovered?'

'No.'

'What about other boats in the area?'

'There weren't any, according to the MAIB.'

'Tell me about the catamaran,' said Dixon.

'It's one of our smaller boats, a Powerglide 46. Four berths, a top speed of twenty-three knots. It was just out for the day to do that survey. I've got all the charts and the GPS track they were on, handed it all over to the MAIB.'

'Fuel?'

'The tanks had been filled that morning; they had plenty. They were both very experienced operatives. Sean had been with us seventeen years and Colin was Colin. He wasn't some bloody idiot.'

There was a big question coming. Finch needed to talk about his brother first, Dixon knew that.

'What d'you think happened to them?' he asked.

'Somebody or something killed them. It was no bloody accident, that much I do know.'

'Was the boat intact, any damage to it?'

'We had it out of the water for the MAIB inspection and there was nothing.'

'What about injuries to Colin and Sean?'

'The post mortem reports found some bruising, but nothing the pathologist thought was of any significance, bearing in mind they both went overboard. The cause of death was drowning for both of them. Sean had a young family, two kids under five, and Colin was married with two teenage boys.'

'Do you have trouble with protestors? Campaigners against offshore wind farms?'

'Some, but not much. Most people seem to recognise that offshore is where these things should be going, rather than blighting the countryside. I mean, once installed, some of them are visible from the coast, but actually they're over five miles out, and some further than that. Local fishermen have caused us a few problems in the past, I suppose, when we've been surveying what they regard as their fishing grounds.'

'What sort of problems?'

'There was a scallop boat out of Braunton that rammed us. Or threatened to, anyway. Bloody nearly did. I was there that time. We were in a much bigger boat, drilling. Shame they didn't go through with it, really. They'd have come off worse. Some of our staff got picked on in a local pub as well; punches were thrown and the local police had to get involved. Then there was a French boat that got a bit arsey once; started getting in the way of a sonar sweep, but the cat just went off and did another area.'

Sarah was still scribbling notes.

'I just refuse to accept that my brother and Sean died in an accident. The MAIB have given up on it, and the local police aren't interested anymore. I've got a campaign website and a Facebook page. I've had a bit of coverage in the local press, asking for any information. There must have been someone else out there; anglers in a small boat, a pleasure yacht even. I've always thought someone must have seen something or *know* something, and I was right.'

'Someone did see what happened?'

'Two weeks ago.' Finch sat up. 'I get a call from a woman – my number's all over social media – she didn't give me her name, just said she had some information about my brother's death that I might be interested in. She didn't say what the information was, how she'd got it, or give me any idea who she was. She said she'd agree to meet me on the strict understanding that she remained anonymous at all times. She wouldn't give evidence at the inquest or put her name to a witness statement. What could I say? I agreed.'

'Did you meet her?'

'No, I didn't. She said she'd be in touch and rang off, so I waited.'

'Have you got her number?'

Finch slid his phone out of his pocket, opened it at recent calls, then scrolled down. 'It's that one there.'

Sarah leaned forward, made a note of the number. Then looked at Dixon, shook her head.

'Eventually I get a voicemail,' continued Finch. 'Still no name, but she said I was to meet her on Sunday evening. I went, got there early, hung around for a couple of hours, and then went home.

She never turned up, then I hear on the news a woman has been murdered and her body left in an open grave.'

'Where was this meeting to take place?' asked Dixon, although he already knew the answer to that question.

'West Bagborough churchyard.' Finch gave a sad nod. 'I remember seeing the grave, covered in planks. And she was in it all the time I was standing there?'

Chapter Nineteen

The questions came thick and fast after that, all of them from Finch.

'It said on the news she was a naval officer?'

'What ship was she on?'

'Whereabouts were they?'

'Can I speak to the captain?'

It took Dixon a few minutes to regain control of the interview, get it back to where he wanted it. There was only so much information he could divulge, not that he knew the answers to Finch's questions anyway. A few minutes of calm descended while Sarah made notes of the relevant details – names and addresses, details of the fishing vessel that had tried to ram their boat, the fishermen who had started the pub fight, the French trawler too.

Dixon finally got rid of Finch with a promise to meet him at his offices in North Devon the following morning, although that was more to give him time to think.

Sarah showed Finch out. 'Are we going back up?' she asked, standing in the doorway with her notebook tucked under her arm.

'No. Sit.'

She closed the door behind her, sat down opposite Dixon.

He was leaning back in his chair, his fingers intertwined on top of his head, staring at the ceiling. 'Puts a different complexion on it, don't you think,' he said.

Sarah didn't answer, perhaps unsure whether Dixon was talking to himself or not.

Victoria Smith's killing had felt different from the outset and now he knew why. It felt different because it *was* different.

She had been about to blow the whistle on something, and that gave her killer a motive; hardly the work of a random predator, but made to look like it.

'It might not have been her,' said Sarah, hesitantly. 'The phone numbers don't match.'

'It was her. She was a lieutenant commander in the Royal Navy and she's hardly going to have been stupid enough to use her own mobile phone. She'd also have known what happened to Finch's brother and his colleague.'

'Communications officer on board a submarine. She'd have been monitoring radio traffic, might have heard something, you mean?'

'*Must've* heard something. Keep it under your hat for the time being. All right? Just until tomorrow.'

'Yes, Sir.'

◆ ◆ ◆

It was a conscious decision – not updating the Policy Log. It was supposed to be an active record of the SIO's decision making process; more of a stick to beat him or her with later when it all went wrong, actually. But this time there would be implications.

Implications.

They were coming at him thick and fast.

Implications for the conduct of the investigation.

Implications for Dixon personally, and his team. Someone who killed a whistleblower would clearly stop at nothing to ensure the information never saw the light of day.

He parked outside the pathology lab at Musgrove Park Hospital. Poland's car was there, and the light was on in the lab so the trip down to Taunton had been worth it. Dixon left Cole sitting in his car, tapped on the lab window, Poland pulling down his face mask as he opened it.

'Oh, it's you. Fire escape.'

A loud clunk from the locking bar inside and the door swung open to reveal Poland head to toe in green, apart from the blood smeared on his apron.

'What is it this time?' asked Dixon.

'Overdose,' replied Poland. 'I could do with a break, and you look like you could do with a Scotch.'

It took Dixon five minutes to bring Poland up to date, perched on the windowsill in his office. He ended with a question. 'How do you drown if you're wearing a life jacket? Assuming it wasn't put on after death.'

'I'll need to look at the post mortem reports, which I can do later on the sys—'

'Will anyone know you've accessed them?'

'From the logs, yes.'

'In that case, leave it for the time being.'

'What have you got yourself into?' Poland took a swig of whisky. '*Again.*'

'It goes with the territory, Roger.'

'I suppose it does.' Poland reached for the bottle. 'The short answer is yes, you can drown with a life jacket on. Heavy seas, hit in the face by wave after wave, strength going, hypothermia setting in, your lungs will soon fill up. People seem to have this idea that you have to go underwater to drown, but you don't. It's just about the lungs filling up with water. The old adage is you can drown in a cup of tea. You don't drown *in* it, obviously, but if it gets in your lungs, the body goes into spasm and . . . secondary drowning, it's called.'

'So, it's perfectly possible it was an accident. They both went into the water, life jackets inflated and they drowned anyway.'

'I'd need to have a look at the bruising you mentioned.'

'There's a timing issue, isn't there.' Dixon was thinking out loud now. 'One of them was found comparatively quickly because the beacon on his life jacket activated, but he still died from drowning.'

'It's possible,' said Poland. 'But it's also possible he was dead already, had the life jacket put on him and then his body was thrown into the sea. If you want to kill someone at sea and make it look like an accident, drown him.'

'The window given for the time of death was so wide as to be bloody useless.'

'When you give me the go ahead, I'll have a look at the PM reports. Just say the word. The reality is, though – and you need to be prepared for it – you'll probably never know what really happened out there.'

'Actually, I think I'm approaching this from the wrong end, aren't I?' Dixon was swirling his whisky around the bottom of the plastic cup. 'The question is what was so important that a lieutenant commander in the Royal Navy, a communications officer on board a nuclear submarine, was prepared to risk her career to blow the whistle on it? And why would she *need* to blow the whistle on it?'

'What is the Navy hiding, you mean?' Poland curled his lip. 'I've heard of submarines getting caught in fishing nets and dragging trawlers down. There was one that went down off the coast of Scotland. Another got snagged in the Channel, but they were able to cut the nets free. These chaps weren't fishing, were they?'

'Surveying the seabed, so there'd have been nothing for a submarine to get caught in. There was no damage to the survey boat, either, so there was no collision.'

'Another?' Poland was holding the bottle in his outstretched hand, gesturing to Dixon's empty cup.

'Better not.'

'Sounds to me like this might get unpleasant. You need to go and have a word with Jane,' said Poland. 'I'm not sure she could cope with another case landing on your doorstep. Not now.'

'Not after last time.'

'Quite.'

◆ ◆ ◆

Cole dropped Dixon back to an empty cottage just as it was getting dark. An exchange of text messages and he caught up with Jane on the beach at Berrow. She was parked on the flats, facing the sea, Peter fast asleep in his car seat in the back.

'He wouldn't stop crying so I took him for a drive,' she said, when Dixon slid silently into the passenger seat. 'Worked a treat.'

'Has Monty had a run?'

'I opened the door, but he wouldn't get out,' replied Jane. She was looking over her shoulder at Monty, sitting on the back seat.

'I've got just the thing.' Dixon slid his hand into his coat pocket, pulled out a tennis ball. 'I'll take him for a walk, see you at home.'

'What d'you want for supper?'

'Pub?'

'Love to.'

Monty took the bait, setting off across the dunes after the ball. Dixon had remembered to unclip the dog's harness from the seat belt; he leaned against the passenger door until the lock clicked softly, mouthed 'half an hour' to Jane, then set off after Monty.

He did his best thinking when he was walking his dog; made no apology for that. There'd been the odd eyebrow raised when he'd disappeared in the middle of an investigation in the past, but Charlesworth and Potter had got the hang of it now, knew the score.

This time it was too early for answers.

Only questions.

A chat with Roger had helped him to crystallise some of them in his mind, see the wood for the trees, and whatever other clichés sprang to mind.

He kicked Monty's ball along the sand, watched the dog ignore it completely, preferring instead to sniff along the line of fetid seaweed left by the tide.

It would be an interesting meeting with Commander Vaughan, the captain of HMS *Agincourt,* when the time came – certainly more interesting than the last one – but he wanted to know as much as he could about the death of Finch's brother and his colleague first; rule out any innocent explanation.

The harsh reality was that if they'd had an accident or been murdered by fishermen, why hadn't the Navy come forward with any information they had right at the outset?

They clearly had *some* information – Victoria Smith had been going to pass it on to Brian Finch when she met him at West Bagborough churchyard. Only someone killed her before she had the chance.

And if something was being covered up, then orders to do so would've come down from on high, which meant it wouldn't be long before Charlesworth was leaning on him.

Dixon arrived home to an empty cottage, found Jane sitting in the corner of the Red Cow, Peter gurgling on the seat next to her and trying to hold an empty crisp packet. Her glass was empty as well, that much was clear from the slice of lemon in the bottom.

'A pint, Rob, thank you. And I'd better have another alcohol-free G and T.'

'I'll bring them over.'

Monty had given up his usual spot in front of the fire, instead stretching out on the floor underneath Peter.

Jane needed to know what Dixon was about to embark on; what was at stake.

'A whistleblower,' she said, under her breath, when Dixon finished. She let the information sink in while Rob placed a plate of fish and chips in front of them both. 'Find out what it was she was going to blow the whistle on, and you find out who killed her and why,' she said. 'You have to do it. It's your job.'

'What about us? We can't have someone else turning up at our home. Not now.'

'The first thing you'll have to deal with is Charlesworth.' Jane spoke through a mouthful of battered fish. 'He'll try the softly softly approach first. Are you sure this, are you sure that. Then he'll suggest transferring the whole case to the Devon and Cornwall lot. They're content to sit on their arses and wait for a DNA match; pin all the attacks on whoever it is they arrest, and the problem goes away.'

'I'm the problem,' mumbled Dixon.

'You always are. Have you updated your Policy Log?'

'Not yet.'

'Who else knows?'

'Just Sarah. Nige will find out tomorrow. We're off to North Devon first thing in the morning.'

'Neither of them will say anything.' She leaned over, picked up the empty crisp packet and handed it back to Peter. 'Keep it to yourself for as long as you can, would be my advice. When will you speak to the submarine captain?'

'When I've found out everything I can. I need to know enough so I can tell if he's lying to me.'

'He'll dodge all your questions; tell you it's classified.'

'At the moment I'm more concerned about this arriving on our doorstep.'

'It won't. And if it looks like it's going to, you let me know and we'll go to my parents' until it blows over. We've had to do it before. Besides, Mum would love it.'

'Victoria Smith might well have been killed for this information,' said Dixon.

'Last time I looked this was a free country. We don't do government cover-ups.' Jane nodded emphatically. 'Fuck 'em.'

Chapter Twenty

Brian Finch was waiting for them when Dixon and Cole pulled into the car park at Finch Geotech the following morning. It had been a wild ride along the North Devon Link Road, Cole making the most of the blue light on the roof of his car and the overtaking lane in the middle of the road.

Dixon had glanced into the back several times at Monty, asleep on the back seat. Cole had insisted. 'Yes, bring him. We might get a chance to give him a run on the beach. Saunton Sands is fabulous.' Then a slightly hesitant 'He doesn't chew, does he?'

The industrial unit was on the edge of Barnstaple, on the road to Braunton. It was clearly an area familiar to Cole, who'd spent much of the drive pointing out this and that, although that was after Dixon had brought him up to speed on the previous evening's developments. That had taken most of the drive south on the M5.

'You were right then,' Cole had said.

'We'll see,' Dixon had replied.

There'd been a couple of text messages from Sarah along the way. One included a link to a naval recruitment video, Victoria Smith talking into the camera about her career, beaming. No dolphins on her uniform, so before she'd qualified as a submariner. Another warning him that Charlesworth was on the prowl.

Dixon unclipped Monty's harness from the seat belt, left the dog standing on the driver's seat, his front paws on the steering wheel.

'You came,' said Finch. He appeared genuinely surprised, his hand outstretched.

'Yes, Sir. We came.'

'It's a refreshing change to have someone take me seriously. I'm sure the local lot think I'm just some nutter.'

There was clearly a lot of money in marine surveying, judging by the cars in the car park. An Aston Martin with a personalised number plate: FIN 1. That was in the space right by the front door. Then came a line of Audis, BMWs and Mercedes. One solitary Land Rover at the far end, and that was brand new; matt black too.

'The Aston belonged to my brother. His wife, Sandy, drives it now. I told her you were coming and she wanted to be here. My parents are here too. They know about the murder of Victoria Smith.'

'That's fine,' said Dixon, although there wasn't a lot else he could say.

'I've printed out their GPS chart for the thirtieth of September, so you can see the track they were on,' continued Finch. 'I've got it upstairs in the conference room.' He noticed the receptionist stand up when they walked in, gesture to the visitors' book on the reception desk. 'There's no need for that, Izzie,' he said. 'We know they're here.'

New furnishings and carpets, leather sofas and chairs, glossy magazines on a glass coffee table, the walls covered in pictures of the Finch Geotech fleet, although Dixon had scrolled through the images on their website the night before. Two small catamarans for the geophysical surveys; four much larger ships for the geotechnical surveys that involved drilling.

There were various business awards too, framed and mounted on the wall above the coffee machine, so you couldn't help but notice them.

'We're upstairs,' said Finch.

Dixon glanced into the compound at the back of the building as he followed Finch up the stairs; a yellow catamaran on a large trailer.

'That's the *Endeavour*,' said Finch, turning on the top step. 'Hasn't been back in the water since she came out for the investigation board inspection. I got them to bring her here so you can see for yourself. I'll show you round a bit later.'

'Thank you.'

An elderly couple at one end of the conference table, holding hands; a woman sitting on her own at the other end who seemed more interested in her red nail polish.

Happy families.

Finch made the introductions.

The father stood up. 'It must've been foul play,' he said, firmly.

'Sit down, Dad.'

'Colin would've had his life jacket on. He always had his life jacket on.'

'It didn't save Sean, did it?'

'Ask yourself why that is. His beacon went off, and he was found within forty minutes.' He ignored his wife pulling at his jacket, trying to get him to sit down. 'My son was murdered, and I want to know who did it. Victoria Smith was going to tell us, wasn't she, and look what's happened to her.' His wife finally got her way, and he dropped back on to his chair.

'This is the chart from the thirtieth of September,' said Finch, gesturing to the map lying on the table. 'They were off the north coast, roughly at the border of Devon and Cornwall, so south of Hartland Point, about eight miles offshore.'

'That put them over the horizon?' asked Dixon.

'Someone on the clifftop might've seen them with binoculars, but the visibility wasn't great that day. From sea level they'd have been over the horizon, yes.'

The chart had been marked off in grids, a red line criss-crossing each in straight lines.

'You can see them going backwards and forwards,' said Finch. 'Not a feat of great seamanship these days; it's all done with GPS and the cat has got the equivalent of an autopilot on it and a full nav package, so . . .' He jabbed his finger at the end of the straight line. 'This is where they stopped. After that they're drifting and you see the track meandering all over the place. Not the end of the world, because they could've easily picked up the survey where they left off, only they never did.'

'Is that a known fishing ground?'

'We've given all this information to PC idiot features from Barnstaple,' said Colin's widow. 'For all the bloody good it's done us.' She spoke without looking up from her fingernails.

'Police Constable Gifford,' offered Finch. 'He's putting the file together for the coroner.'

'He made his mind up straightaway,' said the father. 'Said it sounded like an accident to him. The fellow's a moron.'

'Do be quiet, Keith,' said his wife.

'And, yes, it's a known scalloping area. An even depth of fifty metres; not particularly strong currents and a good firm seabed. It'd be ideal for a wind farm, although it would be close enough for the turbines to be seen from the shore. No doubt the tourist trade would kick up if they got wind of it.' Finch shrugged. 'Pardon the pun.'

'Don't some turbines float?' asked Cole.

'They're more expensive than fixed to the—'

'*Too* expensive,' interrupted Finch's father.

'Can't complain,' said Finch. 'Floating turbines would practically put us out of business.'

'Tell them about where the *Endeavour* was found, Brian.' His father folded his arms, shifted in his chair.

'I was getting to that, Dad.' Finch sighed. 'This is where they stopped,' he said, pointing to the map. 'Thirtieth of September at fifteen-forty-two, and yet the beacon on Sean's life jacket didn't go off until sixteen-twenty-two. That's forty minutes later. What was going on for those forty minutes? That's what I'd like to know. Forty minutes after they stopped before Sean goes into the water.'

'And don't forget,' said the father. '*Endeavour* is drifting when she's spotted by Rescue 187 at seventeen-fifty-two, that's the Coastguard helicopter out of St Athan, but she hasn't got that far from where they stopped. That's two hours and ten minutes; she should've drifted much further away.'

'None of it adds up,' said Finch. 'But we can't seem to get through to PC Gifford. He reckons they stopped, drifted. Colin went into the water first, followed by Sean, probably trying to rescue him. He says the currents aren't that strong there at that time of year and that's why *Endeavour* hadn't drifted further away, but she should still have been further away than she was.'

'The biggest single thing,' said the father, standing up again, 'is that the Man Overboard button on the navigation system hadn't been pressed. That's the first thing you do. Hit that button and it marks the position on the GPS. Then you throw something over the side, either a life raft or a life ring, and yet all of the safety equipment is still on the boat.'

'It's all in the MAIB report,' said Finch, handing Dixon a document about half an inch thick. 'I printed you off a copy.'

'Can I see the *Endeavour*?'

'Yes, of course. This way.'

Bright yellow, 'SURVEY' emblazoned on the side. Dixon counted five aerials on the catamaran as they walked down the fire escape into the yard behind the offices, accompanied by the sound of heels on a metal staircase.

An aluminium ladder was leaning against the side of the *Endeavour*, another lying horizontally in a clamp on the back.

'That's the over-the-side ladder,' said Finch. 'Still in its original position. If someone had gone overboard then it would have been deployed so he could've climbed out.'

Dixon followed him up the stepladder and on to the boat.

'Right, there are two life rafts. Both still here.' Secured in position by straps. Finch pointed them out. 'That's a twelve-man raft and this one's six. Release the straps, chuck it over the side and it automatically opens. Then you've got a life ring here and another up top. Both are still stowed away. This,' he said, lifting the lid on a compartment behind the wheelhouse, 'is a coastal flare pack.' He took out a metal box, unclipped the lid. 'All of them are still here.'

'There were no radio messages, either.' Finch's father was shouting from the safety of the bottom of the ladder. 'They've got satellite communications on there, everything, and yet no mayday was sent.'

'May I?' asked Dixon, gesturing to the wheelhouse.

'Be my guest. It's open.' Finch followed. 'It's got two beds at the front – or berths, I should say. That's where those steps lead.'

A kitchenette on the right, seating area, then what looked like two gaming chairs at the front, one in front of the wheel, the other in front of a bank of screens.

'What are these screens?' asked Dixon.

'Dual frequency echosounders. They're what we use for the surveys.'

'And this door?'

'That's the heads. The loo.'

Dixon closed the door of the wheelhouse now he'd got Finch alone, sat down on one of the chairs. 'Tell me exactly what she said when she rang you.'

'Victoria Smith?' asked Finch.

'Let's assume it was her, yes.'

'She said she had some information she thought I ought to know.' Finch hesitated. '"I can't tell you who I am, or where I've got it from. I can't talk on the phone either." I said that was fine. I said I was happy to meet at a time and place of her choosing. She said she'd be in touch and then rang off.'

'She rang again.'

'She did. Last week. Left a voicemail saying she'd meet me on Sunday at West Bagborough church. Nine o'clock because it'd be getting dark by then. I got there early, hung around for a couple of hours, then left. Didn't see a soul.'

'Have you still got the message?'

'I deleted it, I'm afraid. I delete them as I go.'

'So, what d'you think happened to your brother?'

'I think they encountered someone out there; scallop fishermen, probably. I think there was a confrontation and Sean and my brother were murdered. There are some out of Newlyn and Brixham, but there's a local lot with a processing plant just down the road here. We've had run-ins with them before. The local police will have it all on file.'

'Have you spoken to these scallop fishermen?'

'What good would that do? There'd just be another fight.'

Dixon slid his phone out of his pocket. 'I'm going to play you a short Navy recruitment video now. It's Victoria Smith talking about her career in the Navy. I want you to tell me if it's the same voice you spoke to on the phone.'

Dixon clicked Play, held his phone up in front of Finch.

His reaction was immediate. 'Yes, that's the voice. Definitely.'

Chapter Twenty-One

'You'd think a coastguard station would be overlooking the sea, wouldn't you?' said Cole, when he pulled up outside yet another industrial unit on the edge of Bideford.

A wine merchant on one side and a timber yard on the other. Red brick and green cladding, an HM Coastguard sign over the open roller door.

There was a RNLI Land Rover parked outside, taking the last space, so Cole parked behind it, blocking it in.

'I can always move, if there's a shout.'

'You'll be the police,' said a man walking towards them with a mug in one hand and a biscuit in the other. He'd squeezed down the side of the trailer in the loading bay. 'Kettle's just boiled if you'd like a coffee?'

'Thank you,' said Cole.

'I'm Tom Crowther, senior officer here. Welcome to HM Coastguard Bideford. This is Jack Dodson, he's with the RNLI over at Appledore. It was their boat that launched when we got the shout. I asked him to be here when I heard you were coming.'

A few minutes of small talk over coffee. Cole remarked how far they were from the sea, clearly touching a raw nerve.

'The old station was sold off for holiday cottages. Valuable real estate, apparently, and the days of maintaining a coastal watch are long gone. We used to have people up there with a pair of binoculars twenty-four-seven, but we don't do that anymore, so don't need the clifftop station. That was the reason they gave anyway.' Crowther gave a bitter laugh. 'Sell it off, piss the money up the wall, lease a cheap unit, and we end up here.'

Dixon placed his empty mug on the trailer mudguard. 'Talk me through what happened on the thirtieth of September,' he said.

'First thing was I got a call from Brian. He—'

'You know Brian Finch?'

'We know everyone around here; everyone with anything to do with the sea, anyway. They're extra pairs of eyes for us out there, and Finch Geotech have picked up a few people in distress in the past. Towed a yacht in once. Last time it was a paddleboarder; bloody miles out, he was, with no phone. Idiot. Anyway, Brian rang me, said he couldn't raise his brother on the radio or their sat comms, and the GPS tracker showed the boat was drifting. We'd already been paged because of the beacon, so I put a call into Milford Haven, and they sent Rescue 187. Then I tasked the RNLI and off they went.'

'What time was this?'

'We launched at eighteen-seventeen,' replied Dodson. 'In the Tamar class. That's our big all-weather boat. *Endeavour*'s position was well offshore, and we might have had to tow her in.'

'Sea conditions were nothing special,' said Crowther. 'Visibility wasn't great, but the weather was good enough. Sunset was eighteen-forty-one that night so it was getting dimpsy.'

'We found *Endeavour* exactly where she was supposed to be,' continued Dodson. 'Brian had given us her position, and Rescue 187 went straight there. We got to her just as it was getting dark, came alongside and I transferred with Lynn Hill, another volunteer.'

'What did you see?'

'Nothing. PC Gifford asked me that and I gave a statement for the coroner. I've been warned to appear at the inquest too. There was literally nothing out of place; nothing missing either, that I could see anyway. No sign of a struggle, that's what PC Gifford asked me, and there wasn't. No blood, nothing. Engines started first time too, so we took her into Appledore and the lifeboat went off to pick up Sean Duckworth. Rescue 187 had spotted him from the air.'

'What about the safety equipment?' asked Dixon.

'All stowed away,' replied Crowther. 'I checked her over when she got in.'

'What about Sean Duckworth?'

'Dead when they got to him, sadly. His life jacket had inflated, and he was upright. He should've survived by rights. He hadn't been in the water that long and the sea temperature wasn't that bad.'

'The helicopter picked him up and they kept up CPR all the way in, transferred him to an ambulance, but he was pronounced dead on arrival at Barnstaple Hospital,' said Dodson.

'The search for Colin Finch was called off at ten that night, then started again at first light the following morning,' offered Crowther. 'Turns out he wasn't wearing his life jacket. His body washed up at Crow Point a few days later. It's just round the corner from Saunton Sands; found by an angler out after bass on the early morning tide.'

'According to the Marine Accident Investigation Branch report, *Endeavour* was equipped with twenty life jackets and nineteen were found, including the one Sean Duckworth was wearing, which tends to suggest Colin was wearing one and it came off.'

'It wouldn't have come off,' replied Dodson. 'These were top of the range Baltics with stainless steel buckles, zips and a crotch strap.'

'Brian is adamant his brother would have been wearing his life jacket.'

'So, what are you saying?' Crowther frowned. 'That it was taken off?'

'What d'you think happened to them?'

'We'll probably never know, but the likelihood is one of them went overboard and the other—'

'Oh, come on, Tom,' interrupted Dodson. 'These weren't inexperienced wallies out on a pleasure boat. You knew Colin and Sean. All the safety equipment was stowed away.'

Crowther was staring at Dixon. 'You think they were murdered?'

'The family certainly think that,' replied Dixon. He turned to Dodson. 'Did you see anyone else out there?'

'No.'

'Is the lifeboat equipped with radar?'

'Yes, but the range isn't great. Ten nautical miles at most. There were some bigger ships further out to sea, containers heading for Avonmouth, probably. There was nothing inshore, not when we got there.'

◆ ◆ ◆

'Let's make it official, shall we, Nige?'

'It says it's a temporary station, but they've been here four years already,' replied Cole. 'Used to be an auto parts showroom. And there was me thinking Express Park was a dump.'

He parked on the crosshatches, right outside the front door of Barnstaple police station, underneath a large 'Public Enquiry Office' sign.

Sarah had rung ahead, made sure PC Gifford would be in. She'd also be putting in formal requests for the full police file, the inquest file, and the Marine Accident Investigation Branch file.

That just left updating the Policy Log, not that Dixon would need to. Charlesworth would know soon enough, if he didn't already.

They were greeted in reception by a police inspector in full uniform. There to hold PC Gifford's hand, probably. Gifford couldn't be much older than Sarah; gave the impression he'd never seen a superintendent before, let alone had to deal with one.

'What's your name?' asked Dixon.

'Jason, Sir.'

'Well, Jason. What can you tell me about the deaths of Colin Finch and Sean Duckworth?'

'Jason has made a thorough investigation of the deaths, Sir,' said the inspector, jumping in before the young constable had time to draw breath. 'He's taken statements from all parties, as you would expect, and I gather there's been a formal request for the file from Avon and Somerset.'

'There has,' replied Dixon.

'Our file has gone to the coroner, so you may make more progress by speaking to the coroner's officer for this area. That's a Derek Keatley and he's based in Exeter. We used to have our own coroner up here, but that's all gone now, sadly.'

'I'd like to know what Jason thinks happened to them,' said Dixon, firmly.

'I don't know, Sir. And that's the truth. I suspect they met with foul play, but there's no evidence. I couldn't find any, anyway.'

'Did you know either of the deceased?'

'I went to school with Colin Finch's son, Callum. He's working in Bristol now, and I met his father a few times, mainly when he came to watch us play cricket.'

'The sort of bloke who wouldn't wear a life jacket, was he?'

'No way. Finch Geotech were very hot on that. Everyone said so.'

'Were you involved in the incident in the pub? I'm told there was some sort of disturbance involving Finch Geotech staff and some scallop fishermen.'

'That was something and nothing,' said the inspector, diving in. 'We issued a few cautions and that was it. There was no damage in the pub; a few bruises, but that was all.'

'They were from North Devon Shellfish,' said Jason. 'Over Braunton way. The bloke who owns the processing plant has always been against the offshore wind farms; never made any secret of that.'

'Who started the fight?' asked Dixon.

'It wasn't really a fight,' said the inspector.

'Dean Barker,' said Jason. 'He's the bloke who runs the scallop plant. They've got a couple of their own boats that go out of Newlyn, and they process the catch from other boats as well. It was a Friday afternoon and they'd had a few beers.'

'Look, Sir,' said the inspector. 'We treated the *Endeavour* as a crime scene initially, sent in full forensics and they came up with nothing. It's all in the file.'

Dixon stared at him. 'What d'you think happened?'

'I really don't know, but the idea that they were the victims of some sort of foul play is fanciful nonsense.' He hastily tagged 'with the greatest of respect to the Finch family' on the end. 'The lifeboat saw nothing on their radar as they approached the Endeavour. There was no one else out there, so it must've been an unfortunate accident. There simply can't be any other explanation, can there?'

'Actually, there can,' said Dixon.

'A fight *between* Sean Duckworth and Colin Finch, you mean. We looked at it, but again there was no evidence apart from some inconclusive bruising.'

Dixon had sent a text message to Poland asking him to look at the post mortem reports. No point in holding back now.

'Was there an appeal for information?' asked Cole, more to fill the awkward silence that followed.

'Yes,' replied Jason. 'You did one on the local TV, Guv,' he said, turning to the inspector sitting next to him.

'Not one single piece of useful information came from it,' said the inspector. 'Not one, and to be honest we didn't really expect anything. It was all happening too far offshore for anyone to have seen anything.'

◆ ◆ ◆

'Do you get the feeling we're wasting our time up here, Sir?' asked Cole. He'd turned out of the police station and parked in the Tesco's car park while Dixon rang Sarah.

'A sandwich and a bar of chocolate, if you're going in. Thanks, Nige.'

'Oh, right.'

Dixon had his phone to his ear.

'Thanks for ringing me back, Sir,' Sarah said.

'You left three messages.'

'Right. I was looking at the Finch Geotech Facebook page, the one Brian set up about Colin's death, and there's a new comment on it, made yesterday afternoon by Anonymous Participant. She says she saw a plume of smoke offshore; thirtieth of September at about the right time. Thought nothing of it at the time, and it was gone pretty quickly anyway.'

'How d'you know it's a she who made the post?'

'I replied, tagged her in my reply, explained who I am and asked her to ring me. She did, about twenty minutes ago. Wouldn't give her name, is most anxious not to get involved, but she did say she'd be prepared to meet you, off the record, at Sandymouth Bay at five. She'll be out running with her dog; she said it's a Heinz 57, whatever that means.'

'A cross breed,' replied Dixon. 'Did you get her number?'

'No, she must've dialled 141. It just showed up as a private number.'

'I'll see if I can get her car reg in that case.'

'It looks pretty remote on the map, so she'll probably have to drive down there.'

'Well done.'

'Thank you, Sir.'

'Now, go back on the Facebook page and delete your comment.'

Chapter Twenty-Two

'God, you can smell it from here.' Cole had parked at the far end of the car park, as far as he could get from the scallop processing plant. 'I've even shut all the vents.'

'You don't like fish?'

'I like eating it, preferably covered in batter, with a twist of lemon. But raw . . .'

'Are you going to be all right in there?' asked Dixon. 'I don't want you throwing up everywhere.'

'I'd rather wait here, unless you think you'll need me, Sir,' said Cole, his face ashen.

'I'll be fine.'

The front door was locked, so Dixon rang the bell. Metal cladding, no windows, a large parking area behind with refrigerated lorries, their engines running; two caravans in the far corner, both covered in tarpaulins, and a small yacht on a trailer.

He waited, then walked around the side of the building, past several foul-smelling skips, scallop shells lying crushed on the ground in front of them. A forklift truck was being used to load a pallet of polystyrene boxes into one of the lorries; scallops bound for the restaurants of London, probably.

Dixon waited for the driver to reverse away from the back of the lorry.

'I'm looking for Dean Barker,' he said.

'He's in the office.' The driver waved in the general direction of a first floor window in the back of the building, a flight of metal stairs visible in the open loading bay.

He squeezed past the gaggle of smokers standing just outside, paused to look at the scallop processing operation.

Maybe being a police officer wasn't that bad after all?

A conveyor belt, operatives standing either side dressed in full waterproofs, each with thick gloves and a sharp knife. Pick up a scallop, prise it open, drop the shell in one bin, the flesh in another. Rinse and repeat.

'Who are you?' The voice came from the top of the stairs.

Filthy jeans and a woollen pullover, the sleeves rolled up above his elbows to reveal tattoos. Wellington boots, even indoors, but then the unit was awash with stinking sea water.

Good job Cole had stayed in the car.

'I'm looking for Dean Barker,' replied Dixon, holding up his warrant card. 'Police.'

'You'd better come up.'

Dixon closed the office door behind him, stood with his back to the open window. He was looking at the whiteboard on the wall behind the desk; the fishing schedule for the month, possibly.

Barker sat down behind his desk, an open packet of sandwiches and a can of lager in among the piles of paper, wire baskets overflowing. There were two filing cabinets against the wall on the left, pictures of fishing boats on the wall above.

'What's this about then?' he asked.

'I'm investigating the murder of Victoria Smith. Her body was found in a grave at West Bagborough.'

'That's Somerset, isn't it?' Barker leaned forward, pointed at Dixon's warrant card just as he was sliding it back into his pocket. 'Let me see that again.'

'I'm with the Avon and Somerset force,' said Dixon.

'A detective superintendent.' Barker was examining the warrant card. 'What's that got to do with us?'

'I believe her murder is connected to the deaths of Colin Finch and Sean Duckworth.'

'And you think we killed them?'

'I don't know. Did you?'

'Fuck off, mate. You're well out of order, coming here—'

'There was a fight, wasn't there?'

'It was just a friendly disagreement. I've seen worse round the blind side of a scrum. The pub landlord called the rozzers and it all got out of hand.'

'What was it about?'

'Wind farms in our fishing grounds.' Barker gave an exaggerated shrug. 'Look, it was nothing. A few of the lads were letting off steam, they'd had a few beers and . . . you try spending all day on the production line down there. You'd want a few beers.'

'Can you tell me what boats you had out on the thirtieth of September? Where they were?'

'Yes, I've got all that here. I can give you exact coordinates, crew, everything, but you're pissing in the wind, mate.' He stood up, opened a filing cabinet and took out a lever arch file, began flicking through the contents. Then he unclipped the rings, lifted out a plastic document wallet. 'These are the entries for that day. We had two boats out. One off Ilfracombe and the other went further down the coast, south of Bude. Here.' He handed the wallet to Dixon. 'They've got GPS trackers on them. It's all there.'

'What about that yacht out there?'

'Hasn't moved for three years.'

A cursory glance at the maps. Both boats far too far away to have been involved in whatever happened to the *Endeavour*. Far too far away to have seen anything either.

'Do you have any other boats?'

'Nope.'

'Thank you,' said Dixon, handing the paperwork back to Barker. 'We call it eliminating people from our enquiries.' He gave a conciliatory smile.

'I understand.' Barker was putting the lever arch file back in the filing cabinet. 'So, what happened to this woman then?'

'I really can't say, except that she was found in a newly dug grave similar to the South Devon attacks.'

'And why d'you think it's connected to Sean and Colin's deaths?'

'Again, I can't say.'

'I knew them both. Sean was married to a friend of my wife's, and Colin's kids went to the same school as my daughter. Smart bloke, he spotted a gap in the market and went for it. All credit to him. This climate change bollocks was getting going and wind farms were springing up everywhere, so he mortgaged his house up to his armpits, bought himself his first boat and started doing marine surveys offshore. I think they've got a fleet of eight now.'

'You don't approve of wind farms?'

'Bloody waste of time and money; kill raptors like there's no tomorrow. Solar is fine, but we should be covering car parks and buildings with panels, not fields. Don't get me started on wind turbines. Most of the time the fucking things are either turning too slowly or too fast to generate any electricity anyway. It's all a bloody scam. We've lost two good fishing grounds to offshore wind farms already, but that's all right.' His voice was loaded with sarcasm now. 'We can always import all our food. The French come over here, catch all our fish, and then sell it back to us anyway. You couldn't make this shit up,' said Barker, raising his arms in mock surrender.

'What d'you think happened to Colin and Sean?' asked Dixon. 'You're experienced, know these waters well.'

'I do, but as to what happened to them, who knows? A man overboard recovery that went wrong, probably. And I don't believe that bullshit about Colin not wearing his life jacket. His body had been at sea for days and it could have come off. Easily.'

'What about a submarine?' asked Dixon.

'They steer clear of the fishing grounds, have done since 2015. Don't want to snag nets and stuff. That was after a boat got dragged out in the Channel; they managed to cut themselves free, thank God. The Royal Navy admitted it in the end. Now they stay outside British territorial waters where there's active fishing going on.'

◆ ◆ ◆

Dixon opened the door of Cole's car, dropped into the passenger seat. 'I think it's fair to say Dean Barker is a climate change sceptic,' he said.

'What did he say about—?'

'His boats were miles away at the time. He showed me the charts.' Dixon was scrolling through the messages on his phone. 'Good job you stayed out here. The stench was indescribable.'

'It's on your jacket,' said Cole.

'Nothing a good walk on a beach won't sort out. Do you know Sandymouth Bay?'

'Took the kids there when they were younger. We had a caravan holiday at Bude.'

'There's a beachside cafe.'

'Does a good fry-up, but it'll be closed by now.'

'We're meeting someone there at five. Sarah set it up.' Dixon looked at his watch. 'That gives us thirty-five minutes.'

'Plenty of time,' said Cole, grinning as he reached behind the seat, placed the blue light on the roof of his car.

◆ ◆ ◆

'What are we looking for?' asked Cole.

'A woman with a Heinz 57,' replied Dixon. 'She said she'd meet us here.'

They were sitting at a rickety picnic table in a seating area in the dunes above the beach cafe. It gave a grandstand view out to sea and along the cliff path. Monty was sniffing under the tables, methodically, checking each in turn.

'That was a bit of pastry,' said Cole. 'He won't be sick in the back of my car, will he?'

'He'll be fine.' Dixon was watching the car park, but then whoever it was might have the sense to walk; that's if they really did want to remain anonymous.

And why remain anonymous? That was another question.

There were a couple of cars, parked near the top of the path to the beach. Dog walkers, almost certainly, although you didn't have to be Sherlock Holmes to work that out. A cage in the back of one car, a dog guard in the back of the other.

The tide was out, a vast expanse of sand shimmering in the late afternoon sun. Two small boats were visible, anglers probably; certainly not large enough to be commercial fishermen.

'How far d'you reckon they are offshore, Nige?'

'A mile, I reckon. After bass this time of year. We're raised up a bit here, which means we can see further. Maybe eight miles to the horizon from here. You'd be able to see even further from the top of the cliffs.'

Someone was coming down the coast path from the south. A woman running alone with a dog.

'If that's her,' said Cole, 'she's parked at the end of Northcott Mouth Road.' He held the map on his phone up to Dixon. 'When she leaves, we'll be able to intercept her at this junction, get her number plate.'

'Good thinking, Nige,' replied Dixon. 'You can do that while I give Monty a run on the beach. Pick me up when you've finished.'

'Right.'

The woman reached the junction in the coast path. Left for the beach, right for the cafe.

She turned right, stopped to put her dog on a lead.

Dixon called Monty to him, clipped on the dog's lead, handed it to Cole. 'Wait here, Nige, will you.'

Dixon walked down the steps towards the woman.

She was looking up at the veranda. 'Is the white Staffie your dog?' she asked.

'He is.'

'What's his name?'

'Monty.'

'Your colleague said to look for a white Staffie called Monty, which makes you the superintendent?'

Dixon had his warrant card at the ready.

She was clearly nervous. Dressed in Lycra leggings, running shoes, probably for a quick getaway. 'And you'll be Anonymous Participant from Facebook?' he asked. She'd made an effort to remain anonymous in person too, a neck gaiter pulled up above her nose, muffling her voice, sunglasses and a red baseball cap.

'Sorry,' she said, running on the spot, almost.

'Don't be. I'm just grateful you got in touch.' Dixon leaned over. 'And who's this?'

'Bilbo,' she replied, softening. 'I rescued him from Romania.' Black and tan, he looked like a cross between a Doberman and a Labrador.

'Is he friendly?'

'Better not.' She was wrapping the lead around her hand. 'He can be a bit funny with men sometimes.'

'You told my colleague you saw a plume of smoke?'

'We were out for our usual run, came over the top there and I stopped here to give Bilbo a drink. There's always a bowl of fresh water by the back door.'

'I think Monty's emptied it. Sorry.'

'Anyway, I was standing by the tables and I saw it. Black smoke rising from something, but I couldn't see what it was. It was over the horizon; lasted maybe five or ten minutes, then it was gone, dispersed I suppose.' She pulled her elasticated neck gaiter up to the bridge of her nose. 'I did look when I got back up the top there but couldn't see anything. That's all there is to it, really. I heard about what happened to those surveyors on the boat, never really put two and two together. Then I came across a Facebook page.'

'I'm not going to push you, don't worry, I just want to understand why you wish to remain anonymous.'

'I had a bad experience giving evidence in the past. You do the right thing then get shat on. Never again.'

'I won't ask.'

'Don't.'

'Where was this plume of smoke?' asked Dixon.

'That way,' she said, gesturing to the north. 'It was almost out of sight round the cliff from here. I started running home and by the time I got to the top of the cliff it had gone. I thought I might have got a better view from up there but couldn't see anything. It was a bit hazy, though, I suppose.'

'What time was this?'

'About ten to four; something like that.' She was starting to run on the spot again. 'It said on the news there was no damage to the yellow catamaran thing, the boat the surveyors were on, so I thought it couldn't be anything to do with that anyway. There's no smoke without fire, is there?'

'Actually, there is,' replied Dixon. 'Quite often.'

'Well, that's all I saw, I'm afraid. For what it's worth.'

'Thank you.'

The woman waved, then set off back the way she'd come, her dog following her up the steep hill to the top of the cliff path. Dixon walked with Cole back to his car, then hid behind the hedge with Monty while Cole drove off in the hope of getting her registration number.

He watched the woman disappear out of view, then unclipped Monty's lead and headed for the beach. Down some crumbling steps, and across a band of large shingle; no wellies, which made picking his way through the rock pools a bit of a struggle.

The sand was soft, the walk down to the water's edge leaving deep footprints.

'You're going to get sand all over the back of Nige's car,' said Dixon, brushing his dog's muzzle.

It had been an odd day. It was difficult to pinpoint one thing he'd learned that he didn't know already, wouldn't have got from the files. That wasn't what it had been about, though.

It had been about getting a gut feeling for what had happened.

And he'd got one.

Charlesworth wasn't going to like it. Nor were the Navy for that matter. But as Jane would say, *fuck 'em*.

A figure appeared at the top of the shingle, waving, so Dixon turned back up the beach.

'I got her registration number,' said Cole. 'Haven't run it yet.'

'Don't bother.'

Cole was standing with his hands on his hips, admiring the view. 'A plume of smoke, then,' he said. 'There was no fire damage on the Endeavour.'

'No there wasn't.'

'And the RNLI saw nothing on their radar when they were on the way out. There must've been something else out there, though, mustn't there.'

'There was.'

'Why didn't they see it?'

'That's easy, Nige. It submerged.'

Chapter Twenty-Three

'You are not seriously suggesting that one of His Majesty's Royal Navy's nuclear submarines surfaced, murdered two marine surveyors who happened to be in the vicinity, and then fled the scene submerged to avoid detection?' Charlesworth dropped his glasses on to the table in front of him, folded his arms. 'Please tell me that's not where you're going with this.'

'I'm going wherever it takes me,' replied Dixon.

He'd been warned that Charlesworth was waiting in meeting room 2. 'Like a little trap door spider' was the phrase Louise had used. She'd spotted Cole's car turning into the staff car park at Express Park, intercepted them at the top of the stairs. It turned out Deborah Potter was there too, possibly to referee. It had been a chance of escape, but the reality was the music had to be faced at some point, so why not get it over with now? And he'd probably need Charlesworth as a buffer. Best to have him on side, if he could.

'Victoria Smith contacted the brother of one of the dead marine surveyors and was about to reveal information about what had happened to them. It would be negligent not to follow it up.'

Potter nodded her agreement, when she was sure Charlesworth wasn't looking.

'You've asked Sarah Loveday to set up another meeting with the captain of HMS *Agincourt*.'

'Yes, Sir.'

'I'm hoping you're not going to go marching in there and accuse him of her murder.'

Dixon didn't feel the need to answer that one; let the silence hang.

'Nick's right, Sir,' said Potter, eventually. 'It's a possible motive for her murder and it has to be followed up. Without fear or favour, and all that.'

Charlesworth took a deep breath. 'I know that.' He was rubbing the bridge of his nose. 'It puts us in an impossible position all the same. What time's the meeting?'

'Ten tomorrow morning, Sir,' replied Dixon.

'You can bet the Chief Con will have had the Home Secretary on the phone by eleven in that case. I'll probably have the new Police and Crime Commissioner sticking his bloody oar in as well.' Charlesworth had the look of a man playing poker, staring at his opponent, trying to work out whether he was bluffing. 'How does this fit in with the Devon attacks?'

'It doesn't, Sir,' replied Dixon. 'But then Victoria Smith's murder never has. Not in the manner of her killing, or the location.'

'Surely he suffocated her in the mud because he left the last one alive and didn't want to make the same mistake?'

'Her body wasn't posed like the rest, David,' said Potter. 'That was the one detail about the Devon attacks Hatch held back.'

'Maybe the killer was disturbed before he could—'

'He had time to replace the planks over the grave,' interrupted Dixon. 'Stopped to do that. Nothing looked out of place, according to the gravediggers.'

'What about the DNA? That's pretty conclusive, surely?'

'That the murders are connected, yes. Nothing more.'

'What are you talking about?'

Charlesworth's cap was sitting on the table. Upturned, several grey hairs glinting in the overhead lights. Dixon leaned forward, picked a single hair off the brim of the cap, held it up to the light. 'If Forensics had found this in the grave, would that mean you killed her, Sir?'

'Depends on how it got there.'

'Exactly. And until we know that, relying on the DNA evidence is just making assumptions.'

'All right, all right.' Charlesworth was staring into space, breathing heavily through his nose. 'You do what you've got to do, and I'll watch your back. But remember, that means both our necks are on the chopping block, so you'd better be right about this.'

'Yes, Sir.'

'And try not to ruffle too many feathers.'

◆ ◆ ◆

Jane's message had arrived just after nine.

> *Text me when you're on the way and I'll bung a pizza in the oven Jx*

An hour spent catching up with Louise and Mark, reading the statements on the system. There had been several sightings of a dark saloon. No registration plate, so pretty much meaningless.

There'd been no harm in updating the Policy Log. Not now. It took about half an hour, documenting the new evidence, and the decisions he'd taken based on it. He was supposed to record the investigative direction, instruction, parameters and priorities; made sure he used certain buzz phrases that would keep Charlesworth happy if he, or anyone else for that matter, checked.

The 'SIO's Working Hypothesis' section he left blank. They might just as well have called it 'SIO's Gut Feeling' because that's what it was. He scrolled back up, typed 'Not applicable' in the box.

Actually, he didn't want anyone to know his working hypothesis. Not yet.

There was something else he left out too – something too sensitive for a Sensitive Policy File, even with restricted access. Something that he'd keep to himself; that might become relevant, but might not, in which case no one need ever know.

Yes, he'd leave that out.

For now.

'How's Sarah getting on?' Jane asked. She was standing in the open back door of their cottage, a dog bowl in one hand. 'I'm guessing you haven't fed him?'

'He had half my sandwich at lunch and a couple of digestive biscuits.'

'I bet that's all you've had too, apart from bloody fruit pastilles.' She put the bowl on the kitchen floor, watched Monty demolish the contents. 'Poor little bugger is starving.'

'He had a nice run on the beach at Sandymouth Bay.'

'That's Bude way. What the hell were you doing down there?'

'Long story.' Dixon closed the back door behind him. 'Sarah's doing fine.'

'I thought she would,' replied Jane, dragging a pizza out of the oven and on to a plate. 'What did you find out about that bloke's brother?'

'Enough,' replied Dixon. 'A witness saw a plume of smoke at about the right time and in about the right place.'

'Which means something happened to that boat.'

'I saw the catamaran and there's no fire damage. No damage at all, actually.' Dixon sat down on the sofa, watched Jane rummaging in his jacket pocket for his phone. He'd made the mistake of leaving it in the inside pocket when he'd hung the jacket over the back of a dining chair.

She tapped in the passcode. 'You haven't checked your blood sugar once today. What's the use of having that sensor in your arm if you don't use it? And you've switched off the alerts.'

'I can't have those going off in the middle of—'

'I've switched them back on.'

Best not to argue.

'Does Charlesworth know yet?' She left his phone on the arm of the sofa, sat down next to him.

Dixon gave a positive murmur, his mouth full of pizza.

'How was he about it?'

'Supportive. He told me to do whatever I've got to do, and he'd watch my back.'

'Really? Well, fuck me.'

'Perhaps later.' Dixon smiled. 'If you play your cards right. How's he been?'

'Fine. Squawked a bit earlier, but I put *Goodbye, Mr. Chips* on and he nodded off.' Jane reached over and took a slice of pizza off the edge of Dixon's plate. 'So, where are you with the investigation?'

'There was a submarine out there. Either it was involved in what happened or it knows what happened because it was monitoring radio traffic. Victoria Smith was the comms officer, don't forget. The plume of smoke must've come from something and the RNLI saw nothing on their radar.'

'It might have come from another boat that sank.' Jane bit off the end of the slice of pizza, fed the crust to Monty. 'I'm just thinking out loud, really.'

'Or a boat that submerged. Either way, Victoria knew and was going to tell the family.'

'So, when does the shit hit the fan?' she asked, her mouth full.

'Tomorrow morning at ten. I've got a meeting down at Plymouth.'

'Rather you than me.'

Chapter Twenty-Four

Lieutenant Commander McConochie was waiting for them when Dixon and Cole arrived at HMS *Drake* the following morning. No Monty in the back of the car this time, the dog happier standing guard by Peter's cot – Dixon happier he was there too.

'I still can't get used to calling a naval base "HMS",' Cole had said as he pulled into the parking space opposite the gatehouse. 'I always thought that was reserved for ships.'

'They call this a shore establishment, apparently, Nige.' Dixon had googled it.

Warrant cards, driving licences, the usual drill.

'Park on the parade ground like you did last time. There's a parade at four, but you'll be gone by then,' said McConochie, climbing into the rear passenger seat of Cole's car. 'I've got Commander Vaughan in the conference room, as you asked, and he's brought his XO with him. There's someone coming from Legal too, I'm afraid. You never know what issues might arise.'

Sarah hadn't given a reason for the meeting when she'd set it up the day before. She'd been asked, twice; said she didn't know. That's what Dixon had told her to say.

'I'm afraid I'm not privy to the latest developments in the investigation.'

She'd lied quite convincingly. She'd go far would Sarah.

Commander Vaughan was sitting at the far end of the conference table, flanked by two officers in naval uniform. All three of them stood, offered their hands when introduced by McConochie.

'This is Lieutenant Commander Towers, executive officer on HMS *Agincourt*. Commander Vaughan you know, and this is Lieutenant Bell from our legal department.'

'I hope you don't mind me being here,' said Bell. 'Purely a precaution.'

'Not at all,' replied Dixon.

'Now,' said Vaughan. 'How can we help?'

The door opened and a tray of tea and coffee was carried in, left in the middle of the table by a young rating. 'Thank you, Tricia,' said McConochie, quietly.

Dixon waited. He was being stared at by Vaughan. Assessed.

He used the opportunity to take in the room. Newly refurbished in the old office block; plush salmon-pink carpet, dark wood furniture. It could have been a dining room – probably was given the right occasion. All of the pictures on the wall were of ships at sea.

No submarines, oddly enough.

McConochie pushed a cup of coffee across the table towards him. 'Thank you,' Dixon said, watching the door close behind Tricia.

'New information has come to light that makes an incident that took place on the thirtieth of September last year relevant to the murder of Lieutenant Commander Smith.' Dixon was choosing his words carefully, trying not to give away too much too soon. Looking for a reaction, any indication they knew already.

Bell was making notes, and Vaughan would have made a good poker player; not so his XO. She was deliberately avoiding eye contact.

'What incident?' asked McConochie.

'The deaths of two marine surveyors off Hartland Point,' replied Dixon. 'They were about eight miles out, surveying the seabed, looking for possible wind farm sites. Both drowned, and their catamaran was found drifting.' Dixon paused.

'Did they have some sort of accident?' asked Bell, looking up.

'That's certainly one possibility. Another is they were murdered.'

'Oh, come now, you can't possibly—'

'A plume of smoke was seen from the beach at the relevant time and yet there was no fire damage, no damage at all, on the catamaran. And the RNLI saw nothing on their radar when they approached the area. They got there quickly, albeit too late, sadly.'

'You think this plume of smoke came from a submarine?' asked Vaughan.

Time to lay his cards on the table. 'Yes, I do.'

'Eight miles out is within British territorial waters,' offered McConochie. 'They extend twelve miles from the coast. Beyond that, anything goes, but inside it's British sovereignty.'

'Technically, there's a right of innocent passage, which enables foreign ships to pass through territorial waters,' said Bell. 'But that only applies if the passage is not prejudicial to the peace, good order, or security of the state in question, in this case us.'

'And how is this relevant to Victoria's murder?' Vaughan again, stirring his coffee.

'The family believe their brother, son, father was the victim of foul play, and they've been actively seeking further information, witnesses, anything. The inquest is due to take place shortly. Two weeks before Victoria Smith was murdered, the brother of one of the dead surveyors received an anonymous telephone call from someone claiming to have information about what had happened. They agreed to meet in West Bagborough churchyard the same day

Victoria was murdered. Needless to say, the meeting never took place. The brother has since identified her voice as being the one on the telephone.'

'A whistleblower,' muttered Bell, under his breath.

'I don't believe it,' said Vaughan. 'Not Victoria.'

'A whistleblower implies there is something to blow the whistle on,' said Dixon, matter of fact. 'And killing a whistleblower implies that the information is important.'

'I'm not sure how much help we can be,' said Vaughan, working hard to hide his disappointment. 'I've said before we simply cannot comment on operational matters.'

Dixon had expected that response.

'Anything that might reveal the location of HMS *Agincourt* at the material time would be regarded as operational,' said Bell. 'Details of the deployment of our nuclear submarine fleet are highly classified, as you might imagine.'

'What about the role of communications officer? As a lieutenant commander, I'm guessing Victoria would have been the senior comms officer.'

'We can't talk about that either,' snapped Vaughan.

'She would have been responsible for the operation, maintenance and repair of all communications systems on *Agincourt*, wouldn't she? Including the encryption and decryption of classified messages.'

'Where did you get that information?' demanded Bell.

'Google.'

Vaughan was sitting with his elbows on the table, his fingers intertwined, the knuckles whitening. His XO was still avoiding eye contact with Dixon, neatly folding an empty sachet of sugar before placing it on the edge of her saucer.

'It's reasonable to assume, therefore, that Victoria overheard radio traffic, almost certainly encrypted, that gave her reason to believe she knew what had happened to the marine surveyors.' Dixon was staring at Vaughan. 'Wouldn't you say, Commander?'

'I'm just pleased to learn you're not suggesting *Agincourt* was actively involved in what happened.'

'And what did happen?'

'I am not at liberty to comment one way or the other.' Vaughan took a deep breath. 'Not even to confirm whether or not something did happen.'

Dixon turned to Bell. 'How do we go about getting clearance so you can tell us?'

'You don't,' Bell replied with an apologetic shrug. 'It's an operation deployment matter, I'm afraid. Full stop.'

'Are the private telephones of naval personnel monitored?'

'Not as a matter of routine, no. There may be certain circumstances where permission is granted; welfare issues and stuff like that.'

'Were Victoria's phone calls being tapped?'

'There's no way anyone here would possibly know the answer to that question.'

Lieutenant Commander Towers was looking out of the window now. Short dark hair, just a touch of makeup perhaps. No wedding ring. The naval uniform left few details from which conclusions could be drawn.

'What does the XO do?' asked Dixon.

She looked startled, quickly recovered her composure. 'I'm second-in-command.'

'The first woman to hold that position on a submarine, I might add,' said McConochie.

Dixon had seen her somewhere before. A photograph, on the wall in Victoria's living room at West Bagborough. Three female officers awarded their dolphins at the same time, all of them beaming up at the camera. It had struck Dixon as an odd camera angle when he'd seen it, not that it was supposed to be a formal photograph. It had made the news too; he'd seen the article online.

'I'm responsible for the admin, day-to-day work, drills, exercises. It leaves Commander Vaughan free to focus on strategic command.'

'Was Victoria a good officer?'

'She was a very able colleague; dedicated.'

'Does it surprise you to learn she was apparently intending to reveal classified information to the family of the dead marine surveyors?'

'It surprises me,' interrupted Vaughan.

Dixon looked at Towers.

'She had a strong sense of what was right, and what was wrong,' she said.

'And something was wrong?'

'I'm afraid Lieutenant Commander Towers cannot answer that question,' said Bell, diving in. 'To do so would confirm something we cannot confirm one way or the other.'

'How long is a deployment then?'

'Typically two months,' replied Vaughan. '*Agincourt* is an attack submarine, so we patrol—'

'British territorial waters?'

'Sometimes.'

'Were you out last September, on patrol?'

'Look, this is getting you and us nowhere, I'm afraid,' said Bell. 'You're asking questions we simply cannot answer. We don't know what it is that Lieutenant Commander Smith thought she knew, and couldn't tell you if we did.' He folded his arms. 'It seems you've had a wasted trip.'

◆ ◆ ◆

'I hope you don't think we're being obstructive,' said McConochie. 'It's just that there are things we can talk about and things we can't.' He was standing on the steps of the office block. 'Let me get my cap and I'll take you over to the Wardroom for a snifter – show there's no hard feelings.'

Dixon was conscious that he was being watched from an upstairs window; glanced up just in time to see Commander Vaughan turn away.

'Did you see that, Nige?'

'Yeah. He knows full well what happened out there, what Victoria Smith was going to tell Brian Finch. We just have to hope he's not telling us because he can't, not because he won't.'

'If they admit they know what happened then it reveals their position on an operational deployment.' Dixon was talking to himself, thinking out loud, his voice quietening at the sound of footsteps on the stairs inside the building.

'Right then,' said McConochie, putting on his cap, returning the salute of two sailors walking past the building. 'This way.'

HMS *Agincourt* was visible on the far side of a dock, scaffolding over the conning tower. Work had started to remove the tiles that covered the hull, revealing rusting steel underneath.

'She'll be going into dry dock soon,' said McConochie, when he saw Dixon looking.

'What are those tiles?' asked Cole. 'Looks like the stuff on the outside of a space shuttle.'

'We're not supposed to talk about those.'

'Acoustic tiles,' replied Dixon. 'They absorb and distort sonar. That's what it says on Google anyway. The company that makes them has got a website.'

'It's actually classified.'

'We'll have to hope the Russians don't look on the internet, then, won't we?' said Dixon, with a disarming smile.

They followed McConochie past the parade ground and towards a grey stone building with a grand tower overlooking the River Tamar. In front was a cricket pitch, two sets of stumps standing idle in the middle. 'There's an inter-services T20 later,' said McConochie. 'Always a good excuse for a piss-up.'

He signed them in at reception, then stood in the double doors at the entrance to the mess hall. A large room; oak panelling, oil paintings of naval scenes. 'This is where we hold our mess dinners,' said McConochie. 'I make sure I stay over. There's no driving home after one of those.'

'You said it was at a mess dinner you first met Victoria Smith?' Dixon asked.

'Their decommissioning for refit coincided with Trafalgar Night, so it was a double celebration. Victoria was on the top table with me. There was Commander Vaughan; Judith Towers was there. The Naval Base Commander obviously. He's a marine. Always a cracking night is Trafalgar Night. We hold it on the nearest Thursday night to the anniversary of the battle, then people have only got to survive Friday before they can go home. That's HMS *Victory* there.' McConochie was pointing to a large oil painting over the ornate and vast fireplace. 'And that's a painting we had done of the dinner.'

'Looks like a good night was had by all,' said Cole.

'How many people in total?'

'The mess seats two hundred and it's always a full house for that one.' McConochie handed them both a menu. 'The other one not to be missed is Armada Night. I might be able to swing you an invitation if you fancy it. I'm sure you come in the category of local dignitaries, and you'd be welcome to stay over in the mess. Now, what can I get you?'

◆ ◆ ◆

They were back out on the A38, heading north, when Cole finally broke the silence.

'Well, that was a waste of time, wasn't it, Sir?' he said. 'Should've known, really.'

'Was it?'

Cole stifled a chuckle. 'Go on.'

'An operational deployment for an attack submarine like *Agincourt* lasts two months, and their return coincided with the Trafalgar Night dinner in the mess.' Dixon spoke without looking up from his phone. 'The Battle of Trafalgar took place on the twenty-first of October 1805, which means that *Agincourt* was at sea on the thirtieth of September. But they don't discuss the details of operational deployments, do they?'

'No, Sir.'

'We also know that Vaughan and his XO know full well what Victoria Smith was going to tell Brian Finch.'

'You think they were lying?'

'They didn't actually lie, but they certainly withheld the truth.'

'So, how do we find out?'

'I've got an idea about that.'

There was something else too, but Dixon would keep that to himself.

For now.

'Do you fancy Armada Night, Sir?' asked Cole, mischief in his voice. 'They certainly know how to lay on a good piss-up, by the looks of things.'

Chapter Twenty-Five

Dixon was getting a little too good at lying. Not to Jane, of course, unless it was about sugar. But to everyone else.

'Drop me here, Nige. I've just got to pick up something from the chemist.'

Cole didn't bat an eyelid, said he'd wait in a loading bay round the corner, blue light on the roof of his car.

Dixon had checked Tom Perry's website, and the member of parliament for Bridgwater and North Somerset was running a constituency surgery between two and four that afternoon. 'Appointments should be made in advance, by email or telephone.'

Dixon hadn't done that, but then he didn't want any record of his visit; catch Perry taking his lunch beforehand, that was the plan.

He'd followed Perry's progress since his by-election win the year before; since the murder of his pregnant wife, Elizabeth. Tall, a shock of blond hair, rugby player's ears – the lot of the second row forward. Dixon had watched his maiden speech on the local news. A high flyer, they said, already a parliamentary private secretary in the Housing Department, but then he was an architect. Dixon remembered giving Perry a guided tour of Express Park – remembered catching his wife's killers too.

Dixon found himself following Perry along Bridgwater High Street; popped out for a sandwich judging by the small carrier bag in his right hand. He'd put on a bit of weight, possibly. All those free lunches.

Perry stopped at the front door of his office, noticed Dixon when he turned to put his key in the lock.

'Acting Detective Superintendent Dixon. I've been following your cases with interest,' he said, his hand outstretched. 'It's good to see you, Nick.'

'You may not think so when we've had a chat.'

'Like that, is it?'

It was a warm handshake, all the same.

'Come in, come in,' said Perry. He dropped his carrier bag on the receptionist's desk. 'I got you Brie and cranberry, Prue. Mine's the ploughman's. I'll be back in a minute.' Then he turned to Dixon. 'This way, Nick.'

It was a large office; leather-topped desk, windows overlooking the car park at the back. Dixon stopped in the doorway. 'Let's talk outside.'

'Really?' Perry frowned. 'You're surely not suggesting my office is bugged?'

Dixon had already turned for the back door, Perry's footsteps behind him as he headed along the corridor. Then out into the car park and along the alley.

'Surely this is far enough?'

'This is,' replied Dixon. He stopped, looked up at the back of the building, saw nothing, tucked in behind the wall. 'I'm investigating the murder of Victoria Smith—'

'I know,' said Perry. 'West Bagborough's not my patch, though.'

'She was communications officer on HMS *Agincourt*, about to blow the whistle on something.'

'I thought she was a random vict—?'

'That's what we're supposed to think. She was killed because of what she was about to reveal to the families of two marine surveyors who died in mysterious circumstances off the North Devon coast. There was nothing visible on the RNLI radar when they got out there, no damage whatsoever to the surveyors' boat and yet a walker saw a plume of smoke.'

'Have you spoken to the Navy?'

'I've just come from there. They're saying it was an operational deployment and all details are classified.'

'Maybe they're classified for a reason?'

'Then I want to know what that reason is. I've got one dead submarine officer and two dead marine surveyors.'

'When was this incident?'

'Thirtieth of September,' replied Dixon. 'My guess is Victoria Smith was monitoring radio traffic and heard what happened. *Agincourt* was on deployment at the time.'

Perry took a deep breath. 'Let me make a couple of calls,' he said. 'When I entered parliament, I was paired up with another MP; he's just been made PPS to the armed forces minister, he might know what it's all about. Where will you be at, say, six o'clock?'

'On the beach with my dog.'

'I'll deny all knowledge if this ever comes back to bite me.'

'It won't. Not from me, anyway.'

'All right. I've got this surgery first, then I'll see what I can find out.'

'Thank you. And make sure you use someone else's phone.'

◆ ◆ ◆

Dixon was sitting in the corner of the canteen enjoying his lunch, if it was possible to enjoy a dry baguette with grated cheese in it; yesterday's date on it too. It was gone three by the time he'd got there, and that was all there was left. That or a cold sausage roll.

Insulin injection through his shirt; checked his blood to keep Jane happy. At least there'd be something for her to see when she looked later. And she would look. It was becoming a ritual when he arrived home.

6.7, so it was good too. It was about habits. Breakfast, even if it was a bowl of cereal. A proper lunch; keep the fruit pastilles for emergencies. He'd got a pocket full of them, in among the dog bags.

He'd told Perry he'd be on the beach at six, so he'd need to nip home first, pick up Monty. Literally, probably. The little bugger still wouldn't budge from beside Peter's cot, not according to the text messages from Jane:

Can't get Monty to go out Jx

Throw the ball Nx

I've tried that!

It was oddly reassuring, all the same.

Dixon had checked the visitors' car park when Cole had turned into Express Park. No sign of Charlesworth's car, although Deborah Potter was in the building, so he felt safe enough for the time being.

An easy mistake to make.

'Ah, there you are.'

'Would you like a coffee, Ma'am?' he asked, sweeping up the flakes of cheese with the flat of his hand, dropping them in the remains of the empty packet.

'No, thank you. And it's Deborah when no one else is around, I've told you that before.' She leaned over the table, spoke softly. 'I just came to warn you, David's been summoned to Portishead; a meeting with the Chief Con and the PCC.'

'What about?'

'You. Or rather your visit to Plymouth today. I wouldn't worry too much about it. My understanding is the Navy are just anxious to impress on us they're not being obstructive; they just simply can't talk about operational matters. And besides, David is on your side, as you know.'

As you know was an interesting take on it. Dixon didn't know, actually. *Hoped* was a better way of putting it.

'I gather the partial DNA match was a waste of time,' continued Potter. 'Shame that.'

'It has its limitations,' replied Dixon. 'People need to understand that. This isn't a Netflix documentary.'

'DCI Hatch kept the family under observation after your visit and there's nothing.'

'The mother was telling the truth; she really has no idea who the boy's father is.'

'So, where d'you go from here?'

'I'm convinced Victoria Smith's murder is different from the Devon attacks and was committed by someone else. I'm also convinced the motive was to stop her blowing the whistle on what happened to those two marine surveyors.'

'You've pretty much exhausted every line of enquiry there, I think.'

'Pretty much,' replied Dixon. Actually he hadn't, but he was keeping that to himself.

'Louise and Mark haven't come up with anything either.'

'Not yet, but it's early days.'

'Just tread carefully, Nick, for heaven's sake,' said Potter, standing up. 'If her killing does turn out to be part of the same series of attacks, we're going to look like a right bunch of idiots. And we'll have pissed off our Devon and Cornwall colleagues for nothing.'

'I wasn't aware I had pissed them off.' Feigning innocence.

'You piss everybody off.' Potter put her hand on his shoulder. 'You get away with it because you get results.'

Chapter Twenty-Six

Dixon was standing in front of the whiteboards, staring at the pattern of red pins on the map, when his phone started buzzing in his pocket. He didn't recognise the number, but then he had told Tom Perry to use someone else's phone.

'Nick Dixon.'

'Where on the beach?'

'Park at the end of Allandale Road, walk towards the lighthouse. You know my dog.'

'I'm leaving now.' Perry rang off abruptly.

It was just past three-thirty; a short constituency surgery then. Dixon left Cole returning telephone calls from members of the public who'd rung in with information; stopped at the cottage to pick up Monty. The dog didn't bark, oddly enough, and Dixon managed to get in and out of the cottage without waking either Jane or Peter, both fast asleep in front of the TV. He thought he had anyway, the sound of a baby crying just carrying over the rumble of his diesel engine.

The tide was out, but then he had known it was going to be when he suggested meeting on the beach. He'd had a head start of ten or fifteen minutes on Perry, given that Express Park was on the outskirts of town, and managed to get a long way out across the flats. He hadn't bothered with wellies, which made crossing the muddy channels a bit of a challenge, but he found a way across without getting wet feet.

A tennis ball was keeping Monty busy when Dixon spotted a figure in the distance trying to pick his way across the mud.

'Did you really have to come this far out?' grumbled Perry, looking at his polished black brogues caked in thick grey slime.

'Yes.' Dixon slid his phone out of his pocket, opened a web browser and navigated to YouTube. He held up his hand, silencing Perry when he opened his mouth to speak. 'A little bit of AC/DC, I think,' he said, clicking Play and turning up the volume.

Perry nodded his understanding.

'I thought you had a constituency surgery this afternoon?' Dixon asked, stepping in close to Perry, his voice just audible over the music.

'I cancelled it, wanted to stop you getting yourself in any deeper.'

'Go on.'

'I had a call back from that friend I told you about, who will remain nameless. As will I.'

'Of course.'

'Dropped everything and came to find you,' continued Perry. 'This is . . .' He shook his head. 'Well, I'm not sure what it is, really. But you've stumbled on something with implications, ramifications . . . You need to be very, very careful, old chap. You've got a young son now as well, I hear.'

Dixon hadn't mentioned Peter, not after what had happened to Perry's wife – pregnant with their first child when she was stabbed to death.

'I need to know,' he said. 'What I do with the information is down to me. No one will know where it came from. You have my word on that.'

Perry took a deep breath. '*Agincourt* was out there. She's a hunter-killer, as you know, and she was on the tail of a Russian Kilo-class submarine, the *Novorossiysk*. Now – and this is where we get into really deep, deep shit – the *Novorossiysk* was in British territorial waters, right where your marine surveyors were using their sonar to map the seabed. It goes without saying, Nick, that if this information ever gets out . . .' Perry's voice tailed off. 'Anyway, *Agincourt* was monitoring radio traffic between *Novorossiysk* and its base at Severomorsk, and you don't need to be a rocket scientist to work out that means we have the capability to decrypt Russian radio communications.'

'Also classified information.'

'Very.' Perry raised his eyebrows. 'Anyway, there was a fuel leak and a fire in the engine room on board the *Novorossiysk*. She's nuclear armed, which makes that a big deal, particularly when she was effectively in British territory; she was within twelve miles of our coastline, mapping gas pipelines and undersea cables, they think, but it's best not to ask. I was told not to.'

'I won't.'

'She was forced to the surface, venting smoke from her conning tower, which must've been the plume seen by your witness. That's also when defence intelligence believes she might have encountered your marine surveyors on their catamaran.'

'And what are defence intelligence going to do about it?'

'There's nothing they can do. If it comes out a Russian sub was within eight miles of our coast, and possibly killed two British citizens . . .'

'*Possibly?*'

'That's all it is, Nick. A possibility. I'm told there was no radio traffic from *Novorossiysk* explicitly mentioning any incident on the surface.'

'At least it explains why the RNLI saw nothing when they got out there.'

'The crew got the fire under control, and she was able to submerge, then a couple of days later, she surfaced off the coast of France and was escorted through the Channel by her support tug, under the watchful eye of HMS *Iron Duke*.'

'It also tells me what Victoria Smith was going to blow the whistle on.'

'I am reliably informed, Nick – and I can say no more than that, as you'll understand – that defence intelligence, MI6, call it what you will, had nothing whatsoever to do with Lieutenant Commander Smith's death. She wasn't even under surveillance, apparently, so it wasn't known she was intending to reveal anything to anyone about the incident.'

'What about the Russians?'

'Not their style.' Perry was scuffing the sand with his shoes, trying to get the mud off. 'They'd have used a nerve agent, and her killer would've been *back in the USSR* before anyone had found the body.'

Perry was clearly a Beatles fan.

'The stakes are bigger than you or I can imagine,' continued Perry. 'And you're an intelligent man; you don't need me to tell what you can and can't do with this information.'

'I can't do anything with it, and I can't tell anyone.'

'Exactly.'

'Thank you,' said Dixon.

'My pleasure,' replied Perry, his hand outstretched. 'Now, there's somewhere I need to be, I'm afraid.'

'Go that way.' Dixon was pointing straight up the beach towards the sand dunes. 'You can get across the mud there.'

◆ ◆ ◆

Jane's text arrived as Dixon was watching Perry tiptoeing across the band of mud at the top of the beach.

> *Have u got Monty? Jx*
>
> *Yes. Didn't have time to leave a note sorry Nx PS home in an hour*
>
> *I've made a stew :-) Jx*

Dixon picked up the tennis ball and threw it along the sand, watching his dog tear off after it, leaving paw prints in the smooth sand that had been washed by the tide.

The partial DNA match had been a dead end, and now the deaths of the marine surveyors had led precisely nowhere. There'd been *no radio traffic from Novorossiysk explicitly mentioning any incident on the surface*. That's what Tom Perry had been told to say, probably, and if that was right, then the reality was that no one would ever really know what had happened out there. Yes, it might give some measure of closure to the families to know of the possible Russian involvement, which might explain why Victoria Smith had intended to reveal the information. But that's all it was – *possible* Russian involvement.

There was no reason to disbelieve what Perry had told him. He'd been remarkably forthcoming, actually; recognised that Dixon would have to be told the whole story if he was to believe it.

And the reality was Perry would have got clearance to tell him; assured those higher up the food chain that Dixon could be trusted with the information. Revealing it to anyone would be gross misconduct for a police officer, and an offence under the Official Secrets Act. There was probably a D-Notice in place too, so it would never get in the newspapers anyway.

No, it was about clarity. It was a legitimate line of enquiry and Dixon had been right to pursue it, but it was unlikely to have been the motive for her murder. It was certainly starting to feel that way anyway, and that meant the investigation had gone in the wrong direction; that *he* had taken it in the wrong direction, as Charlesworth would no doubt be quick to point out. It would be a difficult conversation. He would have to tell Charlesworth and Potter he was no longer pursuing it but wouldn't be able to tell them why.

Bollocks.

There was something though, something nagging at him that told him it hadn't all been a complete waste of time.

He was standing under the lighthouse, watching Monty paddling in the filthy water trapped in puddles at the base of the stilts, letting the information Perry had given him sink in. An unfortunate choice of word, perhaps, *sink*. Not that either boat had sunk – not the catamaran or the *Novorossiysk*. A Russian sub sinking off North Devon; now that really would have caused an international incident, whether they bloody well liked it or not.

It would be interesting to know what the *Novorossiysk* had been doing so close to the coast too, although Perry had been told not to ask, and Dixon didn't need to know anyway.

He was reminded of what the First Lieutenant had said about British territorial waters. 'They extend twelve miles from the coast. Beyond that, anything goes.'

Twelve miles.

Bugger.

Chapter Twenty-Seven

'Are you getting anywhere?'

It was an interesting question. Dixon had thought not, had had the wind taken out of his sails well and truly by Perry's revelation. Felt like it at the time, anyway. Not so much now, not after a walk on the beach with Monty. He'd felt like a man who'd just had a door slammed in his face, much as a politician must feel when out canvassing: stand there for a second, slightly bewildered, wondering what to do, then on to the next house.

Always the same question – rarely the same answer.

This time, though, Dixon couldn't shake off the feeling he was standing on the right doorstep. He'd just asked the wrong question. And the only option in that case was to knock on the door again.

Jane was sitting on the sofa, curtains drawn, the top of her head visible in the darkness, the flicker of the TV glinting on her hair.

Peter must be asleep. 'Sort of,' he whispered, standing right behind her.

Monty had taken up his usual position on the rug next to the cot.

'Don't bother whispering,' said Jane, standing up. 'I've got to get him up in a minute anyway.'

The doctors had been right, being at home was doing them both good, although Peter was likely to grow up thinking he lived at Brookfield School. His first word was almost certainly going to be 'chips'.

'Was it a submarine?' asked Jane, idly.

Dixon walked over to the sideboard, opened the door and took out a bottle of vodka, hidden from view when Jane had found out she was pregnant. 'I'm afraid I'm not at liberty to talk about it,' he said, placing the bottle in her hands.

She looked at the label, then looked at him, her eyes wide. 'Fuck.' Under her breath.

'All I can say is that I'm reliably informed the incident had nothing whatsoever to do with the murder.'

'And you believe that?'

'I do, and I don't, as it happens.'

'What about the two blokes in the boat?'

A shrug was the best he had to offer.

'A waste of time then?'

'Not quite.' Dixon lifted the lid of Jane's laptop, the screen lighting up to reveal a web browser open on Mumsnet. 'You need to get out more,' he said, smiling.

'I needed some advice about breastfeeding, so I did a search. Don't take the piss.'

'See if you can find a website that gives us distances between two places as the crow flies.'

'Why?'

'Devon and Cornwall have got their graves marked on separate maps. Put them on the same map and there's a pattern.'

Jane sat down in front of the computer, typed in 'distances as the crow flies'.

'How about "free map tools – how far is it between"? Sounds like it might be it.' She clicked on the link in the search results, clicked away the annoying cookie pop-up. 'From where to where?'

'HMS *Drake* to Modbury,' replied Dixon.

Jane started typing, got as far as 'Modb' before selecting 'Modbury, Devon, England' from the dropdown menu. 'I'm guessing you want miles rather than kilometres?'

He was standing behind her, leaning over with his hands on her shoulders. 'Thirteen-point-zero-eight-six miles. Now try to Peter Tavy.'

'Fifteen-point-three-four-three.'

'Kingston, Devon.'

'Twelve-point-five-six-five miles.' Jane turned on her chair, looked up at Dixon. 'What's the significance of that?'

'It's about British territorial waters. They extend twelve miles from the coast. Beyond that you're into international waters and "anything goes", according to the First Lieutenant at HMS *Drake*. Our killer is a sailor and, for whatever reason, he's sticking to the twelve-mile limit; won't leave a body within twelve miles of HMS *Drake*.'

'They surely had a geographic profiler look at it?'

'They did, but he just said the killer lives in Plymouth.'

'No shit.' Peter had started to stir, so Jane leaned over the cot, picked him up and put him in Dixon's arms. 'Talking of which,' she said, 'the nappies are on the chair.'

'Thanks.'

'What are you going to do?'

'A DNA screen. All male service personnel at *Drake*.'

'How many men is that?'

'A couple of thousand, I expect. It'll vary depending on what ships are in. They'll have a list and we'll only need to test everyone who was ashore for all three of the Devon attacks. It's a sod of a lot better than having to test the entire male population of Plymouth.'

'Are they doing that?'

'Not likely.'

'What about the date of Victoria Smith's murder as well?' Jane was stirring the stew on the hob in the kitchen, although Dixon had lost his appetite for some reason.

'No.'

'What will you do about her murder?'

'Find the Devon attacker and we find her killer.' He tied the nappy bag as tightly as he could without ripping the handles. 'To be able to frame him for Victoria Smith's murder, her killer must know the Devon attacker, must know he's guilty of those attacks.'

'Stew's nearly ready,' said Jane, from the kitchen. 'I'm guessing you'll be off back down to Express Park?'

'Afraid so.'

'I'll eat later in that case.'

'Have we got any pickled onions?'

Jane leaned around the door frame, a quizzical look on her face. 'Pickled onions? Who the bloody hell eats stew with pickled onions?'

'Everyone, surely?'

'Not mine they don't. I'd never have married you if I'd known.'

◆ ◆ ◆

Dixon had thought it might take an hour or so, even on a Saturday night. He checked the time when he clicked 'Save changes' on the Policy Log, left his phone on the corner of his workstation at Express Park. It was less than fifteen minutes in the end, before it started buzzing.

'Yes, Sir.'

'What d'you mean you're no longer pursuing possible whistleblowing by Victoria Smith as a line of enquiry?' demanded Charlesworth.

'I've taken it to its logical conclusion, Sir, and believe it is unlikely to have been the motive for her murder.' Dixon had known the question was coming, had rehearsed his reply.

'Why not?'

He'd known that one was coming too. 'I'm not at liberty to say, I'm afraid. You'll just have to trust my judgement on it.' Evasive, feeble, but there wasn't a lot else he could say without lying, and he'd done enough of that lately.

There was a definite sigh from the other end, no attempt made to mask it. Charlesworth had known the score, though; known where it might lead. 'And this DNA testing you're proposing, they've had a geographic profiler look at it, but you know better, is that it?'

Dixon ignored the jibe, opted for the honest answer. 'Yes, Sir. It's the naval connection and the twelve-mile limit. There was no indication that might be relevant when the profiler looked at the Devon attacks.'

'D'you know how much this is going to cost?'

'I've got a meeting with DCI Hatch in the morning and I'm hoping they'll agree to share the cost. It might be helpful if you were to have a word with your opposite number overnight.'

'And what if they say no?'

'Then we pay for it and solve their case for them. Either that, or you get to sack the idiot who authorised the expenditure.'

'You.'

'You'll also need to discipline the idiot who promoted me to a rank that gives me that level of authorisation.'

Charlesworth cleared his throat. 'Yes, quite.'

'Are you saying we shouldn't be running this DNA testing, Sir?'

'Of course not.'

'Good. Then I can take it the ACC has approved it.'

'I'll make a few calls, see what I can do, but for God's sake, don't rub them up the wrong way. By rights they should be paying seventy-five per cent given they've got three victims to our one, but I suppose we'll have to go fifty-fifty on it. Leave it with me.'

Charlesworth rang off.

It was going to be an interesting meeting in the morning with DCI Hatch at Crownhill. Dixon had set out his reasoning in an email, suggested the geographic profiler look at it overnight and be there as well.

Chapter Twenty-Eight

Everyone had been asleep when Dixon got back to the cottage just after midnight, so he'd stretched out on the sofa. It wasn't until just after three that Peter had them all up anyway. A quick turn around the field with Monty had got him out of another nappy change, but at least it meant he could go to bed afterwards.

Eight o'clock sharp and the familiar rumble of Cole's engine outside woke everyone up again.

'He needs changing.'

'Got to go, sorry.'

Shame that. Dixon had hoped to have got out unnoticed.

They'd talked a lot about being parents in the weeks before Peter was born, about sharing the load. Dixon had been looking forward to it. 'We'll need to find a balance,' Jane had said. All that had gone out of the window in the heat of a multiple murder investigation, though. The best that could be said was that Jane had encouraged him to go back to work.

Back to police work.

She was a police officer herself, knew the job inside out; knew the demands it made. She understood.

First things first, a visit to the home of the First Lieutenant to interrupt his Sunday morning. Hopefully he was an early riser.

Dixon had an address in Wedmore. 'I know it,' Cole said, when Dixon read it out. 'It'll be on the corner, right opposite the church.'

Twenty minutes later he let Dixon out of the passenger seat, then parked tight to the wall opposite a large double-fronted house with steps up to the front door and bay windows either side.

'Is he expecting us?' asked Cole.

It hardly mattered. Dixon rang the doorbell. Twice.

She was a tall woman, wearing a dressing gown and slippers. 'Sorry,' she said. 'I was having a bit of a lie-in. It is a Sunday.'

'Yes, I'm sorry to bother you; we're looking for Lieutenant Commander McConochie,' said Dixon.

'He's around the back,' she replied, examining their warrant cards. 'Is it to do with that submarine officer who was murdered?'

'It is.'

'You'd better come this way. It's easier.' She stepped to one side, allowing them into the porch.

They followed her through to the kitchen and out into the back garden.

'That's our garage. It opens out on to the lane at the back, but there's a side door you can see. He's in there.'

'Thank you.'

McConochie had seen them coming, was standing in the open door wiping his hands with a cloth. 'Good morning, Superintendent,' he said. 'How can I help you?'

It was a large double garage, two cars parked inside, light streaming in from the open up-and-over door.

'We're looking into running a DNA screen of all service personnel at HMS *Drake*, Sir,' replied Dixon. 'Wondered if that would be possible?'

'Certainly,' said McConochie. 'We'll be happy to help in any way we can. The RNP will be able to assist you with the testing, and I should imagine we'd be able to get through it fairly quickly.

Let me speak to Penny Stroud. I'll need to run it past the Naval Base Commander too, but he's not going to object. If it has to be done, then it has to be done.'

'Thank you.'

'It's important you understand we've got a mixed bag at *Drake*,' continued McConochie. 'We've got the crews from the ships at Devonport, the skeleton crews from the ships in for refit, then we've got the base establishment, and others here for other reasons; either they're awaiting the outcome of disciplinary proceedings, or they might be here for further training. Some are ashore for health reasons as well.'

'We test them all,' said Dixon. 'Anyone there at the relevant times.'

'If you email over the dates, I'm sure Warrant Officer Stroud can put together a list. That should be easy enough.'

'I'm sorry if this is going to be disruptive,' said Dixon.

'We'll manage,' replied McConochie. 'The base commander was most anxious that we should cooperate fully with your investigation.'

'How many gates are there at *Drake*?' asked Dixon.

'Several,' replied McConochie. 'And there's access through Devonport as well. We'll put leave restrictions in place, though, so all service personnel leaving the base will be required to show proof they've been tested and sign out. I'll go and make the calls now.'

'Thank you, Sir.'

'Just nip through the garage and you'll be in the lane at the back. Left and left again, to get to your car.'

◆ ◆ ◆

The meeting at Crownhill was about money, basically. The DNA testing would be going ahead, even if Avon and Somerset Police had to fund it themselves; Dixon was clear in his own mind about that.

Yes, that would put his neck on the block, but so be it.

DCI Hatch was sitting at one end of the table, a detective inspector Dixon hadn't met before to his left – Hatch did introduce him, but the name didn't stick. Dixon was good with names, but only those he needed to remember.

To Hatch's right was a tall thin man with a beard, wearing a tweed jacket and wool tie; had the look of a university lecturer, possibly. Dixon would've checked under the table for sandals but thought it might appear rude. Professor Jeremy Fallon, according to the business card on the table. Dixon turned the card over: Criminology Department, Plymouth University.

'Over to you, I think, Jeremy,' said Hatch, looking smug.

'I've read your email.' Fallon picked up a printed copy, waved it in front of him. 'And the twelve-mile limit makes perfect sense to me. Assuming you accept any sort of naval connection to the case. Otherwise it must be random, a coincidence.'

'The naval connection is there. Whether you accept it or not,' said Dixon.

'Well, it is, and it isn't,' said Hatch. 'Victoria Smith was a victim selected at random, just like the others.'

'That presumes that it's the same killer, which it isn't.'

'And therein lies the difference between us.' Hatch leaned back in his chair, folded his arms. 'You thought she was a whistleblower and that was the motive for her murder, but it turned out to be a wild goose chase.'

Cole was sitting next to Dixon, shifting uncomfortably in his seat. 'My colleague Sarah Loveday checked overnight and there were nine burials in the relevant period *within* twelve miles of HMS *Drake*,' he said. 'Why were none of those graves used by the killer?'

It was a good point. Sarah had still been in the incident room when Dixon had left the night before, and he'd wondered what she'd been doing. She'd resisted his attempts to send her home too.

'Maybe he couldn't find a suitable victim,' ventured the DI sitting next to Hatch.

'Or maybe it was because the graves were within the twelve-mile limit?' continued Cole.

'He's using graves more than twelve miles from *Drake*, overlooking any within twelve miles.' Fallon was nodding to himself, scribbling in a notebook on the table in front of him. 'It's certainly the best theory we've come up with yet.'

'That's all it is, I'm afraid.' Hatch dropped his pen on the table. 'There's no evidence, and we simply cannot sanction a mass DNA test on the scale being proposed based on a theory. No matter whose theory it might be.'

◆ ◆ ◆

Dixon arrived at HMS *Drake*'s main gate twenty minutes later, his departure from the meeting abrupt.

A mouthed 'sorry' from Fallon had proved no consolation.

The rumble of Cole's engine at the security barrier brought the Officer of the Watch out of the gatehouse. Mercifully, he recognised Dixon. 'Back again, Sir,' he said.

'I need to see the senior Royal Navy Police officer on the base,' replied Dixon.

'That'll be Warrant Officer Penny Stroud today, Sir. I'll ring her now while you sign in.'

'Thank you.'

A short wheelbase Land Rover was waiting for them outside when they came through security, visitor passes dangling round their necks on lanyards.

'You can leave your car there, Sir,' said the Officer of the Watch. 'Do you want me to let the First Lieutenant know you're here?'

'He's at home today. We've just come from there.'

'They'll be with me, Chief, if anyone wants to know where they are.' Warrant Officer Stroud was leaning across from the driver's seat of her Land Rover, shouting through the open passenger window. 'Hop in, Sir,' she said, looking at Dixon. 'The First Lieutenant rang me, and I've spoken to Sarah Loveday as well, so I know why you're here.'

Dixon's first call had been to Charlesworth, asking him to ring the Naval Base Commander at HMS *Drake*, and no doubt the brigadier would've spoken to his First Lieutenant to give his permission. Dixon had then rung Sarah, asked her to liaise with the RNP.

'Is it doable?' he asked, climbing into the front seat, watching Cole fumbling for the seatbelt in the back.

Stroud was wearing a naval uniform, and yet it was different somehow. Royal Navy Police epaulettes, possibly. Stab vest and a police radio, of course. 'Yes, it's doable, Sir. There are twenty-three of us on site, so we'll soon get through it. It's Sunday today, though, so we'll put everything in place for tomorrow morning if that's all right.'

'It's just the male personnel living on site at the relevant times,' said Dixon. 'How many is that?'

'Eight hundred and ninety-one, at the moment, Sir,' replied Stroud. 'We've got a destroyer in and *Agincourt*, obviously.'

Dixon did the maths in his head; at seven hundred quid a test, that was well over six hundred thousand pounds.

'How will you notify them?'

'Email and text message. I can get those sent out this afternoon. That'll restrict leave for those still on the base and anyone returning.'

Stroud followed a service road at the back of the base, tucked in behind a railway line, accommodation blocks towering over them.

'I spoke to a colleague at Bulford,' said Stroud. 'We've got our own forensics lab there, and he suggested we do it block by block.

We can set up a testing facility in the lounge on the ground floor. Should keep it simple.'

'Sounds ideal,' replied Dixon. 'Can your lab do the testing?'

'Not in the numbers required.'

It had been worth a try.

Actually, Dixon had a plan. An obvious plan, perhaps; more of a hope than a plan, even. Leak it to the press – it wouldn't be long before it was all over social media too – and wait for the killer to make a run for it. It sounded simple, and it was. Might save several hundred thousand pounds too, which would keep Charlesworth happy.

Dixon had been involved in mass DNA testing before, seen it in his time at the Met. Never easy with the civilian population; pick a geographical area, but who knew who was living in it at the material time? The electoral roll was worse than useless for that. Here, though, they'd know exactly who was in the target group, have their contact details, even their photographs.

If he was right, the killer really had no escape. Running was his only option.

The RNP station was a single-storey block, new red brick, tucked under the railway bridge.

Dixon's phone buzzed in his pocket just as he was climbing out of the Land Rover in the car park; turned out to be a text from Sarah, so he read it aloud. 'First batch of testing kits arriving by courier later this afternoon, FAO Warrant Officer Stroud.'

'I'll store them here under lock and key,' said Stroud. 'We'll keep an eye on anyone leaving after the text messages go out too, if that's what you're thinking, Superintendent?'

It was, as it happened.

Chapter Twenty-Nine

Dixon and Cole waited at the Royal Navy Police HQ until the testing kits had arrived and the email and text messages had been sent. The testing was due to start at 8 a.m. the following day in Cornwell Block, which housed submariners ashore from HMS *Agincourt.*

It seemed as good a place to start as any. Some were on leave, some had been redeployed at sea, but that still left seventy-six submariners, among the others accommodated in the block. Some were part of the skeleton crew that had stayed with *Agincourt* during the refit; others were waiting for deployment elsewhere.

Cunningham-Fraser Block would follow in the afternoon, then Ladysmith Block on Tuesday. McConochie had suggested that the Wardroom and senior rates' mess be dealt with separately and had arranged for the testing there to be conducted by the Surgeon Commander and the lieutenant commanding the base RNP.

Dixon had left Penny Stroud watching the CCTV coverage on the various gates, those signing in and out of the base flashing up on the screen in front of her.

'If he's smart,' said Cole, 'he'll wait, take the test and then make a run for it. That way he'll have a couple of days to get as far away as he can before the result comes back. Might even get abroad in that time.'

'Then we'd better hope he doesn't know that,' replied Dixon, watching Exeter Racecourse flashing by. 'And, besides, most killers aren't very smart. Either that or they're too smart for their own good. How d'you think we catch them?'

'Luck, mainly.'

'Our good luck, or their bad luck?'

'A bit of both.' Cole stamped on the brakes before he reached the speed camera at the bottom of the hill, cruised past it at sixty miles an hour. 'Gets the average down,' he said, with a sheepish grin.

Dixon was holding his phone, waiting for a call from Penny Stroud. If he was right, someone would make a run for it; someone would leave the base who shouldn't. Might take days, though, and it would drive him round the bend waiting for his phone to ring.

He was sliding it back into his inside jacket pocket when it started buzzing.

'Nick Dixon.'

'We've got a submariner from *Agincourt* who's left the base, Sir. He's absent without leave, technically, even though it's a Sunday,' said Stroud. 'Leading Hand Andrew Monk. Aged forty-two. A scab lifter.'

Dixon grimaced. 'A scab lifter?'

'Sorry, naval slang for a medic. We call them all that. He's a medical assistant.'

'Are you sure he's not just off to the pub? It's a Sunday evening.'

'We've restricted all service personnel to Cinderella leave today – back by midnight – and he's got a large rucksack on his back. He's also turned right out of the base towards the railway station,' replied Stroud. 'I sent someone over to Cornwell Block to check his room and he's cleared everything out. Just left his uniform.'

'Where does he live?'

'We've got an address in Tower Hamlets. Next of kin there is listed as his mother.'

'Does he have a car?'

'He's got a black Toyota Corolla, but he didn't renew his parking permit at the end of last month, so I'm guessing he's got rid of it. I'll get someone to check.'

'What time's the next train to London?'

'He'd have made the six-fifteen. Last stop is Taunton at seven-fifteen.'

Dixon looked at his watch; nearly half past six – plenty of time. 'Taunton railway station, Nige. Quick as you can.' Then he turned back to his phone. 'Can you email me a photograph of Leading Hand Monk, please, Penny?'

'Of course, Sir. I'll send over his security photo and a screenshot from the CCTV of him leaving the base, so you can see what he's wearing.'

'Thank you.'

'Good luck.'

'Made a run for it already, has he?' asked Cole. He'd opened the driver's window, stuck the blue light on the roof of his car and was now accelerating hard in the outside lane.

'If something sounds too good to be true, Nige, that's probably because it is.'

'Why else has he left the base? And it's a reasonable shout he'd head for London, if that's his home.'

'We'll see.' Dixon was dialling the incident room.

'Yes, Sir,' replied Sarah.

'I need British Transport Police, Taunton station, for the seven-fifteen to London. As many as they can. Ask them to meet me on the platform. And get the local lot there with a custody van as well, please.'

'Has someone made a run for it already?'

'So it seems.'

'The ACC will be pleased.'

◆ ◆ ◆

Cole parked outside the station, left his hazard lights on and the blue light on the roof. Three police vans had beaten them to it; one of them a dog van. It was rocking from side to side, a loud barking coming from inside.

'Someone's raring to go,' muttered Cole.

The vans were lined up along the wall opposite the main entrance, several uniformed officers hovering in the ticket office.

'It's on time, Sir,' one of them said, when Dixon walked in. 'Six carriages, according to our colleagues from BTP. First class at the front, then a buffet car, then four standard class carriages. They've just gone to make sure the train doesn't leave the station until we give them the signal. They wanted to know if we were sure the man is on the train.'

'We *believe* the man is on the train,' replied Dixon, looking at the screens mounted on the wall – arrivals and departures. 'If he's not, we wait for the next train.'

'It's platform five, Sir,' offered the uniformed officer. 'This way.'

'You got any stab vests in the back of your car, Nige?' asked Dixon, turning to Cole.

'No, Sir.'

'We've got some in the back of the van, Sir. Give me a sec.'

Dixon zipped up his stab vest as he walked out on to the platform, made sure Cole was doing the same. People were sitting on benches, some looking up from their phones or books nervously, some taking photos for Instagram; listening to the announcement that came over the Tannoy. 'Due to an ongoing police incident, please do not attempt to board the train arriving at platform five until advised it is safe to do so.' Other passengers standing at the edge of the platform stepped back, a few seeking sanctuary in the waiting room.

Dixon had remembered to take his warrant card and phone out of his inside jacket pocket before he zipped up his stab vest, stuffed them in his trouser pockets. 'How many have we got?' he asked.

'Eight, including the two transport police lads. They're just coming now, Sir.'

'All right. I'd like two of you on the platform opposite, in case he jumps on to the tracks.'

'The doors won't open that side, Sir,' said a uniformed sergeant with British Transport Police epaulettes.

'What about the windows?'

'They open, but it'd be a bit of a squeeze. What's he done, this bloke?'

'Two murders, and one attempted murder.'

'He might try in that case.'

'Then we'll have two on at the front working their way back, two at the back working their way forward, and two staying on the platform. PC Cole and I will get on at the front of the standard class carriages and work our way back through them. Stop anyone who tries to get off the train, and don't forget to check the toilets.' Dixon held his phone out with the CCTV image of Leading Hand Monk leaving HMS *Drake* on it. 'This is the man we're looking for. He's wearing blue jeans, a green coat and a black baseball cap, and he's carrying a large blue rucksack.'

'I've got a message to the guard, Sir,' said the sergeant. 'He's going to ask everyone to remain seated when the train stops, announce it over the intercom just as the train pulls in. He's going to say there's a police incident on the platform. Some people won't hear it because they'll be wearing headphones but just shout at them to sit down.'

Then the Tannoy crackled into life again, the message automated. 'The next train at platform five is the seven-fifteen service to London Paddington, calling at London Paddington only.'

Dixon watched the train approach, suddenly painfully aware of just how far he'd stuck his neck out this time. A mass DNA screen of a naval base, which had immense implications for the credibility of Avon and Somerset Police if it turned out to have been a waste of time. And that was before the cost was added to the mix. Now he was about to arrest a man whose only crime had been going absent without leave, albeit the night before the DNA screening.

It was all out there too; the DNA screen leaked to the press and all over social media. There really was no going back now.

He was due a bit of luck – and, according to Cole, that's how most criminals got caught anyway. Their bad luck, or the police's good luck. Either would do, Dixon wasn't fussy.

He started walking, following the door at the front of carriage D, Cole right behind him. Several people were standing up inside the carriage, some listening to the announcement and sitting back down again. Others oblivious to it.

He stopped in front of the door, thumped the button to open it when the light came on. He glanced along the train, uniformed officers getting on front and back.

The guard on the train was making the same announcement again. 'Please remain in your seats . . .'

A girl was leaning over the luggage rack, wrestling with a suitcase. Dixon showed her his warrant card. 'Please return to your seat.' It turned out to be the window seat just inside the door.

'Loos are empty, Sir,' said Cole, still behind him.

Dixon worked his way back through the carriage, passengers looking up at him as he went past. If Monk was on the train, he wouldn't look up, would he? He'd keep his head down, pull down the peak of his baseball cap. Pretend to be asleep, try to hide his face.

Several people wanted to know what was going on, some anxious not to miss connecting trains, others with people outside waiting for them, apparently.

Dixon checked each passenger in turn, looked at them squarely in the face, a horrible sick feeling rising in the pit of his stomach as he neared the back of the carriage. No sign of Monk. Yet.

On to the next.

Cole was banging the door of a locked toilet behind him.

A woman's voice, but that was an easy ploy, and Cole was alive to it. 'Open the door, please. Police.' He glanced in. 'Thank you.' Then he tapped Dixon on the shoulder. 'It's clear, Sir.'

It was the strap dangling that gave Monk away. Halfway along the carriage, hanging down from the luggage rack above the seats, pointing to where he was. Almost. A blue rucksack, large. It must've been a struggle to get it up there.

Two seats together, facing the direction of travel – facing Dixon as he walked along the aisle, eyes fixed on the baseball cap he could see in the gap between the seats in front. He stopped, turned to Cole and pointed to the rucksack strap.

The uniformed officers who had got on at the back of the train were now approaching the other end of the same carriage, so Dixon waved at them to stop and wait by the luggage rack.

He peered over the back of the seat in front. Monk was sitting there, crumpled, hunched over, the peak of his baseball cap pulled down over his face. It was definitely him, even down to the black trainers, visible in the CCTV image from *Drake*.

The seat next to him was empty, so Dixon sat down, showed Monk his warrant card. 'Are you Leading Hand Andrew Monk?'

He nodded, the peak of his cap moving, just enough.

'You're absent without leave, Andrew.'

No response.

'The night before DNA testing is due to begin. Is that a coincidence?'

Monk shook his head. 'I didn't do the West Bagborough one. You need to know that.'

Dixon stood up, looked down at him. 'Andrew Monk, I am arresting you on suspicion of the murders of Kirsty Franklin and Portia Woodrow, and the attempted murder of Amy Fox.'

Dixon ignored the gasps from the seat behind him, a face appearing in the gap between the seats.

'Sit back, please, madam,' hissed Cole.

'You do not have to say anything, but it may harm your defence if you do not mention when questioned something you later rely on in court. Anything you do say may be given in evidence.'

'How did you know?' asked Monk, his voice little more than a whisper.

'Twelve miles,' replied Dixon.

'They drum it into you.' Monk had pulled his cap down over his face. 'Never break the law within twelve miles of home.'

Chapter Thirty

'We got lucky.'

'Rubbish,' said Charlesworth. 'You make your own luck in this game. I've said it before, and I'll say it again – you make things happen, Nick.'

'Thank you, Sir.'

'Now, we need to give some thought to getting a press release out before Devon and Cornwall beat us to it. We don't want them taking the credit.' Charlesworth was dialling a number on his phone. 'I'll get Vicky to come in; she can draft something and get it out.'

Quite how he had found out about the arrest was a mystery to Dixon, let alone how he'd got to Express Park so quickly on a Sunday evening. He was dressed as if he'd just come off the golf course, which might explain it.

They'd followed the van from Taunton station all the way into the caged enclosure at the back of Express Park, and Dixon had left Monk downstairs in the custody suite, being checked in by Cole.

'Well done, Sir,' said Sarah, beaming at him when he arrived at the top of the stairs. It was a full house in the incident room; a full house being Louise, Mark and Sarah. 'Shall I cancel the DNA testing? Penny Stroud is expecting that call; hasn't opened the boxes yet.'

'Yes, please.'

'Good. She'll send them back to the lab unopened.'

‘The ACC will think all his Christmases have come at once,’ said Mark, stifling a chuckle.

Dixon handed an evidence bag containing Monk’s phone to Louise. ‘His rucksack is already on the way to Forensics, but let’s see what we can get off this. He deactivated the passcode for us, which was nice of him.’

‘You think he’s going to cooperate, then?’ asked Mark.

‘He seemed compliant, but that depends on what advice he gets from his solicitor. There’s one on the way now. In the meantime, we need to find out everything we can about him. We’ll need his service record for a start.’

‘Already on the way, sir,’ said Sarah. ‘Penny Stroud is on it now.’

‘Social media, everything we can get off that phone. We’ll need his internet search history to prove he was looking for suitable graves.’

‘I’ll get a car to take this up to High Tech straightaway.’ Louise was holding up the evidence bag. ‘They can work on it overnight.’

‘And I’ll get on to the mobile company for a cell site analysis,’ said Mark. ‘See if he was daft enough to take his phone with him when he committed the murders.’

‘It’s going to be a late night, I’m afraid.’

‘Do we notify Devon and Cornwall we’ve made an arrest?’ asked Sarah.

‘Not yet.’

‘The ACC will want to get his press release out first.’ Mark, spot on, as always.

The exchange reminded Dixon to let Jane know. He slid his phone out of his pocket, tapped out a text message:

Late night sorry. Made an arrest Nx

No speech bubble – probably asleep in front of the telly.

'What's the plan?' Charlesworth must have tiptoed up the stairs; took them all by surprise.

'I'm going to do the preliminary interview myself, Sir,' replied Dixon. 'As soon as he's finished with his solicitor. I want to see what he's got to say for himself. Mark and Louise can prep for a full interview tomorrow while I go back down to Plymouth. I want to speak to his commanding officer again, among others.'

'The Devon lot will no doubt wish to interview him.'

'They're welcome to do that here. And once we're satisfied he didn't kill Victoria Smith, they can have him.'

'He confessed, surely?'

'What he actually said was "I didn't do the West Bagborough one".'

'Which implies he did the others, I suppose.'

'If you're going to admit to three, then why not four, unless you really didn't do it,' said Mark.

'Just be careful,' said Charlesworth. 'He could be lying; he's Navy, and maybe he doesn't want to admit to killing a senior officer?'

'I've just had an email from Penny Stroud, Sir,' said Sarah. 'She says she'll have his personnel file and service record for us by the morning.'

'Tell her I'll pick it up in that case,' replied Dixon. 'And I'll need meetings with Commander Vaughan and his XO. Monk was a medical assistant on board *Agincourt*, so I'll also need to speak to whoever it was he assisted.'

'Yes, Sir.'

'You've got twenty-four hours remember,' said Charlesworth.

'Thirty-six. DCS Potter will authorise another twelve hours if we need them. I can authorise it myself for that matter.'

'It would be better done by an officer independent of the investigation.' Charlesworth's phone buzzed. He looked at the screen, turned on his heels. 'Vicky Thomas is here. We'll be in meeting room two, Nick. Give me ten minutes then come down, if you will.'

Dixon stifled a sigh. 'Yes, Sir.'

They were already working on a draft when Dixon got down there fifteen minutes later. The canteen had closed hours ago, so it was a bag of crisps and a can of pop from the machine on the landing. That and a couple of fruit pastilles. He'd checked his blood – scanned the sensor in his arm – and his blood sugar level was low and going down.

'Ah, Nick,' said Charlesworth. 'You arrested him for the Devon murders and the attempted murder. What do we say about Victoria Smith's killing?'

'I'd like her killer to think he's safe. He went to a lot of trouble to make it look like Monk attacked them all, and he needs to believe his plan worked.'

'So, we lie to the press. Is that what you're asking me to do?'

'Devon and Cornwall Police will tell you he killed her as well.' Dixon had never got on with the press officer – starched hair and a personality to match; jeans and a leather bomber jacket this time, instead of the usual two-piece suit. 'We withhold information from them when it suits us,' he said. 'This is no different.'

'It makes perfect sense to me,' said Charlesworth.

Vicky Thomas started typing on the laptop open on the table in front of her, reading aloud as she went: '. . . the murders of Kirsty Franklin, Portia Woodrow, Victoria Smith, and the attempted murder of Amy Fox . . .'

'Apart from that, I don't really mind what it says.' Dixon hadn't sat down, turned for the door.

'We'll send this out in a minute,' said Charlesworth. 'Then I'll ring my opposite number at Devon and Cornwall, let them know what's going on.'

No doubt DCI Hatch would jump straight in a car.

◆ ◆ ◆

'All right, Andrew. You're still under caution, obviously, and your solicitor has explained what's going to happen now. This is your chance to tell us what's happened – why it's happened.'

Dixon was sitting next to Andrew Monk; nice and cosy. It was the new interview room layout, supposed to build a rapport with the person being interviewed, less confrontational than having a table in between them. Monk's solicitor was to his right, Cole sitting to Dixon's left.

They were all sitting opposite the recording device. Everyone still referred to it as a tape machine, even though there was no tape. It had meant new wording for the introductions too. 'This interview is being recorded on to a digital hard drive. Please state your name for the recording . . .'

'Where were you on the twenty-eighth of January last year?'

Monk glanced at his solicitor, turned back to Dixon. 'No comment.'

Not a good sign.

'We know where you were, Andrew,' said Dixon. 'You were in the churchyard of St James the Less, Kingston. So why don't you tell us why you were there?'

'No comment.'

'How do you explain your blood and skin cells being found on the thigh of an eighteen-year-old girl called Kirsty Franklin, whose body was found in a freshly dug grave in that churchyard?'

'No comment.'

'When we were on the train, Andrew, I asked you if it was a coincidence that you were going AWOL the night before the DNA screening was due to begin at HMS *Drake* and you shook your head. What did you mean by that?'

'No comment.'

'Your DNA was also found on the body of Portia Woodrow.'

'No comment.' Monk was rocking backwards and forwards on his chair, the plastic creaking.

'What did you mean by "I didn't do the West Bagborough one"?'

'I didn't kill Lieutenant Commander Smith.'

'Does that mean that you *did* kill the others?'

Another glance at his solicitor. 'No comment.'

'Let's talk about Lieutenant Commander Smith then,' said Dixon, expecting Monk's solicitor to intervene – do something useful for his client anyway.

'My client has not been arrested for the murder of Victoria Smith,' said the solicitor, sitting up, looking across at Dixon.

'I'm asking him purely as a witness.'

The solicitor nodded to Monk.

'I didn't kill her.'

'Where were you that night? Last Saturday night.'

'I was on the base, went out to the pub, got back about one, I suppose.'

'Anyone go with you?'

'No.'

'Anyone vouch for your whereabouts?'

'I don't know.'

'Your DNA was found in the grave at West Bag—'

'It must've been planted there.' Monk's breathing was shallow, quickening. 'I don't even know where West Bagborough is, couldn't point to it on a map.'

'Why did you get rid of your car?'

'It failed the MOT and it was going to cost more money than it was worth to fix it.'

'When was this?'

'About a month ago.'

'Where is the car now?'

'The garage gave me two hundred quid for it. Stockton's, down Lee Mill. They'll probably fix it themselves and sell it on.'

Dixon knew Sarah was watching the feed in the adjacent room, making notes; that would be top of her list – sending uniformed officers to see if Monk's car was still there.

'All right, let's assume your DNA was planted at the scene of Lieutenant Commander Smith's murder.' Dixon emphasised her rank. 'For that to happen, her killer must have had access to your DNA.'

'It would be all over the *Agincourt*, my bunk, clothes. And I live on the base.'

'There were carpet fibres too. We're checking to see whether they're a match with your cabin at *Drake*, but whoever did it would also need to have known that you killed the other women, Kirsty and Portia, and attacked Amy. Think about it, otherwise framing you for Victoria Smith's murder makes no sense, does it?'

'We had a death on board, on my first trip. I've been having counselling.'

'I think you've said enough, Andrew.' Monk's solicitor leaned forward, his hand on Monk's shoulder. 'My client needs a comfort break.'

'Who died, Andrew?'

'No comment' just about carried through the tears and shallow breaths.

Dixon had one last card to play. 'DNA is funny stuff, Andrew. Tells us a lot. And there's this database we've got. Did you know you've got a son?'

Brought him up short, did that. 'Who, where?' demanded Monk, wiping the tears from his cheeks with his hands.

'This interview is terminated at . . .'

Stew on that, you tosser, thought Dixon, standing up as Cole dealt with the formalities.

Sarah Loveday was first out of the anteroom when Dixon emerged from the interview room. 'DCI Hatch is in there with the ACC,' she said.

'Monk's car, and make sure we get his medical records.'

'On my list.'

Time to get it over with. Dixon pushed open the door of the anteroom. DS Reddaway was there, with DCI Hatch. Charlesworth was smiling, oddly enough.

'Well done, Superintendent.' Hatch had his hand outstretched in Dixon's direction. 'I'm arranging for two of my officers to come and interview him in the morning. I hope that's all right?'

'Certainly,' replied Dixon. 'Although it seems he's going "*no comment*".'

'It'll just be a formality, anyway,' continued Hatch. 'He can go "*no comment*" as much as he likes. We've got enough to charge him with all four. The CPS will give us the nod on the DNA and what he said when you arrested him, if nothing else.'

'He denies any part in Victoria Smith's murder.'

'That's just because she's a naval officer.' Hatch sighed, loudly. 'Oh God, don't tell me you believe him?'

'We do,' replied Charlesworth.

Hatch looked at Reddaway, shook his head. 'So, where does that leave us?' he asked.

'You're welcome to interview him here, and he can be charged here when Superintendent Dixon is good and ready. Then transferred down to Plymouth when we've finished with him.'

'And when will that be?'

'Has anyone spoken to Amy Fox's family?' asked Dixon, deflecting.

'I did that as soon as I got the call from my ACC,' replied Hatch. 'The other families too.'

Taken some of the credit then.

Twat.

Chapter Thirty-One

Dixon left Louise and Mark to their interview preparation just after midnight, managed a few hours asleep on the sofa before Peter started crying and had them all up anyway.

'Midwife is coming today,' Jane said.

'I'm sorry, I—'

'Of course you can't. I wasn't telling you expecting you to be here.'

Yes, Jane knew the score.

He got back to Express Park at six. Monk was in conference with his solicitor, two Devon and Cornwall officers sitting in the interview room. Hatch was slumped in a chair in the anteroom, his head resting against the wall, eyes closed.

'What's new?' Dixon asked, when he reached the top of the stairs.

'His internet history is full of searches for burials in Devon,' replied Sarah. 'He looked at the announcements for Peter Tavy and Kingston, even went to the funeral directors' websites. Nothing in Somerset at all.'

'Have you been home?'

'No, she hasn't,' replied Louise.

'Go. Now. Get some sleep.'

'Really? Not now, Sir. He's just about to be—'

'He'll answer "no comment" to every question,' interrupted Dixon. 'And he's not our man anyway, he's theirs. Now go home and go to bed.'

They watched Sarah trudge towards the door.

'Are you ready for the interview?' Dixon asked, turning to Louise.

'We haven't come up with anything new on Victoria Smith's murder,' she replied. 'They found his car. It was still at the garage, and it's gone off to Devon and Cornwall's lab. There was a toolbox in the boot, which they're going to be looking at; no ball peen hammer, though. We haven't got cell site analysis yet, but Devon have come up with various images of his car on ANPR cameras at the relevant times and places.'

'We've been back through ours,' said Mark. 'Nothing, but then he said he'd got rid of it before Victoria Smith was murdered anyway.'

'It'll be a complete waste of time, I'm afraid, but we've got to go through the motions, put it to him, line by line.'

Mark shrugged. 'It'll be interesting to see whether he denies everything or just answers "*no comment*". Not that it makes much difference.'

'He'll answer all their questions "*no comment*",' said Dixon. 'Then deny he had anything to do with Victoria Smith's killing.' He was watching the top of the stairs, hoping the footsteps belonged to Cole. 'Either way, I don't want him charged until I get back. I don't care what Hatch says, or the ACC for that matter. All right?'

'Where will you be?' asked Louise.

Cole appeared at the top of the stairs, a coffee in one hand and a bacon roll in the other.

'Plymouth,' replied Dixon.

◆ ◆ ◆

Penny Stroud was waiting for them when they arrived at the main gate. 'I've set up a meeting with his CO, and a separate meeting with his XO, as you asked. And his line manager as well. He was assistant to Surgeon Lieutenant Fisher on board *Agincourt*, so he should know more about Monk than anyone else.'

'What about his service and medical records?'

'I'm just awaiting clearance to release those to you.'

They followed her Land Rover around the perimeter service road, parked in the compound behind the Royal Navy police station.

They had to squeeze past the boxes of DNA testing kits in the corridor to get to her office; still unopened and waiting for a courier to collect them.

'You got lucky,' said Stroud, flicking on the kettle on the windowsill in her office.

'It was always going to go one of two ways,' replied Dixon. 'Either he'd run early or he'd run late.'

'I've arranged the meetings to start with the surgeon lieutenant at nine. The First Lieutenant thought it would be better at his office, rather than dragging them all the way over here.'

'Fine.' Dixon was watching her spooning coffee into three mugs. 'Have you had any dealings with Andrew Monk?'

'Not personally. There have been issues while he's been on the base, though. Behavioural issues, shall we say.'

'Go on.'

'The biggest single issue we have here – in the Navy generally for that matter – is unacceptable sexual behaviour. USB we call it. There's usually alcohol involved as well. A couple of the younger Jennies have reported him for USB in the last year or so. He's been ashore for counselling and there's been a disciplinary process. It's all in his records, and as I say, I'm just waiting for clearance.' She leaned over her desk, clicked a mouse, the screen lighting up. 'Nothing yet, sorry.'

'I didn't think female sailors were called Wrens anymore?'

'We're not, but the nickname stuck.'

'What sort of USB?'

'I'm not aware of an actual physical sexual assault, nothing like that; it was more harassment, staring, taking photos, creepy stuff like that. He's a weird, weird bloke by all accounts.'

'Is it going to be possible to speak to these women?'

'One certainly. The other is at sea, I'm afraid.'

Dixon knew not to ask where.

The phone rang on Stroud's desk. 'Right, thanks.' She replaced the handset, turned to Dixon. 'There's a van at the main gate to collect the boxes. I'll drop you at the First Lieutenant's office on the way. Leave that,' she said, gesturing to the mugs. 'They've got posh coffee over there.'

◆ ◆ ◆

The First Lieutenant must have been watching from a window, was halfway down the stairs when they walked into the office building. 'You've made an arrest, Penny tells me.'

'Yes, Sir,' replied Dixon.

'I looked him up on the system,' said McConochie. 'Can't say I can put a face to the name, but I gather he's been with us a while. An odd fellow, by all accounts.'

'We're still waiting to see his service and medical records.'

'That's the Admiralty for you.' McConochie looked at his watch. 'Nothing happens terribly quickly. Won't be long now. I've got Surgeon Lieutenant Fisher in the meeting room. I'm guessing you don't need me to sit in?'

'No, Sir.'

'Nobody from Legal this time, either, but you know what you can ask about, and what you can't.'

The surgeon lieutenant stood up, introduced himself, hand outstretched. Reuben Fisher was tall, thin, with short hair. A narrow face, dark eyes. Dixon was struggling to find any distinguishing features, apart from the nervous twitch. Bloody uniforms.

'How long have you been in the Navy?' he asked. A couple of easy questions first to put him at his ease.

'I joined straight from medical school,' replied Fisher. 'Finished my qualifications in the Navy, so that would be eight years ago. Just over.'

'And do you have to go through the same training as everyone else to get your dolphins?'

'Oh yes. We're sailors first, doctors second.'

'How long have you been on submarines?'

'Four years.'

Cole was making notes, so Dixon poured him a coffee from the jug in the middle of the table, slid it across to him.

'Always on the Astute class or have you also done tours on the Vanguard class?'

'Two on the Vanguard class. They're longer tours, nine months at a time, so we medics tend to share them around.'

'What sort of issues do you get on board?'

'Minor accidents, had a few burns. Sometimes you get a flu bug going around, but everyone's vaccinated, obviously. A couple of heart attacks, someone had a stroke once. Something serious like that and we tend to head for the nearest friendly port and have them airlifted home.'

'There's a sick bay on board, presumably?'

'It's small, but then everything is on board a sub, as you'd expect. Well equipped, despite that though.'

'And that was your place of work with Leading Hand Andrew Monk?'

'It's him you've arrested, is it? They never said.'

'It is.'

'For Victoria's murder as well?'

Dixon would keep his powder dry on that one for the time being.

'Can't say I'm surprised. He was a weird one.' Fisher glowered at the memory. 'Look, I may as well tell you what happened, because you'll find out soon enough. Eighteen months ago, maybe, we had a death on board *Agincourt*. I can't tell you where we were or what we were doing, but usually we'd have docked somewhere, and the body would've been flown home. That wasn't possible for reasons I can't specify.'

'That's fine,' said Dixon, and he could guess. 'We quite understand.'

'We've got a mortuary of sorts on board – one refrigerated unit – and she was in a body bag, in the refrigerator.'

'How did she die?'

'An accident; quite innocuous. She fell down an internal ladder, bashed in the back of her head, broke her neck. She was dead by the time I got to her, so there was nothing for it but to keep her on board until we got home. That was only a few weeks, and it was quicker than heading for the nearest safe port anyway. The old days of wrapping them in a Union Jack, reciting the Lord's Prayer and firing them out of a torpedo tube are long gone, you'll be pleased to learn.' Fisher sighed. 'Although it might have been better if we had.'

'Go on.'

'Leading Hand Monk developed a fascination with her body. That's the only way I can describe it. Several times when I walked into the sick bay, he was there with the refrigerator door open. I don't know what he was doing, really don't want to know to be frank, but I was forced to make a report to the XO and he was relieved of medical duties for the remainder of the deployment. The sick bay is locked, for obvious reasons, and he was told to surrender his keys, which he did.'

'What happened after that?'

'There was a disciplinary process. I don't know the outcome. I don't think he's been to sea since, not as far as I'm aware. Certainly not on any sub I've been on.'

'Were you aware he was at *Drake*?'

'I've seen him around a couple of times, but I didn't know what he was doing here.' Fisher folded his arms. 'If it had been down to me, he'd have been dishonourably discharged, but he was still in uniform last time our paths crossed.'

'Did you speak to him?' Dixon was seething now, doing his best to hide it, speaking through gritted teeth.

'No. It was all I could do to return his salute to be honest with you.'

'Were you aware of the three attacks in Devon? Two murders early last year and then another attack in November.'

'Yes, I was aware. It was all over the local news and the national news too.'

'The victims were young women, hit over the backs of their heads with a blunt instrument and then left in newly dug graves, posed as if they were in a coffin.' Dixon paused, watching for a reaction. 'Or a body bag.'

There were cogs going round, Dixon could see that; decided to give them a helping hand.

'You're telling me that Leading Hand Andrew Monk developed an unhealthy fascination with the body of a dead woman, and you didn't think it might be worth reporting that to the local police?'

'No, it never—'

'A dead woman who'd hit the back of her head falling down a ladder.'

Fisher reddened. 'Now you point it out, perhaps it might have been worth saying something, but that's with the benefit of hindsight.'

'How old was she, the sailor who died on board the sub?'

'She was a junior rating, on her first operational deployment. Early twenties, maybe. It'll be in her records.'

'Who knew about Monk's behaviour on board the sub?'

'I did, obviously. I reported it to the XO, she'd have reported it to the CO. The Cox'n would've been informed – he's responsible for safety on board. That's it, probably.'

'Who was the Cox'n?'

'You'll have met him,' replied Fisher. 'He's the Officer of the Watch here now, supervises the main gate. Chief Petty Officer Pusser Hill.'

Chapter Thirty-Two

Penny Stroud closed the door behind her. 'The XO isn't here yet,' she said. 'Forgive me, Superintendent, but you appeared to be suggesting Lieutenant Fisher knew – or should have known, perhaps – what Monk was doing.' She looked at Dixon, frowned.

'Fisher said he was a sailor first, doctor second.' He was stirring a fresh cup of coffee. 'Are you a sailor first, police officer second?'

'Police officer first,' she replied. No hesitation either. 'I was with the Met before I joined the Navy.'

'Monk has been arrested for the two Devon murders and the attempted murder of Amy Fox. Not the murder of Lieutenant Commander Victoria Smith.'

'Why not?' demanded Stroud.

'Because he didn't do it,' replied Dixon. 'Someone else here did it. They knew what he was doing, killed Victoria Smith and made a feeble attempt to make it look like Monk had done it.'

'But there's DNA isn't there?'

'From a hair sample.'

'And what about the carpet fibres? There's a match—'

'It proves nothing.'

'Monk is saying they were planted?'

'On Victoria Smith, yes. And I believe him.'

'All right then, why?'

‘I thought, to begin with, it was because she was about to blow the whistle on an incident that took place during *Agincourt*’s recent deployment. I was half right.’ Dixon took a sip of tepid coffee. ‘She was about to blow the whistle, just not about that.’

‘What then?’

‘According to a friend, she was having an affair with a married man. I’m guessing it was a senior officer, but that doesn’t necessarily follow. You call it USB, I think.’

‘So, we’ve got another killer in *Drake*?’

‘You have. Someone who knew about Monk.’

McConochie opened the door, leaned in. ‘Lieutenant Commander Towers is here,’ he said. ‘I’ll get someone to freshen up that coffee as well.’

Uniform again. Irritating. Towers was in her early thirties, much the same age as Victoria Smith, her short hair pinned back. She returned Penny Stroud’s salute, tucked her cap under her arm, then shook hands with Dixon and Cole.

‘The First Lieutenant is organising some fresh coffee,’ said Dixon, when Towers reached for the jug. ‘That’s gone cold.’

Towers sat down. ‘You’ve arrested Leading Hand Monk, I gather,’ she said.

‘What can you tell me about his last deployment on *Agincourt*?’

‘Revolting little man.’ She curled her lip in disgust. ‘We had a female crew member die. It was an accident, poor girl. First deployment, and she falls down a ladder. Tanya McCann, from Liverpool. Got a bit of stick for her accent, but she took it in good part. It was just banter. You have to allow some, otherwise we’d all go mad.’ She waited while a civilian staff member bustled in, cleared away the cups and saucers, and the cold coffee. ‘She was a nice girl. Probably wouldn’t have gone far in the Navy, but then not everybody can, not everybody is able to. She was trying to climb down the ladder backwards, not facing it as you're supposed to, and her heel slipped. Bang, down she went.'

'I won't ask where the sub was when that happened,' said Dixon.

'Couldn't tell you even if you did. All I can say is we had to keep the poor girl on board until we got home, which was enough time for Monk to develop an unhealthy interest in her.'

'Were there any issues with Monk before that?' asked Dixon. He waited while a fresh tray of coffee was brought in. 'Any of the female crew members complain of inappropriate behaviour, for example?'

'You've not seen his file?' asked Towers, pouring herself a coffee.

'Not yet.' Dixon looked blankly at Stroud.

'I'll chase that up now,' she said, reaching for her phone.

'You need to understand, *try* to understand, what it's like on a submarine, particularly on an extended tour, when we can be submerged for weeks at a time. You've got men and women in close proximity, day and night. The submarine service has a bit of reputation for USB, but it's inevitable, I suppose. There have been occasions when I've had to put people in their place, use a well-directed elbow.' She rolled her eyes. 'But there was an issue with Monk, yes. A couple of complaints were made during his last deployment, and there have been others since.'

'I'm aware of the issues at *Drake*,' said Dixon.

'No formal complaints were made on board ship. A couple of the female crew wanted me to know his behaviour was creepy, off the record. Staring, stuff like that. Then we had the business with him interfering with the dead body, of course.'

'Were you aware of the murders in the local area here?'

'Not really. You get so wrapped up in life on the base, on the submarine. I'm sure I was aware there'd been some attacks on women locally. I seem to remember circulating an email to my female colleagues advising them to be alert when off base, but I can't say I knew the details of what had been happening. Can't say I'm surprised it turns out to have been Andrew Monk either.'

'How well did you know Victoria Smith?'

'Very well. We'd come through sub school together, got our dolphins at the same time. There were three of us, the three musketeers they used to call us. *Mouse*keteers, according to some of the cheeky sods.'

'That's sexism,' said Stroud.

'It is, but if you reported all of it you'd spend your life doing nothing else. It's getting better, of course it is, but there's still a long way to go.'

'I've seen a photograph of the three of you,' said Dixon. 'Victoria had it framed on her mantelpiece. Who was the third?'

'Lieutenant Commander Charlotte Fraser. She's at sea on a Vanguard class. Can't say any more than that, I'm afraid.'

'Did the three of you keep in touch?'

'Not so much with Charlotte. I did with Victoria, obviously. We were on the same boat.'

'Was she a friend?'

'Yes, I suppose so. We were work colleagues first and foremost. I was the XO and she was the senior communications officer, so we worked closely together, but yes, we were friends. You can be both.'

'Did you discuss your personal lives?'

'Not really. I haven't got one; married to the Navy, me. Victoria wasn't in a relationship as far as I'm aware, or if she was, she never told me. I knew she was buying her house in West Bagborough; very excited about that, she was. I was supposed to be going over there at some point, but never got round to it.'

'So, it would surprise you to learn that she was in a relationship with a married man?'

'Yes, it would. Who?'

'We don't know.'

Towers looked at Dixon, her brow furrowed. 'Sorry, how is this relevant, if she was murdered by Andrew Monk?'

'Purely background,' replied Dixon.

Towers appeared to accept that as a valid answer, turned back to her coffee.

'How did she get on with her fellow officers on board?'

'Very well. There was never any issue. She was highly regarded. Got on well with the CO and everyone else. Always had a good report. You'll have seen her service record?'

'I have. Was there ever any issue between Monk and Victoria on board?'

'No. She was comms and he was a scab lifter. Their paths might have crossed in the gangway, but he'd have stepped aside to let her pass. That's about it.'

'Was she ever ill on board?'

'Not that I know of.'

'So, there's no reason you can think of why Monk would target three random local women, and then Victoria Smith?'

'Look, he might have become fixated on her while he was on *Agincourt*, I suppose. He's the sort for that, but there was never any sign of it, and if that's the case, even she hadn't spotted it. She'd have said if she was worried by someone like that.'

'Do you have any questions for Lieutenant Commander Towers, Nigel?'

The question took Cole by surprise. 'Er, no, Sir,' he said, pretending to flick back through his notebook.

It hadn't been about that anyway. It had bought Dixon a moment to think. There was something else, but now wasn't the right time. Not with Penny Stroud sitting there, making her own notes.

'Thank you very much,' he said, standing up.

'I'll go and see if the CO is here,' said Stroud, looking at her watch. 'The siren will be going off in a minute.'

Dixon must've looked blank because Towers felt the need to explain. 'It sounds like an old air raid siren,' she said. 'It's tested every Monday at eleven-thirty; supposed to warn of a radiation leak. You can hear it right across the city.'

◆ ◆ ◆

'Sorry to spring that on you, Nige,' said Dixon, when the room emptied.

'I'm guessing there's something you're not telling me,' said Cole.

'Nothing personal. I'm not telling anyone. Yet. It might not be relevant anyway.'

'Commander Vaughan is on his way now, Sir,' said Stroud.

The familiar whine of an air raid siren started in the distance; familiar to Dixon, and to anyone who'd ever watched an old British war film.

'Here they come again.' Dixon couldn't remember the actor, couldn't remember which film, but someone had said it. It might have been Arthur Lowe in *Dad's Army*, even.

Now the siren was being used to warn of a radiation leak, although no one seemed to take much notice, those in the road outside not even breaking stride. It was rising to a crescendo when the CO walked into the conference room.

'Sorry to keep you waiting,' he said, out of breath, red in the face; been running, possibly. 'I was in the Wardroom. You've spoken to the XO and our doc?'

'Yes, Sir,' replied Dixon.

'You've arrested Monk, I gather. Horrifying to think it was one of ours behind those attacks. I'd string him up from the—' He caught himself, thought better of it. 'And what made him kill Victoria Smith is beyond me, frankly. What's he had to say for himself?'

'No comment.'

'Hardly surprising. Bloody lawyers. You know you get feelings about people, and I knew he was a bad lot. Even before that business with the corpse. You know about that, I take it?'

'We do.'

'There was a disciplinary when we got back from patrol and he was given a final written warning, would you believe it. Got off lightly if you ask me – unfortunately they didn't. I know he hasn't been to sea since, had to do some therapy or other.' Vaughan tipped his head, listening to the siren winding down. 'All I can say is he's not getting back on board my boat. You can't have someone like that on a sub.'

'He's not getting on board anybody's boat, Sir.'

'Quite.'

'We've been given to understand that Victoria Smith was in a relationship with a married man. Do you know anything about that?'

'Was it me, you mean?'

Dixon waited.

'No, I didn't know that,' said Vaughan. 'And it wasn't me, before you ask.'

'Were you aware of what was going on outside the base? The attacks on young women.'

'Just that two or three, or whatever it was, had been attacked and left in graves. I think some of my female officers made sure all their colleagues knew about it, to take extra care when off base. They're safe enough when they're here, of course.'

Stroud's phone was buzzing on the table in front of her. 'Sorry,' she said, sheepishly. She let it ring out, turned it over when it started buzzing again.

There was a knock at the door, then Tricia appeared. 'Sorry,' she said. 'You really need to take that, Penny.'

'Go ahead,' said Dixon.

'Warrant Officer Stroud . . . Yes . . . A what? . . . Where? . . . Get it cordoned off at both ends and I'm on my way.' She rang off, her eyes wide. 'I'm sorry, Commander Vaughan, Sir, we're going to need to continue this later. If you'd be kind enough to come with me, Superintendent.'

'What's going on?' demanded Vaughan.

'We've got a body, Sir,' she replied. 'Sounds like a fall from an accommodation block.'

Chapter Thirty-Three

A small crowd had gathered in the narrow service road between two tall accommodation blocks. Grey stone, shuttered doors and bars on the windows on the ground floor. Six storeys possibly, Dixon didn't bother to count them.

High enough.

'Stand back, please,' shouted Stroud, elbowing her way through the throng. 'There's nothing to see here.'

Actually, there was.

Royal Navy Police Land Rovers were parked across the service road at both ends, blue tape being stretched between the downpipes on both sides.

'Back behind the cordon, please.' Stroud had got in front of the crowd, and was trying to move them back, her arms outstretched.

'Everybody, go now, please.' McConochie's voice from the back of the crowd.

Someone was kneeling over the body behind Stroud, about to attempt CPR, clearly unsure whether it was worth it; she put her hand across her forehead, stood up and moved back with the rest.

Way beyond CPR, but then a fall from that height . . .

The service personnel were the first to drift away, obeying a direct order from the First Lieutenant. The civilian staff soon followed.

A visitor's ID card was floating face down on the pool of blood and brain that was seeping across the tarmac, the lanyard still around her neck. She'd landed on her front, had time to turn her face away, close her eyes, put her arms out to break her fall. Her skull had been crushed by the impact; one leg had severed, and was lying a few feet from the body, blood seeping from the stump.

Arms out to break her fall had been instinctive, probably; not that it was going to work from that height. Both had buckled underneath her.

Identification would be easy if she'd passed through the main gate, signed in. But Dixon knew who it was. The arm off a pair of black horn-rimmed glasses and the hairstyle had been enough.

The question was what was she doing here? Who had she come to see?

'Have you got screens, or a tent?' asked Dixon. 'We should get her body covered.'

'Of course,' said Stroud. She'd been staring at the pool of blood, and the question seemed to snap her back to the present. 'There'll be one in the Land Rover.'

McConochie appeared at Dixon's elbow. 'That's one of our visitors' passes,' he said. 'It'll tell you who she was here to see. An ID should be fairly straightforward as well.'

'Her name is Jennifer Drummond. She's a friend of Lieutenant Commander Smith.' Dixon gestured to the accommodation block behind him. 'This is the block where Victoria Smith lived, isn't it?'

'That's right. Some officers we accommodate in the Wardroom, others here for longer stays are on the top floor of this block. I took you up to her cabin.'

'You did.'

'Then I'll leave you in the capable hands of the Royal Navy Police. They'll no doubt keep me abreast of developments, and if you need anything, just ask. I'd better go and let the Naval Base Commander know what's going on.'

Stroud was watching two of her officers putting a tent over the body, checking the windows above for anyone with a camera. 'I've put a call in to the Defence Serious Crime Unit; they've got an office on the other side of the base. They'll be here in a minute.'

That explained the siren in the distance.

'We'd usually liaise with Devon and Cornwall Police when something like this happens, but I'm guessing it'll be you, seeing as you're here.'

'Her name is Jennifer Drummond,' replied Dixon. 'She was a friend of Lieutenant Commander Smith.'

'You know her?'

'I met her as part of my investigation. It was Miss Drummond who told me that Victoria was still in an on-off relationship with a married man.'

'Where to first, then?' asked Stroud.

'Who found the body?'

'One of the cleaners.'

That explained the trolley against the wall at the bottom of the service road.

'He was in a bit of state, so I've put him in the lounge of Hawkins Block. Someone's making him a cup of tea.'

'What time did he find the body?'

'He said it was about eleven-thirty-five. A bit later maybe, because he was a bit behind. That was about all we could get out of him.' Stroud shrugged. 'Do you want to speak to him?'

'Is this road busy at this time of day?'

'Not really. You only come down here if you're going to the back of either of these accommodation blocks, and that's just the cleaners. It's not a short cut to anywhere.'

'In that case, it's reasonable to assume she was killed just after eleven-thirty.'

'The nuclear siren lasts for two minutes,' said Stroud.

'The sound would've masked her scream.'

'We ought to rule suicide out, surely?'

'I have. She wasn't the sort, and even if she was, she's hardly going to have travelled all the way here from Bishops Lydeard to do it. She came here to see someone.'

'And that someone killed her.'

'Is there a pathologist on the way?'

'I put a call in to Derriford and they're paging someone.'

'Let's start up there in that case,' said Dixon, pointing to the top floor of the accommodation block.

Once inside, Cole headed for the lift.

'We'll take the stairs, Nigel,' said Dixon. 'Let's get the lift buttons dusted for prints, although she was on an escorted pass, so whoever signed her in will work here anyway.'

Stroud had the key, opened the door of Victoria Smith's room.

It looked exactly as it had done a few days earlier: uniforms still hanging in the wardrobe, clothes on the bed. The windows were locked, no sign of a struggle, no scuff marks on the frames. Not that it would've been difficult to push an unsuspecting Jennifer Drummond up and out.

'Let's get the latches dusted as well.' Dixon craned his neck, looked down, careful not to touch the window. 'She's directly below here.'

'She's not big, maybe ten stone at most,' said Cole. 'Easy enough to lift.'

'She'd have made an attempt to cling on to something, probably the frame, so even if we don't find his prints, we might find hers,' said Stroud. 'I'll organise it. We've got access to our own forensics over at Bulford.'

'Hello?' Shouted from the doorway, footsteps on the landing outside.

Stroud introduced Lieutenant Carter from the DSCU. 'We've got a jumper, have we?' he asked.

It would take a few minutes for Stroud to bring him up to speed, so Dixon left them to it, found the door to the roof. He pulled on a pair of latex gloves, tried the handle.

It opened.

'It'd be easier to knock her unconscious and carry her up here, don't you think, Nige?' asked Dixon, setting off up the short flight of metal stairs towards the shaft of light streaming through an open door at the top.

The roof was flat, with a low balustrade, scuff marks in the algae on the lead flashing at the edge, directly above where Jennifer Drummond was lying in the road below.

Drill Road, apparently.

Cole was staying well back from the edge.

The view was striking – warships in the Tamar, the *Agincourt*, more of the acoustic tiles stripped off to reveal more rust. But Dixon wasn't there to admire the view. There was a women's court shoe lying in the gutter. A left shoe. In the horror of the sight that had presented itself on the ground, he'd noticed her severed leg, not the missing shoe.

And here it was.

'Is that a shoe I can see?' asked Cole.

'Her left.'

'That's it then. Knock her out, carry her up here and over the edge.'

'Let's hope so, Nige.'

'Hope what?'

'That she was unconscious on the way down.'

Stroud and Carter were just starting up the stairs when Dixon appeared at the top.

'This is the crime scene,' he said. 'Her shoe is in the gutter.'

'I'll seal it off in that case.' Stroud turned back, watching Carter back out on to the landing.

'The door was unlocked,' Dixon said, when he reached the bottom of the stairs. 'Easy to see what happened.'

Carter made his excuses after that. Something about Dixon having it all well in hand, being grateful if he would continue to liaise with Warrant Officer Stroud; all the usual noises about wanting to assist in any way.

Stroud posted an officer at the bottom of the stairs to the roof with strict instructions that no one was to go up there until the forensics team arrived.

Back at ground level, a man was climbing into a set of white overalls outside the tent. Must be the pathologist; he had the same aluminium case that Poland always hauled about everywhere – standard issue, probably. 'Anything you want me to look for in particular?' he asked.

'We need to know if she was knocked unconscious before she was thrown off the roof,' replied Dixon.

The man turned to Stroud, the look on his face screaming 'and who is this?'.

'Detective Superintendent Dixon,' she said. 'Avon and Somerset.'

'Won't be easy, looking at the state of her, but I'll have a go. Anything else?'

'A suicide note,' said Dixon.

'I was told it was a murder.'

'I'm not expecting you to find one.'

'Oh, right.'

'Where to now?' asked Stroud.

'The gatehouse.'

◆ ◆ ◆

'That's the Officer of the Watch over there,' offered Stroud. 'Pusser Hill. He's a chief petty officer, so that's basically one of the most senior NCOs you can get. Apart from the base warrant officer, I suppose.'

He was a tall man, neat beard under his naval cap, a touch of grey at the sideburns, perhaps. He was talking to three armed police officers standing behind the barrier in front of the main gate.

A car pulled up and one walked over to the driver's side.

'They're Ministry of Defence police,' said Stroud. 'They're responsible for the perimeter. He's probably telling them the base is closed to visitors until further notice.' She held up her phone. 'By order of the Naval Base Commander. I've just had a text alert.'

The car was doing a three-point turn now.

Hill ducked under the barrier, marched over to where Dixon and Stroud were standing.

'Pusser, this is—'

'We've met,' said Dixon.

'Of course you have.'

'You'll be wanting to know about Miss Drummond.' Hill was standing with his hands clasped behind his back. 'Definitely *miss*, she was most adamant about that.'

'How d'you know it's her?' asked Dixon.

'There have only been a handful of visitor passes this morning, Sir. You and your colleague, a couple of surveyors, and someone to look at moss on the cricket pitch. I was told it was a woman; couldn't have been anyone else, could it?'

'Who was she here to see?'

'She was asking to see Lieutenant Commander Smith's CO, which as you know is Commander Vaughan. She didn't have an appointment, so I sat her in the waiting room and rang his office.'

'She was able to sign in on an escorted pass without an escort?' asked Dixon.

'She was already on the system, Sir. She was here for a dinner last year as Lieutenant Commander Smith's guest, and the pass names Commander Vaughan as her escort for the day. I was told he was coming over to get her. Presumably you've seen her pass?'

'It's covered in blood, Pusser,' said Stroud, her voice hushed.

'Oh, I see. Sorry.'

'Was she collected by Commander Vaughan?' asked Stroud.

'I couldn't say,' replied Hill. 'Once she'd signed in, I left her in the waiting area and went off to ring Commander Vaughan's office. They said he'd be on the way over to fetch her, and I really didn't give her another thought. I was in my office, dealing with emails. When I came out ten minutes later, she'd gone.'

'What time was this?'

'Twenty past eleven, maybe. She signed in at ten-fifty-six, that's stamped on her pass. All I can tell you is she was collected by a male officer. I saw that much from my office, but I really couldn't tell you who it was.'

Bloody uniforms again.

'Is there CCTV?' asked Dixon.

'Lots covering the perimeter, but once you're inside the base . . . let's just say there could be more.'

'I wanted to ask you about your service on board HMS *Agincourt*.'

The drizzle had forced them inside, into Hill's office; more of a cubbyhole off the back of the gatehouse. It offered a partial view of the waiting area, at best, and if Hill had been sitting at his computer, he'd have had his back to it. The three MoD police officers were out in the road at the front of the security barrier, and the guard sitting behind his Perspex screen would've been unsighted too.

'I can't really talk about that, I'm afraid,' replied Hill.

It was a tight squeeze in his office.

'It's operational detail,' said Stroud, standing with her back to the door.

'I'm given to understand you were tracking a Russian nuclear submarine,' said Dixon. 'Is that right?'

'Who told you that?' demanded Hill.

'There was an article on BBC News, so it's public knowledge. It surfaced in the Channel and was escorted through by a Russian tug and one of our frigates. You're surely not going to tell me *Agincourt* wasn't there as well?'

No reply.

'I'm just keen to understand how much the crew would have known about what was going on,' continued Dixon. 'I'm guessing you'd have moved to action stations, silent running, or whatever it is.'

'You've been watching too many old war films, Sir.'

'Possibly.' Dixon smiled. 'But the crew must've been told something?'

'Just that we were shadowing a hostile submarine. It's what we train for, and this was the real thing,' said Hill. 'We stayed about a thousand yards off her stern. It went on for about forty-eight hours in total, I suppose, but we never knew exactly where we were. She surfaced and a frigate took over the shadowing. That's all we were told about it.'

'I'm guessing the officers would have known more?'

'The captain and the XO, obviously.'

'And the communications officer?'

'Victoria Smith, you mean?' Hill's eyes widened.

Dixon waited.

'She'd have been monitoring radio traffic. Would've reported our position, periodically. None of this is relevant to her murder, surely?'

'How well did you know her?'

'She was an officer and I was the senior NCO on board, so we knew each other, worked together. She was a respected colleague. What more d'you want me to say?'

'Were you aware she was in a relationship with a married man?'

'None of my business.'

'Are you married?'

'Divorced.' There was a bitterness to it, the word almost spat out.

'How well do you know Leading Hand Andrew Monk?'

'I know *of* him, can put a face to the name, but that's about it.' Hill leaned back against his desk, folded his arms.

'You surely served together on *Agincourt*?'

'His last deployment. Two months.'

'Were you aware of the allegations made against him – interfering with the corpse in the sick bay?'

'I was made aware, as the senior NCO on board. I was responsible for safety, discipline. I had to know, particularly when he was relieved of his medical duties. I had to find other work for him for the remainder of the trip. Cleaning, mainly; all he was fit for. Is it him you've arrested?'

'For the Devon attacks.' Dixon gestured to the computer screen behind Hill. 'Are you able to see when service personnel sign in and out of the base?'

'It flashes up in real time and a record is kept.'

'So you'll be able to confirm whether Andrew Monk was off base at the times of the attacks?'

'Certainly. All I need is the dates and times.'

'My colleagues at Devon and Cornwall Police will no doubt want to check that with you, take a witness statement.'

'That'll be fine. Happy to help.'

Chapter Thirty-Four

'Commander Vaughan is asking how much longer you need him for, Sir.' Stroud was holding her phone to her ear.

'I do need to speak to him again, please,' replied Dixon. He was watching two blue vans being waved through at the barrier. Royal Navy Police Forensics; that would keep Charlesworth happy – someone else picking up the bill.

'He needs to leave for London in an hour, but he's back tomorrow.'

'I need to speak to him *before* he leaves.'

'I'll ask him to wait.'

'*Tell* him to wait.'

Present at the time of the murder. That was a first for Dixon. And a male naval officer – in uniform – had collected Jennifer Drummond from the main gate. Hardly narrowed it down much.

'The detective superintendent has asked that you wait, Sir. Please.' Stroud was still grinning when she rang off. 'Not often I get to tell a submarine captain what to do.' She was standing next to Dixon, waiting.

'How many male officers are there in *Drake* at any one time?'

'A couple of hundred, maybe, if you include all the units at Devonport.'

'Let's go and see how the pathologist is getting on.'

A black van, with tinted rear windows, was waiting at the top of the service road between the two accommodation blocks, the road still blocked by RNP Land Rovers and vans.

There was movement inside the tent, the occupants silhouetted by the arc lamps, a camera flash going off periodically. The tent glowed in the gloom of the road – little more than an alley, just wide enough for a car.

RNP officers in overalls were crawling on their hands and knees; a fingertip search. Dixon could hear voices on the roof too.

There were no stepping plates; no crime scene manager either, which was a relief.

He ducked inside the tent, stood behind the mortuary assistant.

Jennifer Drummond's hands had been placed in plastic bags; the severed leg had gone too, placed in a sealed black bag marked 'Human Remains'.

The pathologist was leaning over, using a pair of forceps to lift small white objects out of the pool of blood. He looked up at Dixon. 'Some of her teeth,' he said. 'The force of the impact . . .' He didn't feel the need to explain further. 'We're going to be a while here, if that's what you want to know.'

'Have you found any other injuries?'

'She landed on her front, and it looks like there's an injury to the back of her head. I won't know for sure until I get her back to the lab. She's a bit of a mess, as you can see.' He gestured to Jennifer Drummond's head – misshapen, the skull crushed.

'What about a suicide note?'

'I've checked her pockets and there's nothing.'

◆ ◆ ◆

'Sorry to keep you waiting,' said Dixon, walking into the conference room.

Vaughan was standing in the window, his hands clasped behind his back, staring out across the cricket pitch towards the frigate sheds. His submarine, *Agincourt*, out of view to the right. He turned, his face reddening. 'I don't appreciate being kept waiting. I have to be in London tonight for an important dinner.'

'A woman is dead, Sir,' replied Dixon, matter of fact. 'A woman who'd signed into this base asking to see you.'

'Me?'

'It is your name on her escorted visitor's pass.' Dixon let that hang for a moment. 'Her name is Jennifer Drummond, and she was a friend of Lieutenant Commander Smith.'

'I don't know her,' said Vaughan, shaking his head.

'She was at the Trafalgar Night dinner last October, as a guest of Victoria Smith. My understanding is she was sitting at the top table with you.'

'You've seen the dining tables in the Wardroom. There'd have been at least thirty at my table on Trafalgar Night. Local bigwigs. Guests. I can't seriously be expected to remember them all.'

Dixon turned to Stroud. 'Would you be kind enough to check if there was a seating plan and, if so, whether we might have a copy?'

'Certainly, Sir.'

Vaughan pulled a chair out from under the table, sat down. 'Look, I remember Victoria had a guest, of course I do, but I couldn't pick her out of an identity parade, for heaven's sake. She was a small woman, old before her time. It did cross my mind they might have been in a relationship, but I don't think Victoria was that way inclined. Old school friends, I think is what she said. She was teetotal, I do remember that. Must've had a miserable evening; it's a boozy night, as you might imagine.'

'Do spouses go to the dinner?' asked Dixon.

'Some do.'

'Was your wife there?'

'No. She was at home. We live just outside Portsmouth.'

'It was Jennifer Drummond who told me she believed Victoria was in a relationship with a married man, and it's my belief she came here to report the existence of that relationship to Victoria's commanding officer. You.'

'And you think I killed her?'

'At the moment, I don't know who killed her.'

'Did she have an appointment to see me?' asked Vaughan.

'Not as far as I'm aware.'

'That's right, she didn't. She came here without an appointment; turned up at the main gate demanding to see me. A call was put through to my office, but I'd already left to come and see you, here.'

'Where is your office?'

'Holland Block.'

'How far is that from here?' asked Dixon, turning to Stroud.

'A five-minute walk,' she replied.

'What time did you leave your office, Commander?'

'About twenty past eleven.'

'And yet you arrived here just after eleven-thirty. The nuclear siren was still sounding when you walked in.'

'I went to the loo on the way; in the Wardroom, if you must know.'

'Jennifer Drummond was collected from the main gate at twenty past eleven by a male naval officer.'

'I see where this is going. You're suggesting I picked her up from the gatehouse, took her to the top of whichever accommodation block it was and threw her off.' Vaughan picked up a coffee; set it back down sharply when he realised it was stone cold. 'I'm starting to feel like I need a lawyer.'

'What impact would it have on your career if it was revealed you'd had an affair with a junior officer?'

'Unacceptable sexual behaviour.' Vaughan sighed. 'It would end it.'

'Was there any hint that Victoria Smith was having an affair with anyone on the *Agincourt* while you were at sea?'

Vaughan frowned. 'Certainly not.'

'Would it be possible for an illicit affair to go unnoticed?'

'It's happened before, but it's usually been discovered. That's the nature of the beast. Ninety-plus people living in a very confined space, but the reality is that finding any privacy is all but impossible.'

'What about the sick bay?'

'It's always locked.'

'By the surgeon lieutenant?'

'Oh, come on. They'd be overheard if he locked himself in there with Victoria. The whole idea is absurd.'

'What about your own cabin? I'm guessing you have a door with a lock on it?'

'This is getting ridiculous. A submarine captain, at sea, having it off with his comms officer? A happily married submarine captain, I might add.'

'To what extent were you involved with Andrew Monk, following his departure from *Agincourt*?'

'I had to write a report for his court martial, but not after that. I've got enough on my plate with the current crew without worrying about past crew members. They become someone else's responsibility.'

'So, just to be clear, you left your office at twenty past eleven, stopped off at the Wardroom on the way, and got here just after eleven-thirty.'

'That's right. I was coming across the cricket pitch when the siren started, realised I was late, and jogged the rest of the way.' He raised his arms in mock surrender. 'I can assure you; I haven't killed anyone. Now, I've still got time to get my train, if I leave immediately.'

◆ ◆ ◆

'I gather there's been a murder on the base, Superintendent?' asked the Naval Base Commander, Brigadier Milne. A Royal Marine, as Penny Stroud had pointed out on the way over. The first ever, apparently. The green uniform was a bit of giveaway.

'I was here quite by chance, Sir,' replied Dixon. 'I was interviewing witnesses in connection with the murder of Lieutenant Commander Smith when it happened.'

'Who is it? Do we know?'

'A friend of Lieutenant Commander Smith's. A civilian by the name of Jennifer Drummond.'

'I sat next to her at the Trafalgar dinner last year, I'm sure I did. Either that or she was next to my wife. I'm afraid it's a bit of blur after about nine o'clock. What was she doing here?'

'She'd come to see Commander Vaughan, Sir, without an appointment,' replied Dixon. 'She told them at the main gate she was Lieutenant Commander Smith's executor and needed access to her personal belongings, but she was convinced Lieutenant Commander Smith was having a relationship with a married man; came to confront him, I suspect. Or at least to make sure everybody knew about it.'

'Well, she's certainly done that.'

Dixon had been summoned to the Naval Base Commander's office; not an invitation you turned down, according to Penny Stroud.

A grand suite of offices in a new building behind the Wardroom; the oil paintings of sea battles in gilt frames looking slightly out of place this time, in among the leather sofas and glass partitioning.

There was a fireplace in the base commander's office. A modern one, bolted to the wall, no chimney, but it provided a mantelpiece for his framed photographs.

'I hope the RNP are cooperating with you,' said Milne, looking at Stroud.

'Yes, Sir.'

'I've got Defence Serious Crime on it, Sir,' said Stroud. 'And we've got Forensics down from Bulford.'

'You can rely on our full cooperation, Superintendent. Has she got family?'

'She's not married and there are no children,' replied Dixon. 'Her parents are both dead.'

Milne picked up a piece of paper from his desk. 'Now, I've had a message from Detective Chief Inspector Hatch. Apparently, he's made an arrest and needs statements from anyone who knew Leading Hand Andrew Monk. Do you know anything about this?'

'Yes, Sir,' replied Dixon. 'I made the arrest yesterday evening on a train at Taunton railway station. Leading Hand Monk is currently being held at Bridgwater police station on suspicion of involvement in the Devon attacks. He is also helping us with our enquiries into the murder of Victoria Smith.'

'Hatch makes it sound like a Devon operation.'

'Monk fled when the DNA screening was about to start, Sir,' said Dixon. 'That was organised by Avon and Somerset.'

Dixon had never really been that bothered about who took the credit when an arrest was made, but he was buggered if he was going to let another force claim it, particularly a berk like Hatch.

'Wasn't Victoria Smith killed by Leading Hand Monk? That's what I've been led to understand by the First Lieutenant. He's been keeping me abreast of developments.'

'No, Sir. Although it was made to look as though she had been.'

'A bad business. She was a bloody good officer, a high flyer, destined for great things.' Milne shook his head. 'Now, look, we need to make sure we keep a lid on this as best we can, try and keep it under some sort of control. Obviously, there's going to be news coverage, if and when Monk is charged. And it's bound to get out there's been a murder on the base. It couldn't have come at a worse time for us, what with the bloody Russians mucking about in the Channel. Anyway, I've cancelled the Armada Night dinner. We can't be seen to be hosting a lavish dinner with all this going on. Are you seriously telling me we've had two killers on the base?'

Dixon assumed it was a rhetorical question.

'Please tell me it's not more USB from submariners behind all this,' continued Milne.

'Looks that way, Sir,' said Stroud. 'Jennifer Drummond was collected from the main gate by an unidentified male officer.'

'According to who?'

'The Officer of the Watch, Sir.'

'Hill's a good man. An officer, you say?' Milne stood up. 'It gets better and better, doesn't it?'

'Forensics will take the rest of the day,' continued Stroud. 'And Superintendent Dixon is arranging for colleagues to come down from Bridgwater to help us conduct a room by room search for witnesses.'

'Shame there's not more CCTV,' muttered Milne. 'Another hobby horse of mine. What about the accommodation block?'

'Victoria Smith's room and the roof will remain sealed off. As will Drill Road.'

'That's where she is, is it?'

'Yes, Sir.'

'So, what do I tell DCI Hatch?'

'Once I'm satisfied Leading Hand Monk had nothing to do with Victoria Smith's murder, he'll be charged with the Devon attacks and transferred down to Plymouth,' replied Dixon. 'DCI Hatch's team will need witness statements, but it's entirely a matter for you when that happens. It might be worth waiting a few days.'

'Letting the dust settle, you mean?'

An unfortunate choice of words.

Chapter Thirty-Five

'It's like one of those locked room things with that Poirot bloke. It's got to be one of the officers on the *Agincourt*, so why don't we just sit them down in a room and sort it out that way?'

'Nice idea, Nige,' Dixon replied. 'Two problems with that: firstly, this is the real world. And, secondly, we don't know who did it.'

Apart from that it was a sombre drive back to Express Park. They must have passed Louise and Mark heading south on the M5 at some point; didn't see them on the other carriageway, though. At least they'd both had time for a few hours' sleep.

Sarah had already made a start on a whiteboard for Jennifer Drummond by the time Dixon walked into the incident room, not that there was a lot of information. Just her picture, and an arrow across to Victoria Smith.

'The ACC is here,' Sarah said.

'How did the interviews go this morning?'

'Two officers from Devon and Cornwall went first and he *no commented* the whole way through. "No comment" to everything, except his name. Louise and Mark got denials. No explanation except that his DNA must've been planted at the scene, just denied everything to do with Victoria Smith's murder. Lou and Mark are on their way down to Plymouth now and the Devon lot left about lunchtime.'

'How was Hatch?'

'Fine. Said he wants to be here when Monk is charged.'

'Anything else?'

'Not really. I had a call from a new witness in West Bagborough who says she saw a taxi in the village the night Victoria was murdered. I've got her contact details. She'd been away visiting her sister, lives in one of the houses we got no answer from when we did the house to house.'

'A taxi took her home from the nightclub.'

'This was earlier. About ten, she said.' Sarah gestured to the stairs. 'The ACC,' she whispered. 'I recognise his footsteps now.'

'Ah, there you are, Nick,' said Charlesworth, appearing at the top of the stairs. 'You have done well. Not only was the DNA screening cancelled, but you've got the Royal Navy Police picking up the bill for the forensics on this latest murder.' At least he managed to keep his glee to himself.

'The murder was on their base, which makes it their jurisdiction, technically.'

'And you were there.'

'Still don't know who did it.'

'That Hatch fellow reckons Monk had a grievance with Victoria Smith, from something that happened on the sub; thinks he should be charged with all four. They certainly knew each other, and Hatch doesn't see how you get round the DNA.' Charlesworth glanced up at the clock on the wall. 'He has a point. Are you going to charge him or ask for an extension?'

'Charge him.'

'Just with the Devon attacks?'

Dixon nodded. Charlesworth knew him well enough by now.

'On your head be it.'

'We've got enough and the CPS will go for it.'

'A good result for us all the same, solving Devon and Cornwall's case for them.' A grin; Charlesworth clearly couldn't help himself. 'So, tell me about Jennifer Drummond.'

'She arrived at the main gate demanding to see Victoria's CO; was signed in and collected from the waiting area by an officer in uniform. Next thing we know is she's been thrown off the roof of the accommodation block under cover of the nuclear siren that goes off every Monday at eleven-thirty.'

'The killer must've known that.'

'The whole of Plymouth knows that. You can hear the siren right across the city.'

'Sarah said Jennifer Drummond was behind the belief that Victoria Smith was having an affair with a married man.'

'Kathy Huxtable said it was over long ago. Jennifer Drummond said it was on-off, and it's my belief she went down to the naval base to confront someone with that information, asked to see the captain of the *Agincourt*.'

'Can he account for his whereabouts at the relevant time?'

'Not satisfactorily.' Dixon flicked on the kettle. 'There's a limited pool of suspects, it seems to me. It must be someone who knew what Monk had been up to, so he could make Victoria's murder look like Monk had done it, at least superficially. If we go back to the original incident on board the sub, then that's the surgeon lieutenant, who I'll be speaking to again in the morning, the executive officer and the CO. The Cox'n also knew what had been going on, and he's now the Officer of the Watch, responsible for the main gate.'

'Could it have been him?'

'We've only got his word for it that he saw Jennifer Drummond being collected from the waiting area by an officer in uniform. He might've offered to show her Victoria Smith's rooms himself, taken her up there and . . .'

'What about when Monk left the ship?'

'There was a disciplinary process, but the details of that were kept confidential, and the panel was made up of officers from off base, London and Portsmouth. He was given a final written warning and had to undergo counselling.'

'There's nothing in his medical records,' offered Sarah. 'Just the notes you'd expect to see, really.'

'Have you spoken to Monk's psychiatrist?' asked Charlesworth. 'He'd have known what the filthy little—' He caught himself. '. . . had been up to.'

'Not yet, Sir,' replied Dixon. 'At the moment I'm concentrating our limited resources on people who are likely to have known Victoria Smith as well.'

'And been having an affair with her. Makes sense, I suppose, if it really wasn't Monk.'

The phone was ringing on Sarah's desk.

'Get that,' said Dixon.

'Yes, he's here . . . Oh, right. Yes, I'll tell him straightaway.' She replaced the handset. 'That was the custody sergeant, Sir. Monk's been in with his solicitor again and it seems he's had a change of heart; wants to talk. The custody sergeant thinks it's genuine, reckons he doesn't want to be charged with the murder of Victoria Smith, and this is his best way out. Monk's said he'll only talk to you, though. And he wants to know about his son.'

'You'll need that custody extension in that case,' said Charlesworth. 'Leave it with me and I'll get Deborah Potter to deal with it.'

'Is she in the building?'

'She is.' Charlesworth was dialling a number on his mobile phone. 'I'll need to let Hatch know too. He might want to sit in.'

'If he sits in, Monk won't talk, Sir,' said Dixon. 'You heard what he said. It'll be just me and Nige. He knows us and we can send the recording down to Hatch later.'

'He won't like that.'

'He should've told us about the DNA match then, shouldn't he?'

◆ ◆ ◆

Monk fidgeted throughout the formalities: the usual reminder he was still under caution, the interview was being recorded, introductions. Picking his fingernails, using a long thumbnail he'd chewed off as a toothpick.

His face was flushed; looked like he hadn't slept much either.

'You've had a change of heart, Andrew,' said Dixon.

'You lied to me.'

'Did I?'

'You said I was a witness in the murder of Victoria Smith.' He spoke without looking up. 'Next thing I know, I'm being interviewed as if you think I did it.'

'Your DNA was found at the scene, on Victoria Smith's body, so we have to put that to you formally, give you your chance to have your say. Same with the other allegations that flow from that.'

'That I killed her?'

'And you denied it.'

'D'you believe me?'

'I do, as it happens.'

'I want to know about my son.'

'Let's talk first,' said Dixon.

'My solicitor tells me I'm probably going to be convicted of the other attacks.'

'There's no *probably* about it, Andrew. You will be convicted; two counts of murder, and one of attempted murder.'

'He says I ought to tell you what happened, that I might get a lighter sentence.'

Dixon glanced up at the camera, conscious that Charlesworth and Potter were watching in the adjacent room. Hatch was watching on a live feed too.

The cosy interview room hadn't been available – the *touchy feely* one, as some called it – so they were in one with a table between suspect and police officers. Dixon preferred that, preferred the formality of it. He was sitting opposite Monk, Cole sitting opposite the solicitor, who was scribbling in his notebook.

'When you're ready, Andrew,' said Dixon. 'There's no rush.' He'd managed to grab a sandwich from the canteen, while Potter had dealt with the formalities of the custody extension, and his blood sugar was fine, even though he'd skipped lunch. 'We've got all night, if needs be.'

The solicitor looked up sharply, his 'I bloody well haven't' unspoken.

'It was the submarine,' said Andrew, his voice hardly carrying.

'I'm going to need you to speak up a bit, Andrew, for the tape,' said Dixon.

'It was the submarine.' Louder this time. 'Being down there, day after day, it fucked me up mentally. I thought I'd be all right, but it creeps up on you. The suffocation of it. There's no privacy, people everywhere. You can't even take a shit without someone listening.'

Dixon waited.

'I never thought it would affect me like that,' continued Monk. 'I thought I'd be fine. I thought I was strong, but it gets you, it bloody gets you. I was getting anxiety attacks, my heart would be going ten to the dozen, my head spinning, then I'd be sick. Panic attacks. Then the voices started.'

Dixon sighed to himself. He'd expected something like this; expected Monk to be setting up an insanity plea. Anything to deflect from the true horror of what he'd done. Monk's fate would be decided by psychiatrists now.

He glanced at Cole, who just rolled his eyes.

'There was an outbreak of food poisoning on board too. I got it, diarrhoea and vomiting, fever, and that's when the voices started. I was delirious, and there was no room in the sick bay, so we were just in our bunks – all we had for privacy was a curtain.'

'There were complaints made about you on board. Some of the female submariners said they felt intimidated by you.'

'I was ill.'

'Go on, Andrew.'

'When I got off the ship, I thought I'd be all right, that I'd get better, but I got worse. I was having the panic attacks all the time, and instead of helping me, they had me up on a gross misconduct charge. That just made me worse. I was getting paranoia. I ended up having to see a psychiatrist and he gave me some tablets.'

'What was the outcome of the misconduct charge?' asked Dixon.

'I got a final written warning and was thrown out of the submarine service. Not suited to it, apparently.' Monk sneered. 'I could've fucking well told them that.'

'What did you do then?'

'I just stayed at *Drake*. I don't think they knew what to do with me, to be honest. I was having psychiatric treatment for mental illness brought on by my submarine service, so they probably thought I'd sue them if they sacked me.'

Dixon had heard enough. It was all very interesting, but Monk could bore the psychiatrists with it. 'Tell me about the night of the twenty-eighth of January last year,' he said.

Monk took a deep breath. 'I wanted to meet someone,' he said.

'For what?'

'Sex.'

'Aren't there mobile phone apps for that these days?'

'I'd tried them. Never met anyone.'

Dixon hadn't read the report from High Tech on Monk's phone, just the appendix dealing with his internet search history. And the photos. They'd been enough.

'I'd stolen some magnetic taxi plates off a taxi in Plymouth, stuck them on the side of my car, and parked in Union Street. This girl just got in. She was very drunk, threw up in the back while I was driving out to Kingston. Then she started trying to get out of the car, so I locked the doors. I told her I wasn't going to hurt her. I was just hoping we might have sex in a quiet spot somewhere and then I'd take her home, but she was kicking out at the back of my head with her heels, while I was driving. I stopped the car, went to let her out and she attacked me, so I hit her with a hammer.'

'Where was the hammer?'

'Under the passenger seat. I had some bloke threaten me with a knife after I cut him up at a roundabout, so I put the hammer under the seat, for self defence like, you know.'

'How many times did you hit her?'

'Twice. I panicked. It was self defence.'

Of course it was.

'What did you do then?' asked Dixon.

'I took her to Kingston church and left her in an empty grave there. I was frightened, didn't know what else to do, started having another panic attack.'

'You knew the grave was there, Andrew, it's in your internet searches. You looked for a burial knowing there'd be an empty grave the night before.'

'I wanted to have sex with her in it. It was just a fantasy.'

'Why did you remove her clothes?'

'My DNA would've been on them. I knew that much.'

Dixon thought it best not to press the point; he knew the real reason Monk had removed her clothes. 'What did you do with them?'

'I put them in one of the big wheelie bins behind the Wardroom.'

'And you left her posed in the grave. Why?'

'A mark of respect. I left her as if she was lying in a coffin.'

'What did you do then?'

'I left.' A look of outrage crept across Monk's face. 'What d'you think I did?' He demanded. 'I'm not some sort of pervert.'

'You took photos.'

'That was just so she could be identified later. I had to switch off the flash and use a torch, so you can't see much more than her face anyway.'

So she could be identified later . . .

Given how long Monk had had to come up with this crap, it really was pathetic.

'What about Modbury then?' Dixon asked.

'It was a last-minute thing. There was a burial due the next day, so I went to check the grave, see if it would be any good for . . . Anyway, I came out of the churchyard and there she was. She started shouting at me, accusing me of killing that girl at Kingston. She was fumbling with something in her coat pocket; I thought it was a knife, and she was going to attack me, so I hit her. She had a dog and it ran off, I remember that.' Monk was crunching a piece of fingernail between his teeth.

'What did you hit her with?'

'The hammer.'

'That you just happened to have in your hand?'

'Like I said, I carry it for self defence.' Monk was watching Dixon out of the corner of his eyes, looking for any reaction. 'With the handle up the sleeve of my coat.'

Best poker face on. Any hint of disgust on his face and Monk might clam up, revert to 'no comment' answers.

'So, you left her in the grave?'

'Just like before. I panicked, binned her clothes.'

'And what was in her coat pocket?'

'It was a paint spray, and there was a personal attack alarm in her other pocket.'

'Where is the hammer now?'

'In the bottom of Number Five Basin. There's a ladder down to a landing stage, and I stood at the top of that, threw it as far as I could.'

'Why did you use a ball peen hammer?'

'I found it in the boiler room at the accommodation block; no sharp edges on it so less blood, and the end fitted in my hand, the handle up my sleeve. The voices told me to use it.'

'That was thoughtful of them.'

A flash of anger from Monk.

Dixon ignored it. 'And what about their phones?'

'They're in the basin as well.'

'You left her posed?'

'As a mark of respect, yes.'

Cole shifted in his seat. Sometimes the table between interviewer and suspect was useful to protect the interviewing officer, other times it protected the suspect. This was one of those occasions, Cole's fists clenched in his lap.

'You hit Portia Woodrow on the back of the head. How did you do that if she was attacking you?' asked Dixon.

'She turned to run when she saw the hammer.'

'She was no longer a threat at that point then, surely, if she was running away?'

'I suppose not.'

'But you hit her anyway?'

'I thought she might come back when she'd got the knife out of her pocket.'

'Or was it the fact that she'd seen your face?'

Monk shrugged.

'For the recording, Andrew Monk shrugged,' said Dixon.

'I panicked,' said Monk, hastily. 'The voices told me to hit her.'

'Let's talk about Amy Fox,' said Dixon. 'You left her in Peter Tavy churchyard.'

'I was parked in the middle of Tavistock and she just walked over and got in the back of my car.'

'You had the magnetic taxi plates on the doors?'

'Yes.'

'So, she probably thought you were a taxi?'

'She was drunk and I thought she might be willing to . . . you know . . . Anyway, she was sick in the back of my car, so I told her to get out and walk the rest of the way home. She tried to run, fell and hit her head.'

'According to her medical records, Andrew, she was hit on the head with a hammer.'

'I tried to help her up, but she started screaming, lashing out at me. I had to, it was self defence.'

'Why the gap between Modbury and Peter Tavy?' It was a deliberate ploy, using the place names instead of the victims' names. Made it less personal for Monk, more likely Dixon would get an answer, and that was what it was all about at this stage. Dixon hated it, all the same.

'My treatment made the voices go away for a while.'

'And you thought you were pushing your luck, might get caught?' Dixon could've kicked himself at the question. Too confrontational.

Monk stared at him, a flash of anger in his eyes; the look screaming 'so, you don't believe me after all'.

Dixon didn't, of course he didn't. But he was making progress. They now knew where the murder weapon was – where to send the divers. The victims' phones too. It was also a confession, of sorts. The rest would be for the psychiatrists to sort out. Either way, wherever he was going, Monk wasn't getting out.

'What did you do when you found out Amy Fox was still alive?'

'I got rid of the hammer, dumped the taxi plates in a bin at *Drake*, and sold my car. I was going to apply for a transfer too, somewhere far away, then you come along with your DNA screening.'

'Which bin?'

'It was a wheelie bin behind the Wardroom; they'll be long gone by now.' Monk remembered what was happening, his voice softening. 'The medication was working by then, and the voices were leaving me alone, telling me to stop.'

'Which is it? Leaving you alone or telling you to stop?' Dixon's patience only went so far.

'The last thing they said was "It's time to stop".'

'Let's talk about Victoria Smith's murder then,' said Dixon. 'What do you want to tell me about that?'

'I want to know about my son first.'

'I'll need his permission. You know what the Data Protection Act is like. I can't just give out his personal information.'

'Get his permission then.'

'I will ask the question. When you've told me about Victoria Smith's murder.'

'I didn't do it. I wasn't there. It wasn't me. My DNA was planted at the scene.'

'And I believe that, Andrew. What I'd like to know is who you think did that.'

'I don't know.'

'Who would have had access to your DNA profile?'

'Anyone on the sub, anyone in the accommodation block.'

'That doesn't narrow it down much.'

'Not my problem.'

'I think you'll find it is. Someone knew you'd attacked those girls,' said Dixon. 'Deliberately set out to make it look like you killed Lieutenant Commander Smith as well, and you're telling me you've got no idea who might've done that, who could've done that.'

'It was someone on the sub.'

'Why?'

No reply.

'Is it because they knew about you interfering with the corpse in the sick bay?'

Monk closed his eyes, breathing deeply, his chest heaving. 'You know about that?'

'We do.'

'I was just looking at her. She was beautiful, peaceful, serene.'

'Like the others?'

'Yes, like the others.'

Chapter Thirty-Six

'I thought I was going to lamp him one in the middle there. The little shit,' hissed Cole, when the door closed behind them. 'D'you want me to ring Jordan Harris, see if he wants us to release his details to his father?'

'All in good time, Nige.'

'Not sure I'd want to know that creep was my father.'

Charlesworth was waiting for them in the corridor, his hand outstretched. 'Well done, Nick,' he said. 'What now?'

'We'll get a charging decision out of the CPS, charge him and then ship him off down to Plymouth. Hatch is welcome to him now.'

'You need to be sure about this.'

'I am sure about this.'

'It means Hatch gets to make the calls to the families.'

'He's welcome to that as well.'

'So, where does that leave us with Victoria Smith's murder?'

'High and dry.'

◆ ◆ ◆

'You had a visitor earlier on,' said Jane, when Dixon opened the back door of the cottage just after eleven. 'Our member of parliament, said he'd wait for you in the pub, but he's probably gone home by now.'

'How's Peter been?'

'Fine.'

'Has Monty been out?'

'We all went this afternoon, about teatime.' Jane was craning her neck, talking over the back of the sofa. 'It was the only way I could get the little bugger to go out. We all had to go. It's not easy with Monty in one hand and a pushchair in the other. Have you eaten?'

'I had a sandwich earlier on.'

'How's Sarah getting on?'

'She's doing really well.' Dixon had opened the fridge door, more in hope than expectation.

'I can bung you something in the microwave.'

'I'll be fine.' Dixon took out his phone, swiped it past the sensor in the back of his arm. 'Six-point-four going down. A banana will do.' He dropped on to the sofa next to Jane, kissed her, then looked at Peter, asleep in his cot, dimly lit by the flicker from the black and white film on the television, the sound muted. 'What's that?'

'It's an old Sherlock Holmes I recorded off Talking Pictures.'

'Did Tom Perry say what he wanted?'

'No.' Jane turned in her seat to face Dixon. 'Well, have you charged him?'

'With the Devon attacks, not West Bagborough. There was another killing today as well, at the naval base, and I was bloody well there, wasn't I? Six storeys, off the roof.'

Jane grimaced. 'Not nice.'

'A friend of my dead naval officer.'

It was a tentative knock at the door, from someone who knew there was a baby asleep inside, possibly. Not even Monty barked.

'That'll be Perry,' said Jane.

'There was someone sitting in a car in the pub car park when I got home,' said Dixon, getting up. He opened the front door. 'Come in,' he said.

'Better if we walk,' replied Perry.

Dixon picked up Monty's lead, clipped it on the dog's collar and dragged him outside.

They walked in silence along Brent Street, before turning on to the farm track that led across the fields.

Perry waited until they were clear of the houses and out into open countryside. 'You promised me you wouldn't say anything about . . . you know.'

'And I haven't.'

'Well, someone bloody well has. It's all over social media: a Russian submarine in British territorial waters, suspected of involvement in the deaths of two marine surveyors. The Ministry of Defence is doing their best to keep a lid on it, but the shit's really hit the fan, Nick.'

Dixon let Monty off the lead, the moonlight reflecting on the dog's white fur enough to keep track of him in the darkness.

'I'm not supposed to know,' said Perry. 'I've told you, and you're not supposed to know. And if either of us is suspected of telling anyone else, then we're in deep, deep trouble. It's the Official Secrets Act, up to here.' He was holding his hand above his head for emphasis, to ensure Dixon got the picture. 'There are D-Notices in place, but that only stops the mainstream media printing it. It doesn't stop bloggers and people like that. And it doesn't stop the foreign press, either. If our NATO allies get hold of it, it doesn't bear thinking about.'

'All I can say is it wasn't me.'

'It's trending on bloody Twitter, or X, or whatever we have to call it these days. The Russians haven't denied it yet, either. The whole thing makes us look weak.'

'What were we supposed to do, sink it?'

'Don't ask me, I'm just a PPS in the Housing Department.' Perry kicked a stone along the track. 'My contact at the MoD is coming under pressure, rang me in a right old stew. Look, I don't want to land you in it, old chap, but I'm expecting to come under real pressure.'

'If they want to know who you told, tell them,' said Dixon. 'That's fine with me.'

'You've got a young kiddie.'

'I'll be all right.'

'It may all blow over. The current thinking is to come out and say: *Of course we knew, we shadowed it all the way and it was never a threat.* It was in deep trouble anyway with that fire on board.'

'At least that's true. Maybe the Russians couldn't see their map for the smoke,' said Dixon, smiling.

'I must say you're taking this all rather well. And there's still the issue of those two civilian surveyors.'

'The Russians are hardly going to admit to killing them, are they?'

'Anyway, I thought you should know,' said Perry. He stopped on the track, looked back; wondering if he was being followed, probably. 'I can't go down for this.'

'You won't,' replied Dixon. 'And neither will I.'

◆ ◆ ◆

'What was that all about?' Jane asked, when Dixon got back to the cottage.

'No harm in you knowing now, I suppose. Victoria Smith was about to blow the whistle on a Russian sub in British territorial waters. Classified information, as you might imagine. Tom Perry tipped me off about it, but it's found its way into the public domain now, and the hunt is on to find who leaked it.'

'Oh God, don't tell me you're in the firing line for something else.' She was sitting on the sofa, feeding Peter, her face reddening. 'At best that would be gross misconduct. You might even be prosecuted under the Official Secrets Act.'

'I used the information to make decisions about the direction of the investigation. I did not leak the information to anyone. I didn't even tell you.'

'Perry told you, though.'

'He'll be fine. He's a politician.'

Jane sat Peter in Dixon's lap when he sat down next to her, Dixon holding his son under the arms. 'He smiled at me then, I'm sure he did.'

'They don't do that until they're about three months old.' She budged up, letting Monty hop on to the sofa next to her. 'When this business is over you need to get this dog out and about a bit more.'

'I'm sure I can manage that.'

'That's assuming you don't go to prison. What would it be, two years for something like this?'

'I won't go to prison.'

'How can you be so sure?'

'Because I know who leaked it.'

Chapter Thirty-Seven

Twice in the night. Jane slept through both of them – although, when he thought about it, there might have been other occasions that Dixon had slept through. He was getting the hang of changing nappies too; keeping count, each one a beer Peter would owe him when he was old enough.

Everyone was asleep when he crept out of the cottage, the deep rumble from Cole's exhaust on the pavement outside.

Warrant Officer Penny Stroud was waiting for them when they arrived at *Drake* just before nine. Fresh visitors' passes took a few minutes, then they were clambering into her Land Rover, Cole's car left in the parking space opposite the gatehouse.

'I gather Monk confessed, Sir,' said Stroud.

'Not to the murder of Victoria Smith, and we've still got the murder of Jennifer Drummond.'

'Of course. Your colleagues were here until late, but we haven't come up with anyone who saw anything, I'm afraid. Drill Road is the back of both buildings. No one heard anything, either, except the siren.'

'That's assuming she screamed,' said Cole. 'She might've been unconscious.'

'The accommodation blocks are like ghost towns during the day,' continued Stroud. 'Everyone is out and about, at work on the base.'

'Anything from your Forensics?' asked Dixon.

'Not yet.'

'There are some bins behind the Wardroom. Can we see them?'

'Yes, of course.'

Stroud followed a service road in front of the clock tower, turned behind the Wardroom into a car park, large bins lined up against the back wall of the grey stone building. Blue, green, grey; large wheelie bins. There was a skip too.

'There are more behind the medical centre,' said Stroud. 'What's your interest in these?'

'It's where Monk says he dumped the victims' clothes, and a set of magnetic taxi plates.'

'When was this?'

'Most recently, after the Amy Fox attack.'

'The skip is new, and the bins are emptied every week,' said Stroud. 'Anything thrown in them will be long gone by now.' She'd stopped in the middle of the car park, and was leaning forward in the driver's seat, looking up at the back of the Wardroom.

'Where?'

'A commercial tip. Milehouse Facilities Management. They've got a huge blue bin lorry that comes once a week. The recycling is once a week too; it gets sorted on site, though. What are you thinking?'

'Monk said he threw the magnetic taxi plates in a bin behind the Wardroom. I think someone saw him do that and retrieved them. We know that Victoria Smith went home in a taxi the night she was killed, but a new witness has come forward to say they saw a second taxi in West Bagborough earlier that evening.'

'An officer getting in his car, possibly,' said Stroud, hesitantly.

'What are those windows?' asked Dixon.

'That's the kitchen on the ground floor; officers' accommodation on the upper floors. Short stays mainly, but some of the more senior officers have rooms in the mess.'

'And whose cars are these?'

'This is the officers' car park. Everyone else uses the parade ground.'

Cars were parked along the wall in front of ornate gardens; some had driven in, others had reversed, one was parked in the shade with the rear windows open an inch or so.

Trees screened the mess from the road at the top of a steep bank, the high perimeter wall just visible through the azaleas and rhododendrons, spikes along the top, CCTV cameras on poles.

'Sarah Loveday spoke to you about Number Five Basin?'

'The Royal Navy Diving Unit were just setting up when you arrived,' replied Stroud. 'Would you like to go down there and have a look?'

'Thank you.'

A lone groundsman was mowing the cricket pitch as they drove down towards the vast basin, the open water of the Tamar beyond, several warships alongside the wharf.

HMS *Agincourt* was moored on the far side of the basin, the scaffolding over her conning tower now covered in sheeting that was fluttering in the breeze.

'You can get some pretty big ships in here,' said Stroud.

'What d'you reckon, Nige?' asked Dixon. 'How many rugby pitches?'

'God knows. It's difficult to tell.'

'It's thirty-four acres, Sir,' said Stroud.

'Seventeen, then,' muttered Cole. 'Roughly.'

Two dark blue vans were parked adjacent to the harbour wall, a steel ladder disappearing into the abyss below. The tide was out, that much was clear from the mark on the granite walls of the basin; it meant a drop of twenty feet into the water.

'They'll be putting the divers in from a boat,' said Stroud. She parked behind a van.

Dixon stood at the top of the ladder, looked along the basin. 'This is the only ladder – he definitely said ladder, not steps – so this must be where he was standing. He threw them as far as he could, straight out. The phones will have gone further, if he got them spinning like a Frisbee.'

Stroud introduced the dive team petty officer, O'Connor.

'We're setting up a grid, Sir,' he said. 'Four divers, side by side, fingertip search. They'll be along in a minute; we have to get the boats in the water further down. We'll find them for you, don't you worry. There's a lot of silt at the bottom, but it's routine stuff for us.'

'Thank you.'

'Where to now, Sir?' asked Stroud.

'The medical centre,' replied Dixon. 'I'd like to have a word with the surgeon lieutenant, find out where he was during the nuclear alarm yesterday.'

◆ ◆ ◆

'I did ring him yesterday,' said Stroud. 'Warned him you'd need to speak to him again this morning.'

It looked much like any doctors' or dentists' surgery. It was both at the same time, though, the sound of a dentist's drill not quite masked by the music playing over the speakers above their heads in the waiting room. The other giveaway was the patients, all of them in naval uniform. The doctors and nurses too.

'This way.' Fisher looked embarrassed, spoke softly in the hope no one else in the waiting area would notice. Everyone looked up, all the same. 'We'll go in here,' he said. 'There's more room. The consulting rooms are quite small.'

'You'd be used to that, though, Sir. On a sub,' said Dixon.

'Of course.'

A small meeting room, a round table in the middle.

'This won't take long, Sir,' said Dixon, not bothering to sit down. 'I want to know where you went when you left the conference room yesterday. It was about twenty past eleven.'

'Yes, well . . .' Fisher closed the meeting room door behind him. 'I went across to the Wardroom, got there five or ten minutes later, read the paper for a while.'

'Did you see Commander Vaughan on the way?'

'No, sorry. I hadn't got a clinic yesterday until after lunch, so I had a bit of time to myself.' His face reddened. 'Who was she, the woman who fell?'

'A friend of Victoria Smith, and she was thrown off the roof,' replied Dixon. 'She didn't fall.'

'Oh, I see.'

'Had you ever met Jennifer Drummond?'

'Not that I recall.'

'You were at the Trafalgar Night dinner last October?'

'I was.'

'On the top table?'

'Lord, no. Not senior enough for that.'

'Miss Drummond was at the dinner with Lieutenant Commander Smith.'

'We didn't speak. I was dining with my medical colleagues.'

'Can anyone vouch for you in the Wardroom yesterday?'

Fisher puffed out his cheeks. 'Probably not. The reception area was empty when I arrived, and I sat upstairs in the reading room. There's a bay window overlooking the cricket pitch and the Tamar. I made a coffee from the machine, so someone may remember clearing away a cup and saucer, but that's about the extent of my alibi, I'm afraid.' A hint of sarcasm had crept into his voice.

'What did you do when you left the Wardroom?'

'I went to the gym. You have to sign in there, so there'll be a record of my arrival.'

'And what time did you get there?'

'Eleven-forty-five, possibly. I heard all the sirens and what have you.'

'And how is that time recorded?'

'You have to write it in the book: time in and time out.' Fisher sighed. 'Oh, I get it. I wrote it in the book myself, so I might've lied.'

'You missed your vocation, Sir,' said Dixon. 'You should've been a police officer.'

'I can assure you I didn't falsify the time. I got to the gym, there's a clock on the wall. I checked the time and wrote it in the box. Eleven-forty-five, from memory.' Fisher slid a chair out from under the table, sat down.

'How well did you know Victoria Smith?'

'We were professional colleagues, officers on the same ship. We attended briefings and training courses together, various dinners. I knew her as well as anyone I work with. How well d'you know your colleagues?'

'I married one of them,' replied Dixon. 'How long did you work together?'

'Two tours on *Agincourt.* I knew her before that, though. We were at Dartmouth together for our basic training, but our paths took us in different directions after that. For a time, anyway. I went to sea and she was with NATO in Italy.'

'Let me ask you directly, were you in a relationship with her?'

'Certainly not.' Fisher sat bolt upright. 'I'm married, with two children.'

'Had you ever been in a relationship with her?'

'No. Look, you need to understand the culture in the Navy. Relationships are frowned on, and certainly between senior and junior officers. It's unacceptable sexual behaviour, even with consent. She was my senior, and she'd have been in real trouble if it got out. She wasn't that stupid, at least the Victoria Smith I knew wasn't that stupid. Who knows what goes on behind closed doors?'

'Were there rumours?'

'None.'

'Do you live on the base?'

'Monday night to Thursday night, then I go home to Salisbury. I've got rooms on the top floor of Boscawen Block. Just along from . . .' His voice tailed off. 'Look, I didn't kill her, and I didn't kill this other woman either.'

'Were you involved in Leading Hand Monk's disciplinary process?'

'I gave a statement about what happened on board, but I wasn't called to give evidence at the hearing.'

'Has he been treated at this clinic?' Dixon knew the answer to that one, he'd seen Monk's medical records.

'A couple of times while he's been ashore, but I made damned sure someone else saw him.'

'Can you access his medical records?'

'On the computer, yes.'

'What about his psychiatric records?'

'Yes.'

'Monk said in interview he didn't interfere with the body. He said he just looked at her.'

Fisher curled his lip. 'I really don't want to have to go over all that again. It's all in my statement, which you'll find on the disciplinary file.'

Stroud's phone had been buzzing intermittently in her pocket, then text messages started arriving. She slid it out of her pocket, glanced at the screen, then held it up to Dixon.

Where r u Pen. NBC is asking to see Supt Dixon urgently

'Naval Base Commander?'

Stroud nodded. 'Have you finished here, Sir?'

'Yes, thank you,' replied Dixon.

Chapter Thirty-Eight

'The brigadier has asked to see Superintendent Dixon in private.' The officer turned to Cole and Stroud. 'There's coffee on the side there,' he said, gesturing to a sideboard beneath an oil painting of more ships under sail. 'If you'll follow me, please, Superintendent.'

The brigadier was standing in the window of his office, staring out across the car park. He turned at the sound of the door closing behind Dixon. 'I'm sorry, but I have to ask you to leave the base, Superintendent. Immediately, please.'

Dixon had expected it, after his visit from Tom Perry the night before. 'I'm a security risk, I suppose?'

'You are.'

'Actually, I'm not, but that's for another day.'

'Are you saying it wasn't you?'

'I am.'

'Well, I have my orders, I'm afraid. From the top. Your security clearance is revoked with immediate effect, and you're to be escorted off the base.'

'You still have a killer at *Drake*.'

'That will be DCI Hatch's problem. He'll be here anyway with his team, taking statements from everyone involved with that fellow Monk. I gather the dive team are in the water, looking for mobile phones and the murder weapon. We usually deal with Devon and Cornwall Police when there's an issue. We know them and they know us.'

'The murder of Victoria Smith is still my case, and I intend to find her killer, with or without your help.'

'I'd expect nothing less.' Milne offered a conciliatory smile. 'And may I say, finding Monk was a first class piece of work, however much DCI Hatch might try to take the credit for it. And however embarrassing it might be for the Royal Navy.'

'The embarrassment will get worse, before it gets better.'

'I have no doubt about that.'

'Were you aware of the disciplinary issues involving Leading Hand Monk?'

'That business on board the *Agincourt*, you mean? Yes, I knew about it. Filthy little . . . Most unsavoury.'

Dixon turned for the door. 'I'll get Warrant Officer Stroud to drop me back to the main gate, assuming I don't need an armed guard.'

'That will be fine.'

'One last question, Sir,' said Dixon, his hand on the door handle. 'Are you married?'

◆ ◆ ◆

Dixon had noticed them on the way up the stairs; he stopped halfway down, nudged Cole and gestured to the large window overlooking the car park.

'The bins,' whispered Cole.

'The bins.'

Stroud was waiting for them at the bottom of the stairs. 'Where to now, Sir?' she asked.

'Main gate,' replied Dixon. 'My security clearance has been revoked.'

'Really?'

'I'm suspected of being behind the leak.'

'I saw it on the news this morning. The official line is the Russian sub was drifting without power due to a fire in the engine room. The Defence Secretary has ordered a leak inquiry too.' Stroud was watching Dixon for any reaction. 'It wasn't you, was it?'

'No.'

'But you knew about the sub?'

'I did.'

'Who told you?'

Dixon looked at her, smiled.

'Of course,' she said. 'Well, it's been a pleasure, and an eye-opener. I usually deal with Devon and Cornwall, but you're in a different league.'

'Thank you.'

◆ ◆ ◆

They were out on the A38 before Cole summoned up the courage. 'You knew about that?'

'I didn't say anything, Nige, I'm sorry. But the fewer people who knew about it, the better.'

'I've never been involved in a leak inquiry before.'

'You'll be able to say you didn't know.'

'Who told you?'

'Have you got a charging cable for my phone?'

'Glovebox,' mumbled Cole. 'So, what do we do now? The killer's at the naval base and we've been thrown out.'

'Express Park first. Then we'll go over to Bishops Lydeard, have a look at Jennifer Drummond's house.'

There were several cars in the visitors' car park Dixon didn't recognise when they arrived an hour later. The two black Jaguars either side of Charlesworth's car for starters.

Cole was looking in his rear view mirror while he waited for the electric gates to the staff car park to open. 'They're XE 300 Sports; top of the range. Give me a run for my money in this. I wonder who they belong to?'

'I can guess,' said Dixon. He'd had several text messages from Sarah on the drive up the M5, alerting him to who was in the building.

Charlesworth.

Four men in suits.

They'd never all fit in meeting room 2.

Dixon had got as far as the canteen before Charlesworth caught up with him. 'Meeting room one, when you've got a minute, Nick. There are some people down from London who'd like a word.' He raised his eyebrows. 'Defence intelligence.'

Dixon turned to Cole, behind him in the queue. 'I'll take my coffee. You'd better have my bacon roll, Nige.'

'Good luck, Sir,' said Cole.

The conference table was smaller than the one at *Drake*. Charlesworth in uniform, the four suits – a uniform of sorts. At least there was no Carlisle and Larkin; the Professional Standards Department not involved yet, and hopefully not at all.

Charlesworth made the introductions. Unusually for Dixon, he took out a notepad and wrote down the names; it saved bothering to remember them anyway.

Commander Jenkins – that name had stuck – was staring at him, spoke first. 'What was your interest in the *Novorossiysk*?'

'I'm investigating the murder of Lieutenant Commander Victoria Smith.'

'And?'

'I would have thought it pretty self-explanatory in that case, wouldn't you?'

'I don't think you realise the seriousness of your situation, Superintendent.'

Dixon waited – better that than have the meeting descend into pantomime.

'Who told you about the presence of the *Novorossiysk* in British territorial waters?'

'I am not at liberty to say.'

'We know it was Thomas Perry MP.'

Those early exchanges in a sword fight, looking for an opponent's weaknesses.

'What did you do with the information?' demanded Jenkins.

'Made decisions about the direction of the murder investigation.'

'Nothing else?'

'Nothing else.'

Answer the question, volunteer nothing. All that legal training coming in handy again.

'Who did you tell?'

'No one.'

'Not even your partner, Police Constable . . .' Jenkins snatched a piece of paper off the table. '. . . Cole?'

'No.'

'What did Mr Perry tell you?'

Dixon sighed, his 'you'll have to do better than that' unspoken. Jenkins got the message.

'You went to Finch Geotech, spoke to local fishermen. Why?'

'I was informed that Victoria Smith had made contact with the Finch family and was intending to reveal certain information to them in relation to the deaths of the marine surveyors off Hartland Point. She was killed before she could do so, and I needed to understand what that information was to be able to assess whether or not it might have been a sufficient motive for her murder.'

'And that information concerned the presence of the *Novorossiysk*?'

'Presumably.'

'And was it a sufficient motive for her murder?'

'It remains a possible motive, yes.'

Jenkins was smoothing his moustache with his thumb and index finger, his eyes fixed on Dixon. 'You seem defensive.'

'It's a natural reaction when someone comes under attack.'

'Is it? You feel you're being attacked?'

'I'm being investigated as the possible source of the leak. I've had my security clearance at *Drake* revoked, and now you're here questioning me.'

'And you're hardly cooperating.'

'I'm answering your questions.'

'Barely.'

'Perhaps you're asking the wrong questions.'

'What questions should I be asking?'

'That's entirely a matter for you.'

Jousting now.

'The Defence Secretary will be concerned by your reluctance to help the inquiry.'

Deep breath, count to ten. It was either that or tell them he didn't give a flying fuck about the Defence Secretary.

'Look, this is getting us nowhere,' said Dixon. 'I was aware of the presence of the *Novorossiysk*, told no one. Now, you might not have better things to do, but I have.' Dixon stood up.

'We haven't finished, Superintendent.'

'I think we have,' said Charlesworth. 'Superintendent Dixon is under no obligation to reveal the source of his information. He is an outstanding police officer, and if he says he told no one, then he told no one. That's the end of the matter as far as we're concerned.'

◆ ◆ ◆

Dixon was waiting for a bacon roll when Charlesworth caught up with him in the canteen.

'They've gone,' he said. 'You do need to be careful, Nick. They'll look for a scapegoat, and you can bet your bottom dollar it won't be any of the politicians.'

'It won't be me, either,' replied Dixon.

'Here.' Charlesworth thrust a copy of *The Times* into Dixon's hand. 'The government withdrew the D-Notice and put out a statement saying the Russian sub was on fire, lost power and drifted into British territorial waters. *Agincourt* was shadowing it the whole time, and it was never a threat. And this is what Victoria Smith was going to tell the Finch family, I suppose?'

'She'd have been monitoring radio traffic as the comms officer on *Agincourt*, so she'd have known all about it, radioed in their position periodically. Most of the crew were just told they were shadowing a Russian sub, not where it was, or that it was forced to the surface.'

'You think the Russians killed the marine surveyors?'

'The reality is we'll never know one way or the other. Unless it was in radio messages intercepted by *Agincourt*, but I'm told it wasn't.'

'There's no mention of that in the news.'

'I can see it happening. They're forced to surface, venting smoke from the conning tower, only to find two blokes on a boat taking photos of them on their phones.' A plate with a bacon roll on it was slid across the counter to Dixon. 'Kill them and make it look like an accident. It would explain why the *Endeavour* hadn't drifted as far as expected.'

'Who knew Victoria Smith was about to tell the families?'

'Now that *is* the question.'

'You're going to struggle with *Drake* off limits.' Charlesworth was eyeing up Dixon's bacon roll. 'You can always send DS Willmott and that Pearce fellow, I suppose. What we don't want is the Devon lot making our arrest – not after we made theirs.' He looked at the kitchen assistant. 'A bacon roll for me, please.'

'Yes, Sir.'

'They've found the hammer, apparently,' continued Charlesworth. 'Sarah Loveday had a call earlier while we were in with James Bond and his chums.'

'I really need to . . .' Dixon had picked up his bacon roll, was holding it in the napkin, waving it in the direction of the door.

'You carry on. Just be bloody careful.'

◆ ◆ ◆

'Penny Stroud rang, Sir, said you'd want to know, the hammer was right where he said it would be in Number Five Basin. They're still looking for the phones.'

'Where are Louise and Mark?'

'They've gone back down to Plymouth,' replied Sarah. 'Your security clearance might have been revoked, but theirs hasn't. That's what they said, anyway. The RNP are going to be carrying on with the canvassing for witnesses and they're going to help with that. It means they're on the base too. Just in case something happens.'

'Something else,' said Cole.

'Do me a favour will you, Sarah? Ring round Plymouth taxi firms and see if any of them have had a set of magnetic taxi plates stolen in the last eighteen months or so.'

'Shall I get Reddaway to check if a theft has been reported to police?'

'Might as well. Taxi firms first, though. Chances are they wouldn't have bothered to report it.'

It didn't take long. Dixon was standing in front of the whiteboards, listening to her conversation.

'You have? . . . When?' Sarah was scribbling on a notepad. 'Did you report it to your local police? . . . Why not? Hardly worth it . . . Right. What do they look like, these plates? . . . Right, thank you. And your name is . . . ? . . . Well, thanks again, Tariq.' She rang off. 'First one I rang. Imaginatively called Plymouth Taxis, Sir. They had a set of plates pinched in January last year. The actual taxi licence is bolted to the bumper, but the signs on the car doors are just magnetic; about the size of an A3 piece of paper, bright red with the company name and phone number.'

'You said someone had rung in from West Bagborough?'

'Yes, she'd seen a taxi in the village about ten that evening,' replied Sarah. 'Didn't recognise the firm. I said I'd send someone over to see her, but there hasn't been anybody free, so I haven't got round to it yet.'

Chapter Thirty-Nine

'Bishops Lydeard first, then we'll go over to Corfe.'

'Scientific are in there today,' Sarah had said, when Dixon asked for the keys to Jennifer Drummond's house in Bishops Lydeard. 'Donald Watson's got them.'

He'd parked his van on the junction, blocking the lane.

'I'll have to leave mine here,' said Cole, reversing into a space right outside the window of a small cottage, a figure inside staring out at them through the net curtains.

'Put the blue light on the roof,' said Dixon.

They walked across the road, up the flagstone garden path.

'Well, what've we got?' he asked, standing in the open front door.

'The grandfather clock is a belter,' replied Watson. 'Must be worth about six grand. And there's a lovely mahogany dining table and chairs. Some Meissen in the display cabinet. His and hers Rolex watches in a jewellery box; her late parents', I expect. The gent's is a gold Submariner with the blue dial, so that's twenty grand's worth on its own.'

'I didn't mean the antiques.'

'Oh, sorry. I'm not sure what you're looking for in that case.'

'Miss Drummond was Victoria Smith's executor and collected some of her papers from safe storage at the bank,' said Dixon.

'What do they look like, these papers?'

'No idea. I imagine they'll be in a document wallet of some sort, or an envelope.'

'Have we found her car?' asked Cole.

'It was parked on-street a couple of hundred yards down from HMS *Drake*,' replied Watson. 'Devon and Cornwall have got it on a flatbed lorry; they're bringing it up to our lab, apparently. Our case, our bill. I'll check it for those papers when I get back.'

'Do we need overalls?'

'No. I only put them on through force of habit. It's not the crime scene, is it?' Watson was raising his voice as Dixon walked into the living room. 'We could do with some help, really.'

'There isn't any.'

'Oh, right. Brilliant.'

Everything had flowers on it in the living room. The carpet, the curtains, the wallpaper, even the sofa and chairs. At least the colours matched, so it had clearly been planned; shades of green and pink.

Dixon sat down next to a bookcase, started pulling photograph albums from the bottom shelf, one by one. He'd met Jennifer Drummond only once, but she was the meticulous type, each photograph sitting squarely on a pencil line drawn across the page, held in place by little stickers in the corners; a note in fountain pen underneath each image, the writing small and neat.

In school uniform, with Kathy Huxtable and Victoria Smith, all three of them grinning at the camera. Jennifer Drummond at Kathy Huxtable's wedding; what looked like a hen-do, as well. She'd even been to Victoria's passing out parade at Dartmouth Naval College.

Sisters, almost.

Several officers were milling about in the background of one of the photographs, so Dixon slid it out of the album and left it on the arm of the chair. Another of Victoria Smith, sword in hand, receiving her commission.

Then came an album of photographs Jennifer had taken on holiday in Italy. Dixon knew Kathy and Jennifer had been out to visit Victoria while she'd been on secondment to NATO.

It was pretty obvious, really – to Dixon anyway. Jennifer hadn't known the identity of the officer Victoria had been having an affair with, so if she'd taken his photograph, it would have been unwittingly. And that meant if he was going to be anywhere, it would be in the background of one of these images.

It would need a magnifying glass and a bright light, and there were plenty of those back at Express Park.

A couple taken on a restaurant veranda somewhere; Naples, possibly. There was lots of water in the background. He added those to the pile. Then some taken at the Trafalgar Night dinner Jennifer had attended as Victoria's guest the previous October; several familiar faces, some smiling at the camera, some in conversation in the background.

He slid the photographs into his inside jacket pocket.

'There's an office of sorts upstairs.' Watson was peering around the door. 'Nigel Cole just went up there to have a look.'

Dixon followed, finding Cole in what was once the back bedroom. The bed was still there, as well as a filing cabinet, a desk with an ancient computer and a printer, but not much else. Cole had opened the top drawer of the filing cabinet, was flicking through the contents.

'This is old stuff, Sir. Parents' bank statements going back years, house insurance policies, stuff like that,' he said, closing the drawer and opening the next one. 'Surely if those papers she collected from the bank contained anything relevant she'd have taken them with her when she went to Plymouth, in which case they're either in her car or they're long gone. She had a bag with her when she went through security, remember, and we never found that. Or her phone.'

'She might have made copies, I suppose.' Dixon was looking at the printer on the chest of drawers. 'That's not a copier, so she'd have to have gone to a post office, possibly.'

Cole slammed the top drawer, moved on to the next.

Dixon sat down on the rickety dining chair in front of the computer, opened the small drawers in the plinth beneath the monitor, pulled out a black and white image.

He recognised what it was straightaway. After all, only a few short months ago he'd been looking at another ultrasound scan. Of his own son.

He turned it over, read the handwritten note on the back: *Vic. 12 weeks. Feb 2017.*

'Here, Nige,' he said, handing it to Cole.

'Victoria Smith was pregnant?'

'She was at Dartmouth Naval College in February 2017.'

◆ ◆ ◆

Kathy Huxtable must have recognised Dixon in the passenger seat of Cole's car, the electric gates opening as soon as they pulled up at the entrance.

She was waiting for them in the porch, watched them park behind her Audi. The Range Rover had gone – her husband at work, probably. Shame. Dixon was about to deliver her second death message in little more than a week.

Corduroys tucked into the top of wellington boots; one of those blue padded jackets with no sleeves.

'I was in the garden. Just nipped in for a coffee when I saw you pull up. Any news?'

'Shall we go inside?'

'You make it sound like it's bad news. It is, isn't it?' She slumped on to a pile of logs that had been neatly stacked against the wall under cover of the canopy. 'If you've got something to tell me, best get it over with,' she said, breathing deeply.

'Miss Drummond is dead,' said Dixon, softly.

'First Vic and now Jenny.' She was fighting to keep her composure, wiped away tears with the back of her hand. 'You'd better come in.'

'Is your husband here?'

'He's busy at the racecourse. I'll ring him later.'

She was opening a bottle of white wine by the time they closed the outer and inner doors and caught up with her in the kitchen. 'The coffee machine is on, if you'd like one?'

'Thank you.'

She opened a kitchen drawer; took out a packet of cigarettes from the back. 'These are years old, stale as hell, but I keep them for emergencies.' She lit a ring on the gas hob, leaned over and sucked hard on the filter. 'What happened?' She switched on the fan in the cooker hood, blew the smoke into it.

'Miss Drummond fell from a building and was killed instantly.'

'Fell or was thrown?'

'It was murder.'

Kathy nodded, slowly, filling her wine glass at the same time, right to the brim. 'Where was this?'

'HMS *Drake*.'

'I told her not to go down there.' She took a swig of wine. 'It's got something to do with this business on the news, I know it has,' she said. 'I knew there was something going on when Vic got back from that last tour, but she wouldn't talk about it. She must've known about that Russian submarine.'

'She'd made contact with the family of one of the surveyors and arranged to meet—'

'She was going to blow the whistle.' Kathy gave a sad smile. 'That sounds like our Vic. She hated injustice, hated cover-ups.' She left her cigarette balanced on the edge of the sink. 'Sorry, I was making you a coffee, wasn't I?'

'You know why Miss Drummond might have gone to *Drake*?' asked Dixon.

'Jenny came to see me last week. She was in a bad way; Vic's death – murder – had really upset her. I mean *really* upset her. She kept rabbiting on about a married man Vic was having a fling with. I thought it was over, but Jenny said it was still going on. He's a senior officer, tried to block her promotion to lieutenant commander when Vic tried to end the relationship. She got it anyway, of course she did, but he made it pretty difficult for a time.' She placed two mugs of coffee on the table, then a plastic carton of milk; picked up her glass of wine off the worktop. 'Vic never mentioned any of this to me, although I knew there'd been an affair. Jenny knew. Vic must've confided in her. Jenny was like that – easy to confide in. And they were more like sisters, those two, anyway. It was always them and me, if you know what I mean.'

'What else did Jenny say?'

'She seemed to think it was her responsibility, for some reason. Her job to sort it out.' Kathy was holding her cigarette under the cooker hood, the smoke spiralling into the fan above. 'She said she was going down to *Drake*, tell Vic's CO and expose this man. A senior officer having an affair with a junior colleague; his career was over and she was going to make sure of it. I tried to talk her out of it, but she was determined.' She dragged a pine chair out from under the table, sat down next to Dixon. 'I never thought she'd go through with it, to be honest.'

'But she didn't know who this man was?'

'No.'

'And you've got no idea who it is?'

'I always thought it was someone on the sub, but I may be wrong. Like I said, we had a disagreement about it. Vic never mentioned it to me again. What she did tell me about it was all rather sordid; made it sound illicit and grubby. I think it started when they were at Dartmouth, a drunken fumble, but then he kept coming back for more.' A large swig of wine. 'I got the impression it was just sex, at least as far as Vic was concerned, but she knew he could make her life difficult if she said no, so she just put up with it. "Lie back and think of England", although *lie back* is probably an exaggeration. More often than not it was in cars, from what I could gather.'

Dixon handed her the ultrasound scan.

'Where did you find this?' she asked.

'Jenny's house. There's a date on the back.'

'Vic would've been at Dartmouth then,' said Kathy, with a heavy sigh. 'I remember a long weekend. Just the two of them. Vic had got leave and I wasn't invited. It all makes sense now. Jenny would've gone with her, she was like that – a mother hen. Before the pregnancy started to show, obviously.' She stood up, ran the tap, held her cigarette under it, then dropped it in the bin.

'I take it the pregnancy was terminated,' said Dixon.

'Must've been. I went to Vic's passing out parade in the April and she wasn't pregnant then.'

'And you've got no idea who this man is?'

'She never said, and after our row, I never asked.'

'Do you know what ended the relationship?'

'She got her dolphins, I suppose. I really don't know. I don't know for sure it ever ended, actually. Jenny said it was still going on.'

'Jenny told them at the main gate she was Victoria's executor,' said Dixon.

'Yes, that's right. Vic said I'd be useless at it, and she was probably right.'

'Had she made a start administering the estate?'

'She'd registered Vic's death, using an interim death certificate. The house was still off limits, your blue tape everywhere, but she'd been to her bank. There were some papers in safe storage there, and she'd got those.'

'Do you know what was in them?'

'Jenny didn't say.'

'What happens to Victoria's estate?'

'It goes to her parents. They'll sell the property, I expect. Can't imagine they'll want it, not now.'

Chapter Forty

'Hello? Cooee! Is that the police?'

Dixon was standing in the back garden of Victoria Smith's house in West Bagborough, the voice coming from the path at the side. An elderly woman's voice, tentative.

'Yes,' he replied. 'Stay where you are and I'll come round the front.'

'I was keeping an eye out for you,' she said, her voice softening when Dixon appeared around the corner of the house. 'Margery Reeves. I live further down the lane, rang about the taxi. They said you'd be along at some point this morning and I saw the blue light on your car.'

'Thank you.' Dixon was looking over his shoulder. 'I've got a colleague somewhere, but I think he's rummaging about at the bottom of the garden.'

The path at the side of the property had been cleared by Scientific Services, a jumble of cut brambles thrown on the lawn. The blue tape was still there, across the front door, some of it hanging down, fluttering in the wind.

'You said you saw a taxi at about ten o'clock on the Saturday evening?'

Elderly, but not wearing glasses, which was a good sign. No corresponding mark on the bridge of her nose either. Even better.

'Yes. I'm sorry I've not been in contact before, I've been staying with my sister on the Isle of Wight. Didn't know anything about . . . what happened until I got back, I'm afraid. Ruth told me all about it; she's in the bungalow on the corner.'

'That's fine, don't worry.' Dixon offered his best reassuring smile. 'You said you didn't recognise the taxi firm?'

'That's what struck me as odd. I didn't know there were any others operating around here. I'd let Mabel outside for a wee before I went to bed – round about ten, same as always – and I was watching her from the window.'

'In your front garden?'

'Yes. It's a courtyard behind my house and she doesn't like to go on that.' She was zipping up her waxed coat – thrown on over an apron when she'd seen them arrive, probably. That, and a pair of cut-down wellies. 'Anyway, I was looking out of the window, and I saw this car creep past in the lane. It had taxi plates on the doors, so I just thought it was looking for an address to make a pickup, you know. I don't have a car and always use taxis, but they know me and where I live now.'

'Which firm do you use?'

'Apple. They're based in Taunton. They even send the same driver, most of the time. This one wasn't Apple, though. They've got an orange sign with a red apple as their logo and a Taunton phone number. This was a red sign and I'm sure it said "Plymouth Taxis". I didn't catch the phone number, I'm afraid.'

'Did you see anything else?'

They both turned at the sound of heavy footsteps on the path at the side of the house, Cole appearing, picking thorns out of the sleeve of his coat.

'This is Mrs Reeves, Nige,' said Dixon. 'Telling us about the taxi.'

'Well, it went past again about ten minutes later,' she continued. 'Now I wouldn't want you to think I'm a nosey neighbour, but that struck me as a bit odd, what with the satnav things they've got these days, and he'd have had a phone number for the client. So, I went out to have a look, see where he was going. I thought he might be lost, and I might be able to help. It took me a while to get Mabel in. If I open the front gate when she's in the garden, she's off and I'd never find a Scottie in the dark.'

'Quite so.'

'Anyway, it was there, parked on the corner there, under that tree. No sign of the driver.' Mrs Reeves was pointing along the lane towards a large oak on the junction with an even smaller lane. 'And what I thought was odd was the plates had gone off the side. He must've taken them off and put them in the boot, I suppose. I thought he might've been visiting someone. Thought nothing more about it and went to bed. Then, the next day a taxi picked me up and took me to the station to go to my sister's.'

'Was the car still there?'

'I really don't remember, I'm afraid. Sunday is a difficult day for cars anyway, because we get the church congregation parking in the lane. It's bedlam sometimes.'

'Was there a taxi licence plate bolted to the bumper?'

'Oh, no. I didn't see that. I know what you mean. I really don't remember that, I'm afraid.'

'What else can you tell me about this car?'

'It was one of those ghastly electric things, I know that much. I haven't got double glazing and my hearing's pretty sharp for my age. This thing made no sound, no engine noise at all.'

'Could've been a hybrid using the electric engine, don't forget,' said Cole. 'Most hybrids have a range of fifty miles or so.'

'What colour was it?' asked Dixon.

'It was night time and there's no street lighting here, dear,' replied Mrs Reeves. 'It was dark coloured, I can say that much, but it might have been a dark brown, black or even dark blue, I suppose. It didn't have those silly lights on it that go right across the back, though. Just proper lights.'

'Was it a saloon or an estate car? An SUV, possibly?'

'It was quite small actually, which was another thing I thought odd at the time. No good for several people with luggage, but as for what it was, I'm afraid I'd have no idea about that. Cars all look the same these days.'

'Did you see the driver?'

'No, dear. It was too dark for that.'

'But you said *he* when you referred to the driver.'

'That's an assumption on my part. Sorry. No woman could do what he did to that poor girl.'

◆ ◆ ◆

'Did you find anything, Nige?'

'I found where Scientific reckon he'd been waiting in the garden, and there's a clear view of the back of the house. Certainly enough to see when lights had come on inside. There's also access from the field at the back, so he could've parked on the corner down there, walked along the lane and into the field.'

'Not past the trail camera?'

'No. There's some barbed wire to step over, but that's it. There was some plaster left in some of the prints, but none of the casts were any good, according to the report. Just thought I'd have a look anyway.'

'Who do we know who drives an electric car?' asked Dixon.

'We can check that easily enough,' replied Cole. 'There were several of them plugged in behind the Wardroom at *Drake*, if you remember.'

'I do.'

'Where to now?'

'Express Park, I think.'

Everybody was there when they arrived half an hour later, three of the sixteen workstations occupied.

'What's going on down at *Drake*?' asked Dixon.

'Hatch and his team have been in most of the day, taking statements for the case against Monk,' replied Louise. 'He's not going anywhere. Remanded in custody by Plymouth Magistrates, as you'd expect, and it turns out there are blood traces still on the hammer.'

'As if they needed any more evidence against him,' muttered Mark. 'The ungrateful tossers.'

'I take it you weren't made to feel welcome?'

'The RNP and Penny Stroud have been great,' replied Louise. 'Devon and Cornwall not so much.'

'Rise above it.'

'We kept out of their way, spent the day with Penny, canvassing people living in the accommodation blocks.'

'No one saw anything, I suppose.'

'We'd have rung you if they had.'

'I asked Penny Stroud to check the officers' cars,' said Sarah. 'It occurred to me that driving in muddy lanes with magnetic taxi plates on the doors would leave an outline where the sign had been. No luck, sadly. She checked all the cars in the car park and nothing.'

'What cars do the *Agincourt* officers drive?'

'Give me a sec.' Opening a document on her computer screen. 'Commander Vaughan has a Range Rover, the XO has got a Mercedes, the surgeon lieutenant drives an electric thing, a Nissan Leaf.'

'What about the Naval Base Commander?'

'A Jaguar E-PACE.'

'That's electric,' said Cole.

'And the First Lieutenant?'

'He's got an Audi. Petrol. And the Officer of the Watch has got a BYD Dolphin.'

Mark was scrolling on his phone. 'That's got a real-world range of one hundred and eighty-nine miles. Can't have been him. He'd be lucky if the bloody thing got him from Plymouth to West Bagborough and back.'

'They'd have been heading south in the early hours of Sunday and none of their cars turned up on ANPR cameras anywhere,' said Sarah. 'Their mobile phones didn't move, either.' She looked at Dixon, sheepishly. 'Not that that means anything, I know.'

'Anyone with half a brain would leave their phone behind.' Louise and Mark, in unison, grinning.

'This business with the Russian sub, Sir,' said Sarah. 'I'm guessing that's what Victoria Smith was going to tell that Finch bloke, and you knew about it?'

'Yes.'

'That what those four suits were here for then, part of this leak inquiry?'

'They were from defence intelligence, but it wasn't me who leaked it.'

'It might still be the motive for her murder, though. If someone knew she was going to say something. It could even have been the Russians.'

'They're hardly going to have thrown Jennifer Drummond off the roof of an accommodation block at HMS *Drake*, are they?'

'They'd have used that Novichok stuff,' said Mark.

Dixon was standing in front of the whiteboards, staring at a picture of HMS *Agincourt*. 'She'd been having an affair with a senior officer, got pregnant while she was at the Royal Naval College in Dartmouth, then had whoever the father was trying to block her promotion, which was probably the last straw. She was going to report him for unacceptable sexual behaviour, end his career, and that was why she was killed.'

'Maybe she told him she was going to tell Finch about the Russian sub?' offered Sarah.

'Take this man down with her, in that case.' Dixon turned around. 'You lot head home. Be back here for nine in the morning. We could all do with some sleep.'

Cole waited until the others had left, appearing at Dixon's elbow while he was still staring at the whiteboards. 'Sarah said the XO drives a Mercedes. That's what—'

'I know, Nige. Don't worry about it. You go and get sleep. Pick me up at eight-thirty.'

◆ ◆ ◆

It was still daylight – just – when Dixon arrived back at the cottage in Brent Knoll. He'd sent Cole home, gambled on finding a patrol car heading in the right direction, ended up taking a taxi. Apple, with magnetic signs stuck to the front doors on both sides of the car.

'Do you ever take those off?' he asked, when the driver dropped him off.

'I don't bother, but I've got off-street parking. Some of the lads take them off at night. Why?'

'No reason.'

No Monty on the windowsill, so Dixon looked in the window. His son was asleep in his cot, his dog curled up on the rug, eyes open. Alert, the tip of his tail wagging.

Jane saw him, put her index finger across her lips, got off the sofa as quietly as she could, tiptoed towards the back door.

Only just got Peter off to sleep, probably. Dixon would need to be quiet.

'Please tell me you're in the clear for this leak thing,' said Jane, when she opened the back door.

'I'll be fine. We've had a visit from defence intelligence. I told them it wasn't me, and Charlesworth told them that was the end of the matter.'

'He stood up for you?'

'You could've knocked me down with a feather.'

'You told them who did do it, surely?'

'Not yet.'

Jane sighed. 'Have you eaten?'

'I had a bacon roll from the canteen.'

'When was that?'

'Lunchtime.'

Jane held out her hand. 'Phone.' She snatched it from Dixon, opened the app and held it to the sensor in the back of his arm. 'Four-point-one, going down. You need to eat. I'll put a curry in the microwave. And there's only sugar-free mango chutney, before you ask. I threw the other stuff away.'

Actually, that was a lie. Dixon knew where she'd hidden it – he'd found it when he'd been looking for the secret stash of chocolate her mother had brought for her – but it was best not to argue. Probably replenished too. There were fresh flowers on the dining table.

'Your folks been round?'

'Mum popped in earlier. Offered to babysit for a couple of days a week, if I want to go back to work part-time. I told her I might have to; someone's got to keep you out of trouble.'

'Maybe when he's caught up a bit? He was eight weeks prem—'

'No, not yet.'

Jane had stabbed the film on the frozen curry softly, managed to push the microwave door shut without a sound. Peter stirred, gurgled, then went back to sleep.

'He's been a little bugger today. Just would not sleep. I tried *Goodbye, Mr. Chips*, bloody everything.'

'Has Monty been out?' asked Dixon.

'We had a turn round the field, me carrying Peter.'

'I'll take him out in a bit.'

'Are you making any progress with this case?'

'He used a stolen set of magnetic taxi plates to disguise his car.'

Jane was leaning over, watching the clock on the microwave. 'I need to stop it before it goes ping,' she whispered. 'And don't take it in there, the smell of it might wake him up.'

'Really?'

'If you knew the day I've had. It means he might sleep through the night, I suppose.'

'Sarah had the cars at *Drake* checked for clean patches on the doors, but he's probably run it through a car wash.'

'They might have left tiny scratches in the paintwork, but they'd soon buff out with a bit of T-Cut. I used to get them on the side of my car from brambles, always kept a bottle handy. It was an old trick Dad taught me.'

Dixon reached into his inside jacket pocket, slid out the photographs he'd taken from the albums at Jennifer Drummond's house, held them up to the light and began flicking through them one by one.

Jane turned. 'What?'

He stopped, slid the photos back into his pocket. Then he walked over to her, took her face in both hands and kissed her on the lips.

'What's that for?'

'What would I do without you?'

'Yeah, right.' She slid the curry out of the microwave on to a plate. 'Here you go.'

'Can I have some of your chocolate for pudding?'

'What chocolate?'

Chapter Forty-One

Dixon was standing in the field behind his cottage, watching Monty sniffing along the hedge, when he heard Cole's car in the road. He'd had to pick the dog up, carry him downstairs; managed to get out without waking Jane or Peter up. There'd been a gurgle or two, from both of them, but they'd quickly gone back to sleep.

Peter hadn't woken up in the night either – or, if he had, Dixon had slept through it.

Moments like this were few and far between. The sun low in the sky, birds singing, a huge weight lifted from his shoulders.

And all it had taken was one throwaway remark from Jane.

'When this is over, you're coming with me in the Land Rover, mate,' he said, clipping on his dog's lead. Although it was quite comforting to know that Monty was standing guard, not that there was much chance of their home being broken into; not again. Lightning never strikes twice, and all that. Actually, it already had, but that was incidental.

They'd changed the locks, added bolts top and bottom of both doors. Just in case.

Dixon left Monty in the kitchen eating his breakfast, closed the door softly and walked around the side of the cottage.

'Where to today?' asked Cole, when he climbed into the passenger seat.

'Express Park first, then Plymouth,' replied Dixon. 'It ends today, Nige.'

'Oh, shame. Back to policing in the twenty-first century for me then. My wife will be pleased, though. She thinks you're trouble.'

'So does mine.'

'How are we going to get into *Drake*? You've had your security clearance revoked, remember.'

'Penny Stroud said she was police first, Navy second, so we'll find out, won't we?'

Charlesworth and Potter were waiting for them when they arrived in the incident room, standing side by side in front of the whiteboards, under the watchful eye of Sarah. She looked at Dixon, mouthed 'sorry'.

'Ah, there you are, Nick,' said Charlesworth. 'We need to have a word about this Russian sub business, and it would be a useful opportunity to find out where you are with the investigation as well. The Chief Con is throwing his weight about, wants Deborah to take over as SIO.'

An empty threat, if ever he'd heard one. Dixon sighed. Might as well get it over with. 'We can do it here, Sir, saves us all trooping down to the meeting room. There's nothing my team can't hear.'

'Well, in that case, the Chief Con has had the Home Secretary bending his ear. You're making a nuisance of yourself at one of His Majesty's naval bases and it's got to stop. The Chief Con stuck his neck out for you, told him there's a double murderer on the base; there was a bit of huffing and puffing, but he's bought you twenty-four hours. He also told him you were close to making an arrest, which is possibly a slight exaggeration, but I'm hoping it's true.'

'It is.'

'Good. Well, in that case, I'll see if I can swing it so they'll let you back in. Give me a couple of hours to make some calls.'

'What about the Russian sub business, Sir?' asked Dixon. 'I'm guessing you're referring to the leak inquiry.'

'MI5 have questioned Brian Finch, who refuses to reveal his source, which is frustrating but sort of inevitable. Then we've got foreign newspapers reporting on comments from the NATO Secretary General about the reliability of the Russian submarine fleet. I think the MoD just wants the whole thing to go away.'

'It's hardly going to do that if there's a prosecution under the Official Secrets Act.'

'Quite. Anyway, you'll be pleased to learn the Chief Con is taking a firm line. The leak didn't come from an Avon and Somerset police officer, and they need to look elsewhere.'

Potter was staring at Dixon, watching for a reaction. 'You know where, don't you?'

'I'll deal with it in my own time, Ma'am, when this is over.'

'You said you were close to making an arrest?'

'You have to understand the Navy for it to make sense,' said Dixon. 'We see a naval base, but to them it's a ship. It's even got a mainmast and a quarterdeck. And the same chain of command. Understand that and it all drops into place.'

'Is that it?'

'There are some scratches on car doors left by magnetic taxi plates, but that's basically it. And a dog.'

Potter looked at Charlesworth, frowned.

'Are we making the arrest today?' asked Sarah.

'We are,' replied Dixon.

'Can I come?'

'No.'

◆ ◆ ◆

Sarah had rung ahead and Warrant Officer Penny Stroud was waiting for the convoy when they arrived at the main gate, Louise and Mark following behind.

'We should be all right,' said Stroud, her voice hushed. 'The Officer of the Watch is getting ready for the twenty-one gun salute. It's Coronation Day, sixth May, the anniversary of the King's coronation.'

'What time is that?' asked Dixon.

'Midday.'

'And everyone will be there?'

'Anyone not otherwise engaged will parade. The Naval Base Commander will be there, the officers from the *Agincourt* and the *Diamond* – that's a destroyer in for refit. She's in one of the covered dry docks.'

Dixon looked at his watch. Twenty minutes. Should be enough.

'Let's get you signed in.'

No hesitation; police first, Navy second.

'My ACC was going to make some calls, so I should be all right.'

'You will be if you're with me,' replied Stroud.

It turned out she was right and they were waved through, visitors' passes dangling from lanyards around their necks. There'd been no hint of any hesitation on the part of the security guard when he'd typed Dixon's details into the computer, so maybe Charlesworth had done his bit, after all.

'I've lined up four of us, and there's four of you,' said Stroud, when they cleared the gatehouse. 'Will that be enough?'

'Should be fine.'

'We need to get your cars out of view. Follow me round the back to the RNP station and we can leave them there, go in our Land Rovers.'

They left the cars behind the RNP station, Dixon and Cole climbing in the back of a Land Rover.

'Are you all right with this?' asked Dixon, watching while Louise and Mark climbed in the Land Rover behind them.

'If you're right, Sir, he's killed two people. One of them a serving officer,' replied Stroud. 'No one is above the law.'

'How long does it take, a twenty-one gun salute?'

'About a minute and a half. Ninety seconds. They're old deck guns, small, but they make a hell of a bang. Firing blanks, obviously. There's a box of ear defenders there, on the floor.'

They followed the service road at the back of the base, and parked behind the quarterdeck, hidden from view behind a line of trees. The mainmast was visible, an ensign fluttering in the breeze. It looked like the mast of an old sailing ship, complete with yardarms and rigging, pennants and signal flags on the ropes.

In front of that was the quarterdeck. Figures in naval uniform lining up behind three deck guns, ready for the salute.

'Five minutes to go, so we'll be closing the roads shortly.' Stroud was ducking down, trying to see under low branches of the trees. 'The ones in battle dress are junior ratings. Those anti-flash hoods are fire retardant. The gloves too.'

Only the eyes were visible.

Dixon picked up a pair of ear defenders, handed them to Cole. 'Better had, Nige.'

'What about you?'

'I need to hear what he says.'

'You can hear voices through them,' said Stroud. 'They just muffle the gunshots, reduce it by ten decibels – something like that. You should put them on. Everyone else is wearing them. Even the Naval Base Commander.'

The quarterdeck looked much like a hotel terrace, only there were no tables and chairs. Just the guns and the mainmast. On the far side, beyond the guns, was a balustrade, then a drop down on to the cricket pitch. Fifteen feet, possibly.

'Right then. What's the plan?' asked Stroud.

'We surround the quarterdeck, let him see us,' replied Dixon. 'I'm expecting him to run, but he won't do it until the gun salute is over. He won't interrupt that.'

'It'd be bad form,' said Cole.

'There'll be clouds of smoke, he might try to slip away,' said Stroud.

Two lines of naval officers were standing behind the guns, the Chief of the Guard at the front, ready to give the command. He'd checked his watch twice in the time it took Dixon and Cole to take their places on the quarterdeck, standing off to the left, behind three non-commissioned officers holding flags.

Dixon glanced across at the line, all standing to attention. The Naval Base Commander, in the green uniform of a Royal Marine, was glaring at him, wondering how he'd got on to his base, probably. The CO of the *Agincourt*, Commander Vaughan, his XO, Lieutenant Commander Judith Towers. Surgeon Lieutenant Fisher. Then came the First Lieutenant and, next to him, the Officer of the Watch.

All were wearing their ear defenders – the headbands at the back of their heads rather than on top of their caps.

'Ready!' shouted the Chief of the Guard.

Louise and Mark were on the far side of the quarterdeck; Penny Stroud and another Royal Navy Police officer in position next to the balustrade, well away from the guns. More were behind the ranks of officers on parade.

'Number one gun, fire!'

A loud bang and a flash, a jet of flame and smoke blown out of the muzzle, the smoke drifting back on to the quarterdeck on the breeze off the Tamar.

Cole flinched, but then it was difficult not to, even though he was ready for it.

'Number two gun, fire!'

Another flash and a bang. More smoke.

Three guns, the third a spare in case of a misfire, so it would be number one gun again, Dixon knew that much; should've stood on the other side of the quarterdeck.

The smoke was thick, but he could make out Louise and Mark on the far side, beyond the guns; could still see the officers on parade, all of them standing to attention, saluting.

No gaps in the line. Yet.

He lost count of the rounds fired, tried to count the cartridge cases lying on the quarterdeck behind the guns, the sort you'd have engraved and put umbrellas in. Every now and again the command came – 'Number three gun, fire!' – just to keep the crew on their toes.

'How many is that?'

'Twelve,' replied Cole, in between gunshots. 'Thirteen now.'

Someone had been mowing the cricket pitch, stopped and was standing to attention next to his lawnmower.

Penny Stroud and her colleague had moved forward, along the balustrade, but were still well clear of the guns. Dixon moved forward too, Cole behind him. The movement was noticed, heads turning along the line of officers on parade.

'Eighteen,' said Cole.

'Get ready,' said Dixon.

Louise and Mark had moved in too; their approach had not gone unnoticed.

The Naval Base Commander looked at Dixon, gave an exaggerated frown under his cap. The CO of the *Agincourt* turned.

'Number three gun, fire!'

Movement in the smoke. McConochie running.

Forward, darting between the guns, pushing a junior rating to the ground.

Stroud was sprinting to intercept him. They grappled. McConochie threw himself backwards, taking her with him over the balustrade, a tangle of arms and legs flailing on to the cricket pitch below.

Dixon climbed over the balustrade, jumped, landing heavily on the grass. He helped Stroud to her feet. 'I'm fine,' she said, limping. 'Let's get after him.'

McConochie was sprinting across the cricket pitch towards the covered dry dock, a couple of hundred yards ahead. The RNP Land Rover that had closed the road was speeding towards the harbour wall, siren blaring.

'Where the fuck is he going?' gasped Stroud. 'His car's behind the Wardroom.'

'That shed,' replied Dixon.

'That's got the *Diamond* in it, but all her guns have been removed. What's he after?'

'Height.'

She stopped, breathing hard, her hands on her knees. 'Go, just go. I'll catch you up.'

Chapter Forty-Two

Dixon arrived at the side door of the covered dry dock, just as the RNP Land Rover screeched to a halt.

He could hear footsteps above him, someone running on the steel gangway between the side of the building and the scaffolding that was covering the ship.

'How do we clear the building?' asked Dixon, when Stroud appeared in the doorway.

She slid her radio off her lapel, used it to smash the glass covering the fire alarm.

Workers in overalls started to appear from all parts of the ship, walking briskly along gangways, climbing down ladders.

Only one person was still going up.

McConochie.

The vast grey hull of the ship was towering over them, scaffolding covering the forward superstructure, the mainmast and the bridge.

'She's had all her weapons removed, missile pods, everything,' said Stroud. 'And that tower would usually be covered in radar and satellite dishes. They're all being updated. Even the gun turret.'

Then Cole arrived. 'Is that him up there?' he asked.

McConochie was still climbing – ladders this time – heading for a scaffolding platform at the top of the mainmast.

'Are we going after him?'

'I am, Nige. You get up on deck, make sure you block his escape if he gets away from me.'

Workers were filing past them now, muttering about another bloody fire drill, heading for their assembly points.

Pushing past workers on the flight of steel stairs. Louise and Mark were behind Cole, all keeping left, using the handrail to pull themselves up.

Dixon stopped at a gangway that crossed the void above the dry dock. 'That way to the deck, Nige. You go with him, Lou. Make sure he doesn't do anything stupid.'

'Why me?'

'You've got a kid.'

'So have you!'

Two people behind him now; he spun round to find Mark Pearce and Penny Stroud following him to the upper-level scaffolding, across the gangway to a platform above the bridge.

Two witnesses to what was about to unfold – not a bad thing.

Ladders now, shouts echoing around the shed.

'Alan? What the fuck are you doing up there?'

The figures below were small, getting smaller, the voice coming from a man in a green uniform.

'That's the Naval Base Commander,' said Stroud. She was limping badly now, hardly surprising after that fall.

McConochie had walked out to the edge of the upper platform and was standing on the railing, holding the scaffolding pole in his right hand, rocking backwards and forwards over the void.

All three of them were on the top ladder now.

'Come any closer and I'll jump,' said McConochie, when Dixon climbed on to the platform.

He helped Stroud off the ladder, told Mark to wait at the top.

'Sir, it's me. Penny Stroud,' she said, edging forward. 'Come down, Sir, we can talk about this.'

McConochie had his back to them, was looking down at the figures below, silhouetted in the doorway. Naval uniforms, caps on. He turned, stared at Dixon. 'How did you know?'

'You used your wife's car, the signs left little scratches on the doors; you were polishing them out when I came to your house on Sunday morning. We've got you on an ANPR camera in Bridgwater. You stayed off the motorway, which was clever, but you've still got to cross it to get home to Wedmore. One-fifty-two on the morning Victoria was murdered.'

The text had arrived from Sarah before Dixon had reached *Drake*.

'Unless you're telling me your wife killed her?'

'No.'

'And who else would've known what Monk was up to and had access to the accommodation blocks, to his DNA? Nobody would bat an eyelid seeing the First Lieutenant inspecting Cornwell Block.' Dixon stepped in front of Stroud, edged forward to within a few paces of McConochie. 'I'm guessing you were working late one night, were getting in your car, saw him put something in the wheelie bins behind the Wardroom.'

McConochie shook his head. 'They were looking for a taxi, weren't they? Then he's there dumping a set of magnetic taxi signs. I knew what he'd been up to on the *Agincourt*, of course I did, interfering with that dead body. I'm responsible for discipline on the base. Didn't take much to work out what he'd been doing.'

'So, instead of reporting your suspicions to the local police, you killed Victoria Smith and tried to make it look like Monk did it.'

'She said she was going to tell the family of those marine surveyors about the Russian submarine, and I wasn't having the Navy embarrassed like that. Not on my watch.'

'So, it wasn't about the unacceptable sexual behaviour then?'

'You know about that?'

'We do.'

McConochie sighed. 'She was going to report me. Her career was over and she was bloody well going to take me down with her, but I did it to protect the Navy. It wasn't about me.'

'You told me the first time you met her was at the Trafalgar Night dinner last October.'

'That was a lie,' mumbled McConochie.

'There's a photograph taken at Victoria's passing out parade at Dartmouth. You're in the background, on the dais, taking the salute.'

'I was her divisional officer. I thought it was consensual, but she screamed at me, told me she felt she had to, that all these years I'd basically forced her. It was classic misuse of a position of authority. I've had to sack enough people for it, and all the while . . . I should've stayed in the bloody background.'

'Did she tell you about the pregnancy?'

'Not at the time. She did, the last time I saw her. I went to her house. Waited for her; tried to reason with her. She'd found out I tried to block her promotion, and we had a blazing row. I didn't plan it.'

'You just happened to have a ball peen hammer in your hand?'

McConochie was leaning forward now, tears streaming down his cheeks, dripping off the end of his nose into the abyss. 'This was my ship. I was supply officer for three years. Seems fitting it should end here.'

'It doesn't have to end, Sir,' said Stroud, an urgency in her voice. 'Not here, or anywhere else.'

'What about Jennifer Drummond?' asked Dixon.

'She rang, got put through to me, said she had information she thought Victoria's CO should know. Then all of a sudden, she's here, in the gatehouse. I said I'd take her up to Victoria's rooms.' He let go of the scaffolding pole, lost his balance and started swaying, grabbed hold of it again. 'Do you want me to spell it out?'

'You killed her.'

'What choice did I have? She knew Victoria had been having an affair with someone, and she had an envelope, stuff she'd got from Victoria's bank – private letters, emails, photographs. I'd been out to Italy when Vic was there with NATO. Just holiday snaps. She was going to give them to Vaughan.'

'What did you do with them?' Dixon took a step forward. Stroud followed.

'Threw them in the incinerator. They're gone.'

'Same as her clothes, I suppose?'

'Yes.'

'So, you did it for the Royal Navy?' Dixon managed to hide the sarcasm in his voice; thought he had anyway.

'Not really. Not if I'm being honest. And there's no harm in that now, is there?' McConochie was breathing deeply through his nose, standing to attention, balanced on the scaffolding pole. 'Thirty fucking years,' he said, solemnly, raising his right hand to his brow in a salute.

Then he pitched forward off the scaffolding pole into the void below.

◆ ◆ ◆

A siren in the distance was the first thing to get through. After that, Dixon heard running on the gangways below.

Shouts of 'Get a medic!'

Mark was climbing down the ladder, others climbing up on to the roof of the bridge.

Dixon was looking down at them, down at the body of Lieutenant Commander Alan McConochie lying on top of the bridge, forty feet below. He must've done a half somersault, was lying on his back, eyes staring blankly up at Dixon, blood trickling from the corner of his mouth.

The surgeon lieutenant was the first to get to him, crouched over, felt his neck for a pulse. He looked up at Dixon and Penny Stroud. 'He's alive.'

An ambulance screeched to a halt outside the dry dock, paramedics soon running up the steel stairs.

'Bloody good job he landed on the bridge,' offered Stroud. 'It's another thirty feet down to the deck. He'd never have survived that.'

'I'm not sure he's going to be too pleased about it.'

Dixon watched the gaggle of officers turn away, shaking their heads.

Colleagues, friends, quick to disown.

Quick to distance themselves.

Chapter Forty-Three

'I feel I owe you an apology.'

That came from the Naval Base Commander. A firm handshake too.

It must have been the best part of an hour before McConochie was carried off the ship, handcuffed to a stretcher, his head in a brace, and taken to Derriford Hospital; Mark and Louise following the ambulance.

McConochie had regained consciousness before he'd left, been arrested for the murders of Victoria Smith and Jennifer Drummond. Louise had done the honours in the end.

A broken pelvis, possible spinal injury and internal haemorrhaging, according to the surgeon lieutenant.

'Will he live?'

'Yes.' An easy question, apparently.

Penny Stroud had taken it badly, though. 'I let him get away from us,' she said.

'It wasn't your fault,' Dixon replied. 'If he hadn't done that, he'd have had a go at killing himself some other way.'

'Thank you, Sir.'

'And if the Navy don't appreciate your efforts, there's always a place for you with Avon and Somerset.'

It was late afternoon by the time Dixon got back to Express Park, early evening before he finished his witness statement.

'Did you get the trace on that mobile phone number?'

'Somewhere in West Bagborough,' replied Sarah. 'That's the best we can get from the triangulation. D'you want me to ring—?'

'No. I'm on my way now. Keep me posted if it moves before I get there.'

Cole parked behind a car that was blocking the lychgate half an hour later, left the windscreen wipers running. It still didn't seem right, somehow: a car without a proper handbrake. Dixon hoped he'd never have to get used to it.

'That's—'

'I know,' Dixon said. 'You wait here, Nige.'

'Right.'

There'd been no message from Sarah, so the mobile phone hadn't moved; easy to find too, not that it was going to have been anywhere else, really.

Dixon squeezed past the Mercedes estate, the rear windows open an inch or so, and followed the path up to the church, then left around the tower, found Lieutenant Commander Judith Towers standing in the long grass at the foot of the empty grave. The police tape was still there, the cones replaced with long metal spikes. She was holding a bunch of flowers wrapped in paper; upside down, the rose buds brushing the grass at her feet.

She looked at Dixon, gave a sad smile, then carried on staring at the planks covering the hole in the ground.

Jeans and a blue hooded coat, her naval uniform left behind in her cabin at *Drake*, probably; hadn't bothered to put up the hood either, her short dark hair saturated, rain dripping off the end of her nose.

They stood in silence for what seemed like an age, listening to the patter of the rain on the tarpaulin that was covering the pile of mud.

'You weren't at the dry dock,' said Dixon, eventually. He'd turned up the collar of his coat, thrust his hands deep into his pockets, and was standing at the opposite end of the grave.

'I knew what he'd do when he ran; didn't want to see it.' She sighed. 'I heard what happened. Will he live?'

'He will.'

'I'm not sure whether I'm pleased or disappointed. We were both due to move on to a Vanguard boat, and she'd have been XO on an Astute class after that. I used to pull her leg about it, tell her she was following me around. She just said she was caught in my slipstream.'

'Did you know McConochie had been having an affair with her?'

'No one did.'

'Except Jennifer Drummond,' said Dixon.

'And look what happened to her.' She dropped the bunch of flowers on to the planks covering the grave. 'It seems odd grieving for my friend at an empty grave. It's not even her grave, although it was for a day or two, I suppose.'

'It was dug for a Mrs Henley and the burial will be going ahead next week. It won't be long before Victoria's parents will be able to arrange her funeral.'

'I have a feeling I'll be missing that.'

'Where's Bilbo?' asked Dixon.

Towers looked at him, frowned. 'You knew it was me all the time?'

'I'm a police officer and a dog walker. Police officers never forget a face; dog walkers never forget a dog.'

'I left him in the car. The little bugger hates getting wet.'

'Who will look after him?'

'My mother has him when I'm at sea, so she'll have him when I'm in prison.' She shrugged. 'He knows her, always puts on weight when he's there, but he's happy enough; she's got a big garden, and he gets on with her cats.'

'You said you'd had a bad experience, giving evidence and getting shat on.'

'That was a lie. Sorry.'

'It was all a lie, not that it mattered. You didn't see smoke. How could you? You were on board *Agincourt* at the time. All you really did was keep the Russian sub front and centre.'

'That was the idea. I hoped it would come out that way, but when it didn't, I had to speak to the family. Tell them myself. They had a right to know.' She folded her arms, seemed to crumple in the rain, the harsh reality of her situation taking hold. 'How long d'you think I'll get?'

'Two years is usual for a prosecution under the Official Secrets Act. More if you plead not guilty and are found guilty.'

She inhaled sharply through her nose. 'Worth it, to finish what Vic started. And the families of those two marine surveyors deserve to know what happened to them.'

'What *did* happen to them?'

'It's enough that people know a Russian sub was in British territorial waters, in the right place, at the right time.' Towers looked at Dixon, her eyes narrowing. 'The truth of it is no one will ever really know. We can only *suspect*.'

'There was nothing in the radio transcripts?'

'I can't confirm that one way or the other,' said Towers. 'To do so would mean revealing we can decrypt Russian radio traffic. That's a step too far, even for me.'

'Make sure your lawyer knows that. It will be good mitigation.'

'When it comes to sentencing, you mean?'

'It shows you acted in the public interest, withheld that vital piece of classified information. You didn't go to the press, either. Just the family. It was an act of compassion, letting them know what happened to their loved ones.'

'Then it'll all come out in court, surely?'

'They can deal with the classified stuff behind closed doors.'

'Are you going to arrest me?'

'Someone else can do that. I'm going home to my wife and son.'

'How long have I got?'

'Twenty-four hours. It'll count in your favour if you turn yourself in.'

'Thank you.'

Dixon turned away, stopped, looked back over his shoulder. 'And for my sake, plead guilty. I really don't want to find myself having to give evidence against you.'

Author's Note

I very much hope you enjoyed reading *Seeing Red* as much as I enjoyed writing it.

The research was particularly absorbing this time, offering me a glimpse into another world, although it brought with it the realisation that I had perhaps chosen the wrong career path when I entered the legal profession all those years ago!

I am indebted to Lieutenant Commander Andrew McConochie RN Retired, not only for securing the necessary permission for me to set parts of the novel inside HMS *Drake*, but also for his extraordinary generosity with his knowledge and experience.

I was honoured to have been able to attend the twenty-one-gun salute held on Monday 9th September 2024 to mark the second anniversary of His Majesty's accession to the throne (carried forward from 8th September – gun salutes are not held on a Sunday). For the guided tour of the base, lunch in the Wardroom, and for his time spent checking the manuscript. Thank you, Andy!

All mistakes are mine, of course, although you will not be surprised to learn that I have played fast and loose with some aspects of life at HMS *Drake*. I have simplified the organisational structure somewhat, and glossed over the strict security procedures for entering the base, for obvious reasons. I have also taken some liberties with the geography for the sake of narrative clarity and in the hope of creating a fast moving and entertaining murder mystery. It is a vast site, and the reality is that it would take (me) ten minutes to run from the cricket pitch to the covered dry dock.

I prefer to call it poetic licence!

There will be some readers for whom the idea of Russian submarines operating in British territorial waters is a trifle far-fetched. I can assure you it is not, and a simple Google search will bring up numerous news articles reporting on such incursions.

Likewise, the idea that Monty would adopt the role of young Peter's guardian angel. This is a well-known trait of the Staffordshire Terrier, mentioned specifically in the Kennel Club breed standard.

As always, I am eternally grateful to my wife, Shelley, for reading the manuscript on a daily basis. It has become a routine of sorts; print off what I've written that day, make her a cup of tea, then take the dogs for a walk and leave her in peace!

My sincere thanks also go to my dear friend and harshest critic, Rod Glanville. Thanks, Rodders.

And to David Hall and Clare Paul, who remain willing to share their detailed knowledge of all things Somerset and Land Rovers.

Lastly, I would like to thank my editorial team at Thomas & Mercer, Sammia Hamer and Ian Pindar. I am pleased to report that their patience still hasn't run out. And to my long-suffering copyeditor, Gemma Wain, whose patience must surely have run out by now!

I have, for some time, been thinking of doing something a little different with Nick; taking him abroad, possibly, or to another part of the country. I got as far as Devon in the end but, I hope, managed to achieve something a bit different this time. I do hope you enjoyed it.

Damien Boyd
Devon, UK
February 2026

About the Author

Photo © 2013 Damien Boyd

Damien Boyd is a solicitor by training and draws on his extensive experience of criminal law, along with a spell in the Crown Prosecution Service, to write fast-paced crime thrillers featuring Detective Inspector Nick Dixon.

Follow the Author on Amazon

If you enjoyed this book, follow Damien Boyd on Amazon to be notified when the author releases a new book!
To do this, please follow these instructions:

Desktop:

1) Search for the author's name on Amazon or in the Amazon App.
2) Click on the author's name to arrive on their Amazon page.
3) Click the 'Follow' button.

Mobile and Tablet:

1) Search for the author's name on Amazon or in the Amazon App.
2) Click on one of the author's books.
3) Click on the author's name to arrive on their Amazon page.
4) Click the 'Follow' button.

Kindle eReader and Kindle App:

If you enjoyed this book on a Kindle eReader or in the Kindle App, you will find the author 'Follow' button after the last page.